THE
Sheriffs OF
SAVAGE
WELLS

OTHER PROPER ROMANCE NOVELS
BY SARAH M. EDEN

LONGING FOR HOME

LONGING FOR HOME,
BOOK 2: HOPE SPRINGS

OTHER PROPER ROMANCE NOVELS

BEAUTY AND THE CLOCKWORK BEAST
by Nancy Campbell Allen

MY FAIR GENTLEMAN
by Nancy Campbell Allen

FOREVER AND FOREVER
by Josi S. Kilpack

A HEART REVEALED
by Josi S. Kilpack

A LADY'S FAVOR:
A PROPER ROMANCE NOVELLA
by Josi S. Kilpack (eBook only)

LORD FENTON'S FOLLY
by Josi S. Kilpack

BLACKMOORE
by Julianne Donaldson

EDENBROOKE
by Julianne Donaldson

THE HEIR TO EDENBROOKE:
A PREQUEL NOVELETTE
by Julianne Donaldson (eBook only)

THE *Sheriffs* OF SAVAGE WELLS

A PROPER ROMANCE

SARAH M. EDEN

SHADOW
MOUNTAIN

Visit us at ShadowMountain.com

This is a work of fiction. Characters and events in this book are products of the author's imagination or are represented fictitiously.

Library of Congress Cataloging-in-Publication Data

Names: Eden, Sarah M., author.
Title: The sheriffs of Savage Wells / Sarah M. Eden.
Description: Salt Lake City, Utah : Shadow Mountain, [2016] | ©2016
Identifiers: LCCN 2016003430 (print) | LCCN 2016005425 (ebook) | ISBN 9781629722191 (paperbound) | ISBN 9781629734538 (ebook)
Subjects: LCSH: Sheriffs—Wyoming—History—19th century—Fiction. | Policewomen—Wyoming—History—19th century—Fiction. | LCGFT: Historical fiction. | Romance fiction.
Classification: LCC PS3605.D45365 S54 2016 (print) | LCC PS3605.D45365 (ebook) | DDC 813/.6—dc23
LC record available at http://lccn.loc.gov/2016003430

Printed in the United States of America
Publishers Printing, Salt Lake City, UT

10 9 8 7 6 5 4 3 2

To Sleep
Our relationship suffered in the writing of this book,
and I'd like to make amends . . .
as soon as I finish writing the next one.

Chapter 1

Wyoming Territory, 1875

Sheriff Cade O'Brien was heartily sick of shooting people. Time and again, he'd rounded up a band of outlaws and the imbeciles had refused to come peaceably. Why was the criminal element so blasted stupid? It wasn't as though his reputation hadn't preceded him. He had a revolver named after him, for land's sakes.

He'd spent the past ten years putting holes in the potato-brained law-breakers of the West and reckoned he'd earned a rest. So when a telegram had been sent out across several western territories announcing that the tiny town of Savage Wells was looking to hire a sheriff at an impressive wage, Cade gathered up his meager belongings, his equally meager savings, and his overused gun, and headed out.

The telegram had instructed all interested candidates to report to the jailhouse at a particular time on a particular day. Cade arrived a little ahead of the appointed hour, wanting to take in the lay of the land. He wasn't worried about being beat out for the job. Rather, he wanted time to decide if the job was for him.

He arrived in Savage Wells on a cloudless September afternoon expecting to see a tiny town. But buildings lined either side of an L-shaped street with fields sprawled out in all directions. He'd passed quite a few ranches on his ride in. The signs on each building were large and clear, the storefronts well kept. Mercantile. Blacksmith. Barber. The town even had a combined hotel and restaurant. He might be bored but he'd not go hungry.

Spotting the jailhouse, he rode in that direction. He adjusted his hat to sit a little lower on his head. He hooked his right thumb over his gun belt, keeping the reins in his left hand. He knew perfectly well the picture he and his white stallion, Fintan, made and the impact it had. Most of his confrontations were won before he even opened his mouth.

Not many people were about. Those who were, smiled and waved to each other. A few had stopped to jaw a piece. The conversations were animated, but friendly. No one shoved anyone else. No weapons were brandished. It was quiet. Peaceful. A town that wasn't throwing itself into the fire day after day would take a great deal of getting used to.

Reaching his destination, he dismounted in one fluid movement and tied Fintan's reins to the hitching post. He stood a moment, eyeing the jailhouse with its covered porch and front windows. In a great many towns the glass would've been shot out so often they'd have quit bothering to replace it.

A man stood near the closed door, a pair of wire-rimmed spectacles perched low on his nose and black sleeve protectors over his white shirt. "You must be here about the job of sheriff."

Cade had been a lawman long enough to have the appearance of one. No one ever needed to ask. He gave a single, curt nod. "Anyone else here yet?"

"Oh, yes, yes." The man glanced about, head darting from one side to the other, as he patted at his various pockets. "Mr. Rice, just over there, with the blue bandana around his neck." He motioned toward the post at the far end of the overhang. "Two more men are waiting alongside the building. Two." He pulled off his spectacles and wiped the lenses with a white linen handkerchief. "But there should be more. A few more. A few." He returned his spectacles to his face. "Good, good." He adjusted the brown bowler on his head, then went back to patting his pockets.

Was the pocket-patting a nervous habit or had he misplaced something?

He returned his gaze to Cade, though he continued to fidget. "I am Mayor Brimble." He held out his hand, pulled it back quickly to wipe something off his fingers, then stuck it out once more.

Scatterbrained mayors tended to run scatterbrained towns. That didn't bode particularly well.

Out of the corner of his eye, Cade spied a young lad—twelve years old, he reckoned—standing at Fintan's head, eyeing a bit too closely the horse and the packs it held. Without turning his head fully in that direction, Cade pointed his finger at the boy. "Leave him be, boy. He has a devil of a temper."

The boy's eyes opened wide. "I wasn't gonna hurt him, mister."

"It ain't *you* hurting *him* that I'm worried about."

"Yes, sir." And he backed away.

Cade returned his attention to the mayor, who was watching him with much the same awed expression as had the boy on the street.

"There's no point standing about twiddling our thumbs," Cade told the mayor. "We must be near time to begin."

"Yes, yes." Mayor Brimble patted his pockets once more but didn't find whatever he was looking for.

A man on horseback came up alongside the jail. He tipped his sweat-stained hat back, eyeing them. "Is this the spot for the sheriff job?"

"Yes, yes, yes."

Cade hoped the mayor didn't make a habit of repeating himself all the time. It was likely to grow tiresome.

"I've not seen a saloon or a bawdy house since arriving." Cade had never known a town that didn't have both, often several of each. Most of the trouble he'd encountered as a sheriff had begun at one or the other of those establishments.

The mayor puffed out his chest. "We've never allowed either in Savage Wells."

Now that *did* bode well.

Another man sauntered over, his swagger setting him apart from the families and townspeople. Clearly he was another candidate. Yet another arrived a moment later.

Cade looked at the men awaiting the mayor's instructions. To a man, they looked rough and hardened, comfortable with their weapons. For some it would no doubt prove to be a bluff to cover their own nerves. They'd be weeded out fast enough.

The mayor rocked forward and backward, smiling as though everything was right in the world and he wasn't in any particular hurry. Cade leaned against the front wall of the jailhouse. If the mayor meant to go about this at a pace slower than molasses on a cold winter's day, Cade could accommodate him. Nothing in the peaceful scene laid out in front of him indicated a looming crisis.

A fence post of a man made his way from the barbershop in long, hurried strides.

"Mr. Irving," the mayor said, introducing the newcomer to the would-be sheriffs. "He is our barber and on the town council."

Mr. Irving nodded, but didn't speak.

"And"—Mayor Brimble motioned to a second man approaching from the mercantile—"Mr. Holmes, our merchant, is also on the council. And Dr. MacNamara rounds out our numbers."

The town had a doctor. That was a good thing. Crimes happened even in quiet towns. Cade would rather not kill anyone, but a few too many well-meaning folks had turned a minor gunshot wound into a fatal injury with their amateur doctoring.

"Here comes the doctor now." Mayor Brimble motioned behind Cade.

He turned. He never let anyone sneak up behind him.

Dr. MacNamara couldn't have been any older than Cade, probably not even thirty years old. The town's man of medicine was a puppy. And a city puppy at that. His togs weren't the rough fabric and simple cut of home-sewn fashions. Men from the Eastern cities generally weren't pre-pared for the realities of the West. He'd probably faint dead away at the sight of a bullet hole.

The doctor nodded to the other candidates. Being closest to Cade, he held out his hand. He didn't seem unnerved by Cade, something few could honestly say.

A good firm grip. He might have been young for a doctor, but at least he wasn't a pamby. "You're the doctor, I'm told."

"That's what I'm told as well." Dr. MacNamara's dark eyes danced with mirth. He turned to the others. "Are we all assembled?"

"Yes, yes." Mayor Brimble waved the candidates closer. "We're pleased you've seen fit to apply for this job. We're in need of a new sheriff and had hoped to appeal to the very best candidates."

In need of a new sheriff. Turnover wasn't usually a good sign. "What happened to your last sheriff?"

"He was far too fond of wood," Dr. MacNamara said, a mischievous twinkle in his eye.

Cade folded his arms across his chest and eyed the council members in turn. His stern, impatient glare had never failed to make people spill whatever secret he needed to know.

"He left for Oregon," the mayor explained. "He wanted to be a lumberjack. It was all he ever talked about. Trees. Wood. Lumberjacking. He was hardly paying any attention the last few months he was here. Didn't even always come down to the jail to work."

"Probably best he left then," Cade said. "Most sheriffs leave their posts in a pine box. Seems he did fine for himself."

The other sheriffing hopefuls didn't so much as blink at the reminder of the dangers of the job. They were made of sterner stuff than they seemed to be.

"So why the generous pay?" Mr. Rice spoke up, his blue kerchief flut-tering around his neck in the stiff breeze. "A town as quiet as this don't really need a sheriff good enough to demand that price."

He made exactly the point Cade was mulling over.

"We don't need one *yet*. But we have every reason to believe we will."

Now *that* was intriguing. Something was looming on Savage Wells's horizon, but the council wasn't saying just what. A peaceful place but with a mystery lingering in the air; Cade liked it already.

The mayor patted at his pockets, brow pulled low and deep. The doctor apparently knew what to do. He pulled a folded bit of paper from the pocket of his sharply cut waistcoat along with a small nub of a pencil and held it at the ready.

"Good, good." The mayor nodded triumphantly. "Now, if you men will tell us your names, we'll get started."

The doctor looked at Cade expectantly.

"Cade O'Brien."

An immediate hush fell over the other men. Every pair of eyes pulled wide. More than one mouth dropped open. Cade simply stood there, waiting for their shock to wear off. He'd built enough of a reputation out West to recognize the reaction; it'd pass soon enough.

As if on cue, the silence disappeared as quickly as it had descended and something near chaos erupted in its place. Four of the six men simply threw their hands up and declared themselves out of the running.

"I ain't got a chance against Cade O'Brien," one said, fixing his hat more firmly on his head.

One by one, they passed Cade, dipping their hats or shaking his hand, and declaring it an honor to meet him. The town council looked a bit awed at both him and the exodus he'd caused.

In the end, only Sweaty Hat and Blue Kerchief remained. His respect for the two men increased on the spot. Not everyone was willing to keep at a fight that had suddenly turned lopsided.

"Anyone else?" the mayor asked.

"One more," a feminine voice declared.

Cade turned around.

A woman approached, her nearly black hair pulled into a tidy bun.

Deep brown eyes, a pleasant face—she was a beauty, for sure. Her eyes met his for a moment. She looked him up and down but didn't seem terribly impressed. The final candidate's wife, perhaps? Or sister?

The question faded, however. Hanging low on her hips was a gun belt, a pistol in the holster. He'd known a few women who wore guns, but none who wore it as naturally as she did, or as menacingly.

"One final name for your list of candidates," she said to the doctor, her voice firm and commanding. "Miss Paisley Bell."

Chapter 2

Paisley had learned to appear comfortable under scrutiny. She didn't allow herself to squirm or fret while her declaration sunk into the men around her. She'd kept the sheriff's office running the past few months while their previous lawman had been off dreaming of trees. She'd kept on top of the town's troubles, even rounded up a gang of cattle rustlers. But the town had congratulated the old sheriff on a job well done, and he'd thanked them without mentioning her role in any of it.

When he'd left two weeks ago, she had taken over running the office. She'd made a good temporary sheriff and would be a fine permanent one. And it was time the town realized that.

The mayor's mouth moved silently as he searched for a response. He finally settled on, "This is decidedly odd."

Paisley shrugged. "'Decidedly Odd' is my nickname in this town."

Gideon rolled his eyes at her, the way he had for two years now. They picked at each other the way a pair of siblings might. "No one thinks you're odd," he said.

The broad-shouldered, golden-haired stranger chimed in. "They likely will now."

She'd seen him take note of her gun belt as she'd first approached, but, other than a brief flicker of surprise, he didn't seem particularly shocked by it. A pistol and a lace-edged, flower-print dress weren't generally seen in combination.

His hand hung leisurely near his holster, his thumb hooked casually over his own gun belt. There was a familiarity to it all that spoke volumes of his acquaintance with his weapon. Nothing in his posture was the least bit uncomfortable, neither did he appear to feel threatened.

He was the only candidate who gave her pause. The other two lacked his air of authority. Even the town council lacked it. The position of sheriff was more or less his for the taking, except she didn't mean to simply hand it to him. She'd found something she was good at, something she loved doing, and she'd fight for it.

"Are you in earnest, Miss Bell?" the mayor asked.

She held his uncertain gaze. "Completely." Without looking at Gideon, she said, in the steely, confident tone that generally made people sit up and listen to her, "Write down my name, Gid."

"A woman?" The man with the blue kerchief sputtered. "What kind of a daft town is this?" Someone needed to explain to him that speaking *loudly* under his breath defeated the purpose.

"We're not here to make a spectacle," the authoritative one declared. "Let's move things inside, shall we?"

The town council obeyed him immediately. This was not an encouraging sign.

The three other candidates stopped only a few steps into the jailhouse, staring at the veritable rainbow of ribbons hanging off every cell bar and the spools on shelves and tabletops scattered throughout the place. Paisley, on the other hand, was accustomed to the sight. She took advantage of their distraction and crossed to the sheriff's desk. She stood firm and confident, making certain they all could see how at ease she was in that position. She settled one hand comfortably on her gun belt, slung low on her hips.

The sound of footfalls announced the approach of Paisley's biggest competition. "Why the ribbons?" he asked her. He wasn't one for small talk, that was certain.

He might demand answers, but she didn't have to give them to him straight. "It brightens up the place."

"A jail ain't supposed to be bright." He shook his head as he looked away. He took in every corner of the room. She swore she could see him making future plans for the place.

Did he expect her to simply nod and shuffle off? Her father had been out of work for two years. Their savings were gone. She'd sold furniture and some personal belongings to newly arrived ranchers to help make ends meet, but there was very little left. She needed a job, and she'd found one that suited her. The odds were stacked high against her, she knew that, but she'd never been one to shy away from a seemingly lost cause.

"We haven't actually met," she said, pulling the stranger's sharp blue gaze back to her. "Do you have a name?"

"Cade O'Brien," he answered in clipped tones. "Call me Cade."

"Paisley," she said. "But you can call me Sheriff Bell."

"Don't hold your breath, Miss Bell." He looked away once more.

She needed to regain some hold on the situation. Knowing the council for the hemmers and hawers that they were, she set her sights in that direction. "You'd best get on with it, Mayor Brimble. How is this meant to play out?"

"You really do mean to go ahead?" The mayor looked as unconvinced as ever. "It's odd. Very odd."

"You weren't complaining these past two weeks when I filled the gap left by Sheriff Garrison's departure. And you didn't shout and holler about how odd it was when I stepped in for the previous *three months* when his lumberjack hopes were distracting him from his duties." The town knew she'd been assisting him, they simply hadn't been told just how much she'd done; Sheriff Garrison had been present enough in mind to make certain of that.

Mr. Holmes spoke up for the first time. He only seldom voiced his thoughts. The other member, the barber, Mr. Irving, never spoke at all. He was as silent, and as animated, as the grave.

"But that was temporary," Mr. Holmes said. "Just something to fill in the gap. We need a *real* sheriff."

"I'm here to show you I can be both." She raised an eyebrow in challenge. Her candidacy was every bit as unprecedented as they'd said, but she knew enough of their wishy-washy nature to know they could be persuaded to at least let her try. "Your advertisement for the position didn't say women weren't allowed to apply."

"It was implied," Mayor Brimble insisted.

"Let the woman have a go," Cade said, tossing the declaration out as casually as if he'd been commenting on the weather. "If she feels she's qualified, she ought to be allowed to prove it."

That was unexpectedly supportive, and yet undeniably dismissive at the same time.

"And she does have some experience, which may not be true for the other two men here." That tag-on comment explained a great deal. Cade O'Brien, for all his show of being unimpressed and unsurprised by her appearance and aspirations, was using her to cut at the other candidates. She was to be a tool, then? A weapon? He'd learn differently soon enough.

"What of you, Cade O'Brien?" she asked. "Do you have any experience?"

"A bit," he answered dryly.

The one in desperate need of a new hat chimed in on the spot. "A bit?" He nearly choked on the words. "Sheriff O'Brien's been a lawman for ten years."

Well, bully for Mr. O'Brien. "If I happen upon a 'Ten Years of Sheriffing' medal, I'll be sure to pass it on to him."

Cade didn't respond to the bit of humor. He was either being difficult or was something of a grump.

"It's more than just being a sheriff," Sweaty Hat continued. "He's practically been running the West. He's cleaned up and cleared out more towns than most of us will ever even visit. Rumors of him showing up are enough to send criminals running for their lives. The US Marshals have been begging him to join up for years. Every sheriff on the telegraph system has heard of all the things he's managed and, though it'll make my chances slimmer to tell you as much, he's a legend."

Paisley was already at a disadvantage as a woman, but going up against a man who inspired that level of near-worship was a rather enormous obstacle. But it did raise the question: Why did a man with his qualifications want a job in a sleepy town like Savage Wells?

"As flattering as all this is," Cade drawled, "I'd rather move ahead." He turned toward the mayor. "As Miss Bell asked a moment ago, how's this supposed to play out?"

"Yes. Of course." He nodded a few times the way he always did when collecting his thoughts. "We don't want to take too much time making a decision."

That would be a change for the town council.

"But we also don't want to be hasty." He met the eyes of the other men in quick succession. "Over the next two weeks, we'd like you to take turns being sheriff for a day. That way you can see if the job suits you, and we can see if you suit us."

It was a sensible plan, more or less. Savage Wells was so quiet, Paisley doubted anything would occur to showcase their skills or abilities. Still, that might work to her advantage. Men accustomed to the fast pace of a violent town were more likely to grow antsy and bored, whereas she'd be right at home.

They all agreed to the plan, and Cade, unsurprisingly, was elected to be first to take his turn. The mayor pointed them all in the direction of the hotel atop the restaurant and mentioned that Mrs. Kirkpatrick up the road rented rooms to boarders if that better suited what they wanted for the next fortnight. Hat and Kerchief—she really ought to learn their names—left to secure accommodations. Gideon and the mayor took up a quiet conversation. The other council members left.

Cade, however, remained, his gaze firmly on her. "You're meaning to go head-to-head with me?" He looked at her as though she were plumb out of her mind.

"With all three of you men." She wanted this job, and she meant to give it her best shot. "It's either this competition or a shoot-out on the street."

"I don't shoot women," he said.

"And *I* don't shoot peacocks, so I guess a gunfight between us is out of the question." She offered an overly sweet smile.

"Saints preserve my sanity," he muttered.

"May the best sheriff win," she said.

"I will."

Chapter 3

Paisley Bell was a fine-looking woman, there was no denying that. But she was also a pill. Truth be told, Cade felt bad for her. The town might've been willing to let her fill in a sheriffing gap for a fortnight, but likely if she tried for the job permanently, she'd only be humiliated in the end.

He'd been a bit surprised by the council's two-week trying-on period. He'd not had to prove himself since his very first sheriffing post. Cleaning up the cesspool that was Coalsville in Colorado Territory had earned him a reputation in every corner of the West. From that point on, he'd ridden in to town for each new job, shot, arrested, or run off criminals as needed, and moved on.

He'd almost walked out of Savage Wells, leaving the others to fight for the chance to be blessedly bored in that ribbon-infested jailhouse, but the salary was more than he'd expected a small town would be able to pay. It would provide a comfortable living, that was for sure. And it wasn't as though he couldn't use two weeks of time away from the demands of the law. Besides all that, Paisley Bell was too intriguing for him to simply walk away.

Cade watched her stride to the windows of the jailhouse, her head held high, back straight as a redwood tree, chin at a defiant angle.

Why did she want the job so badly? She had to know her chances were slimmer than a cornstalk in the dry season. Still she was sticking to her guns. He'd enjoy finding out what made her tick.

But first things first. "Dr. MacNamara," he called out. "Would you point me in the direction of the stables?"

"Call me Gideon," the doctor insisted. "And I'll take you to the stables myself, and then on to Mrs. Kirkpatrick's or the hotel, wherever it is you mean to lay your head." He had a very educated way of speaking, this doctor. Although book-learning in a man of medicine wasn't a bad thing.

"And point out the barbershop, as well," Paisley said. "The man needs a haircut."

He and Gideon stepped out into the cool, early evening air. The quiet of the street didn't relieve the tension building in Cade's shoulders. "That Miss Bell's about as stubborn as a Kilkenny cat," he muttered.

Gideon chuckled. "She is very stubborn. She is also a fine woman."

"The wind blows that way, does it?" Cade untied Fintan's reins from the hitching post.

"She is a good friend—the best I have here, in fact—but nothing beyond."

Cade rubbed Fintan's nose in greeting. "A good enough friend that you'd do her dirty work for her?" It was best to know one's enemies from one's allies.

"Paisley doesn't do things that way. No one around here does."

Cade adjusted his hat a touch lower on his head. "I can't say I've ever lived in a town that didn't have its share of villainy under the surface."

"Then Savage Wells will either be heaven to you or a descent into the purgatory of boredom."

Heaven. Definitely heaven.

He followed Gideon up the road, stopping regularly for introductions. Gideon told the various townspeople that Cade was a lawman newly arrived to try on the sheriff badge and see if it stayed pinned on. Everyone seemed intrigued by that and whispered about it amongst themselves as they walked on.

Cade and Gideon reached the corner of the L-shaped street.

"Hold up a moment." Cade wouldn't be able to see this part of town from the jailhouse. He had best make himself familiar with it now. "What's on this end of town?"

"Across the street and down a bit is the schoolhouse, if you want to brush up on your reading or 'ciphering."

"I've not spent a single day in school," Cade said, unashamed. He might not have been formally educated, but he knew a lot of the world.

"What's your attendance record at church?" Gideon asked. "The school doubles as the church on Sundays."

"I've been known to drop in now and then."

He eyed the open expanse of land, liking that he could see for miles. Ne'er-do-wells weren't likely to sneak in to town from this end; they'd be seen long before they arrived.

"The preacher's house sits up behind the school," Gideon said. "The preacher and his wife are friendly. The schoolteacher, who lives with them, is very energetic, sometimes exhaustingly so."

"But they're peaceable?" That mattered most at the moment.

"Unless you consider gossip an act of violence."

Seemed that this part of Savage Wells was sparse and quiet. That would simplify things.

"The stables and blacksmith's forge are directly ahead of us," Gideon said. "There are no other establishments on this side of the bend in the road."

"Your stableman knows what he's about? Takes good care of the animals?"

Cade wouldn't trust Fintan to just anyone. The animal had seen him through hard times. Fintan had been the only constant in his life in recent years.

"The stableman and the blacksmith are brothers," Gideon said. "They're more fond of animals than they are of people."

That was both reassuring and a bit disturbing.

The stable's interior was dim. The smell of animals and hay hung strong in the air, but the place didn't reek with the odor of unkempt stalls or neglected duties. Cade began to feel more at ease about the arrangement.

A man in thick denims and a threadbare gray shirt came out of a nearby stall. He looked them both over before his eyes settled on Fintan. His expression changed from curious to worshipful on the instant.

"Jeb." Gideon held out his hand. "This is Cade O'Brien, and—"

The man shook Gideon's hand absentmindedly, staring at the horse with his mouth agape.

"He's a beauty, to be sure."

Jeb walked directly past Cade without so much a glance in his direction and stood in reverent awe in front of Fintan. "Good carriage. Excellent muscle tone. Clearly this animal's been well cared for. Who had the keeping of him before you brought him here?"

"A stabler in Cordova," Cade said. "Dr. MacNamara says you're qualified. Tell me now if I've been misled."

Jeb poked his head out of the stables and shouted in the direction of the smithy. "Eben. Come see this prize stallion we've got here. Prettier'n a turnip, he is!"

"Turnips being particularly pretty," Gideon said under his breath.

"What's his name?" Jeb asked.

"Fintan," Cade answered. "It's an old Irish name." His grandfather's, in fact.

"Well, your name's about as Irish as a priest." Jeb ran a gentle hand over Fintan's mane. "If you'd given the horse a Russian name or Spanish or some such thing, now that'd be odd."

A moment later a man wearing a blacksmith's leather apron arrived, a look of eager anticipation on his soot-smudged face. He could have been Jeb's twin if not for his enormous build. The two spoke in amazed whispers about Fintan's carriage and withers and made guesses about his lineage. Cade thought he saw tears of joy hovering in the men's eyes.

"I'm worryin' they might kidnap m' horse," he whispered to Gideon.

"They won't, though they might build a shrine to it."

Jeb and Eben peppered him with questions. How long had he had Fintan? What was his pedigree? They knew his breed without asking, very accurately guessed his age, and estimated correctly how many hands he was. The two clearly knew horses. Cade's anxiety disappeared as they spoke.

He worked out the cost of stabling and set out his expectations. They spared only the briefest of glances for Cade.

"How fast can you saddle a horse?" Cade asked. A sheriff needed speed after all.

"Fast as a cat up a tree." Jeb's chest swelled with pride.

"I'll hold you to that," Cade warned, letting his serious expression indicate he was in earnest.

"I'll not let you down," Jeb promised. "You're here trying for the sheriff job, are you?"

A quick nod was sufficient.

Jeb's eyes darted to Gideon. "We heard Paisley put her name on the list."

Word sure spread fast in Savage Wells.

"It's true," Gideon answered. "She is one of our candidates."

Eben folded his massive blacksmith's arms across his burly chest. The man was built like a wall. "She sure is one for getting odd notions in her head. She's a good 'un, though."

"She most definitely is," Gideon said.

Cade rubbed Fintan's nose, then ran his hand down its mane. "I'll check on you in the morning, ol' boy."

Jeb led Fintan to his stall.

"What else do you need to see to?" Gideon asked once they'd stepped back out onto the street again.

"Mostly, I need to learn where everything is in this town. That'll go a long way toward telling me when someone is wandering about where they ought not be." He'd prevented more than a few crimes that way.

They stopped once more, standing with their backs to the smithy, the stables, and the school.

"Here's the bank." Gideon motioned to the building that anchored the corner of the bend on Main Street. "The management changed in recent years, but it is still very well run and efficient."

The bank was on the same side of the street as the jailhouse. That would make keeping an eye on it more difficult. A town with a bank would always need an alert sheriff. He'd drop in on the bank manager later, see what security measures were being taken.

"Directly across the street is the restaurant and hotel." Gideon vaguely motioned in that direction. "Calvin Cooper runs both. He hails from Ohio but pretends he's English. For some reason he thinks that gives him cachet as a chef. I, however, have been to England and know better."

"You don't care for English food?"

"I'm not even sure it *is* food." Gideon made a dramatic show of being sick in his mouth. He finished his bit of playacting and took up his role as town guide again. "Next to the hotel is the post and telegraph office, which doubles as the stage depot. If you ever have business in there, give yourself an extra thirty minutes or so for our esteemed mayor to pull himself together."

Cade kept an eye on the people and businesses that made up Savage Wells's main street. The place was unnervingly quiet. That'd take some getting used to.

"The building beside the post office is the barber shop. Mr. Irving gives great shaves and haircuts, but he's utterly silent. I still don't know how he was elected to the town council."

Cade studied the buildings, committing their location to memory. A small, noticeably plain building sat next to the barber shop. "What's that?"

"The land office," Gideon said. "It is only open a couple of times a month."

That was good to know. If he saw activity there, it'd be reason for suspicion.

"On the other side of the land office is the millinery, run by Mrs. Carol," Gideon said. "She'll regularly and eagerly attempt to sell you feathers and flowers and other adornments for your hat." He gave Cade a pointed look of warning. "She is convinced there is nothing so depressing as an unadorned hat, no matter who is wearing it."

"Hmm."

"Hers is the last business on that side of Main Street. If you follow the road beyond town, you'll pass farms and ranches. On a lucky day, you might even spot our resident attorney, Mr. Larsen. He hardly ever makes an appearance. Some people in town are convinced he doesn't actually live here, simply comes to visit once in a while. Still others think he's nothing more than a specter."

"Is he?" Cade didn't truly believe in specters, but it would be good to know whether Mr. Larsen was an actual person or merely a town legend.

"He is quite real and quite alive," Gideon said. "But you'll be lucky if you see him more than once or twice a year."

"Seems the peace keeps itself around here." Cade liked that.

"We have our moments." Something in Gideon's tone sounded a warning.

Here was more of the mysterious hinting he'd first heard from the mayor. Something was rumbling beneath the surface of this small town, and Cade fully intended to find out what.

"The Holmes family runs the mercantile." Gideon motioned them forward, leaving behind the bank and passing in front of the tall windows of the storefront. "They're good, honest folks. Next is the jailhouse, but you know that. On the other side is the home of one Dr. MacNamara, a likable enough fellow, and handsome as all get out. A sheriff couldn't ask for better neighbors."

"Why's the jail covered in ribbons?" Cade had been pondering that oddity and hadn't yet formulated any kind of explanation. "I asked your friend, but she wouldn't give me a straight answer."

"They belong to Mrs. Wilhite," Gideon said. "A sweet, kindhearted, older woman with an inordinate fondness for ribbons."

"She stores them at the jail?"

Gideon waved to a family across the way while continuing their conversation. "She *sells* them at the jail. Calls it her 'Ribbon Emporium.' She's there three days a week."

"At the jail?" Cade couldn't quite wrap his thoughts around that.

Gideon nodded.

"Sellin' ribbons?"

Another nod.

"This here's a strange ol' town, friend," Cade muttered.

"Ah, but it's quiet. That's worth a great deal."

After years spent in bloody, lawless places, a quiet town was worth its weight in gold. "What about the town doctor? Is he as odd as the rest of 'em?"

"Indeed. He's too young and not nearly somber enough for most people's tastes," Gideon said. "And he refuses to bow to the apparent expertise of one Mr. Wagner, who feels himself far more qualified to be doctoring, by virtue of his vast knowledge of the healing powers of alcohol. Much to Wagner's dismay, however, I don't prescribe a life of drunkenness as a cure for all that ails us."

"How very unScottish of you, *MacNamara*."

"Says the man whose ancestors no doubt hail from the land of Guinness and whiskey."

"You'll find I'm the soberest Irishman in America," Cade answered. Getting liquored up hardly helped one keep the peace.

"That's wise," Gideon said. "You'll need your wits about you if you mean to take on Paisley."

"She ain't likely to simply step aside, then?"

"Not a chance in Hades. She'll fight you tooth and nail for this."

Cade stood on the wooden walkway, thumbs hooked over his belt, thinking. He almost felt sorry for Miss Paisley Bell. He could win their competition with one eye closed and one hand tied behind his back.

She didn't stand a chance.

Chapter 4

Who ties a blasted bow on the door of a jailhouse? Cade yanked the enormous green ribbon from the doorknob. It wasn't the most promising beginning to his day as sheriff.

He stepped inside and saw Paisley at the desk. Did the woman ever leave? He held up the ribbon. "Why don't you toss out a welcome sign and hang some lace curtains? Maybe you could serve tea in the afternoons."

"I hope you are as good at tying bows as you are at untying them," Paisley said calmly. "Mrs. Wilhite spent a great deal of time on that and you've ruined it."

Wilhite? That was the ribbon lady Gideon had mentioned yesterday. "Ribbons don't belong in a jailhouse." That would be one of his first changes.

"One could argue that jail cells don't belong in a Ribbon Emporium." Paisley glanced up at him momentarily. "The last sheriff managed to make it work the past few years. And I easily put up with it since his departure."

"The ribbons need to go."

She leaned back in her chair. "How about *you* go and the ribbons can stay?"

"You shyin' away from a fight?"

"Just giving you a chance to avoid your inevitable defeat." She spun a pencil around in her fingers, amusement tipping one corner of her mouth.

"Mighty big words there, Paisley," Cade said.

"You want me to use smaller ones so you can understand?"

He didn't know whether to laugh or throttle her. "No more ribbons," he said firmly.

Paisley tapped the pencil's eraser against her lips. "I'm not the one you have to tell that to." She pointed behind him. "Consider this your first 'Sheriffing in Savage Wells' challenge."

Cade turned around. Across the room, behind a tall table, stood a woman he'd not noticed until then. Somewhere approaching seventy years old, he'd wager. Bright yellow dress covered in lace and ribbons. Bow in her hair. Tears in her eyes. *Tears?*

"You don't like my ribbons?" she asked, her voice shaky. "Everyone likes my ribbons."

Mrs. Wilhite, no doubt. This could get sticky. "Ribbons and jails don't go together," he said.

She blinked a few times. "But my ribbons make it so lovely."

"Again. 'Lovely' and jails don't go together."

Mrs. Wilhite's pleading gaze turned to Paisley. "Those Grantland boys liked the ribbons in the cells. They told me so."

"The Grantland Gang?" Cade asked under his breath, following Mrs. Wilhite's gaze.

Paisley nodded. "They were rustling cattle out at the Jones's place. I invited them to spend a couple of weeks in here."

"Invited?" He knew enough of the Grantlands to not believe that at all.

"I delivered the invitation with something of a bang." That pencil was swinging around her fingers again.

"Dr. MacNamara spent an entire afternoon digging bullets out of them all," Mrs. Wilhite added.

But Cade hadn't looked away from Paisley. "*You* shot them?" He'd read the report on that roundup, and there'd been no mention of a woman being involved.

"I tried asking nicely, but they refused," Paisley said sweetly. "And since Sheriff Garrison couldn't be bothered with gathering them up, I brought them in. He locked the cells and received the congratulatory telegrams."

She had brought in the Grantlands? He had no evidence of what she was saying, but no reason to doubt her. Indeed, every instinct he had told him she was telling the truth.

"They liked my ribbons." Mrs. Wilhite apparently had no time for other topics. "They said the colors distracted them from the pain of their wounds. And the town likes my ribbons. They're so accustomed to coming here to buy them." She looked to Paisley. "Can he really make me leave?"

"I can—"

Paisley spoke across him. "Not for at least the next two weeks. He's not officially the sheriff."

Mrs. Wilhite breathed a loud sigh of relief. "I don't know what I'd do if he closed down my Ribbon Emporium."

This was getting out of hand. He stepped closer to Mrs. Wilhite. "You'll do just as well in another building as you do here."

Her chin quivered. "But I like it here."

"Ah, saints," he muttered. He'd rather not make enemies on his first day. "We'll sort it out in time."

"There are two other men vying for the position," Paisley said. "They might need just as much convincing."

"Ah, but *they* aren't going to be getting the job in the end," Cade tossed out, letting her see and hear how sure he was of his chances.

Mrs. Wilhite either ignored the rivalry or simply didn't notice it. "I think you might grow fond of the ribbons, Mr. O'Brien, once you've been here for a while."

That wasn't likely. "If you make a crotchety ol' cuss like me fond of ribbons, you'll be a regular miracle worker."

"Challenge accepted." She grinned broadly. "I have a shipment of silver ribbon due by the end of the month. That'll convince you."

"Silver ribbon." He turned back to the desk. "Dream come true."

Paisley made a very deliberate tally mark on a sheet of paper in front of her.

"What have you there?" he asked.

She held the paper up, facing him. She'd written "Sheriff Bell" on one side and "Cade" on the other with a line dividing the paper in half. *Sheriff Bell and Cade.* The woman had gumption, he'd give her that. The tally mark she'd made was under her own name.

"Keepin' score?" he said.

"Ten minutes into your very first day here and I'm winning."

He wasn't entirely sure what to make of her. She wore flowery dresses and lace alongside her gun belt. She wore her black hair up in a feminine bun, but her dark eyes snapped in a way that was anything but soft. She moved with grace, yet commanded attention when she arrived anywhere.

"How long've you lived in Savage Wells?"

"Four years," she answered without hesitation.

"And what brought you here?"

"A wagon."

A pill, for sure and certain.

The other two candidates—Rice with his blue kerchief and Thackery in the sweaty hat; Cade had made a point of learning their names—arrived in quick succession. He'd wondered if they had come to keep an eye on his efforts. He didn't blame them. He fully intended to watch them on their sheriffing days. Know your enemy, and all that.

Rice kept to himself, an abrasive smugness to his attitude. While Cade wasn't eager to spend his free time with the man, it wasn't a mark against him making a fine sheriff. Being sure of himself could warn away criminals.

Thackery was cut from a different cloth. He was quieter, more unassuming. But he also kept an eye on everything and everyone. Cade would wager he didn't miss a single detail. That was a good quality in a sheriff as well.

They'd not even had a moment to settle in when the merchant's little boy hurried inside. "Papa says to come right away."

Trouble at the mercantile. Paisley reached the door just as he did.

"Coming to see how it's done?" Cade drawled.

"I'm coming so I can bail you out when you get in over your head," she said.

"I don't need your help."

Thackery chuckled lightly, but smothered the laugh the moment Cade looked at him. Rice just shook his head and followed along silently.

Cade stepped into the mercantile behind little Billy Holmes. He kept his shooting hand at the ready as he swept the entire shop with his gaze. No one looked shady. Nothing was in disarray. Not a drop of blood anywhere to be seen.

Cade moved directly to the counter. "You sent for the sheriff?"

The merchant didn't look unnerved or worried, but smiled pleasantly like everyone else in this town seemed to. "It's Wednesday."

Mr. Holmes watched him expectantly. Cade watched Mr. Holmes expectantly.

"Wednesday," Mr. Holmes repeated. That clearly was supposed to mean something.

"Wednesday?"

The merchant nodded.

The place seemed calm enough. Why had he been summoned so urgently? "Have you a problem, Mr. Holmes?"

"No problem at all."

They were all watching Cade now—little Billy, Mrs. Holmes, Rice, Thackery, the gathered customers. But "Wednesday" didn't explain anything. His eyes met Paisley's; she was standing not more than a few paces off, leaning against the counter. Blasted woman was laughing at him.

"It's Wednesday, Cade," she said, her voice far too innocent. *"Wednesday."*

"I know how to read a calendar," Cade said.

"Then I'll leave you to it," Mr. Holmes said. He wandered off to see to a customer.

Mrs. Holmes stepped up beside Paisley. "I heard from Mrs. Endicott who heard from Miss Dunkle that you are trying for the job of sheriff. Is it true?"

"It is." Paisley's very patient tone sounded a bit strained.

"But Mrs. Abbott said she'd thought you meant to hang up your temporary badge once the new candidates arrived. Mr. Irving nodded quite emphatically when I asked him." Mrs. Holmes eyed her more closely. "Do you mean to continue on with this odd hitch in your getup?"

"Odd is my favorite kind of getup hitch." A weariness touched Paisley's expression.

Mrs. Holmes stepped away excitedly, pulling a customer aside for an immediate, whispered conversation.

Cade motioned Billy Holmes over with a twitch of his finger. He hunched down, level with the boy. "What is it your pa wanted the sheriff for?" he asked, keeping his voice just between the two of them.

"I thought he was sending for Miss Paisley," Billy said.

Cade kept to the more important topic. "What happens on Wednesdays?"

"She delivers Mr. Gilbert's groceries," Billy replied on a whisper.

"Delivers groceries? As the sheriff?"

Billy nodded. "Sheriff Garrison used to do it, then he got distracted by trees and quit coming around like he was supposed to. So she started doing it for him."

A sheriff delivering groceries. Of course. No gun battles or showdowns in Savage Wells. Just grocery deliveries and ribbons. He'd wanted blessed boredom, and he'd certainly found it. While the grocery assignment had come as a surprise, he was finding himself looking forward to the task.

He turned to the other candidates. "I believe I can handle this job on my own." He tipped his head to them all. "Be back in a shake."

A small crate, packed with goods, sat not twelve inches from where Paisley stood. She indicated it with a dramatic wave of her hand.

Cade sidled right up next to her. He leaned against the countertop. "Good work, there, Paisley. I think you've earned yourself another tally mark."

"Get these to Mr. Gilbert and I'll give *you* a tally for a change," she said.

"Last delivery I made as a sheriff was handing a team of bank robbers over to a federal marshal."

Her eyes opened wide, and her mouth pulled in a perfect circle. It was too theatrical an expression to be the least bit sincere. "Well, aren't you a fancy sheriff." Her look of feigned awe slid away. She pushed the crate closer to him. "Just pretend it's a notorious outlaw. You can even shoot it if you want."

Cade snatched up the crate. He tipped his head to Mr. and Mrs. Holmes, nodded a greeting to the customers who had come inside, then stepped out of the mercantile and down the road, the crate under his arm.

He heard the sound of footsteps and a swishing dress behind him. As he passed in front of the barbershop with its tall windows, he eyed the reflection of the street. Paisley walked not ten strides off his heels.

He slowed his pace with each step, until they were both stopped in the road, her standing not far behind him. He took his time turning to face her.

"Were you needing somethin'?" he asked.

She held a hand over her eyes, blocking the sun. "Just out for a stroll."

"You weren't intendin' to stroll down to Mr. Gilbert's house in case the bumbling would-be sheriff ain't up to the task of delivering a crate of groceries, now were you?"

"I certainly hope that's not my destination," she said.

"Why's that?"

"Because Mr. Gilbert lives"—with a flourish, she pointed over her shoulder in the opposite direction—"*that* way."

"You didn't mention that."

"You said you didn't need my help."

Troublesome woman. "Which house is his?"

"Turn left at the large elm. The Gilbert place is a bit down the road," she said. "You'll recognize it by the rooster-shaped weather vane on the roof and the river-rock chimney, and, of course, the man up in the tree with the shotgun."

"The *what?*"

She gave a quick, dismissive wave of her hand. "His name is Andrew, and he's very sweet. Tell him you've brought the groceries, and he'll let you pass without firing."

"Firing?" Savage Wells was suddenly a heap more interesting.

"Don't fret," she said. "He's generally very reasonable, only a touch protective of the house." She patted his arm in an overdone display of reassurance. "I'll just be off to the Ribbon Emporium." She gave him a laughing smile.

Sure thinks she's funny.

Paisley's directions proved spot-on. Cade turned at the very large elm and, after passing a couple of houses, came upon one with a weather vane and rock chimney. Cade's gaze slid up the tall tree out front and settled on a young man, likely not yet twenty, perched there with a shotgun at the ready.

"Whaddaya want, stranger?"

If I get shot, I'll strangle that woman. "I've come with groceries, Andrew." He held up the crate.

"How d'you know my name?" Wariness hung heavy in his tone.

But quick as lightning, his face lit with excitement, his voice changing to match his expressions. "Do you get premonitions or something? I've always wanted to meet someone with second sight."

Very well. "I knew you were going to say that," Cade answered, nodding sagely.

Andrew climbed down quite agilely, his gun hanging from a strap across his back. Paisley had said Andrew *likely* wouldn't fire. So long as the man had his shotgun near at hand, Cade didn't mean to provoke him.

"You never been up to the house before," Andrew said. "How'd you know where we live?"

Cade tapped his temple with one finger.

Andrew's eyes pulled wide. "How long have you been in town?"

"Since yesterday afternoon."

"And—and—" Excitement cut off his words each time he tried to speak. "Have you had any inklings of things coming?"

Cade eyed the shotgun. He was at something of a disadvantage, having a crate in his hands. It'd slow him down on the draw if pulling his weapon became necessary. There was nothing for it but to play along.

He made a show of thinking deeply. "I've a strong sense we've a powerful cold winter coming."

"I'll make certain we have plenty of firewood." Andrew motioned him toward the house. "I can take the groceries in."

Cade handed the crate over.

"Come by again," Andrew said. "I promise not to shoot you. You ain't one of the enemies."

Andrew walked into the house, his gait slow and uneven, as though he'd sustained an injury that hadn't healed properly. *An armed madman in a tree.* That was a tragedy waiting to happen.

A shotgun-wielding sentinel looking for a fortune teller. A jail filled with ribbons. An impertinent, temporary sheriff. The town grew stranger by the moment. Stranger—and a great deal more fun.

He'd done his time in towns where the undertaker had the most successful business and the graveyard was more full than the church pews. He wouldn't turn down the occasional criminal roundup, but he had no taste left for the exhausting pace he'd been keeping for so long.

He loved being a sheriff. Protecting the innocent, upholding the law, keeping the wheels of a town turning smoothly. It was in his blood, in his lungs, spinning about in his mind. He meant to cling to this chance to do it without all the death and dying. He'd more than earned it.

Chapter 5

"That Cade O'Brien is a very sheriffy kind of person, isn't he?" Mrs. Wilhite had mentioned Cade a full half-dozen times while Paisley helped her dust her shelves of ribbon. "There's a certain air about a sheriff. A bit frightening, but caring too."

Cade did have the frightening part down. Whether or not he would prove caring had yet to be seen.

"What about the other two men trying for the job?" Paisley kept her voice low; the "other two men" were just over by the cells.

Mrs. Wilhite's lips twisted in thought. "I suppose they have the air a bit as well, just not as much."

What about me? Paisley and Mrs. Wilhite had gotten to know each other well during Paisley's time helping Sheriff Garrison and her short tenure filling his shoes. They were friends. But would she view Paisley as a good candidate?

Cade came inside without the crate of groceries. He tossed his hat onto the coatrack. Rice and Thackery watched him closely.

"I see Andrew didn't shoot you." Paisley crossed to the corner where she'd left her broom.

"He's a reasonable fella." Cade sat down in her chair behind the desk.

Andrew was considered an odd duck by most everyone in town. She, herself, had needed several encounters with him to really understand why the man who, according to his family, had once been very levelheaded and reasonable had become so reclusive and irrational. How much did Cade truly understand the situation?

"You didn't threaten him, did you?"

"No need." Cade leaned over the pile of papers on the desk and picked up the first one, reading it.

"And Mr. Gilbert received his groceries?"

"Yes." Cade didn't look up.

He seemed rather intent on the papers. "That's a report of criminals believed to be in the territory sent from the federal—"

"—marshal," he finished her explanation. "I know."

"That one is two weeks out of date, though," she continued. "We should receive another—"

"—next week. I know."

She took a calming breath. Rice and Thackery were watching, and she wanted them to see that she knew as much about running a sheriff's office as any of them did. But Cade was making things difficult. He was so infuriatingly arrogant. "We receive word of captures—"

"—as they occur. I—"

"You know. I know that you know."

He looked up at last. "No need telling me what I'm already aware of, sweetie."

"Don't talk to me as though I were a child, Cade O'Brien." She pointed a finger at him.

"Are we going to have to listen to this for two full weeks?" Rice asked, eyeing them both with impatience.

"You could always chime in now and then," Cade said, still flipping through papers. "Unless you've nothing helpful to say."

Thackery bit back a smile. Paisley liked him better than Rice. She liked them both better than Cade, probably because he was the bigger threat and he knew it.

She approached the desk and set her fingertips on it, leaning in to look Cade in the eye. "I know you have a lot of experience, and I'm not discounting that. But I have more experience with this town. I know them. I'm one of them. *You'd* do well not to discount *that*."

He leaned back in the chair and folded his arms across his chest. "That'd be the same town that can't stop whispering to each other about Paisley Bell and the 'odd hitch in her getup'?"

The pain of his mockery cut deeper than she was willing to let show. "And you were loved in every town you ever sheriffed in, were you?"

"None of them ever laughed at me."

"Hush your bickering, you two," Mrs. Wilhite instructed in her usual sweet voice. "I see a customer coming."

Paisley stepped back from the desk and sent Mrs. Wilhite an apologetic smile. She was a widow without a family. The Ribbon Emporium gave her a purpose and a reason to leave her house. The entire town did all they could to support her in it.

Rice and Thackery had sported smiles ever since Cade's cutting remark. Everyone was laughing at her lately, it seemed. She'd simply have to work that much harder to prove them all wrong.

Mr. Lewis stepped inside. His eyes met Paisley's. "Good day, Miss Bell."

"And to you, Mr. Lewis."

Interactions between them had been awkward from the very beginning. Mr. Lewis had replaced her father as head of the bank. She wasn't entirely certain why Mr. Lewis held that against them; it wasn't as though there'd been tension surrounding Papa's departure.

"I am in need of blue ribbon," Mr. Lewis told Mrs. Wilhite.

"Of course. Blue is in the first cell. I have so many different shades of blue." She fluttered across the room, eagerly guiding him to the blue ribbons.

Several more customers dropped in over the next half hour. Nearly all of them peppered Paisley with questions about why she was trying for the sheriff job, whether or not she was serious, and why her brief two weeks filling in as sheriff full-time hadn't been enough to satisfy her curiosity about the job. She took the questions in stride, keeping her cool throughout. She answered their inquiries then quickly changed the subject by introducing them to Rice, Thackery, and Cade before handing them over to the eager ministrations of the local ribboner.

Through it all, she could feel Cade watching her. He greeted each arrival in his typical gruff, take-charge manner. But quick as the striking of a match, his attention returned to her. She didn't flatter herself that he was mesmerized or enchanted. His expression put her firmly in mind of the eerie calm one feels in the air just before the breaking of a storm.

She'd managed to get enough information from Gideon to know of Cade's vast and impressive background. No man could bring law and order to as many infamous towns as he had and not be rather dangerous himself. Paisley hid all hints of worry, refusing to show in her posture or expression that he'd managed to intimidate her. Fear had never stopped her before—a twinge of worry certainly wouldn't stop her now.

By late that afternoon, Cade had returned to reading through the entire folder of marshal reports and the town's crime logs. He was thorough enough to convince even a skeptic that he fully believed the job would be his in the end. Rice and Thackery were antsy enough that she knew they sensed it as well. The whole town would be sold on the idea of *Sheriff* O'Brien if she didn't find a way to convince them to at least consider her.

The question still hung in the back of her mind that evening as she walked home. The house she shared with her father had once been pristine, filled with fine furnishings and impressive décor. The upstairs rooms were now nearly bare. She'd sold as much of the furniture and decorations in the public rooms as she could without making their straitened circumstances too obvious. They'd once been in a position to fund the building of both the jailhouse and the school and to contribute to the fund to bring a doctor to town. She couldn't bear the thought of becoming the town's charity case, not when she was young and able-bodied enough to work.

The salary the town meant to pay the new sheriff would ease every one of her financial burdens. She and her father would have food on the table, could replace some of the more crucial pieces of furniture they'd parted with. She could replace Papa's threadbare coat before the dangers of winter descended again.

Paisley could smell something frying the moment she stepped inside the house, so she moved immediately to the kitchen. "Papa?"

He stood hunched over two plates with one fish fillet on each, poking them about with a fork.

"Papa, you didn't have to cook." She rather preferred he didn't. There was no knowing if he would remain focused long enough to see his task through to the end or if he would abandon it for some new endeavor.

"I do know how to cook a fine fish. My father taught me not long ago."

Her grandfather had been dead for thirty years. It seemed Papa wasn't quite as firmly himself in that moment as she would have hoped.

"I'll fetch some bread," she said.

He looked over at her, and his brow pulled together in confusion. "Why are you dressed like that? Are you playing at being a soldier again?"

She and her brother had often spent their days as children pretending to be fighting in some imaginary war or another. But that was long ago, before actual warfare had claimed her brother and driven them from their home in Missouri. Papa had, it seemed, spied her gun belt and pistol and in his mind assumed she was still that tiny girl playing a game.

She pulled a loaf from the bread box, cutting two thick slices. "Would you like butter on your bread?"

He made a noise of agreement. She made quick work of the task then carried both plates into the once-elegant dining room. Papa had grieved the change in their circumstances back when it first began. He wasn't really aware of it any longer.

Paisley watched him as they ate, acutely missing the highly polished manners he'd once employed. Not that formality mattered to her; it was simply a recurring reminder that he was not the same person he'd once been.

"I had a busy day in town today," she said. "I believe I'm making progress in my bid to secure a new job."

"A new job? What happened to your last job?"

She hadn't had a job before, not really. They'd been living on their savings. He knew that, or had at some point.

"I am excited about this possibility. It's a job where I can help a lot of people and make a difference in the world."

"Mary-Catherine likes that kind of work," Papa said through his mouthful of fish. "She is forever helping people."

Paisley sighed inwardly. Mary-Catherine was her late mother, and Papa was not only speaking of her in the present but also used her Christian name. Did he not even remember that Paisley was his—and Mary-Catherine's—daughter?

She picked at her meal as he launched in to a retelling of his childhood. How was it he remembered those long-ago moments so well when he more and more often couldn't even recall what they'd done the day before? Gideon had assessed the situation months ago and reluctantly informed her that nothing could be done.

"Prepare yourself, Pais," he'd said. "He will only grow more distant with time. He'll be confused often, likely frustrated. It is impossible to predict how dementia will change him, but one thing I can tell you is that it *will* change him."

At some point, Papa wouldn't recognize her. He wouldn't remember fishing with her in the river behind their house in Missouri. He wouldn't remember teaching her to ride a horse or shoot a gun. Papa had seen her through the loss of her brother and her mother. He'd been her strength after her fiancé, Joshua, had walked out on her. He was the very best of fathers, and she would be a stranger to him.

He finished his meal and sat there, quiet, brow pulled low. His eyelids were heavy and his posture weary. Sometimes he struggled with things as instinctive as knowing what to do when he was tired.

"Perhaps you ought to go lay down," she suggested.

He nodded slowly, vaguely.

Paisley hooked her arm through his and walked with him up the stairs to his room. She paused in the doorway and placed a kiss on his cheek. "I love you, Papa," she said. "Sleep well."

He wandered inside. Would he remember to change into his night-clothes this time? It was impossible to say from day to day how alert he would be.

She closed his door, granting him that privacy, but she couldn't walk away entirely. She leaned against the wall and let the weight of the world settle on her.

She couldn't save her father from the bleak future he faced, but she would see to it he had food to eat and a roof over his head. She would make certain he was warm through the winter. All of that took money.

Oh, heavens, I need this job.

But it was more than the money. The thought of being robbed of one of her few sources of joy—work she enjoyed and was good at—left her with a gnawing sense of dread. The other candidates had a potential livelihood on the line, but Paisley had far more to lose than any of them.

Chapter 6

Cade set the spindle-back chair behind the desk once more and twisted the back a bit, testing its sturdiness. He spun his hammer the way he usually did his gun. Rice was acting as sheriff that day, but Cade never had been one for sitting around doing nothing. Fixing a chair sure beat twiddling his thumbs.

Paisley stepped out of the back room and eyed his handiwork. "George Andrews is the closest thing Savage Wells has to a carpenter. Perhaps when this sheriff job doesn't work out, you could ask to be his apprentice."

There was nothing quite like a sharp-tongued woman to keep a man on his toes.

She continued her trek across the room to the shelves of ribbons. She stretched and dusted the top shelf. Mrs. Wilhite had Paisley wrapped around her finger, even when she wasn't there.

"You're not too shabby with the ribbons," Cade said, leaning against the desk. "When they go, you might ask Mrs. Wilhite for a job."

"The ribbons and I both fit here just fine."

"A stubborn woman can beat the devil," he grumbled.

"My mother used to say 'Often as not, it is a man's mouth that breaks his nose,'" Paisley returned.

He knew the familiar turn of phrase. "You're gonna belt me, then?"

"I imagine I will eventually." She smiled a little. Paisley Bell was decidedly pretty when she smiled. A nag and a thorn, but pretty, just the same. "We had a great deal of wind last night that brought dust in by the bucketful. Seeing as I'm not in charge today"—she acknowledged Rice with a quick nod of her head—"I figure I've more than enough time to see to the sweeping."

"I'm no expert with a broom," Cade said. "I've far more experience with a gun."

"So do I, but a good sheriff hones the skills the job calls for." Paisley dusted yet another shelf of ribbons. There were *a lot* of ribbons.

"You're a pistoleer, then? Or just a terrible housekeeper?"

"It has to be one or the other, doesn't it?" She stepped back, eyeing her work.

"You didn't answer my question."

"No, I didn't." And that was, apparently, all she meant to say about it. She crossed the room as unconcerned as a cow in a green pasture.

Thackery, who had come to see Rice ply his trade as temporary sheriff, jumped up as Paisley approached the stool he sat on. "I can help clean up the dust as well," he said. "The sheriff I was deputy to before coming here had me do a lot of cleaning."

Paisley gave a firm nod of acceptance. "There's a dust rag in the bucket by the back room door."

Somehow the woman already had one of the candidates under her thumb.

Rice sauntered out onto the front porch, no doubt meaning to keep an eye on the street for a time. Cade knew exactly what he'd see; he, himself, had made a study of the view the day before. Well-kept businesses. A great many women and children, the former tending to stop and jaw a while with every person they passed. Cade had seen them do just that during his tour of the town with Gideon. It seemed gossip was Savage Wells's lifeblood.

He moved to the door of the cell Paisley was sweeping out. "So which is it? Gunslinger or Sloppy Sue?"

"Oh, good grief." She didn't even look up at him, and she certainly didn't seem likely to answer his question.

"I don't care for riddles," he warned.

Her smile was more of a smirk. "I'll keep that in mind."

He stepped further inside the cell, stepping around her broom so he could look her more fully in the eye. She knew how to get under his skin. He'd not enjoyed brangling so much in years. "Sharpshooter or lazy housekeeper?" he asked again.

"You're a career lawman," she said. "Use your highly honed powers of discernment and figure out the answer for yourself."

Were she any other woman, he'd never consider that she might be a gunfighter. But this was Paisley Bell. She could say she'd once been a pugilist and he'd believe her.

A broad-shouldered man in mud-speckled trousers stepped inside, his wide-brimmed hat stuffed haphazardly on his head. The man's eyes settled immediately on Paisley. "He's done it again! He's gone and done it, and I won't stand for it."

Cool as a cucumber, Paisley turned to Cade. "This is Mr. Abbott, his farm is north of town. Mr. Abbott, this is Cade O'Brien, a newly arrived lawman and fixer of broken chairs." She pointed to Thackery. "Mr. Thackery, just there, is also a lawman who's come to try his hand at sheriffing this den of villainy we live in."

"Pleasure," Mr. Abbott said quickly and gruffly before turning back to Paisley. "You have to—"

Paisley held up a hand to cut him off. "If you're here about sheriff business, you'll have to bring it up with Mr. Rice out on the front porch. He's filling that role today."

"There's no one out front," Mr. Abbott said.

Cade peeked out the front window. Sure enough, Rice wasn't there.

He'd likely gone out patrolling the streets. Cade himself had done that during his day yesterday.

Abbott jumped directly back into his earlier complaint. "You have to do something about him, Paisley. He's done it again! He's a lying, no-good—no-good—" Abbott struggled for his next word, but his temper didn't seem to cool in the least.

"What's the problem?" Cade strode across the room. Someone needed to take charge. He had rules against hysterics in his jail.

Abbott pointed eagerly as though he'd just stumbled upon something. "Heartless, that's what he is. He's heartless. Write that down, Paisley. He's heartless."

She leaned against the low half-wall that separated the cell area from the rest of the room. A ray of sunlight spilled through the open door, glinting off her high-polished pistol. "The last time you and Mr. Clark were at odds with one another, I wrote down that he was 'heartless,' so rest assured it has been recorded. The two of you swore then that you'd respect Annabelle's decision."

"Oh, I've honored it and respected it, but Clark's a dirty sneak thief."

"Would you like me to write that down as well?" Her question contained the tiniest hint of dryness.

The humor was lost on Abbott. "Yes," he said with emphasis. "A heartless sneak thief!"

A second man stormed inside at that very moment. "Annabelle came on her own, Abbott, and you know it."

Abbott turned on the spot, pointing his stubby finger at the new arrival. "Heartless sneak thief! It's written down, Clark. It's official now."

Paisley glanced down at her fingernails, not the least put out. "Mr. Clark, this is Cade O'Brien. He's come to learn how to be a sheriff. And Mr. Thackery, who, if my guess is correct, already knows how."

Troublesome.

She continued with the introductions. "This is Mr. Clark, whom Mr. Abbott has declared a 'heartless sneak thief.'"

Clark pulled off his shapeless hat and offered a quick bow. "Pleased to meet you." He even smiled, right up until the moment his hat was on his head again and his eyes on Abbott.

"Had her write that down, did you? Well, then she can just write down that you're a black-hearted cajoler. Write *that* down, Paisley." He waved his arms for emphasis. "Write that down!"

"Explain the trouble between you," Cade ordered. He'd not have them come to blows in the jailhouse.

"The trouble is this lily-livered sneak thief has taken my Annabelle," Abbott said.

"Wait just one moment, there," Paisley jumped in. "Is he lily-livered or is he heartless, because, honestly, I'm only going to write down one or the other."

Abbott actually stopped his blustering and thought about it. "Heartless," he finally decided. "Definitely heartless. Clark's not a coward."

"Why, thank you very much," Clark answered, sounding pleased by the compliment.

"Nothing but the truth," Abbott returned in the same friendly tone. "It does take a certain amount of gumption to make off with another man's—"

"She's come to live with me," Clark barked. "She was never happy with you. You don't care for her the way I do."

"You enticed her, tricked her." Abbott pointed an accusatory finger. "She'd never have left me if you hadn't put it in her head to do so."

They were fighting over a woman? No argument was stickier than that variety.

"She was never yours in the first place." Clark was nearly nose-to-chin with his much taller rival. "The judge said as much when he last came through."

Cade caught Paisley's eye. *"Judge?"*

She nodded. "The biggest case our local lawyer has tried in years. Well, nearly the only one, really. And he did have to represent both sides since he's the only attorney we have. Still, it was quite the to-do a few months back, especially since it afforded a rare, in-person glance at Mr. Larsen. Most people around here think he's just a rumor."

She was wandering far afield of the matter at hand. Cade motioned at the argument going on beside them.

Paisley waved it off. "It's an old, familiar dispute."

Years of bad blood made for hot tempers.

"Sheriff Garrison didn't care to be bothered with domestic disputes, so he handed this one over to me. I can easily address this, Cade." He half expected her to pat him on the head and send him off to play. She jumped back into the fray. "The judge ruled that the choice was Annabelle's," she reminded the men. "And you both agreed to honor her decision. Now, if she was with Mr. Abbott"—she looked at Mr. Clark—"then it would be a bit underhanded of you to lure her to your house."

Lure her. Sounded like a blasted kidnapping.

"I didn't lure her," Clark shot back. "She wanted to come. She's stood at the fence for weeks now, begging me. I could see she was unhappy."

Paisley sighed. "You didn't unlock the gate again, did you?"

Unlock the gate? "You keep her locked up?" Cade demanded.

"Of course we do," Abbott answered. "She'd wander all over creation otherwise."

"Annabelle isn't the brightest bird in the flock," Clark said.

Cade glared at the two men long and hard. "Seems to me you're takin' advantage of her simplicity." He'd not stand for that.

"It's not your day to be sheriff," Paisley said.

"Not yours either, and Rice ain't here." The situation was a shambles. "Give over, I'll fix this mess."

"Very well." She turned back to Clark and Abbott, each staring the other down. "Mr. O'Brien's going to sort this out. It'll be a good learning experience for him, I'm sure."

Cade bit his tongue. Annabelle's well-being mattered the most.

"But first," Paisley added, "let me repeat what I have been telling you for months now. You simply need to find a way to share Annabelle."

Share? Was the woman addled?

"Can't do that," Abbott said firmly. "Annabelle's mine. I'll not share her with anyone."

"Neither will I," Clark said.

Cade looked between the three of them. He had to be missing something.

Paisley held up her hands in helplessness. "Well, then, your only solution seems to be the one proposed by the judge when he heard your argument. Settle this trouble with a good, old-fashioned fried chicken dinner."

The men objected immediately and loudly. At least they thought Annabelle worth more than a hastily struck deal made over supper. For his part, Cade silently watched Paisley. He didn't trust the overly solemn expression she wore. She had something up her sleeve. But what?

"Come on then, men." Cade nodded to them both in turn. "Let's see what Annabelle has to say."

"You intend to talk to *Annabelle* about this?" Paisley asked. "Honestly, *talk* to her?"

"She ought to have a say."

"I'm not certain I'd set much store by Annabelle's decision-making skills," Paisley said. "She's likely to go with the first person who feeds her."

The first person who feeds her? It was too odd of a declaration to mean what it appeared to mean. What wasn't he seeing?

"We tried letting Annabelle decide," Abbott said, "but her tiny little chicken brain can't remember what it wants."

"Tiny, little—?" *Wait just one blasted minute.* Chicken brain. Bird. Wanders all over creation. *Wait.* "Annabelle is . . . a chicken, ain't she?"

"Of course she is," Abbott replied. "Best laying hen I've ever seen. And more than that, she's such a sweet bird, scratching about, pretty as a picture."

A chicken.

Clark nodded. "Never known a hen to produce so consistently without exception. And she's not mean like all the others, pecking at people and being ornery. She's a treasure. A prize. And that's why I'm not giving her up to the likes of him." He jerked a thumb in Abbott's direction. "*He* doesn't appreciate her like he ought."

"How dare you—"

Cade held up a single finger. They grew silent on the instant. "She's a chicken? An actual chicken?"

"Mm-hmm." Abbott's drawn brows suddenly shot up. "Ah, Jerusalem crickets!" He grinned broad as the horizon. "You thought Annabelle was a person? That we were fighting over a woman?"

A split second passed before both Clark and Abbott were nearly hunched over with laughter. Thackery didn't manage to stifle his laugh entirely. Paisley grinned. Pleased with herself, was she? He'd deal with her in a minute.

"Here he was thinking we were going to 'share' a woman." Clark choked on the words.

Abbott chortled. "What would my wife think of that?"

Paisley executed a flourishing bow, clearly quite proud of the merry dance she'd led him on.

Enjoy your moment, Paisley Bell. It'll end soon enough.

He turned back to the two men.

"We should have told you right from the start that Annabelle's a hen," Abbott said through his laughter.

"That would've helped, yes."

Paisley had the audacity to speak. "Would you like me to write that down?"

Cade kept his gaze on the men, not trusting himself to look at her at the moment. He let his expression turn good-natured. He stood casually with his thumb hooked in its usual place behind his gun belt. "You'd best settle this, men. I'd suggest a yard all her own, half on each of your properties. That you—" He hated having to use Paisley's exact word, but it was the most fitting one. "That you *share* her."

Thackery, who stood in the nearby cell, dust rag in hand, listening to every word, nodded. "That does seem best."

"We can split the cost of building the yard," Abbott added. "And we can build her a little henhouse."

The men shook hands on it, though their chuckles didn't die down. They made their way up the road once more, talking as though there'd never been a quarrel between them.

Cade waited until Thackery returned to his dusting before addressing Paisley. "That was quite a trick."

"Not a trick at all. I simply knew something you didn't, and you didn't bother asking for my help."

"Chose the perfect words, didn't you? Made sure I thought Annabelle was a person." He turned around slowly, breathing through his frustration. "Quite a trick."

"I suppose I can see how you might have grown confused. Next time, you ought to simply ask for my help."

He folded his arms across his chest. "Keep this up and there'll not be a next time. It would be easy as anything to end this competition right now."

"Just what is that supposed to mean?" Her gaze narrowed.

"There's more than one way to skin a cat, love."

"Remind me to hide the cats," she said dryly.

"It ain't the cats you ought to be worryin' about."

For the first time since he'd met her, Paisley actually looked a little unsettled.

"I'll not have you undermining everything I do, Miss Bell," he warned. "And who's to say you won't start sabotaging the others, too?"

She held her ground, eyeing him defiantly. "And you taking over the chicken dispute when it was Rice's day—isn't that undermining *him*?"

He shook his head. "Trickery ain't my style. Rice was gone. There was a problem. I'm efficient not underhanded. I want your word that you aren't going to be pulling any more of these tricks."

She seemed to ponder a moment.

"I'm not asking for you to consider it," he said. "I'm saving you from yourself. A word or two dropped in the right ears and you'd be out of the running." He'd taken the town council's measure straight off. They'd be easily talked around. "Either start bein' a straight shooter, or this'll end for you real quick."

She didn't look intimidated by his threat, but she also didn't look as defiant either. "Tomorrow's my day as sheriff."

"I know."

She eyed him suspiciously. "No trickery from you on my days?"

"None," he promised.

"This could be interesting." Her mouth tipped upward on one side, and an unmistakable look of mischief entered those brown eyes. "And because I am feeling particularly generous, I'll agree to give you whatever help you eventually realize you need."

"Enjoying this, aren't you?"

"Enjoying *what*?" She spoke far too innocently.

"Brangling with someone." No, that wasn't quite it. She didn't spar with Rice or Thackery. "Brangling with someone who can keep up with you," he amended.

"And you figure that's you?"

He took a step closer to her. The set of her shoulders, the upward twitch of her mouth, the gleam of anticipation in her eyes. It all confirmed his suspicions. She most certainly enjoyed crossing swords with him.

"If it's a challenge you're looking for, darlin', I'll happily oblige." His pulse picked up at the thought. "But don't expect me to go easy on you."

She stood up straighter, closing much of the gap between them. The air crackled over his skin as she held his gaze. He'd wager if he actually touched her, sparks would fly.

"'Go easy on me'?" she scoffed. "Where would be the fun in that?"

"Oh, this'll be a great deal of fun." His voice lowered of its own accord.

Her pert little mouth twisted in the earliest renderings of a smile. "Do you promise?"

"I guarantee it."

Chapter 7

Pull yourself together, Paisley. She leaned against a post outside the jail-house, trying for the hundredth time since the previous afternoon to focus her thoughts. Something had happened between her and Cade the day before, something she couldn't make any sense of. They'd been trading barbs, like they often did, when without warning the exchange had gone from chilly to inarguably warm.

"There's more than one way to skin a cat," he'd warned her just before the change in tone. That was the most likely explanation for what had happened—he was trying to undermine her despite his promises to the contrary. She didn't intend to let him.

Today was her day as sheriff. Paisley didn't know if she'd rather the day be quiet and uneventful or if she'd do more for her cause by tackling a few problems here and there. Sheriff Garrison had left more and more things for her to handle toward the end of his time in Savage Wells. She was good at the work but never received any credit. This was her chance to show the entire town that she could be exactly what they wanted and needed, if only they weren't too thickheaded to acknowledge it. Of course, not even the other candidates had come to see her at work.

"Good morning, Paisley." *Speaking of thickheaded people.* Gideon stood on his front porch next door.

"You appear to be having a lie-about sort of day," Paisley said. "Is there no one with lung inflammation or a sore throat today?"

"*I* am having a lazy day? What about you?" Gideon leaned on the porch railing, grinning at her. "Don't you have a still to break up or a notorious bank robber to smoke out of a cave?"

Paisley turned so her back was pressed to the post. "I'll get around to that this afternoon."

"You think you're up for such a task, do you?" Cade stepped out onto the porch, apparently having overheard.

"I'm more than just a pretty face," she answered.

"You are that," he muttered.

Was she meant to have heard that? She couldn't imagine Cade would offer a compliment on purpose. Still, he *had* said it. "I am *which*? A pretty face or more than?"

"You're wanting to be a lawman," he said, echoing her words from the day before. "Use your highly honed powers of discernment and figure out the answer for yourself."

Mrs. Wilhite suddenly rushed down the street from the millinery, waving her arms frantically. "Paisley!" she called out. "The millinery's been robbed."

Though Mrs. Wilhite knew as well as Paisley did that Mrs. Carol's "emergencies" were never real, she humored her sweet friend and called for the sheriff as the need arose.

Paisley smiled to herself. It had been a few weeks since she'd had to visit the hat shop. And a robbery this time. Those were always vastly enjoyable. She held Mrs. Wilhite's gaze a moment, silently making certain the crisis wasn't a real one. Mrs. Wilhite gave the tiniest shake of her head. *An imaginary emergency, then.*

"Tell Mrs. Carol that I'll be right there, Mrs. Wilhite," Paisley said.

Mrs. Wilhite nodded and headed back to the milliner's shop.

Paisley stepped off the walk and into the road.

Cade was quick on the uptake. He reached her side after only two strides. "What's been taken?"

"My day as sheriff," she reminded him.

"Burglaries ought to be handled by—"

"*My* day," she repeated.

He stopped his protest and held up his hands in a show of surrender. Nothing in his demeanor spoke of defeat, simply annoyed acceptance. He had proposed this arrangement, and she meant to hold him to it.

"Mind if I tag along?" he asked.

"And do what, exactly?" So help her, if he meant to interfere . . .

"Observe. I've not met the milliner yet. Seems a good opportunity to do so."

That was fair enough. She nodded her acceptance, then walked once more in the direction of the millinery shop.

"And I'll be handy should you need m' help," he added.

The blasted man could use a firm knock upside the head. "I won't need it."

She hazarded a brief glance in his direction. He was barely holding back a grin. So he'd been teasing, had he? Did that mean he knew she wouldn't need help and was simply ribbing her? Or was he laughing at her confidence?

Perhaps observing her at work would do him good. She wasn't the helpless female he clearly thought she was.

She pushed open the door to the milliner shop, setting off the bell overhead. She could have predicted with perfect clarity the scene she stepped into. This ordeal had been enacted many times. The shop looked as tidy as ever, with colorful hats and accoutrements arranged masterfully throughout the room. Mrs. Wilhite stood beside Mrs. Carol, the milliner, with the expected look of empathy, holding her friend's hand and whispering the usual words of reassurance.

Mrs. Carol, true to form, held a handkerchief to her heart with a look of almost angelic suffering on her face.

Paisley assumed a posture of clear concern and worry, though she felt neither. She wasn't coldhearted, she'd simply been through enough of these "robberies" to know the entire thing was little more than Mrs. Carol's terribly unreliable memory wreaking havoc on her overblown imagination.

"I understand you've been burglarized," Paisley said.

"I have indeed." Mrs. Carol emphasized the declaration with a nod of her head. "I—" Her gaze narrowed on Paisley. "Are you wearing the sheriff's badge?"

Paisley gave a firm and decisive nod.

"Then the rumors *are* true." She turned to Mrs. Wilhite. "I wasn't sure I believed it—our Paisley trying for sheriff." Mrs. Carol's tone was not one of approval, but neither was it entirely horrified.

"She always did go her own way," Mrs. Wilhite said. "Although a woman sheriff is more odd than she—"

"What is missing, Mrs. Carol?" Paisley would rather not hear about how strange her ambitions were. The town hadn't minded her "assisting" the last sheriff, but taking over the job entirely was more than most were ready to accept.

"Ah, yes. The burglary." Mrs. Carol focused once more. "I haven't a single stem of cherries anywhere in the store. Someone has come in during the dark of the night and made off with them."

"Oh, dear." Paisley had long since perfected the worried tone to use during these conversations. She pulled out her small notebook. "How many ought there to be?"

"Oh, at least two dozen." Mrs. Carol pointed to the palm-sized pad of paper. "And write down that paper cherries are all the rage this year."

Paisley complied. Her notebook was full of Mrs. Carol's misplaced items along with the reasons why each thing was particularly fashionable. There were also several sheets dedicated to Annabelle the Chicken's adventures, as well as customers who didn't care for the food at the restaurant, and changes in Mr. Gilbert's grocery list. This was her "people need someone to complain to" notebook. She had begun keeping it after the chicken trial.

"And is anything else missing besides the cherries?"

"No." Mrs. Carol shook her head, her eyes wide in amazement. "Clearly these criminals have excellent taste." She looked at her dear friend, the alarm in her expression growing. "You had best keep a weather eye out, Thelma. They'll be after your lavender ribbon next."

"Isn't the lavender heavenly?" Mrs. Wilhite sighed a bit. "Just the right stiffness to be shapeable without being cumbersome."

"Oh, simply divine," Mrs. Carol answered. "I fell in love with it the very first moment I saw it. And such a daring shade, as well. Not overly dark, but not so bright it's gaudy."

"I couldn't agree more. Mrs. Holmes ordered it special from a catalog. Wasn't that lovely of her?"

"Simply lovely." Mrs. Carol smiled. "And soon enough you'll have your silver."

"I told her if she sees any other promising colors to be certain to let me know." Mrs. Wilhite was never quite as animated as when she spoke of ribbon. "I could use a new deep red. The one I have now has grown so tiresome."

From behind Paisley, Cade whispered. "Do you mean to start looking for clues?"

Paisley shook her head. "That won't be necessary."

She could feel his incredulous stare though she didn't glance back at him. Mrs. Carol and Mrs. Wilhite had moved on to a discussion of the many uses of blue ribbon. Paisley casually crossed the room and sat on an empty chair. Cade followed, watching her as though she'd lost her mind.

"You ain't gonna solve this crime?" Did Cade always tip his head to the side when scolding someone? She'd likely have ample opportunity to find out.

"On the contrary," she said. "I've solved it already."

And it seemed a lift of one golden eyebrow *while* tipping his head to the side was his personal expression of utter disbelief. He sat in the chair next to hers, watching her through narrowed eyes.

Good heavens, he has beautiful blue eyes.

"You've solved it?" he asked.

She gave a single nod.

Cade lowered his voice to a whisper. "Who's our thief, then?"

Paisley matched his volume. "Mrs. Carol."

And they were back to the uplifted eyebrow and tipped head. "Stole her own supplies?"

"No. She misplaced her own supplies. She does it all the time." Paisley leaned back in the chair, enjoying a moment's relaxation. "After she closes up shop for the day, I'll come back and look through her storage room until I find her cherries, then I'll return them to her in the morning."

He sat in silence, his expression confused. "Does Mrs. Wilhite know the truth?"

Paisley nodded. "But she chooses not to embarrass her friend."

"You do this often?"

She nodded again.

He slumped back in his chair, his posture nearly identical to her own. "It seems a great deal of wasted time."

"Not a bit of it. This is how it's done here."

"Your last sheriff did this?" He motioned toward Mrs. Wilhite and Mrs. Carol who were thumbing through spools of ribbon.

"No. *I* did this because he couldn't be bothered."

"Hmm." It was the same wordless grunt he'd made before declaring Mrs. Wilhite's ribbons would have to move. Apparently he meant to ignore Mrs. Carol's "emergencies" should he become sheriff.

"What are we to do, Paisley?" Mrs. Carol asked.

Toss Cade out before he turns this entire place topsy-turvy. Paisley stood, trading her concerned expression for one of confidence. "I believe this may very well be the same evildoers who struck last time."

Mrs. Carol nodded firmly. "I thought it might be. They made off with all of my blue feathers before, which are also quite fashionable."

"Yes, I remember writing that down."

"Suppose they steal something else?" Mrs. Carol was always a bit frantic at this part of the conversation.

Paisley moved to Mrs. Carol's side. "I will stand guard tonight, as usual."

That suggestion always struck Mrs. Carol as a surprise, though it was Paisley's approach every time.

"I do believe your robbers will see the error of their ways once more."

"And if they don't?"

Paisley patted the milliner's hand. "If the situation grows more dire, I'll employ more aggressive tactics." Meaning, of course, she'd search through more drawers and boxes in the storage room.

Mrs. Carol was clearly relieved. Paisley tossed Cade a triumphant look.

He stood, even as he looked around the shop. "How long've you had a shop here, Mrs. Carol?" he asked.

"Since just after my husband died. He left me money enough and instructions to do something with it that I'd always wanted to do." She pressed her open palm to her heart. "Wasn't that sweet of him?"

He smiled—a genuine, real smile—and for a moment, Paisley could hardly breathe. She'd noticed his handsomeness from the first moment she'd seen him standing outside the jail, but that smile was enough to send her pulse into a sprint.

"He sounds like he was a fine man," Cade said. "I wish I could've known him."

"He was. You seem a good sort, yourself, though a little intimidating."

Cade nodded and said, "A crucial part of being a sheriff. Being a bit frightening can win a lot of battles before they're even fought."

Mrs. Wilhite tipped her head to the side, watching them both. "But Paisley isn't frightening."

"I'll do just fine," Paisley insisted.

"A pleasure to meet you, ma'am." He emphasized the word with a quick nod of his head. "Paisley seems to have this current trouble firmly in hand. If you're needing anything else, let me know."

"I will, thank you." Mrs. Carol smiled sweetly. "And it's very nice to meet you, Sheriff O'Brien."

She is already calling him "Sheriff." Am I even going to be given a chance?

He slipped his hat on his head then pulled the door open. "Whenever you're ready, Paisley."

So much for not taking over when it's my day. She glared at him as she strode through the doorway. Mrs. Wilhite remained in the shop with her friend. Paisley fumed as she headed down the street to the jailhouse. Cade walked silently at her side.

One step inside the jail and she spun about, facing him. "*My* day, Cade O'Brien. You set down the rules for this treaty we're living under and then broke them the very first day."

"Rein in your temper." His hat was on the coatrack again. "I've done nothing of the sort."

"Oh, haven't you?" She overdid her look of contemplation. "I do believe your exact words were, 'If you're needing anything else, let *me* know.' My day, Cade." She pointed an angry finger at him. "It's my day today."

"Don't get your petticoats in a knot." He slipped his hand around hers, gently folding her pointed finger back down. "I didn't undermine you on purpose. It was habit, that's all."

She didn't believe it for a moment. "Well, you had better rid yourself of that habit, Cade O'Brien. You have a week and a half left, then you'll be on your way."

Far from threatened, he watched her with curiosity. "Would you miss me?"

"Not for a moment."

He shook his head slowly and tugged her toward him. "I don't believe you."

"Why not?" She hated how his nearness rendered even her most forceful words a bit breathless.

"For one thing, your eyes sparkle when we banter." His eyes traveled over her face, likely seeing the blush she felt creeping over her cheeks. "And for another"—he slid up beside her, his cheek actually touching hers, and whispered in her ear—"you're still holdin' my hand."

She yanked her hand free of his, though he didn't put up any sort of a fight. "I hate you," she muttered.

"I know." He swaggered toward the back room. "Have a good day of sheriffing. Day after tomorrow I'll show you how it's really done."

She clenched her fists as he disappeared through the doorway. That no-good, arrogant polecat. He was playing dirtier than she'd expected. Talking himself up to the locals. Speaking to her in a way that set her pulse strumming and clouded her thinking. If only he'd taken the same approach as Rice and Thackery and hadn't shown up today at all.

She paced the room. Somehow Cade had discovered her greatest vulnerability. She was lonely. Showing her some personal attention, even feigned, even fleeting, played right to that weakness.

So what is Cade's weakness?

"He's arrogant, for starters," she muttered under her breath. The man clearly thought he had his victory already in hand despite having three competitors. Overconfidence was certainly a weakness.

Perhaps that was her answer. She would let him continue to think his little tricks were working, allowing him to focus his efforts on upending her rather than proving himself. He had no idea how good she really could be at this job. While he was strutting about, she'd be proving her worth.

The more she thought on it, the more sure she was. Cade could keep up his smug efforts; she was aware of his game now. And she would beat him at it.

Chapter 8

"Paisley's currently breaking into the hat shop," Cade said between bites of his dinner.

Gideon grinned as he spooned up a bite of potatoes and gravy. The two of them had become regulars at the restaurant. "She does have a lock-picking kit and is quite adept at using it."

That didn't surprise Cade in the least. "She's an odd sort of woman, and she'd make an odd sort of sheriff."

"Most sheriffs you know don't pick locks?"

He shook his head. "Or smell nice." And Paisley *did*. A tangy, flowery scent. He could still recall it from earlier that afternoon when he'd whispered in her ear. "And she doesn't dress the part."

"You expect her to wear trousers and a leather vest?"

"It's not the dress." Cade took a drink of water. "It's all the lace and ribbons. It don't fit the sheriffin' mold."

Gideon laughed. "I'd say, in terms of a female sheriff, Paisley's creating the mold, not trying to fit into it."

The man had a point. "Still, she's a puzzle." He took a bite of his steak, the best dish the restaurant served. "Why's she so stubborn about this job? Does she need the pay?"

"That's a complicated question to answer," Gideon said. "She did a lot of work for Sheriff Garrison, but wasn't paid. So while I think the money would be helpful, it's unlikely she's pursuing the post strictly for the sake of the income."

Which explained why she wasn't setting her sights on a more traditional job. There was more to it than money.

"If she worked for your last sheriff so much, why's everyone so astounded to see her vying for the job now?"

Gideon thought on it a while. "Partly because no one has ever heard of a woman sheriff before, and new things are always a little unnerving. And partly because most of the things she did for our last sheriff went unseen. He took credit for everything he thought would reflect well on him."

That wasn't surprising. Women were often given the short end of the stick. "But you seem to know. Are you intending to preach to the council on her behalf?"

"I already did," Gideon said. "We met last night, not to make a decision, but the topic did come up unofficially."

"She's fortunate to have you as a friend." Cade wondered if there was more to Paisley and Gideon's connection than mere friendship. That might tip at least Gideon's vote in her favor.

They paid for their meals and headed toward Gideon's house.

"Sure is quiet in this town." Cade filled his lungs with air free of the smell of saloons and gunpowder. "That's a rare enough thing this side of the Mississippi."

"It's rare on the other side as well, you know." They stepped up onto Gideon's porch. "I grew up in the nation's capital, and it's *never* quiet in that city."

"Boston was like that as well."

"Do you miss it?" Gideon asked.

"My sister's still there, and I miss her. But I'd not trade the openness of the West for those cramped quarters again." Just the thought of being trapped between buildings so tall a body could hardly see the sky made him feel closed in and panicky. No, he didn't miss that at all.

"Last time I visited Washington, I felt as though everyone in the entire city was stepping on my toes." Gideon dropped onto his porch swing. "My family couldn't understand why I was so anxious to leave again."

"Not everyone's suited to life out here," Cade said, leaning against the porch post. He most certainly was. It suited him perfectly.

Paisley emerged from the back of the millinery shop, a small box in her arms. The paper cherries, he'd reckon. She stopped in front of Gideon's porch.

"Good evening, boys. How's everything?"

"Just dandy." Gideon motioned for her to join him on the swing. "And how are you?"

"Can't complain. I'm nearly done for the day. Nothing brings a twinkle to my eye quite like picking a lock," Paisley added with a smile.

She sat beside Gideon. Right beside him without any of the hesitation a young, unmarried woman would usually have cozying up to a young, unmarried man. Yes, there was definitely something more there than friendship.

Gideon looked more closely at her. "How is everything at home?"

Her expression instantly grew more solemn. "A little better of late. It's hard not to get my hopes up."

Gideon nodded even as he sighed. What was happening in Paisley's home? Something serious, it seemed.

The two didn't dwell on the topic long enough for Cade to gather any clues. "That's quite a few cherries." Gideon motioned to her open-topped box. "Making a pie or something?"

"You've had my pie, Gideon. Are you really hoping the answer to that question is 'yes'?"

Gideon grinned. "Definitely not."

"You don't bake, then?" Cade pressed.

"Do you?" she tossed back.

"Some."

"I'm no gourmet, but I can cook a few things. I guess that's another tally mark for me." She tapped her fingers on the top of the box. "I'm winning, you know."

"Are you?"

Her pert little mouth twitched upward on one side. "Yes, I am."

"She is," Gideon said.

"You've seen the tallies?"

"Seen them?" Paisley scoffed. "He's added marks. For *me*."

Cade eyed Gideon. "So, you're a dirty-double crosser, then?"

"Can I help it if I'm such a likable fellow that I make friends on both sides of any argument?" Gideon straightened his cuffs. "It's a curse."

"I can think of a few curses myself," Cade muttered.

"I have a Ribbon Emporium to lock up for the night." Paisley stood and shifted her box to her other arm. "I'll see you tomorrow, Cade."

"You're coming to see if Thackery is likely to best you in this competition?" he asked.

Her smile broadened, her eyes dancing anew. "To see if he's likely to best *you*." With that parting shot, she walked away.

Lands, but he enjoyed quarreling with her.

"Is that something people in Savage Wells do?" Cade asked Gideon. "Keep score?"

"No, my friend. I believe that is something *women* do."

Cade looked out over the darkening horizon. The sun had dipped behind the distant mountains. A person didn't see sunsets in the city to rival any out West. Cade wasn't ever going back. Even with its tendency toward lawlessness and the uncertainty of new towns in untried places, the West was home to him.

"I should call it a night myself." He ambled in the direction of the hotel where he'd be staying until the contest was over. He paused across the street from the jailhouse, watching Paisley through the front windows. She could be prickly as a porcupine, but there were moments . . .

He shook off the thought before it fully formed.

His hand tingled with the remembered warmth of touching hers earlier that afternoon. He'd meant it as nothing more than a bit of banter. But he'd nearly pulled her into his arms. Nearly held her close to him. He'd nearly kissed her.

"Careful, Cade O'Brien. It's a dangerous game you're playing," he said to himself.

* * *

Cade sat on the edge of his bed, his elbows on his knees, his head hanging down. A sudden storm had broken not long after he'd crawled into bed. Flashes of lightning lit his room. Crashes of thunder shook the windows. He pushed out one tense breath after another. The breaking of a storm never failed to dredge up memories of battle.

He knew the sights and sounds were nothing but the storm. He wasn't actually afraid. His was a battle with memories and regrets. He rubbed at his temples, flinching when a clap of thunder shook the room.

The sound of men shouting frantic orders filled his mind. Screams of pain. Saints, he could still smell the gunpowder, the blood. So much blood.

He stood, pacing around the room. Tension twisted inside him. He rubbed at the back of his neck. Another flash lit the curtains. Cade took a calming breath. He knew some former soldiers who went into a panic during storms or at the sight of a uniform. He wasn't in such a shambles, himself, but he still didn't enjoy the memories.

He'd endured his share of thunderstorms over the past decade. But he'd sat through them in violent towns. The claps of thunder had been joined by gunshots. The drunken shouts from the streets had nearly drowned out the remembered groans of death and suffering in his mind.

A few more circuits around the room and a few more breaths calmed him. Between the crashes of thunder, all was silent. Still. Peaceful. Not only was the war over, his years of gunning down an endless stream of criminals was as well. Life was going to be far less brutal now.

He was on the cusp of claiming the perfect way of living out his life. He could make a difference, keep the peace, and use his skills, all without needing to live every moment with his hand hovering over his weapon. He could be a sheriff without also being a killer.

Chapter 9

Cade stood at the open door of the jailhouse. The morning was a quiet one after the stormy night that had passed. Blessedly quiet.

A woman walked by, holding the hand of a little boy. Cade tipped his hat. She offered a good morning. Her son watched him, turning his head as they continued down the walk. Cade hooked a thumb over his gun belt and gave the lad a friendly wink. He received a wide-eyed look of excitement in return.

He stepped out to the edge of the overhang, resting his shoulder against the front post. Paisley made her way over from the millinery shop. Her thick, dark hair, fine features, and slim figure would be enough to catch any man's eye. But it was more than that with her. She snatched his entire attention every time. It frustrated him to no end. No woman had ever captivated him the way she did.

Cade shook off the spell she cast even from across the street. It was Thackery's day as sheriff, and Cade meant to see how the man went about it. Rice had done well enough two days earlier, though not much had happened.

Paisley stepped up onto the porch and leaned against the opposite post. "You're doing it again."

"Doing what?"

She motioned to him, then out at the street. "Taking over for another sheriff."

"I'm just keeping an eye on things is all." He adjusted his hat. "I'm letting Thackery run things, just as I let you run things. I keep my promises, Paisley Bell."

"Promises are like smoke," she tossed back. "Easy to produce and quickly waved away."

"I'm a man of m' word."

"I've known a few 'men of their word' in my life," she said. "The only thing they taught me was never to take anyone at his word."

Now that was a telling revelation. "There's a story behind that."

She turned away from him. "You don't know what it's like to keep a town safe only to have them all look at you askance for being different."

How little she understood. "You've not been at this long enough." He crossed to where she stood. "In this job, you're always a bit different. You're the hard one, the cold one. You're the wall between the citizens and the criminals, and that's often a lonely position to be in."

"So why do we keep doing it?"

He'd asked himself that very question off and on for nearly a decade. "Because they need us. And neither of us are the sort to turn our backs on people in need." He moved toward the jailhouse door.

"They need us, but they keep us at arm's length." She followed on his heels. "Painfully ironic, isn't it?"

She'd dredged up a topic he generally kept buried. "It is what it is, Paisley. Either learn to live with it or search out a new line of work."

He nodded to Thackery seated at the desk, then made his way to a tall stool near the back. Paisley did the same.

"You couldn't allow even one moment of agreement between us?" Very little amusement touched her scolding tone.

He glanced at her and allowed the smallest of smiles. "Where would be the fun in that?"

"We might as well have fun while we're trying to beat each other out for this job, is that it?"

That was about what it had come to. "We're friendly enemies."

Something in that didn't sit well with her at all. Contemplation pulled at her features, and not a happy sort either. Paisley Bell was as puzzling as she was stubborn.

A young girl rushed into the building. "Help! Help!"

For such a quiet town, this sort of thing seemed rather common.

Cade, Paisley, and Thackery all jumped up and asked her in unison what the matter was. The poor girl's confusion only added to her panic. If ever there was evidence that the council's trial period was an idiotic notion, this was it.

After only a moment, she crossed directly to *him*. Paisley frowned, but Cade was used to people pegging him as the one in charge. "What's the trouble?"

"He's stuck in the tree," the girl said.

Cade hunched down in front of her. "Who's stuck in a tree?"

"Rupert."

"Is Rupert a person or an animal?" Before Savage Wells that hadn't been a necessary question.

"He's my brother." The worry on her freckled face couldn't be mistaken. "He climbed up there, and he can't come back down. Will you help him, please?"

"Of course, sweetie." He stood and held out his hand to her. "We'll all help you. Mr. Thackery, here, is our sheriff today. He'll lead the way."

"Oh, please hurry." She tugged Cade toward the door.

Cade motioned for Thackery to step out ahead of them. Rice was just then stepping up onto the porch.

"Are we headed somewhere?" he asked.

"We're on a rescue mission," Thackery said.

Thackery was the quietest of them all, but it was good to see he could take charge when need be.

"What's your name?" Cade asked his young guide as she pulled him forward.

"Jenny Fletcher."

"I'm very pleased to meet you, Miss Fletcher. I'm Sheriff O'Brien." That was likely a little presumptuous, but it was habit. And it might set her mind at ease to feel she'd made an ally of a sheriff.

She kept the pace swift. "Can you climb a tree, Sheriff O'Brien?"

"I haven't in some time."

She dropped his hand and looked up at him, wide-eyed. "Well, what good are you, then?"

"I'll sort this out. Just give me a chance."

She looked unconvinced. "I suppose. But you gotta help Rupert."

"We will."

Every child in the school must've been standing about when Jenny pulled Cade into the yard.

"Now, where's this brother of yours?" he asked Jenny.

She pointed at the tallest tree he'd seen in that part of Wyoming Territory. Rupert didn't do things halfway.

He looked to Thackery. "What's the plan?"

"I'll talk with the teacher," Thackery said. "She'll likely know what happened. And I'll ask her to keep the children inside. Having them roaming about will make this more complicated."

It wasn't a bad plan. Cade positioned himself at the trunk, glancing up. He recognized the woman standing at the base of the tree; he had nodded to her and her boy outside the jailhouse earlier. She wrung her hands, her eyes not leaving the branches above.

"Rupert's your little one, then?" Cade asked.

She nodded. "I can't even say how he got up so far. He's never climbed so high before."

Cade could hardly make him out, the boy was so far out of reach. High as he was, Rupert might not be sitting on the sturdiest of limbs. Getting to him without adding to the danger would be tricky at best.

"How are we ever to get him down?" Mrs. Fletcher's voice held a note of panic.

"Don't fret, ma'am. We'll manage the thing." Just how, Cade couldn't say. It wouldn't be an easy climb.

His gaze fell on Paisley, standing among them all. Their eyes met.

"I doubt either of us could make that climb safely," she said.

Thackery rejoined the group. "Even if we could, it'd be a risk to the boy. What we need is an expert climber, if there is such a thing."

Cade snapped his fingers. "Andrew Gilbert."

Paisley nodded immediately. "Of course."

Quick as that, she was gone. Cade turned to Thackery. "We should also send for Dr. MacNamara."

Thackery pointed at Rice. "Go fetch Doc."

Rice nodded his understanding and left with haste.

"You think we'll need the doctor?" Mrs. Fletcher's voice was hardly audible.

"Rupert might've scratched himself or something, that's all." Cade sincerely hoped they weren't faced with anything more serious than that.

Chapter 10

"Sit tight, Rupert," Cade called up into the branches. "We'll have you down quicker'n a cat with her tail on fire."

"Yes, sir," a tiny voice echoed down to him.

"I should have been watching more closely," Mrs. Fletcher said, her palm pressed to her heart. "I should have."

"It's nothing too different than the mischief every child gets into," Cade said. "Some more than others."

A moment of wearied amusement crossed her features. "Rupert is always getting himself into scrapes."

"Reminds me of another young boy whose mother swore each day he'd be the death of her."

"Was that young boy you?" Mrs. Fletcher asked.

"Indeed." Cade took a slow walk around the thick tree trunk. The lowest branches looked sturdy. He could only hope that held true up higher. A few onlookers had drawn near. Thackery sent them scattering with a quick command. That was wise. It'd be dangerous for anyone to spook the boy before Andrew arrived.

Mrs. Fletcher pushed out a deep, tense breath. "I don't think I'll even breathe until he's back on solid ground."

Thackery stepped in. "I've heard from Miss Bell that Andrew Gilbert is an excellent tree climber. I think we can count on him to help us out."

Mrs. Fletcher didn't look convinced. "Yes, but Andrew is—" Her gaze dropped as she thought through whatever it was she meant to say. "Andrew is Andrew," she finally settled on.

What does that mean?

Rice arrived with Gideon at his side. They moved directly to Cade.

"Rupert?" Gideon asked.

Cade pointed up into the branches. "Nearly to the very top of the tree."

"Let's hope he keeps still. That's a long fall for such a little body."

Paisley returned. Alone.

"Where's Andrew?" Thackery asked.

Paisley pointed a thumb over her shoulder. Sure enough, Andrew stood at least twenty feet off. He eyed the scene with thick wariness.

"Andrew," Thackery called out. "We need your help."

The entire group turned toward Andrew, watching, waiting.

"Come on, then." Rice waved him over. "Look lively."

Andrew didn't take a single step.

"He won't come," Paisley said.

"You explained the situation to him?" Thackery asked.

"Of course. He is waiting on the two of you," she said, pointing to Rice and Thackery.

"Waiting on us to do what?" Thackery asked.

"Back away. He doesn't like strangers."

"But only the two of us?" Thackery pressed. "Not O'Brien?"

Paisley shook her head. "He trusts Cade."

Now everyone was watching *him.* "Do what needs to be done to get Andrew over here and up that tree."

Thackery, to his credit, hesitated only a moment. "Rice, you stand outside the schoolhouse and make sure none of the children come darting out. Miss Bell, would you stand friend to Mrs. Fletcher? This day's work likely has her tied in knots."

Paisley guided Mrs. Fletcher and Jenny away from the tree. Gideon had already stepped back.

Only Cade remained at the tree. One, slow step at a time, Andrew drew nearer. His eyes darted about. Voices sounded from across the street. Andrew stopped in his tracks.

A piece of the puzzle fell into place. "Andrew doesn't like to be around people," Cade said.

Paisley was near enough to overhear. "He *can't* be around people," she corrected.

"He's not dangerous, is he?" Cade'd been greeted with a shotgun the first time they'd met, after all.

"No, he's not dangerous." Paisley offered Andrew an encouraging smile.

Cade kept as quiet as Andrew. The man finally reached the tree and looked up into the branches.

"He's up high," Andrew said.

"Higher than any of us can climb," Cade answered. "Can you?"

He nodded firmly. After one more study of the tree, Andrew turned to Cade. "Any premonitions?"

"Only good ones."

That seemed enough. Andrew pulled off his jacket, folded it carefully, and laid it on the ground. He walked one-quarter of the way around the tree then pulled himself up onto the lowest branch. After that, he moved so swiftly Cade could hardly follow his progress.

Gideon came and stood beside Cade. Thackery stayed several paces away and motioned for Rice to do the same. Cade held his breath. Getting to Rupert was the easy part. Getting him down was another story.

"Will being near Rupert be a problem for Andrew?" Cade asked Gideon.

"He is happiest in the trees. Rupert will be back on the ground in no time, but Andrew might not come all the way down for a while."

Andrew guided Rupert down one branch at a time. The treetop rustled with their movements. Cade followed their progress anxiously. Mrs. Fletcher didn't move, didn't seem to breathe. Andrew and Rupert were nearly down when Paisley guided Mrs. Fletcher over.

"He'll be with you again in only a moment." She put an arm around Mrs. Fletcher's shoulders.

"Thank the heavens."

They were only two branches up. Cade moved to the trunk, directly below them. Firmly perched on the lowest branch, Andrew laid on his belly and lowered Rupert down, holding tight to his hands, directly into Cade's open arms.

The boy's tearstained face was a welcome sight indeed. "You've frightened your mother out of her wits," he told Rupert. "Best throw your arms around her neck and say you're sorry."

He set Rupert on his feet, and the boy ran to his mother. Satisfied that Thackery would handle the situation from that point forward, Cade turned his attention back to Andrew, seated just above his head.

"Well done, Andrew."

Andrew didn't say a word. He climbed further up the tree. *He* can't *be around people.* Why was that? "Can I do anything for you?"

Andrew still didn't say anything.

Cade turned his back to the tree and looked out over the children spilling out of the schoolhouse. He folded his arms across his chest. He set his feet as wide as his shoulders, standing guard. If Andrew needed to be left in peace, Cade would make certain that happened.

Gideon knelt in front of little Rupert, giving the boy a thorough examination. Rice stood a pace away, directing the schoolchildren toward the road and on their way home. Paisley kept close to Mrs. Fletcher, who'd gone white as snow, as though the full danger of the situation had only just settled on her. Paisley did understand these people better than he did.

She'd known Andrew would need peace and quiet. She'd kept to Mrs. Fletcher's side when anyone else would have assumed the crisis had passed.

That knowledge was helpful. It gave her an advantage, for sure. But that knowledge could be gained with time. The town needed more than that. He'd seen peaceful places turn to chaos overnight. He'd confronted armed criminals who'd ridden without warning into a town. He'd kept the peace in places ripped to their very seams by war. Even quiet Savage Wells would bow to the advantage of a seasoned sheriff.

Gideon finished his examination and declared Rupert hale and hardy. Paisley was the focus of the doctor's attention next. Their conversation was low and private. *Yes. There's more than friendship there.*

Gideon joined Cade next. "Rupert is shaken but not hurt. Andrew can climb down on his own without incident. Is there anything else you need?"

"Why's Andrew so afraid of people?"

"He's not afraid of people," Gideon said. "He's frightened by the noise they make."

"Noise?"

"He was, according to Mr. Gilbert, quite a friendly sort of boy before the war, but the fighting changed him. Andrew keeps to himself, in a fantasyland of sorts, up among the trees and the birds, away from the noises below."

Cade swallowed down a few of his own memories of bloody conflict. "They lived near a battle, did they?"

Gideon shook his head. "Andrew was a soldier. He ran off to fight when he was only twelve years old."

Saints above. Cade had been only a few years older than that and had quickly realized war was no place for children. "How old is he now?"

"Twenty-four."

Cade would never've guessed Andrew was any older than eighteen or nineteen years old. "He don't look it."

"He does if you're close enough to see him properly. Older, even."

Gideon looked back at the tree. "He seems childlike because he clings so much to his dreamworld. But when you truly understand what that world is, and *why* it is, he becomes this fragile old soul stuck in the darkest memories of his own past."

"The war?" Cade quietly asked.

"Andrew spends his days up in a tree with his gun, not because he's playing some unending game. He's up there waiting, terrified."

"Waiting for what?"

"For the enemy to come down the street with their guns and their cannons and slaughter the people the way he saw them do far too often."

Cade knew that memory well. War left scars not even a doctor could see.

"So he climbs as high as he dares and watches," Gideon said. "He figures his lofty vantage point will give him a few precious moments of warning, that he'll be prepared earlier than he otherwise might. He clings to the reassurance of forewarning because, in his mind, it is only a matter of time before the soldiers come again and the suffering he saw in the war finds him here."

"He's looking for a premonition."

Gideon took a long breath. "Exactly."

Cade had told Andrew he had that gift. What he'd thought was just another odd character in this strange town was actually a soul torn to bits, looking for the right kind of paste to put himself together again. And, in his foolishness, Cade had set himself up to be just that.

What have I done?

Chapter 11

Being charitable in one's thoughts was particularly difficult when one was surrounded by mule-headed people. And Paisley was most definitely surrounded.

Rice, Thackery, and Cade were all exchanging stories of their past heroic deeds, each accomplishment more impressive than the last. The many townspeople who'd come by the jailhouse were listening in wide-eyed awe. The stories would be repeated over and over again by nightfall.

The mayor was present, looking extremely impressed. The men were making headway in their efforts to secure the sheriff job. Paisley needed to make her case as well.

At the first lull in the discussion, she jumped in. "About six months ago, when the Grantland Gang—"

"We heard all about that, Paisley," Mayor Brimble said. "And Sheriff Garrison said you were helpful."

Helpful. She'd done all the work and was only given credit for being "helpful."

"I'm the one who brought them in," she insisted. "Gideon knows that. Mrs. Wilhite was in the jail that day; she knows it as well."

Whispers began quickly circulating. Rice and Thackery looked completely doubtful. Cade mostly looked intrigued. She hoped that meant he believed her, or was at least willing to consider the possibility.

"Sheriff Garrison was rather useless those last few months," Paisley continued. "You all know I stepped in."

"Of course. Of course." The mayor's tone couldn't have been more dismissive. "But very little happened during those months. Grocery deliveries. The little spat about the chicken. Nothing like these men have done."

Quick as that, everyone's attention was on the others. *I am never going to get a fair shake. Not ever.*

Paisley slipped out onto the front porch. The street looked very much like it always did. Calm. Peaceful. She didn't look back at the sound of boots thumping on the boardwalk. She knew the rhythm of Cade's stride.

He stood next to her, leaning forward with his arms resting on the porch railing, sunlight glinting off his polished sheriff's badge. "A quiet afternoon," he said.

"They generally are." She was not at all in the mood for pointless chatter.

Apparently he wasn't either. They stood as they were, neither speaking. It wasn't a comfortable silence in the least. A few people passed, unspoken greetings exchanged between them all. A cold breeze whipped through the trees planted about town. They were likely in for a difficult winter.

"The mayor shouldn't've made light of the work you've done," Cade said. "This whole town owes you a lot, whether or not they're willing to admit it."

"That doesn't do me much good, now, does it?" She leaned her elbows on the railing, mimicking his posture, and rubbed her face with her hands. "Did you have heaps of friends in the towns you lived in before coming here?"

"Not many. The people I interacted with either came by just to make a demand or they were criminals."

She shot him a knowing look. "Now imagine you're a woman holding a man's job along with all the barriers sheriffing puts up on its own."

"Hmm. That'd be a predicament, for sure."

"I've learned over the past months not to listen to their dismissals and doubts. Otherwise, their doubts will fuel mine. Doubt in oneself is a sheriff's worst enemy."

He turned around so he was half-sitting on the railing, not quite facing her but not really facing away either. He folded his arms across his chest. "Did you really bring in the Grantland Gang?"

He actually sounded impressed. That soothed her frustrations a bit. "I did."

"Reports of their capture reached Colorado, where I was working at the time, but there was no mention that the arresting lawman was a law-*woman*."

She stood straight once again. "I do a lot of things I don't get credit for."

"Then why do them?"

She threw back his words from the day before. "Because they need me to."

A gaggle of women came hurrying down the street toward the jail, eager excitement on all their faces. Seeing the town's social committee together could only mean one thing—they were making plans.

"Good afternoon," Paisley greeted.

Miss Dunkle, the schoolteacher, spoke on behalf of the group; she always did. "Good afternoon. We've come to issue an invitation."

Her eyes stayed on Cade, not wandering in Paisley's direction for even a moment.

"What's your invitation?" Cade asked the women.

Miss Dunkle's smile was broad and unwavering. "There is to be a dance at the end of next week. We, of course, wish for all the sheriff candidates to attend. Though the town already has a great many bachelors, three more who are new in town are certainly welcome."

"I'll pass your invitation on to Mr. Rice and Mr. Thackery," Cade said. "Miss Bell, I'm assuming, is part of your invitation, though I'm certain you know she ain't a *bachelor.*"

Miss Dunkle waved that off. "She's also not new in town."

Paisley knew when she wasn't wanted. "I know it's your day," she said to Cade, "but I'll make the rounds and report back anything I find."

He nodded. The social committee didn't give him time to say anything as they launched immediately into a detailed account of the upcoming dance.

Paisley told herself not to let it get her dander up. Cade was new and intriguing with his fancy horse and flashy weapon. He was handsome enough to draw the ladies' eyes and rough enough around the edges to warrant the admiration of the men. Rice and Thackery might not have been as striking as Cade, but they had enough of his air to draw attention as well. And she, on the other hand, had lived in town for years, kept more or less to herself, did her work without pomp or show. She was as commonplace in their lives as the wind. Of course she was being overlooked.

The town liked her well enough. She was a friend, a neighbor. She simply wasn't what they thought of when picturing a sheriff. How did a person convince an entire town to change everything they thought they knew about her and about what made a good leader, a good protector? Maybe it wasn't even possible.

She set off down the walk, checking the businesses as she passed, stopping to talk with the owners. She asked Mr. Jones how his wife and newly arrived son were getting on, making certain they didn't need anything. Mr. Irving's barbershop had a bit of a line, which was good news for him. Money had been tight earlier in the year for his family. The mercantile was bustling as always, and none of the customers hovering about looked shady. All was well at the stables. The school was closed for the day.

"Paisley!" Mrs. Endicott, the preacher's wife, came upon her as she turned back in the direction of the jailhouse. "Have you heard about the social? A few of the ladies meant to go by the jailhouse and issue invitations."

Paisley nodded. "They came by just before I left. Everyone is very excited." *Even those of us who aren't bachelors.*

"I've heard that Mrs. Carol has agreed to make her famous punch and that Mr. Cooper will supply chocolate cakes. What a treat. Now, you didn't hear this from me"—her eyes darted about, checking for listening ears—"but I heard from a reliable source that Mr. Billings is going to ask the Joneses' oldest daughter to the social. In fact, it is commonly believed that he is smitten with her, and there might be wedding bells before the year is out."

All that from a rumored invitation to a social? "Everyone loves a wedding," Paisley said.

"I haven't heard if you are going with anyone," Mrs. Endicott said, watching her with concern.

"I don't have plans to go with anyone," Paisley said. "I never do."

Mrs. Endicott kept pace with Paisley's quick strides. "But you used to. When you first came, you attended socials with Mr. Cooper, and Eben, Mr. Holdst out toward Luthy, and Mr. McMasters. Even once with Mr. Clark."

Paisley shrugged. "They were decent company, but nothing came of those invitations in the end."

"And Jeb walked you home from church a few times, as did a number of ranch hands, and Mr. Larsen."

Mrs. Endicott's list was both impressive and disheartening. Paisley had certainly had a lot of opportunities to find love in Savage Wells. None of them had worked out.

"Perhaps you'll find a good match with whoever becomes the next sheriff," Mrs. Endicott suggested.

Paisley managed not to roll her eyes. "Perhaps, but I believe loving oneself should only be taken so far."

Mrs. Endicott only looked confused. Did anyone in town think she had a chance at winning the competition?

"I'd best be getting home," Mrs. Endicott said. "It was good to talk with you, Paisley. Say hello to your father for me."

"I will."

Though it wasn't very charitable of her, Paisley was grateful to see Mrs. Endicott walk away. She had enough doubts of her own without well-meaning townsfolk adding to them.

Only a few strides later, she spotted Ned Perkins. He strutted about in his usually ridiculous way. The man was like a gnat, hovering about at the most inopportune times, coming back again and again no matter how many times she swatted him away.

When he saw her, he added an extra degree of swagger to his gait. His boots scraped on the planks of the walk as he ambled over, his hands hovering just behind his holsters. Honestly, the man was practically begging to be shot. Fortunately for him she'd taken his measure long ago.

"Good afternoon," she greeted as he approached.

He spat a stream of tobacco juice onto the street. "I'm hearing whispers."

"Have you mentioned that to Dr. MacNamara?" she asked dryly.

His gaze narrowed, his eyes shifting even as his mouth opened and closed a few times. She saved him the trouble of trying to sort out whether her response was in jest or in earnest.

"What whispers are you hearing, Ned?"

"Rumor has it, we're gonna have ourselves a new sheriff." He nodded slow and deliberate. A glimmer of excitement in his eyes ruined the cool and calculated demeanor he was affecting. "And the whispers say he's likely to be a rough-and-tumble, shoots-from-the-hip sort." Ned slipped his fingers around either side of his vest, his stubbly chin stuck a bit forward.

"We have four people trying on the position," Paisley said. "Myself included."

Ned shook his head. "This town needs the skills of a dangerous sheriff, one who'd as soon draw his weapon as look at you." His smile widened, showing off his tobacco-stained teeth. "He'll find I ain't no shavetail. I've bested tougher men than he's likely to be."

He spat another mouthful of juice, but with less success. It dribbled down his chin and stuck to his lips.

"You've a bit, just there," Paisley said, pointing at his mouth.

"Daggummit," he muttered, wiping at it with the back of his hand. "Did I get it all?"

"Much better. But I think you should do away with the tobacco altogether. It's more disgusting than it is intimidating."

Disappointment pulled at his features. "But I've been doin' better at it. That's the first time I've dribbled on myself in days."

"An accomplishment, to be sure," Paisley said. "But I don't think it has quite the effect you're hoping for."

"Well, you just tell those sheriffing types to keep their distance." Ned was back in character, resuming his "dangerous" stance. "Tell them they've met their match in me."

"Walk with me," she instructed. "I'll tell you about them."

He did, swaggering as always.

"Mr. Rice is a tough character, not likely to go along with a joke, but probably quick with his weapon. Mr. Thackery is soft around the edges, but I still wouldn't push him too hard."

Ned nodded eagerly.

"The one you need to be careful of, though, is Cade O'Brien. He has worked in lawless and bloodthirsty towns. It would do you no good to leave him with the impression that he ought to greet you with the business end of his pistol."

"Sounds like a sheriff who's worthy of the badge," Ned declared.

"And by 'worthy of the badge' you mean 'willing to shoot you'?"

His unshaven chin jutted out once more. "I ain't afraid."

"Keep running your mouth like you are and you'll have reason to be afraid," she warned him.

The front porch of the jailhouse was empty. Cade had either returned inside or left to take care of some sheriffing business.

"Would you like to meet the others?" Introducing Ned was a far safer approach than waiting for him to approach Cade with his hands hovering over his holsters.

Ned nodded enthusiastically. He gave himself the once over, adding a slouch to his posture. "Ready," he said.

Paisley stepped inside. Mrs. Wilhite was helping a ribbon customer. Cade sat in the sheriff's chair with his boots up on the desk, ankles crossed. His hands were folded on his stomach, the chair tipped backward.

"Did Rice and Thackery call it a day?" Paisley asked.

"Mm-hmm. Seems they figure they've seen all they need to."

"You have a visitor," Paisley told him.

He moved nothing but his eyebrow.

"Cade, this is Ned—"

"Use the name," he insisted under his breath.

"I am not calling you that," Paisley said.

Ned turned away from Cade and loudly whispered, "You wrote it down. That makes it official. You have to call me it."

She really needed to stop writing things down. Paisley met Cade's intrigued gaze. "Cade, this is 'Dead Ned, the Wyoming Kid.'"

Cade didn't even blink. "If those persuaders are loaded, I'll have your head before you've a chance to so much as look at them."

Ned's eyes pulled wide. His hands dropped from their position above his holsters.

Cade stood in one fluid motion and slowly crossed to where Ned stood. The purposeful sound of his footfalls couldn't have been more different from the shuffling noise Ned made when he walked about.

Cade stopped directly in front of Ned. Everything about Cade shouted his authority and control of the situation no matter that he stood completely silent and still. Then he reached out and pulled both of Ned's pistols from their holsters. He spun the barrels one at a time.

"Unloaded." He eyed Ned unflinchingly.

Ned cleared his throat, staring at the wholly intimidating man. Paisley had warned Ned for years that walking about as though he were a loose cannon, armed to the teeth, was bound to cause trouble for him. Embarrassment if he was lucky, far worse if he wasn't.

"I—er—" Ned's swallow was audible, even from several feet away. "I wasn't—"

Paisley felt bad for him. He put such store in his imagined reputation as a swaggering villain. Cade had pulled that out from under him in an instant.

"Why do they call you Dead Ned?" Cade asked.

Ned swallowed loudly. "'Cause I'm . . . dangerous?"

Cade nodded, then dropped Ned's impotent weapons back in their holsters. "Leave the 'dangerous' outside this jail. Understood?"

Ned nodded. "No loaded weapons in here. Understood, Sheriff."

"Good."

Ned made to spit another mouthful of tobacco.

"Spit on my floor and I'll shoot you myself," Cade warned.

Ned's mouth closed on the instant.

Cade motioned toward the door. "Off with you. And don't let me hear you've been causing trouble."

Ned hurried outside, but only after one last look at Cade. There was no mistaking the eagerness in Ned's eyes. His imagined outlaw persona had longed for a sheriff just like Cade. It seemed half the town was falling all over themselves with gratitude for Cade's arrival.

"Please tell me you've more like him scattered about town."

She leaned against the wall near the desk. "There is *no one* like Dead Ned."

"'The Wyoming Kid.' Don't forget that part." The rare bit of humor helped her resent him a little less in that moment. A very little.

"Savage Wells is unique, and so are the people who live here," she answered.

He sat on the edge of the desk, facing her. "Who do I get to meet next? Have you a soothsayer or a resident ghost?"

"A valiant effort, Cade, but I'm not spilling all of our secrets."

"Is that so?" He slid off the desk, standing at his full height not far in front of her. He was taller than she was, but he didn't tower over her. There were a few advantages to being an uncommonly tall woman. "Not even one secret? One little, tiny clue?"

"About the town?"

He tipped his head a bit, his mouth turning in contemplation. "About you."

"Me?" She hadn't been expecting that.

"You have at least one secret, I'm assuming."

"Well." She let her eyes dart about as if making certain no one could overhear. "I do have a secret, one that isn't common knowledge." She had several, truth be told.

"Do you, now?" He made the same show of looking about for eaves-droppers. "I hope it's somethin' shocking."

"You sound like Mrs. Endicott. She stopped me just today to tell me 'something shocking.'"

He stepped closer, almost touching her. Her pulse pounded warmth all through her. No matter that he drove her mad at times and had set himself up as her rival, her mind didn't seem to have fully received that message. Still, there was some much needed relief from her worries in their bit of banter.

"There's no one else around to overhear," he whispered. He set an arm against the wall beside her and leaned in closer. "Spill it."

The man could flirt, she'd give him that. Further still, she enjoyed it.

"Don't tell anyone," she whispered, filling her words with intrigue and mystery, "but—now, brace yourself—Sheriff Garrison didn't actually capture the Grantland Gang."

A sly grin slowly spread across his face. "You know, I think I heard that somewhere before."

"Are you going to tell me a secret now?" she pressed. "I think you owe me one, Cade."

He raised an eyebrow. "You want a secret? Very well. My name is not actually Cade."

"It's not?" She didn't believe him.

But he shook his head and looked entirely sincere. "And before you ask, I've no plans to tell you what my given name is."

"I'll be the sheriff again in two days," she reminded him playfully. "You'll have to tell me then." She tapped the badge he wore pinned to his black leather vest.

He threaded his fingers through hers and lowered her hand from his badge, keeping their fingers entwined. "I'm finding myself in a charitable mood so I'll share another secret."

Her pulse pounded in her neck. It wasn't the first time he'd stood so close to her or held her hand in his, but there was an intensity to the moment. His gaze was fervid. His breathing was nearly as unsteady as hers.

His free hand slipped behind her neck and pulled her the last inch to him. His breath danced on her lips. All lucid thoughts fled.

"My secret—" His lips brushed past hers as he spoke.

"Yes?" The word spilled out as a breathy whisper.

"My secret is—"

He lifted their clasped hands to his chest.

"—I never—"

Heavens, he was torturing her!

"—kiss a fellow lawman." He stepped back immediately. A hint of a smile shone in his blue eyes. "Personal rule of mine."

Disappointment surged through her. He'd been teasing her the whole time. And, lonely fool that she was, she'd fallen for the ruse. Still, it didn't seem like a mean-spirited trick.

But she didn't mean to let him have the last laugh. She slipped past him, summoning her most feminine smile. "Just so you know, Cade—or whatever your name actually is—"

He looked intrigued.

"I don't have the same rule about kissing lawmen." She mimed an air kiss.

His eyes widened.

Oh, yes. Two could play at this game.

Chapter 12

Gideon had invited Cade to a dinner party of sorts a week after his arrival in town. Parties weren't his cup of tea, but if Savage Wells was to be his home, he'd best make connections where he could.

He looked over the spread of dishes on Gideon's table. "You didn't make this."

"Are you implying that I can't cook?"

"I ain't *implying* anything. I'm stating a fact."

Gideon tossed himself casually into a chair. "When have I ever disappointed you? Culinarily speaking?"

"Soggy toast yesterday afternoon. Lunch a few days back that put the 'sand' in sandwich."

"Even a master has a few bad days." Gideon was far too amused to be serious. "Actually, Paisley cooked tonight's dinner."

"Paisley?" Did Gideon never give a serious answer? "Gun-toting, sharp-tongued Paisley?"

"The very same," Gideon said. "She's a woman of many talents, though she's hardly ever applauded for them. And she's not one to shirk her responsibilities." A knock sounded from the front door. Gideon rose to answer it. "We've done this off and on the past few years, ever since her father stopped working at the bank. She cooks an enormous amount of food—always the same menu since her repertoire is fairly limited—and I invite a few people over. It allows her to pay me for whatever medical expenses she and her father incur, and it helps me come to know the town. She's been my biggest supporter since I arrived."

The fondness in Gideon's tone couldn't be mistaken. He had declared earlier that he and Paisley were nothing more than friends, but Cade wasn't convinced. Paisley's feelings on the matter weren't easily sorted. She kept such things rather firmly tucked away.

Cade hadn't seen much of Paisley since their flirting banter at the jail. She'd taken the teasing well. Saints, the saucy look she'd tossed at him had more than paid him back for his moment of mischief. It had hovered in his thoughts nearly every moment since. Not exactly the best reaction to a woman one's closest friend might very well be courting.

Gideon stepped out of the dining room as a second knock sounded at the front door. Paisley was likely in the kitchen, so Cade headed in that direction. He left the dining room but didn't get past the front entryway. The preacher and his wife had just come inside.

"Sheriff O'Brien," Mrs. Endicott said. "What a pleasure to see you again."

He gave a quick nod.

Before Gideon could close the door, Miss Dunkle, the schoolteacher, arrived as well. "I am not late, I hope," she said. "I was afraid I might be."

"You are right on time," Gideon said and motioned her inside. "I'll just step into the kitchen and let Paisley know we're all here."

"Let me," Cade insisted, before he could stop himself. He probably should've let Gideon, but he'd missed Paisley. He hadn't had a good bit of banter all day.

Gideon didn't seem at all bothered by the lost chance to see Paisley. Cade wasn't quite sure what to make of their connection.

He stepped down the corridor and pushed open the kitchen door. He'd not come fully inside before voices stopped him. Paisley wasn't in the kitchen alone.

"But why are you in here rather than out with the guests?" The man's voice wasn't familiar.

"I will join them when my work is done, Papa," Paisley answered. "They know to start without me if need be."

Cade hadn't yet met Mr. Bell. He stepped quietly into the kitchen. Paisley stood at the table, gingerly moving hot rolls from a baking dish to a serving bowl. She looked up at him. Her father stood at the kitchen window, dressed in a fine three-piece suit. Paisley's height, it seemed, came from her father, as did her thick dark hair.

"Beginning the meal without one of the guests would be rude." Mr. Bell shook his head forcefully. "I'm certain you're mistaken."

"I'm not truly a guest," she said. "I'm working. But Dr. MacNamara insists we take our dinner out there."

"Working? But you said these people were your friends."

These people? Did he not know Gideon or the Endicotts?

Mr. Bell's eyes darted about the kitchen, as if searching out an answer. "Why would you be working at your friends' dinner party?"

"Please try to understand, Papa." Strain colored her tone. "I need to work tonight, but I'm also a guest. It's both."

Mr. Bell spied Cade standing in the doorway. He scratched at his temple. "Who're you?"

He stuck out his hand. "Cade O'Brien."

Mr. Bell didn't seem to notice his offer to shake hands. "Do you live near Abilene?"

Cade knew of only one Abilene, a notorious town back in Kansas. Murders rampant on the streets. Shoot-outs left and right. The worst of criminals running the place unchecked. One city marshal assassinated. The next spending his days in the saloon with the criminal element. Blood flowing like water. There were crime-riddled cities that were better known than Abilene, but few were as dangerous.

"Savage Wells," Paisley said. "We're in Savage Wells."

Mr. Bell's lips pursed. He took on a defensive posture. "I think I know my own town, Paisley."

Clearly he didn't.

"We can discuss this later, Papa. Please."

"But you are being nonsensical." His words were clipped, abrupt.

Paisley abandoned her rolls and stepped over to her father. She took his hands in hers. "I know I'm not making any sense, and I am sorry for that. But please be patient. I am doing the best I can."

Mr. Bell nodded, but the gesture didn't seem to mean anything in particular. He smoothed the front of his vest. "I'll greet the other guests. You will only be a moment or so, I hope."

He stepped past Cade and out of the kitchen. Paisley shook her head, watching her father's exit. Her pinched mouth and creased forehead told a story of worry.

"I'm sorry about that," she said quietly. "He is . . ." She brushed a loose strand of hair out of her eyes, still watching the empty doorway where her pa had been standing. "He grows confused very easily."

After a moment, she let out a long, anguished breath. She returned to the table, her expression still heavy. She finished placing dinner rolls in the bowl.

"Smells good." Cade couldn't think of anything else to say.

"I certainly hope it tastes good as well." She took up the bowl and handed it to him. "Would you mind carrying these in for me, whatever your name is?"

"Still trying to sort that out, I see."

She eyed him sidelong. "You could just tell me."

He shook his head. "Not so long as the puzzle nags at you."

"You enjoy my discomfort, do you?"

"About as much as you enjoy mine, I'd wager." He pushed open the kitchen door, holding it for her.

"Do you have any puzzles I can nag you with?" she asked, stepping into the hallway. "Seems only fair."

"What's Dead Ned's story? He's not a real criminal. But how far does he go with his pretending?"

"He swaggers and talks tough but never anything beyond. He's an annoyance but not a threat. So you don't need to shoot him," Paisley added in a tone as dry as Arizona Territory.

"I think you will find I rarely shoot anyone."

"Is that so?" She looked him up and down, stopping just outside the dining room door. "You strike me as someone who doesn't carry a pistol simply to add color to your appearance."

"I'm no cold-blooded killer, Paisley Bell, and I don't take kindly to being called one." He'd taken lives in the line of duty, but he was no heartless murderer.

She was unmoved. "I didn't say you were a cold-blooded killer."

"You hinted at it."

"I didn't, actually."

He pointed at her with the bowl of rolls. "Wrap it up in all the fine paper you want, we both know what you were aiming at."

"As fascinating as it is watching the two of you come to blows, the rest of us are hungry." Gideon's tease floated over from inside the dining room. "At least set the rolls on the table before you have a shoot-out."

Mrs. Endicott's hand flew to her heart. "Shoot-out?" Her gaze settled on Paisley. "I said you shouldn't wear that gun."

Paisley gestured to her empty hips. No pistol in sight.

It was an odd sight, her without her gun belt.

"I do leave off the pistol once in a while." She shook her head in annoyance, snatching the bowl from his hands. "Do you?"

With that parting shot, she entered the dining room and set the rolls on the table. She chose the empty chair next to her father. That left one choice for Cade—the empty seat directly across from hers.

"What if the town becomes more violent?" Mrs. Endicott's hand hadn't left her heart, her tone hadn't lightened. "This sheriff business wouldn't end well for you, Paisley. I'm so worried."

"Are you not worried about Mr. O'Brien?"

Everyone at the table—everyone except Gideon—looked surprised that Paisley would even hint that the danger would be as much an issue for Cade as it would be for her.

"Of course you aren't," Paisley muttered.

She pulled his attention throughout dinner. She had fine manners and sat with perfect posture. Everything about her spoke of a genteel upbringing. She might have been vying for a position as a sheriff now, but at some point she'd been a lady of some refinement.

Paisley's father had fancy manners as well. The Bells came from money and privilege, Cade would bet his life on it. So what had brought them to this? Paisley working as the sheriff, cooking meals to pay doctor bills?

"Where are you from originally, Mr. O'Brien?" Mrs. Endicott asked. "I can't quite place your manner of speaking."

"Yes, indeed," Miss Dunkle jumped in. "Some of your words are more formal, like from back East, but mostly you sound as though you hail from the West." Miss Dunkle had a way of staring a body down that put one firmly in mind of a coyote keeping its eye on a rabbit.

"I grew up in Boston," he said. "But not in any of the finer parts of town. I lived in a rundown tenement and worked long hours in a factory. Then I fought in the war and lost what little refinement I might've once had in my words." He shrugged as he stabbed a steamed carrot with his fork. "A decade out West dirtied it up even more."

"You have lived in so many places," Miss Dunkle said. "You must have fascinating stories to tell."

"Ain't nothing fascinating about death and dying, Miss Dunkle. And that's all a war is. Too often, it's an inescapable part of sheriffing too. You're fortunate to live in a town peaceful enough to not know that harsh truth."

Silence descended on the gathering. Miss Dunkle and Mrs. Endicott exchanged shocked glances. Even the preacher looked up from his plate. Cade ought to have kept his mouth shut. People didn't care to know the price paid for their peace. It made them uncomfortable. Paisley's gaze was unsettling. Hers was a studying glance, as though with those few words he'd offered her a look into his soul.

"I wonder that you would want a job such as that, Paisley," Miss Dunkle said. "It seems a terrible thing to me."

"Those things Cade mentioned aren't all there is to it," she said. "There's getting little boys out of trees. And locking up chickens."

"And dusting shelves of ribbons," Cade added. "Don't forget the ribbons."

She shook her head. "I've written them down, Cade. They're official."

"You do realize they'll have to go."

"We'll just have to see who's around to make that decision, won't we?" She took a bite of potatoes, her eyes gleaming with a challenge. He appreciated the lighter tone she'd struck. He'd needed it.

"How will the decision be made in the end?" Miss Dunkle asked. "Do the citizens get to vote?"

"The town council votes," Cade answered. "In another week."

"What's all this about sheriffs?" Mr. Bell looked from Paisley to Cade and back again. "Abilene has a marshal not a sheriff."

"I know, Papa. Don't fret over it."

Miss Dunkle seized control of the conversation. "I know who *I* would choose if the choice were mine."

"I know who you'd choose as well," Paisley muttered.

Cade acknowledged the truth with a quick nod of his head. "What do you say we give the council a little push?"

Paisley's gaze narrowed. "What did you have in mind?"

"A head-to-head show of skills."

"Such as?"

He thought for a moment. "Maybe a race to see who can disassemble, clean, and reassemble their weapon the fastest."

She didn't look the least intimidated by that challenge. Very intriguing.

"Or," she said, "a quiz over the most recent fugitive reports and wanted posters."

She would most certainly win that challenge; the woman seemed to enjoy the paperwork.

He tapped his fingers on the table as he thought. The promise of an honest-to-goodness competition had him excited.

"Tests of horsemanship," Mr. Endicott suggested. "A sheriff needs to be good in the saddle."

"Agreed." Paisley said. Did she ride as well, then?

"A test of everyone's knowledge of the townspeople and their particular needs and oddities," Gideon suggested.

Of course Gideon picked something Paisley would win.

"What else?" Paisley asked.

"Quickest draw and truest aim." He'd win that one blindfolded.

The entire gathering got into the spirit of the competition. "Best arrangements for a bank delivery," Mrs. Endicott said.

That one could actually be close. Cade had the brawn and the advantage of being intimidating and quick with his weapon. Paisley had a knack for strategizing.

"Lifting heavy items," Cade said. "Heaviest item hefted wins."

"What in heaven's name does that have to do with being a sheriff?" Paisley demanded.

He shrugged. "I've needed brute strength many times over the past decade."

"Do you honestly believe I could ever best you in that challenge?" She shook her head and rolled her eyes. She took a drink of water.

"If you feel yourself unequal to—"

She swallowed quickly. "I accept." The stubborn set of her shoulders told him she knew she would lose but refused to shy away from the challenge.

"What about sewing?" Mrs. Endicott suggested.

"Sewing?" Paisley and Cade scoffed back in perfect unison.

Mrs. Endicott blushed in slight embarrassment. "I suppose that is an odd challenge for a sheriff."

A sewing competition among lawmen? What utter nonsense.

"I'll take it on if you will," Paisley said to him.

She couldn't be serious. Could she? "What has sewing to do with anything? It's absurd."

"I'm certain I'd need my sewing skills many times over the next decade." She mimicked the exact inflection he'd used when explaining his strength challenge.

Saints, she kept a man guessing. "I ain't having a sewing contest, and I doubt Rice or Thackery'll agree to it either, so you can set your mind to thinking of a different challenge."

Her expression turned mulish, and he knew she was digging in her heels. "Afraid, O'Brien?"

"Hardly. I'm simply not interested in wasting m' time."

She shrugged. "I could see how public humiliation would be deemed a waste of your time."

"Supposing you did win," he asked, "what would that prove?"

"Supposing you were too yellow to even try?" Paisley tossed back. "What would that prove?"

Chicken, was he? Backing down from a challenge wasn't at all his style. "What shall we sew, assuming we can convince our comrades to join in?"

"A dress."

"Have you been breathin' in turpentine fumes, woman? My sewing a dress ain't gonna prove nothing."

She twisted her mouth to one side as she pondered. It wasn't quite the saucy look she'd sent him a few days earlier, but he was enjoyin' it just the same.

"You can sew a shirt, then," she said. "It'll show you have a knack for self-sufficiency."

He could accept that challenge, ridiculous as it was. "Agreed."

Mrs. Endicott and Miss Dunkle shared a look of confused surprise. Mr. Endicott had returned to his meal.

Gideon, true to form, simply grinned, his eyes dancing with mirth. "I can't guarantee the council will make any decisions based on sewing, but it might be interesting, just the same."

"The sewing competition could be judged at the social," Miss Dunkle suggested with loud enthusiasm. "You can each come wearing your creations."

"A social?" Mr. Bell's eyes locked with Paisley's. "You should wear your purple dress. You look pretty in that one."

You look pretty in that one. As if she didn't look mighty fine in anything she chose to wear. He'd wager Paisley hadn't looked merely "pretty" a day in her life.

"I no longer have the purple dress, Father, so I'm of a mind to take up Miss Dunkle's suggestion." Her gaze met Cade's. "What do you say? Shall we wear our wares to the social?"

"I'm game if you are." His willingness clearly surprised her. *Perfect.*

"The social is going to be lovely," Miss Dunkle said. "Everyone will want to see how your sewing turns out."

As dinner continued, Paisley ate quietly, not reacting at all to the discussion around her. Her occasional smiles were quick and often forced. She didn't look up at any of them for any length of time. What was stuck in her craw now?

"I hope you will not choose to spend the entire social in the role of lawman, Sheriff O'Brien," Mrs. Endicott said, coyly. "I know quite a few young ladies will be disappointed if you do."

Miss Dunkle colored up immediately.

"I might spare a moment here or there," he conceded. "Our bachelor doctor'll be around, I'd wager."

"I never feel quite so loved as I do at the sociables," Gideon said. "It's nearly the only time people are pleased to be seeing a doctor."

The dinner guests spent the remainder of the meal swapping stories of social disasters from younger years. Even Mr. Bell joined in the reminiscing. Only Paisley remained aloof.

As the guests finished their meal, she began clearing the table. Gideon offered his farewells to his guests. After a moment, only he and Cade remained in the entry.

Cade let his gaze wander to the closed door of the kitchen, where Paisley had gone to finish her work. "Paisley doesn't try very hard to defend her ambitions to the town."

"She's not as self-confident as she seems. Not remotely." There was a surprising weariness to Gideon's words. "Underneath that tough exterior is an awful lot of doubt."

Cade had seen hints of that in her himself. "And getting this job'll help? Seems it might only put more walls between her and the town."

Gideon pulled off his fashionably-cut coat and tossed it onto the back of a chair in his parlor. "Her doubts aren't in the town, but in herself." He dropped into the chair himself. "I worry less about her *getting* the job than I do about her *not* getting it."

"Why's that?" Cade sat on the sofa nearby.

"She's had a tough few years. Though she's holding up admirably, she looks burdened every time I see her. Another blow might very well break her."

Cade rubbed the back of his neck, not liking the picture Gideon painted. "Do you think the council would ever hire a female sheriff, provided she made a good showing and such?"

Gideon leaned forward, his elbows on his knees. "No. I honestly don't think they will. It took an exhausting amount of convincing on my part just to let her try."

Cade had never intended to lose the competition, but he didn't like that it was rigged against her. "So it doesn't matter how well she does?"

"I think it matters to *her*."

Chapter 13

The evening of the social arrived quicker than Paisley would have liked. Fortunately, she'd been working on a dress already and had only needed, over the past three nights, to add the finishing touches. If she hadn't had something very nearly done already, she never would have completed the project in time.

This ridiculous sewing challenge. How did this become part of the sheriff competition?

The answer, of course, was that she'd let her pride get the best of her. She'd wanted to best Cade at something as handily as he would best her at the "feats of strength" challenge and, though it pained her to admit it, likely at the speedy weapon-cleaning challenge.

Still, the task meant she had a new dress to wear. It wasn't perfectly pieced together, but it would certainly pass muster. The forest green fabric she'd chosen added a richness to her eyes and hair. She'd styled her dress with the waist a touch higher than was fashionable. That cut flattered her best. From an older dress, no longer in prime condition, she'd pulled a lovely bit of lace to trim the collar and cuffs. After a long and detailed consultation with Mrs. Wilhite, she'd settled on a length of reddish-brown ribbon to tie about the waistline with a smaller matching bow for her hair, though that adornment had cost her a few precious coins.

Paisley smoothed and tugged and adjusted her dress. It had turned out well, if she did say so herself. Rice and Thackery had bowed out of this particular challenge, no surprise, but Cade had insisted he meant to give it his best. His shirt ought to be an entertaining sight. Beyond her desire to win their competition, she wanted to look her best that night.

She wasn't foolish enough to read more into Cade's flirtations than a bit of fun, an attempt at slipping her up in her bid for sheriff, and yet her heart flipped at the memory of his hand holding hers, his breath on her lips. She had committed to memory the way he sometimes called her "love," though it was never meant as a true endearment.

He was teasing her, and she wasn't falling for it. But that didn't mean she couldn't enjoy his attention. She'd enjoyed dancing at the socials with the bachelors in town and being walked home from church now and then.

"Cade will dance with me," she told herself. "I'd wager he's a good dancer, too." She smiled at the prospect. It had been a while.

She stepped out of her bedroom and into the hallway. Papa had just emerged from his bedroom, wearing his black, nip-waist jacket and pin-striped trousers. His black necktie hung untied, the ends dangling over his gray-and-black plaid vest. He planned to attend the social, it seemed. She only hoped that didn't prove disastrous.

"How are you this evening, Papa?"

He flipped one end of his necktie in the air, allowing it to fall limply against his chest. "I can't seem to tie this. It looks worse with every attempt."

Paisley took a good look at him; his eyes generally told her the most about his state of mind. There was an inarguable vagueness there, but without the argumentative frustration that too often tiptoed in. Her father had always been even-tempered before his mind began to slip. She hated that the illness was changing that integral part of him.

"Let me help with the necktie," she said.

He raised his chin and allowed her to work.

"Are you looking forward to the social?" she asked as she tied.

"I certainly am. Your mother enjoys dancing."

He'd said *enjoys*, not *enjoyed*.

Paisley adjusted his tie and smoothed his lapels. His expression wandered, unfocused and unsure. How she missed the sharp man he'd once been. She hugged him, holding tight.

"Are you unwell?" he asked, his arms wrapped lightly around her.

"I'm just excited about the social." With a forced lightness in her smile, she suggested they be on their way.

It seemed that the whole town had spilled into the restaurant when Paisley and her father arrived. This was likely to be the last large social before winter arrived. The brutal Wyoming winters kept ranchers and homesteaders from making the long trek into town unless it was absolutely necessary.

She greeted those she passed, and they returned the pleasantries. Papa, despite his wandering thoughts, had enough presence of mind to civilly interact with the others. His manners were beyond reproach. He was friendly and happy. Perhaps it would be a better night than she'd feared.

Paisley linked her arm with her father's, relief settling on her heart. Too many days had been spent in worry over him. She cherished those times when caring for him was easier. He would never be the man he'd once been, but there were nice moments now and then.

"Shall we see if Mrs. Carol brought her famous punch?"

He looked intrigued. "Does she make punch?"

"She does," Paisley said. "Come try a cup."

Papa looked at her sidelong as they wove through the crowd toward the refreshment table. "Is this punch made with spirits?"

"No, thank the heavens." Having the entire town three sheets to the wind would be a nightmare.

"Well, now, Paisley, is this your 'sheriffing competition' dress?" Gideon stood just ahead of them.

"It is, indeed." Paisley slipped her arm from Papa's and motioned to her new dress with a flourish. "Is it enough to win the competition, do you think?"

"I think it might be." He nodded his approval. "You really do look lovely."

"And you really do look surprised." She pulled him aside and lowered her voice. "Did it truly turn out well? I think it did, but I don't want to get my hopes up."

"Pais." That was his "You are needlessly worrying" voice. She knew it all too well.

"I realize this won't have any actual bearing on the council's decision, I simply want to make a good showing." She glanced down at her dress one more time. "I think it did turn out well."

He pressed his hand to her back and nudged her toward the other people gathered around. "There are a number of social-goers waiting to see your entry in the first round of competition. Shall we go satisfy their curiosity?"

"What competition is this, Paisley?" Papa's silver eyebrows pulled sharply down.

Paisley set a calming hand on his arm. "Nothing of significance. Simply a sewing project."

"Oh." But he still looked confused.

"The punch is just there on the table. Why don't you have a glass and take a seat?"

"Will your mother be arriving soon?" He searched the crowd earnestly. "She isn't usually late."

Your mother. Pain seared through her at those two words. He would spend the entire night watching for her, asking where she was, worrying about her absence. Nothing Paisley ever said seemed to ease his concern. He simply could not comprehend the situation. So she pretended, again and again, that her mother was still alive. And it hurt more every time.

"I am sure she will be here directly." Paisley knew she would be telling him that for hours to come.

Gideon's gaze was empathetic. He had some idea of the pain Papa's illness caused her; they'd spoke of it often enough. "Of course she will be," he said to Papa. "She's likely fussing over her hair, wanting it to look just perfect."

Papa smiled fondly. "Mary-Catherine always looks perfect to me." He took a glass of punch and sat in a chair offering a full view of the door. He was waiting for Mama. Papa was always waiting for her.

Paisley swallowed down a thick lump of emotion. If only Mama truly could walk through that door. There had been so many times Paisley had needed her mother's advice, her encouragement, even just a hug. Oh, how she needed a hug!

"I am going to assume explaining things to your father doesn't help," Gideon said as he led her away.

"Lately, trying to make him understand only makes things worse. The more confused he gets, the angrier he becomes." She glanced back at Papa. "It's easier just to pretend."

"Easier for him, certainly, but I'd guess it's harder on you. It is a painful thing to be unable to help someone, whether a family member or a patient."

"We are a maudlin pair, aren't we?" Paisley shook off the heavy emotions, not wishing to dwell on them. She had no desire to grow teary at a town social. "Has Cade arrived yet?"

"He has."

"And did he come in a shirt he sewed himself?"

Gideon nodded.

It would do the absurdly confident Cade a world of good to be forced to admit he wasn't particularly good at something, especially when she happened to be relatively good at that same something.

They joined a small gathering of townsfolk.

"Is this your new dress?" Mrs. Endicott asked.

"It is."

"Lovely," Mrs. Endicott said. "And I see you've left off the pistol this evening." Her gaze dropped to where Paisley usually wore her gun belt.

"I am not acting as sheriff today," Paisley explained. "Mr. O'Brien will have to do all of the shooting this evening."

From just behind Mrs. Endicott, Miss Dunkle's voice joined the conversation. "I hope that doesn't prove necessary. It would be a shame to risk tearing or dirtying his lovely new shirt."

Lovely new shirt?

Mrs. Endicott stepped aside, offering Paisley a clear view of Cade standing there, watching her. Beneath his plain-cut jacket and black vest, he wore what looked like a perfectly acceptable shirt.

Cade pulled off his jacket, giving everyone a more detailed look at his entry in their match of skill. Though the bulk of the shirt was tucked out of sight beneath his badge-bearing vest, the most difficult parts of the endeavor were clearly visible. The collar fit well. The sleeves were the proper length. His cuffs were even.

Surprise tied her tongue for a moment. She popped her hands on her hips and circled about him, studying the shirt he had apparently sewed himself. "You made this on your own?"

"Don't sound so shocked. I'm a man of hidden talents."

She met his laughing gaze. "I was not at all expecting this. You can sew." Voicing that declaration drove home the truth of it. This was *her* challenge, the only one she was sure to win, and he hadn't told her the truth.

He smiled triumphantly. "Did I ever mention the factory I worked in during my childhood?"

"Vaguely," she said warily.

"Horrid place," he continued. "Nothing but tiny children's hands running great, big machines, making clothes we couldn't even afford."

"Making clothes? Let me guess, you specialized in shirts."

"Fastest seven-year-old shirtmaker in Boston." He bowed ever-so-slightly.

"I hate you," she muttered.

"No, you don't." He turned to Gideon. "You're not necessarily neutral, but you are on the town council, Doc. Who do you declare the winner?"

Not necessarily neutral. What did Cade mean by that?

Miss Dunkle replied before Gideon could. "Mr. O'Brien did wonderful work. And that talent is so uncommon for a man, I think he deserves extra consideration."

Cade waved off her argument. "Skill against skill alone."

As if the admission pained her, Miss Dunkle added, "Well. There is some unevenness in the seams of the dress. The workmanship isn't perfect, but it isn't terrible, either."

Paisley knew the description was accurate, but Miss Dunkle added more than the necessary amount of doubt to her tone.

"Looks like a fine bit of work to me," Thackery chimed in. The more Paisley got to know him, the more she liked him. He was a good-hearted sort of person. And he'd left off his sweat-stained hat tonight in favor of slicked back hair. He looked almost like a different person.

Rice was eyeing her and Cade far more critically than Thackery had. The man seldom had anything positive to say, so Paisley braced herself for the inevitable. "The shirt was a surprise," he said. "But Miss Bell's is the better entry. I'd give this victory to her."

Cade's look of surprise no doubt matched her own. Rice offering a compliment? Maybe there was more to him than sour expressions and strutting about.

"Your shirt is impressive, Cade." Gideon stepped up even with the both of them. "But, though it apparently would not meet the most scrutinizing eye of one demanding perfection, I have to declare that Paisley's dress is remarkable. I give this victory to her."

Did he mean it? She'd been lied to often enough.

Gideon held up his hands in a show of innocence. "I don't know what it is you suspect me of, but that is an accusatory look if ever I saw one."

"I'm only trying to be certain you are sincere in declaring me the winner." She watched him closely. "I'll not accept a pity win."

"Dagnabbit, you're stubborn." Cade took a step closer and spoke under his breath. "You did fine work and won handily. All four of us agreed on that." He motioned to Gideon, Thackery, and Rice. "It's for you to accept the victory so we can all get on with the social."

Why was it her cautiousness always seemed to prick men's impatience? Gideon was forever telling her, in tones of exasperation, that she needed to stop second-guessing everything. She didn't think she was as bad as all that, but it kept happening.

As Rice and Thackery wandered back into the crowd, Paisley heard Rice say under his breath, "It isn't as though tonight's competition is going to count for anything."

"Don't listen to him, Pais," Gideon said. "He's just grumbling because he knew he would have lost."

Even if he had, it wouldn't have mattered. Paisley was willing to accept the win, she just wished it could have been a victory that would matter.

"Sheriff O'Brien." Miss Dunkle was suddenly there, placing herself between Paisley and Cade. She slipped her arm through his, sparing only a momentary glance for Paisley. "I believe this is our dance. It seems to have arrived swifter than you anticipated."

"Moments of reckoning often do," Cade muttered. "Come on, then."

Miss Dunkle blinked a few times at Cade's less-than-enthusiastic tone. Paisley bit back a smile. He ought to at least pretend the prospect wasn't horrible.

Miss Dunkle pulled him toward the dance floor. Several couples stepped out as well. Paisley stood alone along the outskirts. The pattern held true as the evening dragged on.

Gideon passed by after a half hour. "You look upset."

"Only a little disappointed. I had hoped to dance tonight, but no one's asked me."

He chuckled. "Probably because you're glaring at everyone. The poor fellows are likely scared out of their wits."

Her shoulders dropped in a sigh. "I have never been any good at this. Set me in a room with a dance floor and I'm lost. Put a gun in my hand and tell me to track down an outlaw, well, that's another thing entirely."

"And you do it in dresses you sewed yourself." Gideon never could resist a jesting response.

"Fine dresses seem more suited to these occasions, don't you think?" There were certainly quite a few of them in the room. "Maybe I'm just not well suited to—"

"I swear, if Petulant Paisley makes an appearance tonight—"

"You know I hate it when you call me that."

"Then quit deserving it," he said. "Enjoy yourself. Stop assuming the worst in everyone, including yourself."

She took a deep breath. This was an old argument, one best left in the past. "Miss Green has been eyeing you for the better part of five minutes, Gid. You should ask her to dance."

He shook his head, his good humor somewhat restored. "If I dance with her, she'll assume I'm courting her, a notion I've been trying to disabuse her of for a year now. I'll just go chat with Mrs. Wilhite and Mrs. Carol for a time. They won't try to sink their claws into me."

"I don't know about that. You're quite the catch, Doc." She smiled at him.

"Give the men of Savage Wells a fighting chance, will you, Pais?" he said. "Try to look like you wouldn't be entirely put out if they asked you to dance."

"I'll summon every acting skill I possess," she replied. When he looked as though he thought she was serious, she gave his shoulder a shove. "I really would enjoy being asked to dance, and I'll work at making sure it shows in my face. Good enough?"

"Good enough." He gave her fingers a quick squeeze before making his way toward Mrs. Wilhite and Mrs. Carol sitting by the punch bowl.

Paisley made certain she wasn't scowling. She kept herself from crossing her arms in a look of defiance. Gideon was right: She'd never get to dance if she kept scaring people off.

Not a moment later, Cade caught her eye from across the room. He was dancing with Miss Dunkle. Again. Paisley smiled, expecting a look of commiseration or shared humor. His expression, however, was one of a sheriff seeing to a problem.

He pulled his hand free of Miss Dunkle's long enough to point at something behind Paisley.

She looked over her shoulder and knew in an instant what had drawn Cade's attention. Her papa was engaged in a rather heated discussion with Ned Perkins, and neither of them appeared likely to keep things civilized.

She crossed to where they stood nearly nose to nose. "Men." She addressed them in her firmest, most authoritative tone. "What seems to be the difficulty?"

"He's a blustering old fool." Ned swayed as he made the accusation.

"I'm a fool, am I?" Papa seemed every bit as unstable. "No more of a fool than . . . a fool."

The slightly slurred words combined with both men's inability to stand entirely upright were her first clues. The real clincher, though, was the smell on their breaths.

She stepped over to the punch bowl and lifted up a ladleful. The fumes were strong and unmistakable. "Did you add any liquor to the punch?" she asked Mrs. Carol.

"None at all."

"Well, then, someone else has done it for you." She set the ladle back.

In a flurry of skirts and gloves, Mrs. Endicott, Mrs. Carol, and Mrs.

Wilhite bustled about Gideon as he lifted the heavy punch bowl and headed out to dispose of the tainted liquid.

"You went an' got the punch tossed out," Ned growled at Papa. "I worked hard at that!"

She might have known Ned had been the one to add spirits.

"I didn't do anything," Papa slurred. "And you're nothing but a scoundrel."

Ned shoved Papa. "Better a scoundrel than brain-scrambled."

Paisley only just managed to keep Papa on his feet. "You'd best keep a civil tongue, Ned," she warned.

"He's a loon," Ned said. He stumbled on his next lunge at Papa. "Drunken old fool."

"I'm not a fool." Papa's declaration was too slurred to be authoritative.

"Are too. Waiting around for a wife who's dead."

That was way beyond the line.

"Don't you talk about my wife." Papa swung at Ned, losing his precarious balance. He bumped into the table. A slice of cake tumbled onto the floor.

"Now look what you've done!" Ned pointed at the cake with growing fury. "You killed the cake!"

Ned pushed Papa again, starting a shoving match between them. Partygoers scrambled away. A few of the ladies gasped. Gideon rejoined the scene in that very moment.

"Sorry about this," Paisley said and tugged at his necktie, untying it in one smooth motion and pulling it from his neck.

She quickly looped it about and slung it around one of Ned's wrists. His surprise gave her enough time to tie up his other hand as well, pinning both his arms to his back.

"Paisley, what are you doing?" Papa slurred.

"Keeping the peace." She eyed her father pointedly. "Come along. Don't make me tie you up as well."

"Tie me—?" He stared in shock.

"Just come along, please," she insisted.

Cade reached her side just as she stepped out of the restaurant with the two combatants. "I can take over from here. You're not the one on duty tonight."

"No, but I am the one you asked to see to this. I'll manage this lot; you straighten up the mess in there." She motioned toward the restaurant with her head. "We don't have enough room in the jail for the entire town to sober up."

He hesitated, as though unconvinced she was equal to the task of escorting two drunks, who were quickly growing more maudlin than anything else, to a couple of quiet cells across the street.

"I've locked people up before," she told him. "I can manage it again."

Rice stepped out and joined them as well. "It's not your day, though. It's hardly sporting to make a show of doing sheriff work when you aren't the one acting as sheriff."

Maybe that was the real reason Cade was objecting. "I'm not trying to take over or make a show," she said. "I just know these two, and I know how to handle them."

Rice didn't care for that explanation. "Know them or not, it's not your day."

She could see this wouldn't be an easily won argument. She turned her attention fully to Cade. "If you insist on taking them in, I won't stop you. But Ned'll be passed out shortly, and my father will still need looking after. And he is my *father*. I think you can allow me to see to his welfare without feeling threatened by it."

His brow furrowed. "You're certain you don't mind missing the rest of the social?"

"Believe me, I'm not heartbroken over it." She was disappointed, certainly, but not devastated. She might have secured a dancing partner once she'd gotten her scowl under control, but there would be other chances.

She gave Ned a nudge. "One foot in front of the other, Ned. You're gonna sleep it off behind bars."

Ned pulled at his cloth shackles. The man was desperate to be seen as a rough-and-tumble outlaw. He'd managed it for one night, anyway.

"You'll rue the day you arrested Dead Ned—"

"—the Wyoming Kid," Paisley finished for him. "I rue it already, compadre."

Chapter 14

Cade had little patience for women who sat around weeping and waiting for someone to solve all of their problems. His ma and her fiery determination had neatly destroyed for him the notion of women as the "weaker" sex. He didn't expect women to be pugilists or steel drivers, but he far preferred when they showed a little backbone. Paisley's cool handling of the disturbance that night placed her firmly on his list of fiery women.

The approach of Miss Dunkle—once again—forced him to amend his requirements. The schoolteacher certainly was one to take charge but not in a way that inspired admiration. Truth be told, the woman was a bit terrifying. She had the single-mindedness of a bird of prey with none of the elegant grace.

"I still can hardly believe you sewed that shirt yourself." Miss Dunkle's talons sunk into his arm.

"This shirt is the lingering remains of my childhood, miss." He managed to detach her. "I hadn't the opportunity of attending school as some people do."

"I am sorry for that," she said. "As a teacher, I, of course, wish all children could have a chance for learning."

"The children of this town are fortunate." He watched a few of them, spinning about in the corner, laughing with one another. The children of Savage Wells were quite fortunate in a lot of things. Not all the young ones in the West had the luxury of play and laughter.

"I think the social has been a success," Miss Dunkle said. "I do wish Ned Perkins hadn't undertaken his bit of mischief, but otherwise, the evening has been a fine one. And the music has been perfect for dancing."

Miss Dunkle had corralled him into dancing with her twice that evening. He wouldn't be roped into a third.

"I'll just be off to check in at the jailhouse." He tipped his head and slipped from the restaurant with a speed that likely reeked of fear. He could see Miss Dunkle had designs on him, and while he could easily douse her enthusiasm, he didn't care to hurt a woman's feelings if he could avoid it. Even if avoiding *it* required avoiding *her*.

A light burned inside the jailhouse. He pushed open the door. All was quiet. Ned had been rather tossed when Paisley had led him off, and her father hadn't been far behind. Paisley sat at the desk, reading a book.

"Is the social over already?" she asked, turning a page.

"Not yet." He stepped over to the first cell and glanced inside. Ned laid on his back on the cot, mouth hanging open, snoring quietly. "I've come to relieve you."

"And give up all this excitement for the dull, monotony of a town social?" She turned another page.

Cade checked the next cell. Mr. Bell was also sleeping.

"How many times did Miss Dunkle get you to dance with her?" Paisley asked. "Three? Four? A cool dozen?"

He sat on the edge of the desk. "Laughing at me, are you?"

She answered with a barely concealed smile.

"Twice," he said. "She made a stab at three. I don't know whether to be flattered or frightened."

"Definitely frightened." She looked entirely serious. "She is doggedly determined to snag herself a husband by fair means, thus far, though foul can't be far off."

He shook his head even as he unbuckled his gun belt. He stood and hung it on its peg behind the desk. "Seems I was lucky I escaped the social with my life. Although seems to me there are a great many bachelors around these parts. My disinterest shouldn't shake her prospects too greatly."

"Were she any other woman, it might not," Paisley said. "But she's not interested in a farmer or a rancher. She's set her sights on something more sophisticated."

"Then she's far off her mark, I'll tell you that. I'm no farmer, but I ain't sophisticated by any stretch of the mind."

She closed her book but kept one finger to mark her place. "Fortunately for you, most women in these parts don't have her requirements."

"Do you?"

That surprised her into a moment's silence. "Are you offering?" The question was just dry enough for humor, but just serious enough to tell him she wanted a straight answer.

"Only making conversation, darlin'. There are a lot of single men, as you've pointed out. And you've been here four years now but aren't attached to anyone. I'm only wondering which of your requirements have played a role in that."

Far from offended, she leaned back in her chair, eyes narrowed and lips pursed. "I can't rightly say. I've not turned up my nose at anyone; I've simply not found the love of my life in any of them either."

He sat on the tall stool. "Is that what you're looking for, then? The love of your life?"

She laughed humorously. "At this point, I'd settle for someone who helped pay the bills and would look after Papa, and, if I'm really lucky, doesn't fully expect to be miserable in my company."

Gideon fit that bill nicely. Yet their relationship didn't seem a solid thing by any means. What was getting in the way, he wondered.

"And what about you?" she asked. "What is it you're looking for? A schoolteacher with the tenacity of a bulldog, perhaps?"

"Fighting off an attack is not my idea of a romantic tryst."

She smiled the tiniest bit. "When you first arrived, I would never have believed you could have a lighthearted conversation. You were always in such a terrible mood."

"You weren't exactly a ray of sunshine yourself, darlin'."

"And yet you keep coming back to my jail." She stood and crossed to her father's cell.

"*Your* jail?"

"I'm being optimistic," she answered, looking in on each of the prisoners. "Someone needs to cheer for me."

She always did seem to assume people were against her, or at least not on her side. Where did that doubt come from? She seemed so confident at first glance.

"I'm impressed with your handling of Dead Ned tonight," he told her. "I can't say I've ever seen anyone cuffed with a necktie before."

The tiniest hint of a blush touched her face. "He will be overjoyed when he wakes in the morning and realizes he spent the night in jail; it'll be a dream come true for him."

It sounded more like a nightmare. "People long for strange things."

She stood beside his stool, holding her book, but looking at him. An odd aura of contemplation entered her expression. "Do you?" she asked.

"Do I what?"

"Long for unusual things?"

He shrugged. "I'm a career lawman hoping to settle in a town quieter than a mountaintop. That's near about as unusual as it comes."

Her searching gaze seemed to see clear into him. "Is that why you chose to have a go in Savage Wells? Because it's quiet?"

"Exactly." A weary weight settled over him. "I've waded knee-deep in death and suffering for too many years."

"During your time sheriffing or as a soldier?"

He let his posture slip, his shoulders rounding in a slump. "Both."

"We fled the bloodstained battlefields of Missouri only to land in Abilene, Kansas."

Her father had said something about Abilene, but Cade hadn't realized the Bells had actually lived in that infamous town.

"It was out of the frying pan and into the most vicious fire I can possibly imagine," she said. "What was it you said at Gideon's dinner party? 'There ain't nothing fascinating about death and dying.' Let's just say I spent a lot of years not being fascinated."

He reached out and took her hand. "Were you living in Abilene when the marshal was—"

"Decapitated by bank robbers? Yes." Her shoulders rose and fell with a deep breath. "My father ran *the bank*, which I'm sure you can imagine was a rather dangerous thing in a town like that."

A town like that? There were few towns that equaled the villainy of Abilene. And Mr. Bell had been a banker in that cesspool.

"Sakes alive," he muttered.

"He came here to open a new branch," Paisley said, "and I felt like I could breathe for the first time in years."

He knew that feeling well. Violence tended to suffocate a person.

"So," Paisley went on, "despite being unsure of how I fit here—the town has been welcoming and kind; I don't want you to think otherwise—and even though I feel like something of an oddity, I like living here more than any place I've lived before. There's a happiness that comes from simply being safe."

"And are you happy?" He suspected she wasn't entirely.

"As much as can be expected under the circumstances."

He rubbed her hand between his. "And which circumstances would those be?"

A mischievous smile tugged at her lips. "The circumstances of not having been asked to dance even once tonight. I've some right to be distraught, don't you think?"

"You'll get no argument from me there. Any woman who wants to dance ought to." He slipped off the tall stool and took the book from her hands, setting it on the desk.

If looks could kill, he'd be a dead man. "If you are mocking me—"

"Nothing of the sort, love."

"I don't believe you," she said.

"Believe this, then—I'd like very much to dance with you, you stubborn woman."

He clasped her hand in his. She made no effort to tug free. He slipped one arm around her waist and pulled her close to him in a dancing position. She was tall for a woman and had only to tip her head to look him in the eye.

She fit nicely in his arms. It was a fine way to end a night. His pounding pulse certainly agreed. *Brown eyes.* He'd always been a bit mad for brown eyes.

"You smell nice," he said. "For a sheriff, anyway."

She laughed. "Perhaps that should be added to our list of challenges: who smells the best."

"And who dances the best," he added.

Her hand rested on his shoulder. "You would win that challenge, hands down. I have never been very graceful."

"I'll let you in on a secret." He leaned in so his cheek brushed against hers and whispered. "I am not very graceful myself."

She lowered her voice to the same level as his. "Perhaps we should skip the dance."

"Do you want to skip it?" Gosh-a-mighty, he hoped she didn't.

"Do you?" she asked, sounding nearly as breathless as he felt.

He slipped his hand higher on her back. Her breath tickled the side of his face. A tiny turn of his head would find their lips meeting, their breaths mingling. One slight adjustment. One small movement. It would be the easiest thing in all the world.

He let the corner of his mouth brush against hers. Not a kiss. Hardly even a touch. The breath she took shuddered through her, as unsteady as his own.

"This is probably a bad idea," she whispered.

His mouth hovered over hers. "You'd rather I stopped?"

"I . . . I don't know."

"An 'I don't know' is the same as a 'no' in my book." He was trembling. Saints, he'd not been this upended by a woman in all his life. "Seems we'll have to wait until another time."

"You're not missing much." There she went again, assuming the worst in herself. What made her do that?

Her hands dropped away, as did his. They still stood close to one another but no longer touched. "I'm a bit out of practice," she confessed. "I haven't been kissed in years."

"Any time you're ready to end that drought, dear, you come find me." He made the remark as a tease but couldn't deny he meant it. And though he'd enjoy kissing her, he knew the idea was a bad one.

Gideon had fast become Cade's closest friend, and there was no doubt in his mind Gideon had a tender spot for Paisley. That'd get sticky as molasses right quick. Beyond that, he and Paisley were rivals, candidates for the same job. Nothing about their situation could end in a way that kissing wouldn't make worse.

"I'd say our dancing challenge was a draw," he said.

"We both win, then?" she asked.

There was the rub. They couldn't both win. In the end, someone had to lose.

Chapter 15

Paisley was all turned around. She'd not been kissed in half a decade, and she missed it. She missed being held, missed hearing whispered words of adoration. She longed for companionship and tenderness. She missed the feeling of truly belonging with someone.

She'd lost so many people in her life. Her mother. Her brother. The man she would have married. And, slowly but surely, her father. Her loneliness often ate away at her.

The townspeople were kind. They smiled indulgently at her oddities, asked sincerely after her father. But there was no one in town she felt truly close to. Gideon was the truest friend she had and even he felt a step or two removed.

She made her way to the jailhouse the morning after the social, not at all sure what she'd find or how she'd feel seeing Cade again. He was just then handing the sheriff's badge to Rice. She slipped quietly inside but not quietly enough.

"A fine good morning to you, Paisley," Cade greeted.

"And to you." She forced a smile despite her swirling thoughts. "Did Dead Ned wake up in good spirits?"

"I caught him doing a victory dance this morning just before I let him out." Cade shook his head with a smile. "Of course, he acted surly and put out."

"I would expect nothing else." Paisley took up a position on the stool between the empty cells.

"And your pa?" Cade asked.

"He was confused," she said. "But not overly so. He's better this morning."

He leaned against the wall near her stool. "Does it worry you to leave him alone?"

"A little." Beyond simply worrying her, it weighed on her conscience. But what else was to be done? She needed a job if they were to keep eating and be able to heat the house during the winter. She hadn't the money to pay someone to look after him during the day. The situation was moving from worrisome to downright frightening. Another month and they would be in dire straits indeed.

"If you're so concerned about it," Rice said, jumping into the conversation from his spot at the sheriff's desk, "maybe you ought to be home watching out for him."

She might have expected that from Rice. He reminded her of an ill-tempered dog, snapping at anyone he didn't like.

"Don't heed him," Cade said. "He just figures now that Thackery's dropped out of the competition he'd do well to convince you to as well. He's threatened is all."

"Thackery dropped out?" Paisley didn't know whether to be relieved or disappointed. She liked Thackery far better than she liked Rice, but one fewer competitor helped her chances. That was probably uncharitable of her.

"He was offered a position at the Billings Ranch and decided to accept it," Cade said. "It seems he likes Savage Wells enough to stay even if he ain't the sheriff."

"You ought to borrow a page out of that particular book, Cade." She couldn't quite bite back her laughing grin. "Savage Wells would be a fine place for you, even when you aren't the sheriff."

His eyebrows shot up even as his mouth twisted to the side. "You certainly have experience in that area. Tell me how it works out for you in the long run, will you?"

Paisley shot him a dry look. "It would be a change, actually. I acted as sheriff even before Garrison left."

"Acting as sheriff and being sheriff aren't the same thing, darlin'."

"And yet you've been *acting* as sheriff every fourth day since coming here," she pointed out. "Should we not have thought of you as the sheriff on those days?"

"That wasn't what I meant, and I think you know it."

"But it *is* what you said."

He held up his hands. "If you're wanting to pick a fight, you'll have to find another way of going about it."

From across the room, Mrs. Wilhite laughed. "The two of you should give off the bickering and jump right to the courtship. You'd save yourselves a lot of time."

Paisley let her disbelief show. "There's no courtship," she said firmly.

Mrs. Wilhite smiled as she always did. "The way the sparks fly between the two of you, I assumed—"

"These sparks ain't nothin' but a brush fire," Cade said. "A quick moment of clearing out the weeds."

"Ah." Mrs. Wilhite's voice rose with enthusiasm for the topic. "But a brush fire isn't such a terrible thing."

Paisley shook her head at the odd logic. "Tell that to the brush."

Gideon entered the jailhouse with his usual aura of barely contained energy. "The town is all abuzz," he said. "What is today's Clash of the Sheriffs event?"

"Clash of the Sheriffs?" Paisley met Cade's confused gaze.

Rice looked just as confused.

"Your feats of strength and skill," Gideon explained. "The sewing contest caught everyone's attention, but now they're wanting something a bit more sheriffy. What is today's task? You have a crowd assembled outside, including the entire town council."

Cade folded his arms across his chest. "I had almost forgotten about that. What do you say, Rice, Paisley? Shall we take up another challenge?"

She was game if they were. "Which one do you have in mind?"

"We could pick one of the boring ones—paperwork or cleaning weapons. Or we could have a marksmanship match," Cade said.

Ah, there was that smirk again. The man clearly thought he'd win a shooting contest without hardly trying. Had he chosen the weapon-cleaning race or a chess match or baking a pie, he likely could have made quite a fool of her. But shooting was one thing she *could* do.

"Marksmanship sounds just fine to me."

"And me," Rice said.

She'd never been outmatched in that area. She'd seldom even been challenged. This could be a lot of fun.

"So how shall we judge this competition of ours?" she asked. "Shooting bottles off a fence?"

Cade stood, his posture so confident it was almost cocky. "That'll work."

Rice beat them both to the door. Paisley grabbed her bonnet. It wouldn't do to have the sun in her eyes.

Cade stopped in the doorway, forcing her to stop as well. "I'll try not to be too distracting, love."

"I'd promise to try," she tossed back, "but I'm not sure I can help being a distraction."

Mrs. Wilhite smiled amusedly. "Sparks and more sparks."

Cade chuckled. Paisley wasn't nearly so amused. She *did* feel sparks with him around, and she didn't like it one bit.

Gideon had spoken true. Quite a crowd had gathered outside the jailhouse. Paisley pulled on her jacket, then tied her bonnet securely under her chin.

Eben, the blacksmith, hurried to the mercantile, intent on begging a few empty bottles. Everyone else followed Gideon to the Albertsons' place at the south of town; it had the nearest fence that edged an open field.

Whispers followed them all the way there. A few people in town knew Paisley had exceptional aim, but Rice and Cade's abilities were completely unknown. There were likely a few among them who were as curious as she was.

Gideon marked off twenty paces from the fence then dragged his foot across the dirt, making a line for them to shoot from. Paisley smiled at the excitement bubbling in Gideon's eyes. Sometimes he was exactly like a little boy who'd been promised a shiny new toy.

Paisley scanned the crowd. How many of the townspeople were rooting for her? She hoped at least a few. Gideon, she knew, would at least not be rooting *against* her. She was nearly certain Cade was the favored candidate. Rice seemed confident enough, but he wasn't as personable.

The town council was there, just as Gideon had said they'd be. Perfect. These results would likely be weighed in the final decision. At least in this, she knew she would make a good showing.

Eben joined them a moment later, a crate of bottles in his arms. Gideon all but skipped over to the fence, helping the blacksmith set up a row of bottles.

Cade slid up next to her. "There's still time to forfeit," he whispered in her ear.

"Is this you trying to distract me?"

He laughed quietly. "How'm I doing, love?"

"Better than you realize," she muttered.

His gaze narrowed. "Truly?"

She might have admitted to herself that Cade was beginning to intertwine himself in her emotions, but she wasn't at all ready to admit it to him.

Gideon sidled up to her on her other side. "Just pretend the bottles are the Grantland Gang, and you'll do fine."

"I mean to do more than fine," she answered. "I mean to turn a few heads."

"I look forward to it."

The bottles were set up and ready. Rice was studying them. "Five bottles each, I'm guessing. Are we leaning toward hitting the most or hitting them the cleanest?"

Gideon conferred with the rest of the council. After a moment, the mayor made his declaration. "We'll start with the number that are shot down. In case of a draw, then we'll look at accuracy."

That was good enough for Paisley. Rice announced he ought to go first, since he was acting as sheriff that day. He eyed the bottles, making quite a study of them.

Paisley took several steps back. Her ears rang with the memory of having stood too close when a gun was fired; it was an experience she didn't mean to repeat.

Rice raised his weapon, steadied his aim, and shot. When all was said and done, only one bottle still sat on the fence. Four out of five. Not bad shooting at all.

Cade caught her eye, his unspoken question clear. She motioned for him to go next. He agreed without argument and stepped up to the shooting line.

The crowd grew quiet with anticipation. Paisley was more than a touch curious herself. She set her hands on her hips, just above her gun belt, and watched with bated breath.

Cade drew his pistol, flourishing and spinning it about. Casual as could be, he shot, knocking the first bottle from its position. The crowd oohed. Cade's arm shifted, and he shot the next bottle, then the next, then the next. Plenty of oohs and aahs followed each successful shot. Four bottles in a row was no small thing.

He looked over his shoulder at her, a question in his gaze. She gave him a nod of acknowledgment. He winked at her then swung his head around and, with only a flicker of a pause to check his aim, fired off his fifth and final shot. He knocked the bottle clean off.

The crowd erupted in applause. Paisley joined in. He was good. He was most definitely good.

"Five out of five," Paisley said. "You're a good shot."

"Good enough to be honored with this." He indicated his pistol before spinning it back into its holster. "An O'Brien six-shooter."

"You have a pistol named after you?" It sounded so ridiculous, and yet she believed it.

He shrugged. "I've obtained something of a reputation."

"Apparently."

He motioned toward the bottles on the fence. "Your turn, Miss Bell."

She moseyed up to the firing line. Five bottles stood in a row, waiting for her to knock them down. Before she'd so much as reached for her pistol, she caught sight of a familiar, but seldom seen face out of the corner of her eye. The town lawyer, Mr. Larsen.

She was shocked enough to stop everything and turn at his approach. The entire crowd did the same. Whispers quickly filled the air, a common sound in Savage Wells. People loved news, and the arrival of Mr. Larsen was certainly that. Their resident man of law seldom left his house. Indeed, Paisley felt certain he actually left town altogether for long stretches. The man made hermits seem social.

"Mr. Larsen," she said as he approached her. "I haven't seen you in months. What brings you around?"

"I rode past Tansy's place," Mr. Larsen said.

"Oh, dear." Paisley knew precisely what that meant, but she wasn't sure what to do about it. "How close do you think she is to making her deliveries?"

"She had only just begun loading her wagon."

She thought on that for a second. "We have thirty minutes at least, then."

Mr. Larsen nodded.

"Care to fill me in?" Cade watched the two of them expectantly.

"Cade, this is Thomas Larsen, Savage Wells's resident lawyer. Mr. Larsen, this is Cade O'Brien, candidate for sheriff. And Mr. Rice, also a candidate, though he is the one acting in that capacity today."

"Nice to meet you both." Mr. Larsen shook their hands.

"Who is this Tansy, and what's she delivering?" Cade pressed.

"She is our resident moonshiner," Paisley said. "Nothing to fret over."

"A moonshiner?" Rice's eyes pulled wide.

"She isn't a threat," Paisley insisted. "But she does make a rumpus."

"Moonshining ain't nothing to sneeze at," Cade said. "Besides being against the law, it's a violent trade."

"He's right there," Rice said. "We need to take care of this straight off."

"The both of you are blowing this all out of proportion."

"I'll not stand by and wait for a moonshiner to descend upon the town." The smiling, winking, laughing Cade had disappeared. "You can hem and haw all you want, but I'm going to introduce myself to this Tansy, whether you're there or not."

"I'm sheriff today," Rice said. "If anyone'll be doing any introducing, it'll be me."

They were going to get someone shot, and it'd likely be the both of them. Maybe not Cade; he was quicker with his weapon than Rice.

"Fine, I'll come along," Paisley said. "Give me half a minute to finish up here."

"Half a min—"

She pulled her pistol as she turned back to the bottles. She popped off one shot after another, not bothering to double-check her aim, dropping all five bottles in the length of a breath.

Silence descended over the crowd. Cade stared, dumbstruck. Rice fairly had steam pouring out of his ears.

Paisley slammed her pistol back in its holster. "Shall we go harass a harmless moonshiner?" She stormed past the lot of them. Why was it Cade couldn't ever take her at her word?

He caught up to her with little effort. "I have never—Where did you learn to shoot like that?"

"As someone once said, Cade, I am more than just a pretty face." She continued in the direction of the stables. Tansy lived too far from town for a leisurely walk.

"I never doubted you could shoot," Cade said, "but, by Harry, you took those bottles down faster than a bird in a gale."

"You know a lot of birds that fire guns, do you?"

Paisley stepped into the stables. Jeb had been among the crowd left behind at the shooting match, so there'd be no help from that quarter. Fortunately, she knew how to saddle a horse. She pulled a saddle off its hook, setting it on her shoulder, then crossed to the stall where Butterscotch was stabled. She'd already arranged for a rancher near Luthy to purchase the mare at the end of the month. Paisley couldn't afford to keep her any longer.

"Hello, there, girl." She rubbed the mare's nose. "Shall we go trot out to Tansy's place and see how she's doing?"

"You seem right chummy with this moonshiner." Rice stood just outside Butterscotch's stall.

"I have had several years to make her acquaintance," Paisley said. "I know how she thinks and what she's likely to do." She began the task of preparing Butterscotch to be saddled.

"Moonshiners are criminals." Rice glared her down. "A good sheriff doesn't take the side of criminals."

"A good sheriff also doesn't jump to unwarranted conclusions," Paisley said.

Rice pointed at her. "I won't take lectures from a batty woman."

"Enough," Cade growled. "Go saddle up, and quit wasting time."

Rice's mouth pulled tight, but he obeyed. There was something to be said for Cade's intimidating air.

Paisley couldn't claim that and it picked at her. "I don't need you to fight my battles, Cade O'Brien."

He leaned against the top of the stall door. "What's crawled into your boots? We passed a fine evening last night, you and I. But today you're bristly as a porcupine in a cactus field."

"Do you want to meet our moonshiner or not?" Paisley asked.

"Do you regret it? Is that what's got you fit to be boiled?"

"Regret what? Distracting you while you were on duty?" She tightened the cinch.

"Not kissing me while you had the chance."

Part of her did regret it, though she knew it would have been a mistake. She covered the awkwardness of her own thoughts with gruff instructions. "I'm nearly done here. If you mean to come along, you'd best get a move on."

He tapped the top of the stable door as he stepped away. He disappeared into his horse's stall, and Paisley felt like she could breathe again. Plenty of twisted up, confused feelings had surfaced at the reminder of that kiss. That *almost* kiss. She'd never keep her focus if he kept bringing it up.

A moment more and they were riding down Main Street toward the edge of town. Cade rode as though he'd been born in the saddle. He kept complete control of his mount without looking as if he was even trying. He sat with his hat tipped casually on his head, one hand on the reins, the other hooked over his gun belt. There was no mistaking he was a man of action, one not to be taken lightly.

Rice mostly looked mulish. After a moment, he rode up beside her. "I shouldn't've snapped at you like I did, Miss Bell," he said. "Being a lawman doesn't teach a fellow to be soft."

It was likely as close as he'd come to apologizing. Still, she'd take it. A simple nod seemed to satisfy him. He rode a pace ahead, though eventually he'd have to hang back; he didn't know where Tansy lived. Paisley chose to enjoy the separation for as long as it lasted.

"You never answered m' question," Cade said.

They kept their horses to a slow trot, a leisurely enough pace to allow conversation.

"Which question?" she asked. "You have had an awful lot of them."

Cade tipped his hat to Mrs. Carol as they passed the millinery. "Where'd you learn to shoot like that?"

"I've always been a good shot."

But Cade didn't accept that explanation. "Natural talent only goes so far. No one shoots as well as you did without working at it. Laws a'mighty, you didn't pause for even a second to aim."

"I honed my skills at a time when pausing for a single second could have meant the difference between life and death," Paisley said. "You learned to always line up a shot so you didn't need to stop to aim. Those who were slow didn't live long."

He glanced her way as they rode past the first of the outlying farms. "Sounds as though you learned to shoot on a battlefield." A change had come over him in the last week. He'd seemed less burdened, less unhappy. But talk of the war weighed him down once more. She missed the friendlier Cade.

You've gone soft, Paisley.

"I learned to shoot as a child in Missouri. When the war reached us there, I learned to be faster and more accurate."

He kept his gaze forward. "Missouri was not a peaceful place during the war. But, then, Abilene isn't a pattern card of calm itself."

She nudged Butterscotch, picking up the pace. "Tansy's place is just up the road. When she's preparing for a run, she keeps her shotgun close at hand."

Cade's hand settled more firmly near his pistol.

"You won't need that," Paisley said.

His mouth twisted in obvious doubt, but his posture relaxed. Perhaps she'd managed to earn a sliver of his trust. "What's her story?"

"She grew up in the Appalachians in a family whose history boasts generations of moonshiners. She moved out West with her brother and his wife—who promptly decided she was an unwanted burden and up and left her behind. They even deeded her the homestead in their haste to be rid of her. She turned to the only occupation she'd really ever heard of."

He nodded his understanding. "Making bootleg whiskey."

"She doesn't make whiskey," Paisley said.

"Beer?"

Paisley shook her head.

"Ale? Wine?"

Paisley couldn't help a grin. "You'll simply have to take a look for yourself."

As Paisley expected, Tansy met them at the fence, her shotgun propped up on one shoulder. Rice's hand dropped to his holster.

"Leave your weapon where it is," Paisley said. "Tansy's calm most of the time. But if you rush in there, weapons ablaze, she'll likely respond in kind. Defending herself, as it were."

"She's a criminal—"

"Do you always rush in without any information? That seems a fool-hardy way to be a sheriff."

Cade cut off whatever Rice intended to say. "Let's see what this Tansy has to say."

Tansy moseyed over, wearing the same mud-stained bowler hat and work boots she always wore. "I knew that weaselly lawyer'd rat me out. Told you I was loading my wagon, didn't he?"

Paisley slid from her saddle and stood at the fence, looking over it at Tansy. "Mr. Larsen did mention it, but you know that he is required to. The judge asked that he keep the sheriff informed of your activities." Seeing as Garrison found checking on Tansy tiresome, Paisley had taken on that responsibility as well.

Tansy pushed her hat back. "That ol' judge had no right stickin' his nose in my business. I've a right to earn an honest living."

"That you do," Paisley acknowledged. "But so long as you identify yourself as a moonshiner, the law around these parts is going to keep a close eye on you."

Tansy's hard gaze settled on Cade. "Who's the pretty boy?"

A deep laugh rumbled in Cade's chest. "I ain't never in all my life been called a 'pretty boy.'"

"You been livin' with people what can't see, have you?" She turned to Paisley. "Is he your fella?"

"Not at all." The admission unexpectedly pained her. "His name's Cade O'Brien, and he's making a run for sheriff."

"That one, too?" Tansy pointed at Rice with her chin.

"That one, too. And me, while we're on the subject."

Tansy made a noise of approval. "You did plenty of work for that lazy dog who wore the badge before ya."

Tansy was enough of an oddity herself to not be bothered by Paisley's "odd hitch in her getup," as Mrs. Holmes insisted on calling it.

She tied Butterscotch's reins to the fence post. "Since there is a possibility one of these two will be filling this role in the near future, would you mind if I showed them around your operation? They need to be familiar with what you do."

"Just don't let 'em tamper with any of my Savage Wells White Lightning," Tansy warned. "I'll not stand for it." She walked off, her shotgun still resting on her shoulder.

"Was that her giving us permission?" Rice asked.

"More or less." She walked up the path toward Tansy's barn, where she housed her operation.

"Tansy named her moonshine after the town?" Rice asked. "In honor of everyone turnin' a blind eye, I'd wager."

"On the contrary," Paisley said. "The town is named after her moonshine."

Cade stopped on the spot, mouth agape. "Savage Wells is named after bootleg whiskey?"

Did he never listen to her? "She doesn't make whiskey."

She kept walking. Rice kept pace with her. After a moment, Cade caught up as well, reaching her in several long strides.

"Her father was a moonshiner, and he had a saying, something along the lines of 'Water on its own is civilized, and it's a moonshiner's duty to bring out the savage in it.' That's where she got the name. The town didn't have a name until about six years ago. The handful of families here at the time thought 'Savage Wells' had a ring to it, even if it was the name of the local moonshine."

"Strange ol' town," Cade muttered.

Rice's gaze took in the wide horizon. "She's very isolated out here. How did anyone ever find out what she was doing?" He squinted, motioning south. "Those look like her nearest neighbors. Did they turn her in?"

"That's the old Parker place," Paisley said. "They arrived after Tansy began openly selling her moonshine and left before the circuit judge ordered these checks on Tansy. They weren't part of it."

"She openly sells it?" Rice's expression was thunderous. "That's far too bold for my liking."

"Get a good look at what she sells, and then tell me if you still think she's too bold." She pushed open the barn door. She waved at the crates and pots and the potbellied stove. "This is her still. No spiral tubing, no copper pots."

Cade eyed it all, his mouth thinned in thought. "She can't possibly be brewing white lightning with this setup. I'd wager it's not even alcoholic."

"It isn't."

Rice peeked into one of the crates and pulled out dried leaves. He smelled one. "Tea?"

"Sweet tea. Iced tea. Light tea. Dark tea. Tansy bottles it up and drives around, selling it clandestinely."

Rice dropped the leaves back inside the crate, wiping his hand on his ever-present blue kerchief.

"Why the secrecy?" Cade asked, looking around the barn. "There's no law against selling tea."

"Moonshining is all she's ever known. It was her family's pride and joy. And, yet, she isn't terribly keen on actually breaking the law." She peeked inside a few more crates and bags. The judge required that they make certain the operation wasn't producing actual whiskey. "I told you how her family dropped her like a hot rock, basically telling her she wasn't wanted or needed or useful. I think moonshining is her way of proving she's still one of them."

Rice set his hat on his head. "Savage Wells seems to collect the runts of the human litter." He shook his head in disapproval as he stomped out.

Cade remained behind.

"We have enough strange characters here in our tiny town to fill an entire state, but behind each of them is a story, an often tragic history." Paisley caught and held his gaze. He needed to understand the importance of what she was telling him. "If you take over as sheriff, that is what you are inheriting. It is more than keeping the peace. It is more than wearing a badge and collecting your pay. You'll have the keeping of this town of misfits and outcasts. They don't deserve to be patronized or laughed at. They need someone who watches out for them because he cares what happens to them. If you can't be that, then you'd best pack up and go."

Cade closed the gap between them. He wasn't the sort to take kindly to being told what to do, but he needed to hear it. He needed to understand. She looked him in the eye, communicating without words that she wasn't afraid of his disapproval.

He surprised her. There were no scolding words or haughty dismissals. He simply took her hand and raised it to his lips, pressing a light kiss to the backs of her fingers. "This town doesn't deserve you, Paisley Bell."

Chapter 16

Cade had a close acquaintance with the scum of the earth. Too close. The world had taught him to view things in terms of good or bad, upright or criminal.

You'll have the keeping of this town of misfits and outcasts. Paisley had knocked his feet right out from under him with that plea. Sheriffing in Savage Wells had always been about escaping towns drowning in their own violence, about using his skills and his passion for the job in a less horrific setting. He'd not given much more than a moment's thought to the people he'd sworn to protect.

Thoughts of little Rupert Fletcher, Mrs. Wilhite and Mrs. Carol, Andrew, and Tansy ran through his mind. These people needed someone to care what happened to them. He meant to be that kind of someone, that kind of sheriff.

"Is your mind wandering already?" Paisley's voice pulled him back to the present. "The council meeting hasn't even started."

He stood outside the town council room. "Just getting a bit of practice in beforehand."

"You have to act interested for at least the first five minutes, even if they aren't set to make their sheriff decision tonight," Paisley said.

"In the law books, is it?" Cade asked.

She shrugged. "Run that by our resident attorney."

Which brought up yet another question. "Why is it Mr. Larsen plays least in sight? Is he shy?"

"No one sees him often enough to know." Paisley's eyes darted to the stairwell. "Unlike our town banker, who is most certainly *not* shy."

The head of the bank, Ellis Lewis, had just stepped from the stairs. What Cade had seen of Lewis he didn't like. The man was arrogant, self-absorbed, and as aggravating as a week-old splinter.

"Good evening, Sheriff O'Brien," Lewis said. Then, turning to Paisley, he added, "And to you."

He passed them both and stepped into the council room.

"Two guesses as to which of us he'd vote for if he was on the council," Paisley muttered. Her features were drawn with strain. Her posture was as rigid as it was exhausted. Yet, Cade didn't think it was only Lewis who inspired the reaction.

"You look worn thinner than paper," he whispered.

She rubbed her face and let out a long breath. "Papa isn't doing well today. He's not ill; he's simply not himself. Even more so than usual."

Watching a parent fade away must be a terrible burden. He set his hands on her arms just below the shoulders. "I'm sorry. I truly am."

She took the final step toward him and, to his surprise, into his embrace. He held her, aching for her pain yet, at the same time, enjoying the feel of her in his arms.

"I need a nap, Cade." She leaned her head heavily on his shoulder.

Heavens, she felt good to hold. A man could quickly grow accustomed to the warmth of a fiery woman at his side, one who challenged him and tugged at him and made him laugh as often as she made him spittin' mad. Yes, sir, he could most certainly get used to that.

"If you need to go home and be with your pa, Paisley, you go on ahead. I can fill you in on the meeting when we see each other tomorrow."

"It is tempting, I assure you."

"Whaddaya say the two of us skip out on this mind-numbing meeting and go shooting or something."

"Shooting?"

He shrugged a shoulder. "Or something."

Her dark eyes held his. "What did you have in mind?"

A great many foolish things. And, unexpectedly, he found himself acting on one of those things. He let his hand slip from her face and settle at the back of her neck, tipping her head up toward him. Her lips parted with a breath. He leaned in close, his mouth almost touching hers.

"We're looking to start a brush fire here, Paisley," he whispered huskily.

She slid her hands up his chest. "Brush fires aren't so bad."

She raised herself up enough to press her mouth to his. Her arms wrapped around his neck. He kissed her, slowly, savoring every moment.

Cade's pulse pounded hard in his neck. The air around them crackled and jumped. The flowery scent she wore drove him nearly out of his mind. He stopped himself an instant before threading his fingers through her hair. His brain, foggy as it was, called a halt, and his lips obeyed.

They were in public, by Jove. Anyone might walk past at any moment. Besides that, Paisley was Gideon's sweetheart, or at least Gideon seemed to want her to be. Cade couldn't go around kissing his best friend's woman.

He stepped back, dropping his hands from her face to her shoulders. His lungs wouldn't stay entirely steady. Rice chose that exact moment to come up the stairs to the council room door. He didn't say a word, but eyed them both suspiciously before stepping through the door.

Cade motioned for Paisley to proceed him into the room. He took a moment before following her. What had come over him? He knew Gideon's feelings. Paisley had fully participated in that kiss, or at least it seemed that way, but betraying his best friend made him a cad.

With his pulse calm and his breathing normal, Cade stepped inside the council room. He returned the nods he received, then took his seat beside Paisley. The smallest hint of a blush still stained her cheeks.

"Let's begin," Mayor Brimble said. "Mr. Lewis, I assume you've come with a matter concerning the bank."

Lewis rose from his chair. He smoothed his sleeves and cuffs. He puffed out his chest like a rooster in a henhouse.

"The Western Bank of Omaha has decided that this branch will serve as the head of operations in this area of the country," Mr. Lewis announced. "Large amounts of money will be passing through this town on a regular basis. I am concerned that the town is not ready to receive it." He eyed them as though they were all bacon-brained.

Paisley sighed impatiently. "The delivery will, no doubt, go exactly as it always does: just fine."

"Your confidence is adorable." Had he been closer, Lewis likely would have pinched her cheek or offered her a sweet.

"She's wearin' the badge today, pup," Cade said. "You're to address her as Sheriff Bell."

But Lewis's attention was back on the men at the table. *Mangy ol' dog.*

"Head of operations?" The mayor's eyes grew large. "Well. Well, well. That sounds quite important. Quite. What does it mean, exactly?"

"All of the money intended for branches in western Wyoming and the Montana Territory will be deposited here, and then picked up by those branches to be taken back to their respective towns." Lewis was clearly pleased with himself. "Our branch will be receiving its first significant shipment of money this week."

Rice whistled appreciatively. "That'll be a challenge. Securing even small deliveries takes effort."

Too right.

"How much money are you talkin' here?" Cade set his elbows on the table.

Lewis's expression twisted with enough pride to choke a largemouth bass. "The amount will exceed one thousand dollars on the first delivery," he said.

"A thousand dollars passing through this town?" A lead weight settled in Cade's gut.

Billy Carpenter in Arizona Territory had been gunned down over a fifty-dollar poker match. Cade had come upon the scene of a two-hundred-dollar robbery that ended in a triple murder. When a man had arrived in a town in Nevada with a rumored eight hundred dollars to his name intended as payment on a ranch, Cade had restored peace only after three solid days of warfare in the streets. A thousand dollars passing through a town as ill-prepared as Savage Wells was a disaster waiting to happen.

"I anticipate four or five times that in a few years' time," Lewis added. "Perhaps another—"

"You." Cade pointed at him. "Sit."

The banker could save his braggin' for another time. Savage Wells was in over its head.

Cade turned immediately to the mayor and council members. "You've a mess on your hands."

"Mess?" the mayor asked. "What m—?"

"You're a town without a sheriff," Cade said. "And you'll soon have more money passing through here than many people will see in their lives. No more time for games. You need to settle the issue of sheriff so this bank business can be dealt with decisively."

"We have another two days to make our choice." Mayor Brimble looked almost frantic at the possibility of having to make a decision. "And we haven't finished with all the challenges you were going to do. How are we supposed to know—"

"Were your mother a tortoise she'd be proud of your pace," Cade said, "but I ain't overly fond of it."

He looked at Paisley, and she nodded her agreement without the slightest hesitation. "He is absolutely right. Omaha likely chose Savage Wells to operate its local business because it has a reputation for being peaceful and stable. Not having a firmly decided sheriff makes this town anything but solid and steady."

"But we haven't—We weren't expecting to—" The mayor fiddled with the corner of his papers. "Springing this on us—"

"Why can't we take the two days we were anticipating and make the decision then?" Mr. Holmes suggested.

"I'll give you a thousand reasons," Cade said.

"I agree," Lewis said. "My bank is poised to—"

Cade cut him off with a look. "You've said your piece, Lewis. Your bank'll be looked after. You can go now."

"I have a vested interest in the outcome of this decision," Lewis insisted.

"An interest, yes, but not a vote. Get out."

Lewis simply stared.

"We'll wait," Cade said. He folded his arms on the table in front of him and watched the banker start to squirm.

After a long, awkward moment, Lewis stood. "At least let me know who will be in charge of securing the delivery."

Cade gave a single, shallow nod, but didn't bother repeating his earlier instructions. He watched the banker, waiting. Lewis finally accepted his dismissal. He stepped out, glancing back repeatedly.

"Time for this council to undertake a miracle: decision making." Cade eyed them all. "This has to be sorted before you leave this room."

"I don't know that we can," the mayor said, shaking his head over and over again.

"Then I hope you brought along pillows and a blanket. We're going to be here a long time."

"But how would we go about making such a quick decision?" Mr. Holmes asked. "A debate and then a vote? A vote, some debate, and another vote?"

They couldn't even decide how to decide. "I've seen men get filled with lead over far less than a thousand dollars," Cade said. "Word of the money shipments will spread. Every criminal in the area will circle like vultures."

The council paled. Gideon, to his credit, managed to look a little less frightened than the others.

"Do we really want to force them to make a decision they're not ready to make?" Rice asked.

"Here's the hand you've been dealt," Cade said, eyeing the council. "Your good cards, for starters. This'll bring in more businesses, which'll likely bring in more citizens. In time, that'll bring more money for the town to use in ways it needs. But you've a few bad cards in there as well. Every bank robber, stagecoach holdup man, and criminal gang in the entire territory'll hear about Savage Wells and the money to be had here. They'll watch. Check. Plan. Decide if the bank and the town are an easy target."

Rice nodded reluctantly. "That's true enough. The town needs a strong arm."

"It ain't as simple as that," Cade said. Paisley was going to be as angry as a pig in a cactus patch, but there was no avoiding that. He couldn't allow innocent people to be killed over money, not if he could prevent it. "Any weak link'll be spotted. The town needs to be seen as anything but an easy target. The quickest glance should discourage criminals from *even trying*. We need to make certain no one thinks twice about it."

"What are you saying?" Paisley's tone turned suspicious.

"That we haven't the luxury of playing this game any longer."

"What game?" Her posture had gone rigid.

He hated how this was playing out, but thousands of dollars passing down Main Street couldn't be ignored. He had blood enough on his hands. "The council has only one option now."

Paisley's mouth pulled into a tight line. "And that option is you?"

"Not quite," Rice said. "He means that option is *not you*."

"Why ever not?" she demanded. "I've held my own. I've made as good a showing as either of you. Why should I be eliminated so handily?"

The explanation would sting, he knew that much. "Would-be criminals will think this town is an easy target. But they won't be as likely to try anything if—"

"If the sheriff is a man," she finished for him.

"I know it's not fair," he said. "But the Western Bank of Omaha lit a fuse, and this town's sitting directly over the dynamite."

"Dynamite?" Mayor Brimble tugged at his collar. "I don't think we had better delay. Mr. O'Brien is right. We need to think about the safety of this town. That is, after all, the reason we advertised for the best sheriff money could buy. We want this town to stay peaceful."

"Wait just one minute—" Paisley tried to interrupt.

"By a show of hands," Mayor Brimble continued. "All in agreement that Mr. O'Brien and Mr. Rice are the best choices in front of us just now."

Mr. Irving, Mr. Holmes, and Mayor Brimble all raised their hands without hesitation. Paisley's eyes slid to Gideon. Her gaze was intense. She didn't blink.

"I'm sorry, Pais," Gideon said. He slowly raised his hand.

"That decision is made, then. Please leave the badge, Paisley." The mayor made the request as if asking someone to pass the salt.

She didn't move so much as an inch. "That's it? I held things together for months while Sheriff Garrison daydreamed. I stepped in and took over during those weeks after he left. And all you can say is 'Leave the badge'?"

The council exchanged confused looks.

"Leave the badge, *please*." The mayor tagged on the "please" almost as a question.

Paisley unpinned the badge in jerky motions. She held it for a moment in her hand, fingers wrapped almost reverently around it. With a sigh, she tossed it onto the table.

"It seems I no longer have a purpose at this meeting." She looked at the mayor and councilmen in turn. Her eyes avoided Cade. "I'll see you men around town."

Cade tried to stop her. "Paisley, I'm sorry."

"Oh, I bet you are." She walked out of the room without a backward glance.

Gideon's gaze was focused on the tabletop. Mayor Brimble's mouth turned down in a fierce frown. Everyone in the entire room looked uncomfortable. This had been rather badly done.

"We didn't mean to offend her," Mayor Brimble said. "Not at all. Not at all."

What needed doing was best done quickly. Cade had an angry woman with a white-hot temper to find and cool off. "You've one more decision to make tonight, men. You need a sheriff. Now, I needn't remind you of my qualifications—"

Rice jumped in. "I could do just as well if you gave me the chance."

"You don't have the luxury of taking a risk on the unknown." Cade eyed each council member in turn.

"He's right," Gideon said, slumping low in his chair. "It's the same argument we used against Paisley. We don't want anyone who looks at this town to even remotely doubt it is defended. Cade's very name tells them that. His presence tells them that."

The council required only a moment to cast their next vote, and Cade found himself a sheriff again. He'd done this so often it hardly felt exciting any longer. Rice was more emotional than Cade; he stormed out.

Cade hadn't time for hysterics. He stood, snatching up the sheriff badge. "I'll make arrangements with Lewis. You lot can handle the rest of the town business."

He left quickly. This was not at all the way he'd expected the sheriff decision to be made. He honestly wished it hadn't come down to this, but the money forced the issue. He really had been the only choice after that.

He found Paisley pacing Gideon's porch. Of course she'd gone to his home. There'd be an almighty row at that house as soon as the council meeting ended.

"I hadn't meant for—" He got no further.

"I'm not particularly in charity with you right now, Cade O'Brien, so I'd suggest you head back up to the meeting and leave me in peace."

"I just need you to understand—"

"Understand what? That I am out of a job? Or maybe that, unlike you, I was plowed over in that meeting, without having a single moment to argue in my favor?" She paced ever faster. "Or perhaps you think I ought to understand that I was only fooling myself all this time, thinking I had any shot at being named sheriff."

"You'd be a fine sheriff," he said. "But a woman sheriff doesn't inspire confidence. I realize that ain't fair, but it's reality. If criminals staked out this town and found a woman in charge of law and order, I promise you they'd make a try for the money every time. *Every single time.*"

"I could have dealt with that," Paisley insisted.

"At first, certainly, when only a few tried their hand. But what about when it kept happening? You'd spend every hour of every day with your pistol drawn, shooting every shady-looking character, hoping to stop them before they shot you."

"It wouldn't have reached that point. Savage Wells is a quiet town, it—"

"Do you think Abilene started out as a despicable place?" She had to understand what was at stake here—it was more than a job, more than a badge. "Towns go bad, Paisley, and it happens quickly. It's far easier to prevent than reverse."

"And it goes without saying, does it, that I couldn't possibly have prevented it?"

"There are few criminals who would have taken you seriously," he said. "Not because you can't do the job, but because no woman ever has. They'd figure there was nothing to worry about."

She folded her arms across her chest. "How is anyone ever going to realize a woman *can* do this job if no woman is ever allowed to do it?"

"What was the town supposed to do? Issue a challenge to every cold-hearted villain to come see if they could best Savage Wells's female sheriff?

How many of the people in this town would be caught in the cross fires while you proved a point?"

"I never get to prove anything. Never." She slammed her hands onto her hips. "And the few times I do accomplish something, no one notices."

"No one notices, do they? Mrs. Wilhite mentioning how much you help her with her ribbons, that's not noticing? Or Mrs. Carol knowing the minute you came into her shop that you would take her worries seriously? Or Andrew looking to you to know if he was safe to approach Rupert's tree? Or Gideon—" He scratched at the back of his head just below his hat. "Well, Gideon certainly notices plenty."

"A blasted lot of good his notice does me." She spun about, starting yet another circuit of the porch.

"Do I need to stay here and protect the good doctor against your wrath?"

She glared at him with enough fire to singe. "You, sir, are in my black books right now, so you'd best watch yourself."

He stopped her with a hand on her arm. "I know you're upset about the job, but there's no call for turning that against me personally."

"You made this personal, Cade." She pulled free of his grasp. "The first time you started flirting with me, I wondered if it was just a strategy for you. But I started believing you actually meant it. And then kissing me only to turn around and feed me to the dogs not ten minutes later—" She shook her head, her mouth pulling in a tense line. "It may not have been personal to you, but you made it personal to me."

"That ain't fair." He hadn't known what would happen at that meeting. And he certainly hadn't kissed her as a strategic move.

"Life is never fair." She leaned against the wall at the far end of the porch, her back turned to him. "Just go, Cade. You've done enough for one day."

He stood rooted to the spot, not knowing what to do. He had taken the income she needed. He suspected he'd dealt a blow to her pride as well. He'd meant what he'd said. She would make a good sheriff, and if it weren't for the money, she might've been given the chance to prove it. But they hadn't the luxury of an experiment like that. He'd not let Savage Wells become another Abilene.

Gideon arrived in the midst of their tense silence. He spared Cade a fleeting glance before crossing to Paisley. Cade couldn't hear what they said; he didn't stay long enough to try.

He walked slowly back to the hotel and up to his room. His thoughts were heavy as he packed his few belongings, getting them ready to be moved to the sheriff's rooms above the jail.

You've done enough. She fully blamed him for what had happened. She'd likely never talk to him again. And though he knew he hadn't the right to hold her in his arms or kiss her one more time, the knowledge that she wouldn't have allowed it cut deep.

He couldn't blame her. Getting this job and preserving the peace he'd sought for so long had cost him Paisley, and that was proving a steep price to pay.

Chapter 17

The town's weak link. Cade had called her that. Gideon voting against her had hurt, but Cade plowing her over like he had pained her the most. He'd allowed no discussion, offered her no opportunity to make her case. He'd simply taken charge and made the decision for everyone.

His earlier compliments had, it seemed, been rather empty. Perhaps he'd been attempting to distract her, to get her to let her guard down. Heavens, she'd actually kissed him right before the meeting. He'd been a more than willing participant, for sure, and he'd been the one to tighten the embrace. But *she* had kissed *him*. She'd believed in that moment there was reason for it.

There's more than one way to skin a cat, love. Little had she known then that she was the cat.

"Come inside, Pais," Gideon insisted. "I'll make you some coffee."

She let him guide her to the front door. Cade had already left.

She followed Gideon to the kitchen. He motioned for her to sit at the table. She didn't need a second invitation. She was tired. So very tired.

She leaned her head back and closed her eyes. When had life become so hard? Only five years ago Mama had still been alive, Papa was healthy and whole. Even living in Abilene, there'd been a certain steadiness to their lives that she missed. And there'd been Joshua. They were going to be married. The future had looked unendingly bright.

"How has your father been feeling?" Gideon broke into her sad reminiscence.

"Poorly, truth be told," she said. "He has been coughing again."

He nodded, waiting at the stove while the coffeepot heated. "If his cough grows worrisome, let me know."

"I will."

Gideon stirred the contents of the coffeepot. "Is his mind wandering more than usual?"

"Not more frequently, but more drastically." She rubbed at her aching neck. "He used to at least realize he was forgetting something, even if he couldn't sort out what that something was. Now when his memory slips, he doesn't seem to realize it. It's as if he's stepping further and further into a fog. I know someday soon I won't be able to see him at all, only the outline of a man I used to know."

"I wish I could do something to make this all go away, Pais. I really do."

She could manage a smile for him at that sentiment. "Mama often said, 'Wishing doesn't turn sour milk into cream.' Life certainly has poured me a great deal of sour milk lately."

He watched her from the stove. "I am sorry about how the votes played out. It should have been handled better."

"I won't argue with you on that." She gave a humorless laugh. "I would have liked to have been given even a single minute to speak for myself. More than that, even, I'd have liked to have received at least one vote. I'd have accepted even a halfhearted one."

"The council had to vote the way it did," he insisted. "Like it or not, the changes at the bank forced our hand."

"If not for the bank, would the votes really have gone differently in another two days?"

His immediate discomfort answered her question.

"The council was never going to choose me, were they?" She should have realized as much.

"No, Paisley. I don't think so."

That certainly didn't add a silver lining to anything. "Do you think women will ever be given a fair shake, Gid? We'd make fine sheriffs and council members and even doctors, but no one ever gives us a chance."

He thought about it a moment. "Women can vote in this territory. That's a step in the right direction. And I'd guess, in time, women will start inching their way into those professions in which they aren't currently welcome. Change is like that. It's often very slow."

"Are you telling me to be patient? Because that's not one of my virtues."

He smiled for the first time since his return. "Maybe I'm just trying to get out of your black books so you won't shoot me the next time we run into each other down a dark alley."

"Savage Wells doesn't have any dark alleys."

He wiped his brow with more than a touch of melodrama. "What a relief."

"You are just about the nuttiest doctor I've ever known." She liked that about him. He made the harsh realities of life and illness and suffering a little easier to take.

He poured a cup of coffee and handed it to her. "I'll likely get my nose cut off for sticking it where it doesn't belong, but I suspect your finances are tighter than you've been letting on."

She held her hands around the blessedly warm cup and let the steam cloud on her face. "I have less than twenty dollars left," she admitted. "Not nearly enough for the new coat Papa needs or for fuel for the winter, let alone food and repairs to the roof."

He poured himself a cup and sat near her at the table. "So the job was more than a matter of pride."

"I was simply excited to have found work I'd truly enjoy. I could have made a difference and helped people." She sipped at the hot coffee. "I'm not sure what I'm going to do now."

Gideon blew on his own coffee, the steam wafting away from him. "You could come help me, now and then. I get overrun more and more often. I'll have a few slow days in a row followed by an unending flood of people. I could use a nurse."

It was a kind offer but ultimately a foolish one. "I don't know anything about being a nurse. I'd be very little help to you."

"You're bright and clever and a hard worker," he insisted. "You would catch on quickly."

"And in the meantime, I'd be a cross between a burden and a charity case."

He set his cup on the table, shaking his head at her. "Is that how this is going to play out? Tonight's decision will mean you spend the next who knows how long wallowing in self-pity again?"

"I am not wallowing. I'm being realistic."

He held up his hands in defeat. "I don't want to hash out this old argument. We've both had a tough day. Will you at least consider my offer? There's plenty of work outside of actual nursing that you could do."

"I'll think about it."

And she did. She thought about a lot of things as she made her way home. Heavens, she'd wanted the sheriff job, and not just for the money. She could have been good. She could have helped people. She could have supported herself and her father doing something she loved.

She'd allowed herself to actually believe she'd had a chance, that she might have come out the victor. And she'd tried so hard. That was what hurt deepest. She'd done her very best and tried her very hardest. And it wasn't good enough.

She would let herself "wallow," as Gideon had called it, but only for one night. In the morning, she needed to have a plan. She'd see to it Papa had what he needed. She'd find income enough to pay their bills. And somewhere in the midst of it, she'd find a way to be happy with the hand life had dealt her.

Chapter 18

Savage Wells was every bit as short on jobs as Paisley had suspected when first tossing her hat into the sheriff ring. What the town was no longer short on was reasons to whisper as she passed or chances to pat her hand consolingly when talking to her. Not only had she lost her bid in a public way, but her money troubles could no longer be hidden.

"I'll just tuck in an extra couple of eggs," Mrs. Holmes said in her "I'm terribly sorry" voice.

"It was an extra bit of ribbon I didn't need anyway," Mrs. Wilhite insisted while dropping a length of burgundy into Paisley's hand.

"Bring your father by for a haircut, no charge," Mrs. Irving offered on behalf of her husband.

Paisley was grateful, she really was, but subsisting on charity was a difficult thing. The town's kindness would help her get by for a time, but what she really needed was an every-day, long-term job, and everyone was fresh out of those.

Her job search took her past the Gilbert house late the second afternoon following the council's decision. Andrew was in his usual perch, his shotgun laying across his lap. Fall had dropped enough leaves to make him visible in the treetop.

"How are things up there, Andrew?" she called out to him.

"Saw a couple of strangers riding into town," Andrew said, his eyes scanning the horizon.

Instinct took over in an instant. "Did they look like shady characters?"

"Don't know."

Hmm. "On horseback or driving a wagon?"

"Horseback," he said. "Will you tell Sheriff O'Brien about them?" Andrew looked down at her for the first time. "They didn't look dangerous, but they're strangers. I'm not fond of strangers."

"Sure enough," she said. "Can you tell me what they looked like?"

Andrew thought a minute. "Kinda dirty and dusty. They wore chaps and leather vests and wide-brimmed hats."

Sounded like a couple of ranch hands.

"I'll let the sheriff know, Andrew." Calling someone else "the sheriff" felt odd. She'd let herself imagine being the sheriff too many times. "I think you can come down, Andrew. Cade'll watch out for the town. You know he will."

Andrew shook his head immediately. "Can't do that. I have to keep watch."

"You don't have to now. You really don't."

His intent gaze was back on the horizon. "Bad things happen when I stop watching."

Oh, Andrew. I worry about you. "Promise me you won't climb up there during any lightning storms."

"Everybody knows that, Paisley," he said.

"Say howdy to your folks for me."

"I will."

She'd need to stop by now and then to check on Andrew. He always grew more frantic as the end of autumn approached. Wyoming didn't allow a person to spend hours on end in a tree during the winter. Instead, he spent those months pacing and panicking inside his parents' home. Cade wouldn't know how to settle him down.

A few trips out to Tansy's place would be a good idea as well. And dropping in on Mrs. Carol might help keep her from fretting over her missing items. Mrs. Wilhite would appreciate a chat as well. Perhaps she could manage that between earning a living and taking care of her father. Sleeping was rather overrated.

In the meantime, she still had a job to secure.

Mr. Cooper was at a table in the corner of the restaurant bent over some papers when she stepped inside.

"Are you still looking for a waitress?" she asked.

He looked up. "Are you applying for the position?" His feigned English accent hadn't improved over the years. "I have heard that you need a job."

"I do," Paisley said. "If you don't have anyone yet, I'm applying."

"Well, then, it seems we've solved two problems." He turned back to his papers. "You can start tonight at dinner. Be here at four o'clock on the dot."

Relief mingled with resignation.

"And don't wear your gun," Mr. Cooper added. "We don't want to scare away the customers."

Oh, yes. This was going to be just fabulous.

* * *

Paisley's first customer at the restaurant was Mr. Thackery, whom she'd not seen since he'd dropped out of the sheriffing race. "I'd heard you were working at the Billings Ranch nearby," she said. "It's good to see you again."

"And you, Miss Bell." He set his hat on the table beside him. "I got my first pay today and thought I'd come celebrate."

"An excellent idea. What'll you have?"

He rattled off a quick couple of things. She wrote down his order in the notepad she'd once used for her sheriffing notes. There was a painful irony in that. *At least you have a job. Things could be worse.*

"I was sorry to hear you were voted out of the running," Thackery said. "Though it won't mean much, I thought you made a fine showing for yourself."

His eyes reflected a kindness devoid of pity. She appreciated that. "I suppose in the end all any of us can hope to do is make a fine showing for ourselves."

He nodded a bit sadly. Perhaps he'd wanted the job more than his early departure indicated.

Not wishing to dwell on their mutual disappointments, she jumped back to the business at hand. "I'll let Mr. Cooper know your order, and we'll have it out as soon as can be."

She'd made it as far as the next table when Thackery spoke again. "Will you be working here from now on?"

"That's the plan."

His Adam's apple bobbed awkwardly. "Maybe I could come have a slice of cake sometime. We could share stories about being a sheriff's second fiddle."

She nodded with full empathy. "I think I'd enjoy talking to someone who understands that."

She'd only just set Thackery's plate of chicken-fried steak in front of him when Cade and Gideon came in. She knew they often ate at the restaurant, but somehow she'd not expected to see them, at least not on her first night. She and Cade hadn't spoken since the night he'd run roughshod over her at the council meeting. If he meant to gloat, she'd have a difficult time not tipping a bowl of soup into his lap.

"Well, howdy there, Cade. Gideon. Do you two know what you want tonight?"

Their surprise was even greater than her own.

"Are you working here now?" Cade asked.

"Wednesdays and Fridays during the day and every night," she said.

Gideon watched her closely. "Does this mean you won't come by and help at my place now and then?"

"On the contrary." She'd thought it through and knew she'd do well to rebuild her savings. If that meant working smaller jobs between her hours at the restaurant, then she'd do it. She pulled her notepad from her apron pocket along with the nub of a pencil she'd been using. "What can I get for you two?"

"Careful what you order, Gideon. Anything Paisley writes in her notebook is gospel in this town."

She narrowed her gaze on Cade. Was he mocking her or teasing? It was impossible to tell. She'd do best to act as though she saw it as one great joke. He had seen enough of the holes in her armor. She didn't need to point out any others.

"That's right. No changing your mind on your meals." She held her pencil at the ready, watching them both with patient expectation.

Gideon jumped right in. "T-bone steak, baked potato with a pat of butter, steamed carrots, and a dinner roll."

She jotted it down. "To drink?"

"Lemonade, I think."

Paisley raised an eyebrow. "You think, or you're sure? Once I write it down—"

He chuckled. "I know, I know. Once you write it down, it's official. Lemonade. I'm sure."

She turned to Cade but refused to allow her gaze to linger on his shiny badge. She missed wearing it. She missed Cade and the connection she thought had been growing between them.

"For you?" she asked, her eyes firmly fixed on her notepad.

"Fried chicken, baked potato, dinner roll, a slice of apple pie, and sarsaparilla. And I'm sure of that, so go ahead and write it down."

"I already have." She slipped the notepad in her apron pocket. "I'll be back directly with your lemonade and sarsaparilla."

She passed Thackery's table. He'd finished his meal. "Any good?" Cooper's meals could go either way.

"Better than anything Old Tom out at the ranch makes." He set his napkin on the table and stood up. He pulled a few bills from his jacket pocket and handed them to her. "I'll come by for that cake sometime."

She slipped the bills into her apron pocket. "I hope you do."

His eyes widened for a moment. "You do? Ur—Yes. I will." He cleared his throat. "Maybe I could walk you home after services on Sunday, if you don't have someone doing that already, of course."

"My papa always walks home with me," she said.

He nodded quickly, fidgeting. "Well, I'll see you for that cake, anyway."

Paisley did her best to clean tables and sweep as far from Cade and Gideon as she could get. Neither was being particularly difficult or pitying, but she'd rather not give them the opportunity.

It had been a hard few days, and she wasn't holding up well.

She stepped out of the restaurant late that night. One day on the job and she was already exhausted. She'd spent many hours the night before listening to Papa cough, wondering if it warranted talking with Gideon. In the end, the cough hadn't sounded like much more than a tickle in the throat, but she couldn't be certain.

Cade stood nearby, leaning against a post. She walked directly past him.

"You've avoided me for two days, Paisley." He walked alongside her, his long strides keeping easy pace with hers. "Though you've tossed a few glares toward the jail as you've passed."

"How do you know those weren't wistful glances inspired by a deep longing and—No. I can't even continue with that one." She pulled her coat more tightly around herself.

"I've missed having you around." His tone and expression were fully serious.

"If I promise to get myself arrested next time you're lonely, will you quit crying yourself to sleep at night?" They'd not yet reached the edge of town.

"So we're back to this, are we?"

"Back to what?" The cold wind bit at her face. The walks home each night would grow more miserable as winter drew closer.

"To decidin' which of us is the porcupine and which is the pincushion."

She folded her arms across her chest, though she didn't stop her onward march. "Are you calling me prickly?"

"Let's just say that chip on your shoulder is turning into a boulder."

Cade didn't give off walking with her. The ground was muddy enough to muffle their footsteps as they left the town behind. The only sound was the branches blowing in the wind. The scene was serene and peaceful, but it didn't soothe Paisley's battered soul. She was tired of always coming out the loser.

"I'm doing the best I can," she insisted.

"I've a feeling you can do far better, Chip."

"Chip? As in that 'chip on my shoulder' you were just mentioning?"

"A fitting nickname, don't you think?" He was unapologetic. "You are convinced this town dislikes you, shuns you, but they bend over backwards for you. They care about you. Not every town does that. And if you keep pushing them away, this one will stop. Then you'll have real reason to feel sorry for yourself."

Feel sorry for myself? How dare he twist my troubles into nothing but self-pity. I am struggling, but I'm surviving.

"The council meeting should have had more give-and-take, you were right on that score," Cade said. "You ought to have been given the chance to make your case, and I'm sorry you weren't."

Did he mean it?

"But more than that, I'm sorry you see the world through tinted lenses, convinced that everyone looks down on you and thinks the worst of you." What little sympathy had touched his words before evaporated.

He was back to stern, businesslike Cade O'Brien in a flash. "Life's tough on everyone, Chip. Everyone. You got to let the hurt go, or it'll eat you up."

It was the last thing he said before walking away, and the last thing she heard echoing in her mind before drifting off that night into a restless sleep.

Chapter 19

Cade sat astride Fintan at the edge of town, watching a stagecoach approach. He had his rifle resting across his legs. Today was the bank delivery. His badge was in full view, polished to a shine that ensured every ray of sunshine glinted off it. He meant to make certain that anyone watching would walk away knowing Savage Wells was well protected.

To that end, he'd temporarily deputized four others to stand guard throughout the town. Bill Nelson, who'd made cattle runs in these parts for years and had a steady hand on his weapon and a calm head on his shoulders, was stationed at a window above the mercantile. Cade had spoken with the man a number of times since coming to Savage Wells and had taken his measure straight off. Nelson said little, but didn't miss a detail. He was a straight shooter in every sense of the phrase. Bringing him in for the deliveries would add a much needed layer of safety.

The stagecoach slowed as it reached the edge of town. The driver dipped his head in Cade's direction. Cade answered with a dip of his own and turned Fintan to follow alongside the coach. Up beside the driver was a man with a dark brown hat pulled low over his eyes, a dust-covered kerchief about his neck, and a shotgun resting on his lap. The stage was guarded as well.

Cade kept pace as they made their way to the bank. He eyed the street and surrounding buildings. Nelson was at his post. Cade recognized the townspeople standing about. No one looked out of place.

Clark stood at an open window above the restaurant, just where Cade had asked him to be. Though the man was a bit too attached to his chicken, Clark had impressed Cade on other occasions with his logical mind and firmness of character. Add to that Clark's reputation as the best hunter in all of Savage Wells and he was an easy choice to be temporarily deputized and placed as a lookout during the delivery.

Paisley would have been his best and first choice, but she was still as angry as a hornet the last time they'd spoken. Her grievances with him and her easily bruised pride would likely have prevented her from accepting.

The stage pulled up in front of the bank. Cade dismounted, his calculating gaze sweeping the street. He kept his weapon at the ready. The man riding next to the driver climbed down, a heavy box under one arm, his shotgun held in the other hand.

"You the new sheriff?" he asked, eyeing Cade's badge.

"O'Brien."

"I'm Stevenson," the man answered.

"Have you been doing these deliveries long?" Cade watched the street as he spoke, keeping close to Stevenson as they walked the few steps toward the bank.

"Two years now," he said. "I come up from Laramie."

Cade nodded. That's what he'd been told as well. Hearing a consistent story was always reassuring. He opened the door to the bank and stepped inside with the delivery. This was a crucial moment. Once inside, Cade couldn't watch the street. He'd depend on his lookouts to make certain no one came inside while the money was handed over.

Nelson would watch the north. Clark would watch the street. Andrew was stationed in the schoolhouse tree, keeping an eye on anyone approaching town from the south.

Mr. Lewis waited inside. He closed the bank during deliveries so the place was empty except for the three of them.

"You can set the box here." Lewis motioned to the clerk's counter. He pulled out his keyring and flipped through them. The strongbox Stevenson set down had two locks, and Cade'd wager only the bank officials in Omaha and Lewis here had keys. A good system.

"I'll stand guard out front," Cade said.

"Thank you, Sheriff O'Brien," Lewis said. "And send Mr. Nelson down once he's done."

Cade stepped out, pulling the door closed behind him. The stage had pulled over to the post and telegraph office where it usually let down passengers. The street was quiet again. Cade hadn't expected any trouble with this first delivery. He had no worries over the next one, for that matter. Or the next one. But he was convinced the town's response would be watched and noted and discussed. He knew the lawlessness of the West too well to expect anything else.

Anyone watching today would realize Cade O'Brien wasn't taking a lazy approach to his new position. Savage Wells would be protected just as fiercely as every other town he'd sheriffed.

Stevenson stepped out of the bank. He carried his weapon and strongbox again. "You've an impressive setup here, Sheriff," he said. "More lookouts than I've ever seen in such a tiny place."

"I don't take chances."

Stevenson's eyes filled with both respect and agreement. "I appreciate that. It'd be my life, after all, you'd be taken the chance with."

"Lewis said these deliveries may very well start coming in almost weekly," Cade said. "Would you be the one making the delivery each time?" He intended to make certain he could identify everyone who was supposed to be part of these risky endeavors.

Stevenson nodded. "But I don't make deliveries out to the smaller banks. They'll send their own men."

That was good to know. He'd have to make certain Lewis introduced him to everyone coming for their portion of the funds.

As Stevenson made his way back to the stage, Cade crossed to the restaurant, where Clark had come out front.

"Any reason I need to stay nearby?" he asked Cade.

"None. Thank you for agreeing to help." He shook Clark's hand.

"Any time, Sheriff. None of us wants to see Savage Wells turn in to a den of thieves."

Clark made his way down the walk, heading home. Nelson was out front of the mercantile, so Cade went there next. Andrew had told him he'd simply climb down from his tree once everything was quiet again.

"Delivery went off peaceful as a newborn kitten," Nelson said, nodding toward the bank.

"Just the way I like it." Cade would rather avoid trouble than fix it later. "Lewis has seen the wisdom of keeping a guard posted while the funds are waiting to be picked up by the other banks. He's agreed to take you on at the rate I suggested."

Nelson set his rifle on his shoulder. "He'll not be disappointed. And I'm grateful for the pay. Cowboys don't find as much work during the winter."

Cade jerked his head toward the bank. "Get to it, then."

Nelson walked away without another word. There was no small talk with him. Cade liked that.

The rest of the day was uneventful, leaving Cade plenty of time to think over his strategy for the deliveries. As the cash amount increased, the security would have to as well. He needed to think about placing someone behind the bank should anyone try to get in, or out, that way. Paisley would have a good idea who he should talk to.

But after their last conversation, when he'd ripped into her the way he had, he'd not be surprised if she never spoke to him again. He shouldn't have let his frustrations run off with him that way, but that blasted chip on her shoulder irked him to no end.

He'd never met anyone like Paisley Bell. She was tough but caring. She fought for the things she wanted even when the deck was stacked against her. Sharp-witted. Strong. Determined. Beautiful. Brave. She was surprising in the best way.

And she didn't see it.

She didn't see it.

Chapter 20

Paisley worked herself to the bone over the next week. She worked at the restaurant both days the stagecoach stopped in Savage Wells. All of the riders ate their midday meals there, though none of them seemed very happy about it. They complained about the food, the speed of service, the comfort of the chairs, the color of the tablecloths. Paisley realized they were tired and sore from long hours cramped in a stagecoach. They were hungry and anxious and that made people impatient. She understood that. But she was tired and sore and hungry and anxious, herself. Cade's scold had stayed with her. Life was hard on everyone, and she needed to buck up under the weight of it.

She didn't enjoy her job, but it was the reason she'd been able to re-stock the pantry and begin preparing for the coming winter. And though the townspeople still watched her with the sad expressions usually reserved for the very ill or destitute, they were helping her and offering encouragement. She could focus on their good intentions even if she chafed against their sympathy.

She returned home late one night after a week at her job, desperately tired. She meant to check on Papa, have a cup of tea, and drop into her bed. She stood at the bottom of the stairs, trying to convince herself she had the energy to climb them. She had never been a layabout by any means, but being a waitress was proving taxing.

She dragged herself up the stairs. The hallway needed sweeping. She'd have to see to that the next morning before she left for the restaurant. And she needed to make Papa a sandwich for his lunch; he sometimes forgot to eat when she was gone. And she'd fallen behind with the laundry as well.

It's little wonder you're so tired.

Papa's bedroom door was ajar. No light spilled out into the hallway. She hoped that meant he was sleeping. His cough still hadn't cleared up, and it had her concerned.

"Papa?" she whispered as she poked her head inside.

She didn't hear a response. After a moment she realized she didn't hear anything at all. No rustling or movement. Not even breathing.

Oh, good heavens. Panic surged through every inch of her. He wasn't breathing!

She rushed in, but couldn't make out much in the dimness. She felt around in the blankets on his bed. He wasn't there. She was relieved, but only momentarily. Where was he? She turned about, searching every corner of the room.

He was definitely not inside the room. She checked her bedroom, just in case, then she checked all the other rooms on the upper story. He wasn't in any of them.

She rushed down the stairs. Not in the parlor. Where could he possibly be? Only by sheer willpower did she prevent her mind from dwelling on the worst possibilities. She moved swiftly to the kitchen—no sign of him there—then opened the back door. Papa wasn't out on the porch, either.

Where was he? He never ventured in to town. Perhaps he was in the barn. Paisley snatched up a lantern and lit it.

She pulled on her coat and headed out into the dark night. The wind blew fiercely as she crossed the yard. Ominous clouds had hung overhead all day. Though they'd reached November, they'd not had their first snow. That looked likely to change overnight.

The barn was dim. "Papa? Are you in here?"

He was nowhere to be found. His fishing pole wasn't in its usual spot. Had he gone fishing? Heaven help him if he'd headed for the river at night in the cold. He didn't always remember to wear his coat.

Paisley rushed back to the house. His coat wasn't on its usual hook. At least he had some protection from the elements. But, then, his coat would only be sufficient for so long, and there was no way of knowing how long he'd been gone.

Oh, Papa. Where are you?

She couldn't possibly find him on her own; there were too many places he might have gone. Her only choice was to go back to town and get help.

Savage Wells was dark when she arrived. That would make gathering a posse a bit harder. No one answered Gideon's door when she knocked. What if he was making a house call? She glanced at the jailhouse. The downstairs windows were dark. But the back upstairs windows glowed with lantern light. Cade was awake.

Paisley hurried up the exterior wooden staircase that led to the sheriff's personal rooms. She knocked at the door, worry building to painful levels inside her. The door opened.

"Cade, I—Oh, Gideon, you're here."

Gideon must have seen the concern in her face. "What's happened?"

"Papa is missing. I can't find him anywhere. His fishing pole is gone, and I think he headed to the river. There's miles of bank and hardly any moonlight tonight." Saying it out loud brought a surge of panic nearly to the surface. "If he went anywhere other than the river, who knows how far he might have wandered."

"We'll help you look." Cade turned to Gideon. "Grab your medical bag and a couple of blankets. Paisley and I will head to the stables and grab horses. Meet us there."

Thank the heavens.

Gideon stopped just long enough to give her shoulders a reassuring squeeze. Paisley and Cade rushed to the stables.

"I'm trying not to worry," she said, "but Papa gets disoriented easily, and his mind wanders, and—"

"We'll find him, Paisley. With all three of us looking, we'll find him."

She rubbed her hands repeatedly over her legs and forced the air from her tight lungs. "I thought I was hiding the panic pretty well."

"You were," he said. "If not for the narrowing of your eyes, I'd not have sorted it out."

"I've lost every member of my immediate family, Cade. I can't lose my father too."

"I doubt he's wandered far."

She tried to breathe. "I hope you're right."

"Hold it together as best you can, love," Cade said. "Even if you have to pretend this ain't worrying you, we need you thinking clearly."

Love. Her heart warmed at the sound of that. He hadn't called her "Chip" even once. Maybe her doubtfulness hadn't pushed him away entirely.

"We oughtta go on horseback," Cade said. "Then we can split up."

"Jeb should have a lantern. We can use that one, plus I brought one with me. Gideon has one too."

They didn't bother waking Jeb, but quickly saddled the horses themselves to use. Since Paisley had been forced to sell her beloved Butterscotch, she borrowed the Holmes's mare. She assured Cade they wouldn't mind.

Paisley rocked back and forth while they waited for Gideon to arrive. The need to be moving and working and seeing to the crisis had her wound so tightly she couldn't keep still.

Cade set his hand on her arm and caught her gaze with his own. "I'd bet the farm he's gone to the river."

"But the river's so long." She rubbed at her forehead. "And it's so dark."

His hand slipped up her arm, coming to rest on her cheek. "We'll find him."

His touch was calming in a way she wouldn't have expected. It was as though he was giving her strength, as if his own certainty and focus was flowing directly into her. She took a deep breath and felt her pulse slow.

Gideon came inside, his saddlebag on his shoulder. Cade's hand dropped away immediately, and he led his and Gideon's horses out by their leads.

"Lead the way, Paisley," Cade instructed.

She led the three of them southward, toward the river. It was the best place to begin looking.

"Gideon and Paisley, you head north along the river," Cade said. "I'll go south."

Cade was thinking more clearly than she was. *Pull yourself together, Paisley.* "How do we signal to you if we find him?"

"Give me a whistle. Sound carries over water."

"We'll try that, then," Paisley said. The moon, barely peeking out from behind the clouds, shone on the water. "Otherwise, we'll double back after three miles or so."

Cade nodded then set his stallion southward. Paisley and Gideon headed north.

"Has your father done this before?" Gideon asked.

"Not to this extent. He sometimes gets turned around, but nothing too drastic. I sometimes have to remind him where his room is, or I find him in the barn and he doesn't know why he's there, but he's never gone so far away that I couldn't find him. And he's never wandered away at night."

Gideon didn't seem surprised to hear it. Was this the natural course of things, then? Was this her first glimpse of things to come?

"He's growing worse, isn't he?" She knew the answer but needed to hear it from him.

"It seems he is." Gideon scanned the area. "It is happening faster than I expected."

She swallowed against the lump in her throat. "And before I was at all ready." She was losing her father. How could a person ever truly be "ready" for that?

She held her lantern high as she slowly rode along the riverbank. The wind bit at her. Paisley patted her horse's neck, wordlessly thanking the mare for braving the weather. She couldn't have done this without her.

"Perhaps your father was merely sneaking out for a bit of courting," Gideon said after a minute. "Did you ever think of that?"

"If that's what this is, I'll kill him." And, yet, she almost hoped his disappearance was something as ridiculous as that.

They rode on, each searching the banks and the clumps of bushes they passed. She spotted no footprints, no indication anyone had been that way. Nothing to point her in the right direction. Her mind spun with horrible possibilities. She needed a distraction.

"What about you, Gideon?" she asked. "Is there anyone in town you'd enjoy courting?"

He laughed. "Not a soul. Single women aren't exactly thick on the ground around here."

"And none of them would have you, anyway," she teased. "You're too particular."

He grinned. "I may have to order one through the mail."

She appreciated his humor in that moment. They'd covered a mile already, and she'd seen no sign of her father. Having an excuse to smile helped her stay calm.

"How long do you think Papa can be out here with just his coat before he is in danger from the cold?"

"So long as he stays dry and it doesn't start snowing, he can last for a while." Gideon's eyes stayed focused ahead. "He'll be cold and uncomfortable, but he won't be in danger."

"That helps keep the worry at manageable levels." Paisley searched the opposite bank, though she sincerely hoped Papa hadn't crossed the river. There were no bridges this far from town. If he'd crossed, he'd either wandered very far afield or he was very, very wet.

"There, Pais."

She spun her head to follow Gideon's gaze. Papa sat not thirty feet ahead of them on the riverbank. *Thank heavens!* Paisley nudged the mare forward.

She dismounted as soon as she reached him. "Papa, you—" Oh, heavens. He was soaked. "Have you been in the river?"

"I lost my footing." He watched the slow-moving river as he spoke. "I was watching for fish." He coughed. "I fell in."

Paisley knew that tone. Papa's mind was lost in fog.

Gideon crouched in front of him, setting his lantern on the ground beside them. "Did you see any fish?" He tested the soundness of Papa's legs.

Papa coughed again. "Not a one. There are usually some in the . . . uh . . . the lake?" He seemed to know "lake" wasn't the right word but couldn't come up with "river."

"Grab the blanket off my horse, Paisley. He's shivering."

She snatched it off and hurried back to wrap it around Papa's shoulders. He coughed again. Paisley didn't like the sound of it.

"How long has his chest been rattling like this?" Gideon asked.

"I first noticed it this morning," she said.

Gideon took one of Papa's arms, and Paisley took the other. Papa didn't seem entirely steady on his feet. Gideon studied Papa's face; what he saw clearly didn't reassure him.

"Can he ride your horse?" Gideon asked. "I want to get him to my house as quickly as I can."

"That sounds worrisome."

Gideon shook his head, but Paisley didn't fully believe it. "I just don't want to take any chances."

Another deep, rattling cough shook Papa's frame. With a little assistance, he was able to get into the saddle.

"Go on ahead with him," Paisley said to Gideon. "Tie up the horses out front and I'll walk them to the stables when I arrive."

Gideon nodded. "Head up by way of the river, so you can let Cade know."

"I will." Her gaze settled on Papa. His coloring was bad and that cough of his didn't sound good at all.

The two men rode off toward town. Paisley couldn't seem to move from the spot. How ill was Papa? Was he in danger? She'd worried so much about his mind, she hadn't given much thought to whether or not he was healthy in body.

Gideon was a good doctor, as good as any she'd ever known. Better even. Her father was in good hands. She told herself that again and again.

The wind picked up, chilling her through. There would be time enough for worrying after she was inside and warm again. She set two fingers in her mouth and let out a long, shrill whistle, then two short ones. With any luck Cade had heard that.

She braced herself against the wind and walked back along the riverbank in the direction of town. Gideon would look after Papa. It would all be fine in the end. This was merely a temporary setback. He'd be better soon. The cough would clear. She wanted to believe his mind would as well.

She rubbed her hands to fight off the cold. Mama had been much more ill when she'd passed away than Papa was now. Surely that meant there was no real cause for worry.

The sound of horse's hooves pulled her attention forward. Absolute, undeniable relief flooded over her. She felt calmer with Cade around. It was more than just the reassurance of a level head. He'd seen her deepest flaw and hadn't given up on her, but had challenged her to be better. He hadn't simply walked away.

He also hadn't returned to flirting and teasing and bantering with her. He'd not even come close to kissing her again. The brief moment when he'd touched her face at the stable had felt more like reaching out in empathy than in affection.

But he's here. That meant more to her than almost anything else could have. He was there when she needed someone.

"Where's your horse?" he asked as he reached her. "You've not been thrown, have you?" He dismounted in an instant, his hands on her arms as he studied her face.

"No, I haven't." His concern soothed her further. "We found Papa. He had fallen in the river and was wet and coughing."

"Laws a'mighty. How bad off was he?"

She forced herself to breathe, though her lungs protested the effort. "Gideon was as casual as ever, but there was real worry in his eyes. He took Papa back to town."

Cade nodded his understanding. "On your horse, I assume."

"Yes, so I'm walking back. It's not as crucial that I get there quickly."

"Walkin' back, my aunt Nellie." He set a hand on her back and moved her closer to Fintan. "We'll ride together."

Heavens, it was tempting. "Most horses don't enjoy being ridden double." She didn't want to get her hopes up if things with Cade weren't going to work out.

"Fintan has done it before. And we'll move slowly." His arm slipped fully around her shoulders. It was likely no more than the comfort given from one friend to another. Even so, she let herself soak it in. She'd needed a measure of reassurance lately, *his* reassurance in particular.

Cade mounted, then held out his hand to help her up. She settled in behind him.

He clicked his tongue, and the horse obediently began walking. Cade guided his stallion around. They ambled back toward town.

"Put your arms about me. No point fallin' off and breaking all your bones."

She wrapped her arms around him. He was blessedly warm.

"Not too awful for you?" he asked.

"Awful? You're blocking the wind," she answered. "And you smell nice. For a sheriff, anyway."

She felt him chuckle.

"Should we ask Fintan what he thinks?" Cade patted the stallion's neck.

"Fintan loves me," Paisley said. "Don't deny it."

Cade laid his arm across hers where they rested at his waist. His thumb rubbed a gentle circle against her hand. How quickly she could forget all of the troubles that plagued her, the hard words they'd exchanged, if only he'd hold her and take some of her worries away.

You'd best stop this now, Paisley. You know the kind of heartache that waits down this path. You know it far too well.

Chapter 21

Cade had never seen Paisley so agitated. She grew irritated now and then, certainly, but she'd never fallen clear to pieces like this before. She rocked back and forth in her seat, watching Gideon listen to her pa's breathing with one of his doctoring instruments. Cade wasn't a man of medicine, but even he knew the raspy sound wasn't a good sign.

"An inflammation of the lungs," Gideon said after a long moment. "I'd recommend keeping him here rather than making him brave the cold to return home."

Paisley kept rocking, her hands clasped so tight her knuckles had gone white. "How long do you think he'll need to stay?"

"That will depend a great deal on how he gets on tonight. If his fever doesn't grow worse, he should be able to—"

"He's running a fever?" Paisley leapt to her feet.

Cade stood as well, keeping close to her side. He wasn't much use in a sickroom, but no one ought to be left uncomforted in such a situation.

"A small one, Pais. Enough to know he's ill but not enough to be worried."

"So help me, Gideon, if you are coddling me I'll wring your neck."
There's my Paisley.

"No coddling," Gideon said. "I swear it to you."

"Fine words coming from a politician's son," Paisley muttered.

Cade shrugged. "She has a point there. Lying's in your blood."

Gideon shook his head at them. "I'll be downstairs if you need anything."

"Thank you," Paisley said. She stood at her father's bedside, looking down on him with drawn brows.

Gideon paused, a hand on her arm. "Pais?"

She offered a fleeting smile. "I'm holding up, I promise."

It was apparently enough for Gideon. Cade wasn't so easily satisfied. Her expression was still too burdened for his peace of mind.

"Papa didn't know where he was." She didn't look away from the bed. "He couldn't come up with the word 'river.' He didn't have the presence of mind to return home after he fell in. He just sat there, shivering in the dark for who knows how long."

She painted a bleak picture, for sure. Very little could be done. Mr. Bell's mind was breaking more every day, and she had to watch it happen.

"I can't leave him alone." She pushed a breath out and paced to the window. "But I have a job I can't afford to lose or quit. And when I'm not at the restaurant, I'm doing other odd jobs around town. Even with all of that, I can't pay anyone to sit with him all day and most nights."

Cade sat on the window seat, facing her. "What're you planning to do, lock him in the house?"

"What if he sets the place on fire?" She paced away from her father's bedside. "I can't guarantee he would know enough to put the fire out or unlock the door so he doesn't—" She took another tense breath. She sat next to him, her eyes unfocused. "What am I going to do?"

"Bring your pa to the jail during the day," he offered. "It's quiet there most of the time."

"But I work every single dinner hour. I don't get home until ten o'clock most nights."

"I know it ain't dignified, but if it'll help you out, he can sleep in one of the cells." It wasn't a great solution, he knew. "Or we might scrounge up a cot somewhere and set it up in the back room."

She propped her elbows on her knees and leaned her face into her upturned palms. "I need a more permanent solution. And I'd like for him to be at home while he still realizes it is home."

"Bring him by during the day, at least while you're sorting this out."

She leaned her head against his shoulder. Cade pulled her up close. She needed the reassurance; he enjoyed the nearness.

"Perhaps you could find other work and stop at the restaurant all together," he said.

"No one else is hiring right now. Only odd jobs here and there, and I've accepted all of those I could find. It simply wouldn't be enough."

A thought occurred to him, half-formed and undetailed, but a thought just the same. If the stage passed through more often, as he suspected it would eventually do, and the bank deliveries increased in amount and frequency, the town would do well to hire a deputy sheriff. He didn't know how much they would pay or if it would be enough to meet her needs. Heck, he didn't even know if she'd accept the job. She'd probably see it as charity. But he'd think on it, just the same.

"I should see if I can help Gideon with anything." She stood, forcing his arm to fall away from her shoulders.

Everything seemed to go back to Gideon with her. And Gideon seemed forever focused on Paisley. There was no denying it any longer: Cade was growing alarmingly attached to his best friend's sweetheart. That couldn't end well.

"Gideon's a good man," Cade acknowledged, reminding *himself* as much as anything.

"He is," she said fondly before leaving the room.

She'd only been gone a moment, when Mr. Bell asked, in a raspy voice, "Where's Paisley going?"

Mr. Bell looked tired and more than a bit pale. But he'd remembered

Paisley's name. That was an encouraging sign. "She's off to seek some comfort from her sweetheart." He didn't like the sound of that at all.

"Joshua has come for a visit?"

Joshua?

Mr. Bell shifted about under his blankets, not fully tossing and turning, but twisting, like one who's not comfortable but not miserable either. He finally settled. His gaze narrowed. "Who are you?"

Mr. Bell's mind wasn't entirely clear it seemed.

"I'm Cade O'Brien. I'm the sheriff in these parts and a friend to your daughter."

Mr. Bell mouthed Cade's name a couple of times before his brows pulled together. He shook his head. "I've never heard of you."

"I'm new here."

"Does Joshua know you're a friend of Paisley's?" Mr. Bell asked.

Cade pulled a chair up next to the bed. "I've not had a chance to meet Joshua yet. Will he disapprove of her being my friend?"

Mr. Bell coughed. Cade poured a glass of water from the pitcher on the bedside table and helped Mr. Bell take a few sips.

"Joshua won't be jealous if that's what you're worried about." Mr. Bell coughed again. "When he was first courting Paisley, he was a bit possessive, but he seems more secure with things now."

Courting?

"But ever since they became engaged, Joshua—" Mr. Bell coughed hard and deep.

Cade helped him take another sip of water, forcing himself not to ask any questions, though he had plenty. Was Mr. Bell confused about this Joshua fellow or had Paisley actually been engaged? Where was the man now? Where did Gideon fit in to that picture?

"Are you married?" Mr. Bell asked.

"No, I ain't."

Mr. Bell gazed up at the ceiling. "If you loved someone, loved her enough to marry her, would you wait months and months and—" His cough would not let up. "Would you keep putting off marrying her?"

"Not a snowball's chance in Tucson, Mr. Bell. I'd not wait one day longer than necessary."

Mr. Bell nodded firmly. "Exactly. While I was engaged to my wife, I begged her every day to simply run away with me and get married without waiting another moment. But she's stubborn and has a mind of her own."

"I love that in a woman."

Mr. Bell's smile grew. "So do I." In a heartbeat his smile disappeared. "She's ill."

"Your wife?" Cade knew Mrs. Bell was dead.

"Yes. It's nothing she can't beat, though. She'll be fine, don't you think?" Mr. Bell's expression was bleak.

"She'll be grand," Cade said. "I'm full certain of it."

Tears filled Mr. Bell's eyes. "She's very, very ill." His voice broke on the words.

Heavens, how often did Paisley relive these moments with him? It was little wonder she so often looked worn thin. It was a burden that went beyond the physical.

"I've lost my son," Mr. Bell said. "We left behind all of our family in Missouri. Mary-Catherine and Paisley are all I have left." After another round of coughs, Mr. Bell slid more fully under his blankets. "If Mary-Catherine should . . . If . . ." Emotion cut off his words for a moment. "Paisley has lost so many people she cares about. She dies a little each time."

The death of a brother as well as a mother. Leaving behind a home to live in a town like Abilene. Losing a fiancé somewhere along the way. And now she was struggling to make ends meet, all while slowly losing her father. It was a great deal too much loss and pain for one person.

Mr. Bell's eyelids were heavy. Cade saw to it he was comfortable, then slipped from the room as quietly as he could.

She dies a little each time. That was not something he'd expected to hear about the steel-nerved Paisley Bell.

Chapter 22

Paisley had only an hour between lunch and dinner at the restaurant. Pa was still recovering at Gideon's, so Paisley headed in that direction. She couldn't continue keeping such late hours, not while Papa needed so much attention. Until a job with more suitable hours miraculously appeared, she would have to make the best of it.

Gideon sat behind his desk on the side of his parlor where his shelves of medicines and examination table were. "How are things at the restaurant?" he asked.

"Same as ever." Paisley was an expert at masking worry and pain. Grumbling and grouchiness worked with most people. Gideon was duped far more easily by cheerfulness. "I've been thinking about your offer to do some work around here, and I've a mind to take you up on it as a means of paying for the doctoring you're giving Papa."

He looked pleased.

"I am quite good at alphabetizing paper and organizing shelves of jars by color," she said, her relief lightening her mood. "Or I could arrange them by potency or severity of disease they treat."

"I prefer organizing them by how horrible they taste."

She appreciated his humor. She'd had precious little reason to smile during the past twenty-four hours. "I can also sweep floors, wash windows, and polish banisters."

"That is an impressive skill set." He took up his stack of papers and crossed to the tallboy up against the nearby wall. "I'll gladly put you to work." He set the papers in a shallow drawer.

Work was something she could do, something she knew well. "What do you want me to do first?"

He took her cue without argument. "The upstairs rooms could use a good cleaning."

She nodded firmly. She knew where the cleaning supplies were kept from her times cooking meals for Gideon and his guests. She grabbed what she needed and headed upstairs. Papa was awake and sitting up in bed when she stepped inside his room.

"How are you, Papa?" she asked as she set her supplies down near the door.

"My throat hurts and I have a miserable cough, but otherwise I'm not terribly ill."

Lucid thoughts and complete sentences. Thank the heavens. She began straightening the items on the bureau. "Do you need more water or something to eat?"

"No."

Paisley checked the extra linens kept in the cedar chest at the end of the bed. They didn't appear to need laundering.

"Were you out with Joshua?" Papa asked.

Her heart dropped at that simple sentence. Joshua. That name never failed to bring with it a flood of difficult memories. Close on its heels came the realization that Papa was not as whole of mind as she'd hoped. Joshua had been out of their lives for years.

"No, not this time," Paisley answered. She pulled a rag from her pile of supplies and began dusting the surfaces.

"The two of you seem to be getting on well," Papa said. "Your mother is convinced he intends to ask me for your hand."

Papa was at least five years back, then. Sometimes he was clear back to his childhood. She never knew from one day to the next.

"Do you think he will?" Papa asked.

"Ask for my hand?"

Papa nodded.

"If I had to guess, I would say he will." She, of course, didn't have to guess. She knew exactly how it had played out.

She distracted herself by setting to work.

"Does Jane have the day off today?" Papa asked, watching her soap the windows.

Jane had been their girl-of-all-work back in Abilene. Papa often grew agitated when things didn't make sense to him. His decline into senility was changing his personality. He wasn't as patient and understanding. He fluctuated between almost simplistic and argumentative. Where would he settle in the end?

"Yes, Papa. Jane has the day off."

"Why not leave the windows for when she returns?" He sounded so confused. Before his mind began declining, he would have told her with an indulgent smile that she was being illogical.

"Washing windows gives me an excuse to stay in here and talk to you without Mama telling me you need your rest." Over the months, she'd grown adept at smiling when speaking of her mother as though she weren't gone, at appearing cheerful while her heart was breaking. Papa would never guess how much it hurt to speak of Mama as though she were simply in the next room. "But she would be right. You *do* need your rest. I'll finish up in here quickly."

Papa laid back down, not even arguing that he felt fine. He'd once been remarkably stubborn about his endurance.

She washed the soap off the windows then tossed her wet rag back into her bucket. She watched him as she swept the floor. The last year had aged him. His hair was nearly all silver now. The lines on his face were deeper. She had always known those changes would occur. She had looked forward to it, having been robbed of the chance to see her mother and brother grow old.

Paisley gathered up her cleaning things. "I love you, Papa," she said, kissing him on the forehead. "I hope you remember that."

He smiled indulgently. "Good night, my girl."

Good night? It wasn't even yet dusk. "Good night, Papa."

She watched him a moment longer. She still loved having him near, but at the same time, she missed him acutely. She missed him despite the fact that she saw him every day.

Chapter 23

Cade had his rifle disassembled for cleaning when the sound of footsteps on the porch pulled his attention to the jailhouse door. His hand dropped to his holster, where his pistol sat at the ready. He'd learned in the war to never be caught without a weapon.

Andrew Gilbert stepped inside.

"A fine good afternoon to you," Cade said. "Is there a problem?"

"Nothing like that." Andrew shoved his hands in his jacket pockets and dug the toe of his shoe against the wood floor. "I've been wondering if you've looked into those strangers that came to town a while back."

Cade motioned toward the empty stool. "Come have a seat. We'll shoot the breeze a bit."

Andrew came closer but didn't sit. "I got real good at cleaning a weapon while I was a soldier," he said. "I can help if you have another one."

Cade nodded. "In the cabinet in the back room. Fetch it here. We'll work while we talk."

Andrew seemed more at ease, at least with the handful of people who regularly sat about the jailhouse. That was progress. And he'd spoken of the war, which was more than some soldiers were able to do afterward. A good sign, that.

Andrew returned with the other rifle and pulled up the stool. He set directly to his work.

"I've learned a bit about those men you spotted," Cade said. "I can't say they *aren't* villainous, but so far they've not been any trouble."

Andrew nodded, bent over the gun he was slowly disassembling. He'd likely been quicker during the war, but time or difficult memories had dulled his movements. "I'll keep an eye out," he said. "And I'll let you know what I see."

Still up in that tree, then. "How late in the year are you able to climb up there?"

Andrew's hands moved faster, but without panic or franticness. There was something like calm familiarity in his movements. "Not much longer. The branches get icy, so it's not safe. And—" Andrew pressed his lips together. His brows plunged downward.

Cade kept at his own cleaning, not pushing the man. The weight never seemed to leave Andrew's posture, nor the pain from his eyes. The war had broken far too many people and had left far too many scars.

"My leg don't work right," Andrew muttered. "I got shot at the Battle of Shiloh. The sawbones never could get the ball out."

Cade had seen that before. "Those battlefield docs surely tried, but it was a rough business."

Andrew's tense posture relaxed the tiniest bit, even as his expression tightened. Cade understood the dilemma raging inside the man. Sometimes talking of the war helped. Sometimes it only made things worse.

"I wasn't old enough to be fighting," Andrew said. "Not really. After Shiloh, they set me up as a lookout, seeing as I couldn't march too far or too fast."

"Up in the trees?" Cade guessed.

"I'd whistle down to them if I saw anyone coming." He took a deep breath, then rolled his shoulders forward and backward as if getting comfortable. "I liked being up there. It was quiet. No one could sneak up on me."

It was little wonder, then, he still returned to the trees. "All the noise was hard, wasn't it? Even between battles. All the men drunk as wheelbarrows, talkin' loud and singing rowdy songs, or mourning their loved ones at home or comrades in the ground."

Andrew gave a tiny nod, now fully focused on his task. It was the longest conversation he'd ever had with Andrew. Perhaps in time, the man would open up more. He might even come down out of the trees.

"When you were a boy, what was it you dreamed of doing with your life?" Cade asked.

Andrew stopped long enough to really ponder. His lips pursed and twisted. "My father is a farmer. I guess I always figured on doing that as well."

Cade heard a lack of excitement in the retelling. "If not a farmer, then what?"

Andrew smiled a bit, a crooked, half-formed smile. "I used to imagine myself leading a charge against a castle."

"A knight of the Round Table, were you?" Cade smiled. He'd had similar dreams during his days at the factory. "Was it the armor that intrigued you or the shiny swords and lances?"

Andrew leaned his elbows on the desk. "I always pictured scores of people being kept prisoner on the other side of the moat."

"You were a rescuer." Cade could appreciate that. It was exactly the sort of thing he'd dreamed of doing all his life, and the thing he liked best about sheriffing. Helping people pushed him on like nothing else.

Color stained Andrew's cheeks. He dropped his gaze to the disassembled rifle. "I was only daydreaming. I turned out to be no kind of hero."

Cade wagered something other than getting shot had gone terribly wrong for Andrew in the war, something that haunted him. How long would the country bear the scars of that conflict?

"I look back on my time on the battlefield and wonder if anyone felt like he was a hero," Cade said. "I think every soldier wishes he had done things differently."

"You were a fine soldier, I'd wager my last penny on it." Andrew spoke with conviction. "You wouldn't have been scared or confused or unsure what to do. Even with the cannon smoke and gunfire and shouting, you would have known exactly what to do."

The praise made Cade feel guilty as sin. "I need to confess something. Despite what I told you all those weeks ago, I don't—"

"Have the second sight?" Andrew offered a half-smile. "I know. I figured it out."

"I shouldn't have lied to you. I didn't know you very well then, and you had a shotgun. I couldn't be certain you wouldn't shoot me."

Andrew's eyes widened with surprise. "I wouldn't have shot you. You're one of the good ones."

"You're a good one yourself, Andrew. I thank you for your help here."

"I have a knack for this sort of thing," Andrew said, hesitation in his voice. "So, if you ever need or want someone to give you a hand around the jail—" He swallowed nervously. "Well, I can't be up in my tree, so I guess I could use something to do. I wouldn't expect any pay or anything. I just like to help."

"I couldn't pay you as it is," Cade said. "I asked the town council about hiring on a deputy, and they said they couldn't afford one right now. But, if you're willing to work, I'll accept your help."

Andrew squared his shoulders. "I'm not afraid of hard work."

Good man. "Well, then, you come by any time, and I'll set you to it."

For the first time since Cade had met him, Andrew held himself proudly. "I have the rest of today free."

"Finish up your work on that rifle," Cade said. "Then, see if you can't find a way to make this jailhouse look less like a maypole."

Andrew eyed the yards and yards of ribbon, and a grin spread across his face. "Mrs. Wilhite surely does love her ribbons."

"That she does. And we love her too well to take them away from her." Cade had resigned himself to the ribbons. "I suppose there's not much to be done on that score."

They kept at their weapon cleaning. Cade had his rifle reassembled and back in the cabinet, just as Andrew began putting his together.

Cade dropped a hand on Andrew's shoulder as he passed. "Thank you for helping."

Andrew gave a quick nod. "Any time."

Cade had known too many broken soldiers. In a small way, he was one himself. If he could help Andrew heal, help him in any way, he would. And he might start healing a little as well.

*   *   *

Six people standing about constituted a crowd in Savage Wells. Thus when an even dozen gathered around the entrance to the mercantile, Cade knew he'd best go see what the trouble was. A robbery attempt? An accident?

He kept his strides casual but quick. The crowd was agitated, frustrated. Cade wove through them and headed for the center, where the trouble would be.

"No, I insist," someone said.

"No, *I* insist."

Cade reached the mercantile door just as the two men standing there repeated themselves. "What're you standing about here for, men?"

They both turned to look at him. Their expressions filled with apology. "I'm sorry," they both said in unison.

"I ain't requirin' an apology, only an explanation."

"Sorry to have troubled you, Sheriff," the first man said. "Mr. Oliver was here before me, and I simply meant to let him step inside first."

"Oh, but I don't mind letting Mr. Jones go ahead of me," the second man said. "Please, I insist."

"No, I insist."

"No, *I* insist."

A crime of politeness. That was new. "This is what you're going on about? Who steps inside ahead of the other?" Cade indicated the growing crowd. "You're snagging things up somethin' terrible."

Mr. Jones and Mr. Oliver's looks of regret grew. They immediately began apologizing to the entire crowd. They invited every last person to go inside first. A great many "I insist"s filled the cold air.

Cade met Clark's eyes, who stood nearby in the crowd. Clark had come by the jailhouse a few times since settling his argument over Annabelle and had helped out with the bank deliveries. Cade liked the man. Trusted him.

Under his breath, Clark explained the entire thing in two words: "They're Canadian."

Ah. He'd known a few Canadians; these apologies could go on forever. "Men," Cade addressed the two. "Someone has to go first."

"I'm so sor—"

Cade cut off yet another apology. "I'll sort it for you. Whoever's oldest goes in first. Next time make it the younger of you." He eyed them, and they quickly agreed. "No more of these 'arguments.' Understood?"

They agreed and apologized all in the same breath. Mr. Jones stepped inside first then Mr. Oliver. In no time, the crowd was flowing once more.

"This happens often, does it?" Cade asked Clark.

"Every time they're in town. No one has the heart to tell them their kindness is causing a great deal of trouble."

"It's a full miracle anything ever gets done in Canada," Cade said.

"I'd wager Canadians aren't all quite like that," Clark said with a smile. "But it seems like a right friendly place to live."

Clark followed the crowd inside. The walk and the street were clear once more. All was as it should be.

Aren't you the problem solver, Cade O'Brien? Savin' the world from politeness.

Cade set himself in the direction of the jail, whistling a jaunty tune as he walked. He took in a lungful of cold, fresh air. This town was precisely what he needed. Peaceful. Welcoming. But still in need of his help.

Paisley was crossing the road from the millinery. She'd taken on a great many small jobs about town, mostly cleaning and laundry. Cade's father had often said there was no shame in a job well done, but, truth was, Paisley's talents were wasted as a maid-for-hire.

He tipped his hat as she came closer. They'd not spoken since the night her father had wandered away.

"Good day to you," he said. "How's your pa?"

"Recovering. How is the exciting world of sheriffing in Savage Wells?"

"I bravely saved the town from a couple of Canadians," he said.

Her smile made an immediate appearance. *Thank heavens.* He'd not thought to see her smile any time soon with all the worries she carried about. "Oliver and Jones. While I was working at the restaurant I accidentally knocked over Mr. Jones's cup of water, and *he* apologized to *me* for a full ten minutes."

He loved her smile and was more grateful than he could say to see it again. But he knew how easily he fell under her spell. He'd do better to keep his head. A bit of light banter seemed the safest approach.

"It's an odd thing living in a town where most everyone *isn't* going to shoot me." He patted his holster. "This little beauty is going to start feeling neglected."

"I can't say I have much call to use mine while scrubbing floors and washing windows. And yet, in a very real way, I am still 'cleaning up' the town." She cringed at the bit of humor. "How did the bank delivery go?"

Cade motioned for her to walk with him as they spoke. "Fine enough. Though I'm planning to have a few more guards stationed about. The delivery attracted more attention this time than last, and the new teller hasn't arrived yet to add to our numbers."

"Ask Tansy. She may be a moonshiner, but she never shied away from helping me out when I was acting on behalf of Sheriff Garrison."

That was a good idea. Cade had spoken with Tansy a couple of times since taking over as sheriff. She was a tough old bird and, he'd wager, didn't have a cowardly bone in her entire body. "She'd work on *this* side of the law, you think?"

"She's done it before." Paisley's brows shot up as though she'd just thought of something. "You ought to ask Mr. Oliver as well. He is mild-mannered and polite, but he's also good with a gun and quick on his feet. Not a soul would suspect he was a guard, seeing as he's so sweet-tempered."

Brilliant. "He'd be the ace up our sleeve."

"Exactly."

He and Paisley reached the porch of the jail. "I visited with Andrew yesterday," she said. "He said you'd checked on the strangers who came in to town."

He nodded. "Two brothers looking to take up farming. They're the sort who're content to keep to themselves. Still, I'll keep an eye on things."

"Bill Nelson seems happy with his new post as guard at the bank." Paisley's eyes darted away from him for just a moment. "Annabelle has her own henhouse now, so there's peace again amongst the chickens." Again Paisley's gaze moved from his face to just over his shoulder in the direction of the land office.

Quick as a desert hare, Paisley flipped back her jacket and pulled her pistol from its holster. Cade had just enough time to cover his ears before she shot at something behind him. He spun around. A man he'd not seen before laid on the road.

He and Paisley rushed off the porch and to the prostrate man. A six-shooter sat next to his outstretched hand. Paisley nudged it away with her foot. The stranger moaned, clutching his shoulder.

"I spotted him sneaking out from behind the land office," Paisley said.

"I know that makes him suspicious," Cade said, "but it ain't quite enough reason to shoot him."

"This here's Gary Burton." Her pistol was already in its holster again.

"He's a cattle rustler. He was arrested here in Savage Wells about six months ago. He's supposed to still be in prison."

Cade recognized the name. "Word came last week of his escape. Marshal Hawking suspected he might be in the area."

Paisley nodded. "Then I'd say it's a very good thing for you *I* was in the area."

Cade grabbed the man by his unwounded arm and pulled him to his feet. The sound of gunfire had brought people out onto the walk. Cade spotted Mrs. Wilhite on the porch of the millinery. "Fetch the doc," he instructed.

"I ain't going back to prison," Burton mumbled.

"Fine. I'll have her just shoot you dead," Cade said, nodding to Paisley. "That'd save me a great deal of trouble."

Burton groaned.

"I'll take that as a 'No, I thank you kindly, Sheriff.'"

He and Paisley dragged the man to the jailhouse. The next thirty minutes were the most familiar Cade had spent in Savage Wells: an outlaw had a bullet dug out of his shoulder while tied down to a bed so he wouldn't escape. Cade arranged a cell for him then prepared a telegram.

But running through his mind was an unsettling thought. If not for Paisley's sharp eye and lightning-fast draw, he'd've been shot in the back. He'd left himself open, not keeping an eye on the street like he'd always done before. Savage Wells had lulled him into putting his guard down. That had to change, else next time he wouldn't be so lucky.

Chapter 24

Paisley's mind hadn't stopped reliving the moment she'd spotted Burton on the street though more than two hours had passed since she'd shot him. He'd arrived unkempt and unshaven, so she'd not recognized him straight off. But the moment she'd realized who he was, she'd known exactly why he'd come back to town. The two days he'd spent in Savage Wells's jailhouse had been filled with detailed threats of what he meant to do to the person responsible for sending him to prison in the first place.

Sheriff Garrison had taken credit for apprehending Burton, but Paisley—and Burton—knew better.

And now Burton had come back to kill her.

She hadn't had enough time to be scared. Her heart had made up for its calm in the moment by pounding a touch harder whenever she thought back on the encounter. Keeping cool while in the heat of the moment was a crucial part of being a sheriff, but eventually a person had to feel that worry and realize the danger of it all.

Papa was spending the afternoon at the jail with Cade. She wasn't entirely sure of the arrangement, but Gideon had let Papa stay at his house every day that week. She owed him at least one day on his own.

She stepped inside the jail, ready to whisk Papa away if things had turned out as badly as she feared. But what she found stopped her in the doorway. Papa and Cade sat across from one another at the desk with a checkerboard between them.

Papa is playing checkers? He must have been having one of his better days. He'd been so distant, so vague over the past week.

Papa moved a checker.

"A triple jump?" Cade threw his hands up in the air. "Here I was thinking I had a chance this time."

Papa smiled. "I warned you I am a very good checker player."

"I've a knack for the game myself," Cade said.

"My four victories to your one say otherwise."

Cade chuckled good-naturedly. Burton, still locked up in a cell, twitched in his sleep but settled back into a loud, buzzing snore. Papa and Cade both turned their heads in the direction of the cell, then sputtered in unison, barely keeping back laughs.

"It is cruel to laugh at a man for snoring like an ailing raccoon," Paisley said.

The two men looked at her, both grinning. "He's been snoring for at least thirty minutes," Papa said. "Your brother used to snore so loudly we feared the riverboats would think it was a foghorn."

He was thinking of Tom in the past tense. Papa really was more lucid than usual. Paisley treasured these days. It was as if the heavens were smiling down on her for a moment, letting her cling to her father for a little longer.

"Do you two mind if I join you?" She crossed to them even as she asked the question.

"Pull up a stool, love."

"Love?" Papa looked at the two of them with curiosity.

"Don't read too much into it, Mr. Bell. I'm only one of dozens of unattached men in these parts. Miss Paisley could have her pick of any one of them." Cade grinned at her. Was he mocking her? But his own scold from a week before wiped that thought from her mind. He'd insisted she was too quick to take offense, and she was working on that.

"My pick of any of them?" she tossed back. "I like the sound of that. But I probably should cross off my list the bachelors I've shot. They aren't likely to come courting."

"Shot?" Papa was immediately on alert.

Cade slipped his hand around hers. Heavens, she liked it when he did that. "You saved my life from that ailing raccoon over there," he said. "So I'm voting you shoot all the men you feel deserve it."

She moved a little closer, keeping her hand in his. "What if I decide *you* deserve it?"

His smile turned lazy. "I've a feeling I'd enjoy convincing you otherwise."

Heat crept over her face. She was not usually a blusher, but Cade managed to bring that out in her time and again.

"Now, give me back my hand, woman. I've a checker match to win."

She did just that. "What was that I heard about Papa winning four games against you?"

Cade bent over the checkerboard. "I used to be quite proud of my checkers skills."

"When I was a girl, he used to let me win," Paisley said.

Papa smiled at her fondly.

"The man won't even let me come close," Cade muttered.

"Don't be a sore loser," Papa said.

Paisley couldn't remember the last time he'd been in a laughing mood. It was wonderful to see again.

Cade's eyes darted in her direction. "Why're you smilin' at me like that?"

"Like what?"

"Like I'm a cream pie or a newborn puppy or something." He moved a checker. "I ain't complaining. It sure beats the death glares you sometimes give me."

Papa took his turn. "I think you're in trouble already, son."

"With you or with your daughter?" Cade pushed one of his red checkers ahead.

"Looks like both." Papa jumped Cade's piece. He spun the checker around in his fingers. "You had best make up with Paisley because you're not likely to win against me."

Cade caught her eye. "How would you propose I make up sweet to you? Shall I buy you a length of ribbon?" He motioned around the room. "I know where I can get some."

She enjoyed being back on friendly terms with him. "Sew me a shirt and we'll call it even."

He focused on the game once more, though he continued talking to her. "The look on your face when you saw my shirt that night was priceless."

She could finally look back on that moment with humor. "Probably much like the look on yours when I shot down those bottles without the slightest effort."

"We are full of surprises, you and I."

Mr. Lewis chose that exact moment to storm into the jail. Livid didn't begin to describe his expression.

"See here, O'Brien," he nearly shouted. "The delivery strategy you—"

"Clap your trap, man." Cade didn't even look up from the checkerboard. "I don't abide chaos in my jail. If you've a comment, make it calmly and civilly."

"I don't have a comment," he said. "I have a complaint."

Cade leaned back casually in his chair. "Do you? Well, I've needed a good laugh lately, so let's hear it."

Mr. Lewis stumbled over a reply. Paisley rather appreciated seeing him upended.

"Our next bank delivery will be noticeably larger than the last," Mr. Lewis said. "And you have only increased the number of guards by one. And to suggest—"

"Two," Cade said. "I've increased the number by two. If you're going to complain, do it accurately."

"Well, two perhaps, but one of those hardly counts," Mr. Lewis said. "Mr. Oliver couldn't scare off a mouse, and you've placed him inside the bank—*inside.* To have a mild-mannered Canadian overseeing the most important—"

"That mild-mannered Canadian came highly recommended by Miss Bell." Cade's tone was casual, but nothing in his expression was. "I'd wager Burton over there could give you an accounting of how sharp she is."

Mr. Lewis shot Paisley a look of painful condescension. "You Bells just can't stand to let the bank go, can you? You push your way back in by whatever means possible."

Paisley knew better than to defend herself. Mr. Lewis always managed to twist it around.

"Your father nearly ran the place into the ground with his incompetency."

Papa's face flushed. His gaze dropped to his hands. He had, of course, done absolutely nothing resembling Mr. Lewis's accusation, though things had been chaotic during his last few months at the bank. He'd simply grown too scattered and too forgetful for a job so dependent on details. He'd been humble enough to step down before things grew truly bad.

"I'll shoot him, Cade," she muttered under her breath. "I swear I will."

"Believe me, shooting people quickly loses its appeal." Cade stood up. He motioned for Mr. Lewis to walk with him back toward the door. "Clearly you've no confidence in my abilities. So I'll leave you to guard your deliveries from now on. But, to show I've no hard feelings, I promise to attend your funeral."

He slapped Mr. Lewis on the shoulder then pivoted as if to return to his desk.

"I beg your pardon? Keeping this town safe is your job—your *only* job. I suggest you do it."

Cade turned his hard glare on Mr. Lewis. He hooked his thumb over his gun belt, a posture Paisley hadn't seen him take in a few weeks. Everything about him spoke of danger and barely restrained temper. "Are you feeling lucky enough to say that again, Lewis?"

Mr. Lewis stood mute and shocked. "That, er . . ." His Adam's apple bounced twice in his throat.

"You've insulted my judgment. Called into question the services I've offered your bank. You've insulted a family I hold in regard. Now you've implied I've shirked my duties to this town." A growl hung low in his words. "I don't tell you how to run your bank. I'd suggest you don't come around here telling me how to be a sheriff."

Cade stood stock-still and watched Mr. Lewis with impatient expectation. After a moment, Mr. Lewis shifted his weight from one foot to the other. His eyes darted about.

"I'd—" Mr. Lewis cleared his throat. "I'd appreciate if you would continue to oversee the deliveries."

"I'll oversee it," Cade said, "but not because it's my 'only job.' I'll do it so that your idiocy doesn't destroy what Mr. Bell created. I don't bow to the opinions of a louse. Understood?"

For the first time since he'd moved to Savage Wells and taken over the bank, Mr. Lewis appeared truly cowed. Almost humble. "I'm sorry, Sheriff. This is a big opportunity for the bank—for me. I'm letting my nervousness run away with my judgment. I'm sorry."

"Don't let it happen again," Cade said. "Now, off with you. I've work enough to do."

Mr. Lewis, to Paisley's great surprise, left without further comment, without bothering to take one more shot at her or Papa.

Cade returned to his desk not looking the least bothered by the banker's attack. "Whose turn is it?" he asked Papa.

"I think it was yours."

Poor Papa. He still hadn't looked up from his clasped hands.

"'Tis a shame our game was interrupted by the ravings of a madman.

I wasn't sure Lewis would ever stop blatherin'." Cade steepled his hands in front of him and eyed the checkerboard. "I believe I'll win this game."

"I've seen you play, son. Don't hold your breath." Papa looked as though he might smile.

"Don't count me out. I might suddenly become the greatest checker player who ever liv—You can't start laughing before I've even finished my speech, man."

But Papa was most definitely laughing, a sound that did Paisley's heart good. The men continued their game, tossing back and forth their predictions of the other's defeat. Papa looked happier than she'd seen him in quite some time, despite Mr. Lewis's visit.

When Cade had first sauntered into town, Paisley hadn't pegged him as the type to spend an afternoon playing checkers with a man whose mind wandered relentlessly or to defend a family whose circumstances grew more humble by the day. She was happy to be wrong.

Cade had set up the checkerboard for another game when Andrew Gilbert stepped inside, though he didn't come in more than a few feet.

"Howdy, Andrew," Cade said. "Thought you'd drop in."

Andrew stuffed his hands in his pockets. He dug his toe against the wood floor. "The weather's too cold for climbing."

The war had done something terrible to Andrew, had left cracks in his mind that nothing seemed able to heal. Paisley worried fiercely about him.

"Do you play checkers, Andrew?" Cade asked.

He nodded.

"Mr. Bell has won the last five games we've played," Cade said. "I think he deserves a new challenger."

"I like checkers." Andrew crossed to the desk, his limp more pronounced than it had been recently. The coming of winter always seemed to make that worse.

Andrew tended to hover at the edges of rooms, when he was willing to enter at all. He didn't usually move *closer* to people. And though he was still obviously worried about their safety now that winter had arrived, he wasn't panicking. That was almost miraculous.

Cade moved to the occupied cell. "Dinner'll be in about an hour, then lights out," he told the prisoner.

"Wouldn't want to waste kerosene on a prisoner," Burton spat.

Cade shrugged. "Mostly, I just don't want to see your face."

Paisley moved to Cade's side. "Could I have a word?"

"Come to shoot me again?" Burton grumbled.

"Once a day is my limit with most people," Paisley answered.

Cade's expression remained hard and unyielding. "Pull a gun on me again, Burton, and you'll discover *I* don't have a daily limit."

"I was aiming for *her*," Burton growled.

"And yet," Paisley said, "of the two of us, only *you* got shot." She motioned Cade into the back room. "I—"

"He meant to shoot *you*?" He closed the back room door. "If I'd known that—" He paced away. "I don't like the idea of scum like that threatening you."

"He's not the first." She laughed a little at his indignation. "Did you think I wore my gun belt because I preferred it to jewelry?"

He shook his head. "What does Gideon have to say about it all? The threats and the danger?"

What did Gideon have to do with any of this? "He generally says, 'Don't get shot.'"

Cade kept up his tense pacing. Did this really upset him so much? No one had ever shown that much concern for her, not since Papa's mind began to slip.

Paisley stopped Cade's pacing with a hand on his arm. "I don't have a lot of talents, but I am good with a gun. I realize that isn't a very feminine skill, but I'm proud of it."

"You should be. You shoot better than any man I've ever known."

She wasn't about to let that compliment pass without rubbing it in a bit. "Better than you?"

"Well, I don't know about that." His tone was gruff, but the corner of his mouth twitched with amusement.

"I wanted to thank you for spending time with Papa. Most people either ignore him or talk to him like he's a child, and—" She swallowed against an unexpected lump of emotion. "Sometimes I feel like I'm the only one who sees the person he still is underneath it all. He did a fine job running the bank, no matter what Mr. Lewis says. He only had to step down because his mind grew ill."

He slipped his hand in hers and squeezed her fingers. "He's welcome any time."

"Thank you." She pressed a light kiss to his cheek.

Her heart leapt at the brief contact. She knew she ought to pull back and place a friendly distance between them, but somehow she couldn't. His free hand brushed her waist, settling low on her back. Her lungs squeezed tight—not a drop of air came in or out.

She met his deep blue eyes. He looked confused, almost displeased. Did he not want her to be near him? To embrace him? She still remembered their kiss outside the town council room and how melting it had been. Three weeks had passed since then, with only brief, occasional contact. What she wouldn't give to have that connection back again, even for an instant.

But he'd only looked less welcoming of her attentions. She let her hands drop away from him.

He stepped around her stiffly. "I'll go check on Andrew and your father." He didn't glance back, but left as if he couldn't get away fast enough. Why was it that kept happening to her?

She'd loved Joshua, and he'd run out on her. She'd made the acquaintance of scores of bachelors in Savage Wells, and nothing had come of any of it. Those disappointments had certainly stung, but the ache she felt standing there after Cade had left the room was surprisingly acute. He was a good man, she saw more evidence of it all the time. She longed for his company and hoped to earn his good opinion.

She'd begun loving Cade, those early droplets of love that either led to a storm or petered out into nothing, though one could never tell early on which it would be. He, on the other hand, seemed to be putting distance between them with all possible haste.

Chapter 25

"What the blue blazes are you doing in a backwater town like this?" Marshal Hawking fingered a length of ribbon tied to the cell bars. "You're a legend, Cade, and you've settled in Savage Wells? You must be bored plumb out of your mind here."

"Well, Hawk, after a decade mucking out the dirtiest towns of the West, I'd say I've earned a touch of boredom." He leaned back in his chair, linking his hands behind his head.

"While I was dropping a fugitive off at the territorial prison in Laramie, I heard a rumor that one of the candidates for sheriff of this place was a woman." Hawk let the ribbon drop. "The inmates were convinced it was true, but—" He shook his head as if to toss aside the very idea and secured the cuffs around Burton's wrists.

"That woman put the bullet through your prisoner's arm," Cade said.

Hawk's brows rose. "Did she?"

"And she's the one who rounded up the Grantland Gang, though the 'official' sheriff at the time took credit for it. I've gone over the records, and I'd wager most of the work done here the past six months was done by her, including catching a stage robber, smoking out a fugitive hiding on the edge of town, and capturing Burton the first time." He let that sink in a minute.

Hawk's expression changed from surprised to impressed. He made a thoughtful sound. "Well, since she didn't end up becoming sheriff, perhaps she ought to consider bounty hunting."

Paisley chasing down the most violent of killers in the country? The idea tied his stomach in knots.

"You think I'd have a future in it?" Paisley asked from the doorway.

When had she come in?

"Are you the sharpshooter that took this lowlife down?" Hawk asked.

"Both times." She sauntered in; something in her swagger was equal parts rugged and alluring.

Hawk's mouth tipped in appreciation as he watched Paisley approach.

Cade dropped his relaxed posture and sat more rigidly in his chair, watching Hawk watch Paisley.

"Paisley Bell." She held out her hand.

"Marshal Hawking." He shook her hand just as he would have done with a fellow lawman.

Cade ought to have appreciated the respectful gesture—Paisley certainly did—but instead found himself resisting the urge to growl. He'd need to warn Hawk that Gideon was there before him—before both of them.

"Obviously you have good aim," Hawk said. "How quick is your draw?"

"Ask Cade, there. He saw it in action a few days ago."

Hawk looked at him. Honesty compelled him to answer. "Lightning fast."

"Cool head in a crisis?" Hawk asked her.

"Usually," Paisley replied. "The only time I can ever say it faltered was when my father went missing. But I bucked up."

"I'd like to see your credentials, Miss Bell," Hawk said. "Cade, here, had quite a lot to say in your favor. Seems to me you'd make a fine bounty hunter or even a deputy marshal."

Her eyes narrowed. "If you're patronizing me, I swear—"

Hawk held his hands up in a show of innocence. "I do know of one lady bounty hunter," he said. "And she's a deucedly good one."

"Does it pay well?"

The infuriating woman seemed serious.

Hawk shrugged. "Depending on who you catch."

"And depending on whether or not you get yourself killed catchin' him," Cade added. "Now can we get this scum outta my jail?" He jerked his thumb in Burton's direction.

"Sure enough." Hawk sent Paisley one more smile before returning to the business at hand. They had Burton out of the cell and out of the jailhouse in a flash. Once the prisoner was secured in the wagon that Hawk and his deputy marshal would be hauling him away in, Hawk turned to Cade, who stood in the doorway.

"Good seeing you again. If the peace and quiet of this place gets to be too much for you, send word. The offer to join the marshals still stands. We could use a man with your skills and experience."

Paisley stepped out alongside Hawk and the two engaged in a quick conversation. Cade couldn't make out what they said to each other, but he had a guess as to the topic.

Hawk and his deputy rode off down the street with its drifts of snow in the shadows and thick mud down the middle. Cade didn't envy them the ride to Laramie.

Paisley stood on the porch, watching the wagon lumber away from town. Was she really considering Hawk's suggestion? She certainly seemed to be.

"Bounty hunting?" Cade tossed out. "Are you full mad, woman?"

She didn't flinch. "It'd pay a far sight better than washing windows."

"It pays a lot because so few people live to collect the bounties."

She leaned against the doorway, unimpressed by his logic. "Not a lot of Western sheriffs live long, either, Cade, and you didn't raise an objection when I was considering that job."

"This is Savage Wells, for land's sake. This place is a cakewalk compared to the rest of the West."

She folded her arms across her chest. "Marshal Hawking seemed to think I could handle it."

"He was flirtin' with you, love."

"Hawking said he wasn't fooling with me," she insisted. "And you said yourself I could shoot as good as any man you've ever known."

He stepped past her into the jail. "It ain't a matter of ability."

She followed him inside. "Then what? I know I wasn't entirely level-headed when my father disappeared, but I'm good in a crisis otherwise."

"Bounty hunting ain't like keeping the peace." Cade shoved at the desk chair with his boot. "It's chasing down murderers for the price on their heads. It's lurking in shadows, knowing you might have to kill them to keep them from killing you."

"If it came to that—"

"Have you ever killed a man, Paisley?"

"Well, no. I haven't had to."

He met her gaze, needing her to understand what he was saying. "It changes you. That first time, you never forget. Or the second, or third. It's a weight on your soul."

She watched him intently but didn't speak. He had to make her understand the nature of what she was contemplating.

"You're a good shot and you've a cool head, but putting holes in people strictly for money would turn you into someone cold and sick inside."

"Did you ever put holes in people strictly for money?" She stepped closer, her gaze never wavering.

He sat on the edge of the desk. "Are you saying I'm cold and sick inside?"

"Not at all." She stopped directly in front of him. "Your objection sounded personal."

"Not personal on *my* account." He took her hand in his. "I've seen what killing does to people. I don't want to see that happen to you."

"If I didn't know better, Cade O'Brien, I'd think you cared about me."

He did. Heaven help him, he did. In that moment, even thoughts of Gideon's position couldn't force Cade to release Paisley's hand. Maybe he was a terrible friend. More likely, his feelings for Paisley were simply deeper than he'd been letting himself acknowledge. Either way, he held fast to her hand, relishing the moment he knew would be all too brief.

"I'm sorry you're stuck washing windows and serving meals rather than doing what you love." He caressed her hand as he spoke. "But I've seen good people take the path you're contemplating, and I know what being a gun for hire turned them into."

"Were you ever a bounty hunter?" she asked.

"That's one thing I've kept my hands clean of." He dropped his gaze to their entwined fingers.

"You talk like you're ashamed of the things you've done."

He didn't look up at her. "I'm no saint, I'll say that much."

"But you're a decent sort of person," she said.

He closed his eyes at the touch of her fingers along his cheek. "A decent sort, am I? You accused me recently of kissing you as part of a strategy."

"Did you?"

"That you even need to ask tells me a heap." And it wasn't at all flattering. He'd kissed her because he'd wanted to and because he'd thought she'd wanted that as well. But his conscience had stopped him every time since. He didn't really know where her heart lay. Until he did, things had to stay merely friendly between them.

"I never know what to think about men," she said quietly. "They've been breaking their word to me for years."

That Joshua bloke, no doubt. Perhaps others. She deserved better than that. She deserved someone who treasured her and admired her.

"Paisley, I—"

A voice interrupted. "Pardon me, I'm looking for the bank."

Cade shot a glare toward the door. A sharply dressed man stood a single step inside the door. "Why're you looking for the bank, stranger? Do you have business there?"

"I'm the new teller."

Ah, yes. Lewis had said he'd be arriving this week ahead of the money delivery. "Delancey, right?"

"Yes."

Paisley stiffened and spun around. The stranger's mouth dropped open. Paisley's expression turned shocked.

"Good heavens," she whispered, staring. "Joshua."

Chapter 26

Paisley couldn't entirely think straight.

Joshua Delancey was in Savage Wells. He was standing right there in front of her. Joshua, the first man she'd ever loved. The man who'd wanted to marry her. The man who had walked out on her.

"Paisley?" He looked as shocked as she felt.

"Joshua?"

"Paisley." The truth seemed to be sinking in.

"Joshua."

From behind her came the addition, "Cade."

Her thoughts were jumbled. A weight settled in her stomach. *Joshua.* After four and a half years, Joshua was right there. But why?

Joshua stepped up to her and set his hands on her arms. His gaze darted all over her face. "Why are—What are you doing here of all places?"

"What am *I* doing here?" She stepped back, forcing his hands to drop from her arms. "You are supposed to be in Omaha."

"I *was* in Omaha," he said as though that ought to have been obvious. "But you aren't in Abilene."

"We left Abilene four years ago."

"You left—?" He shook his head almost impulsively. "I—Wh—" His gaze remained on her face, studying her, watching her, almost caressing her features.

Too many years and too many broken promises stood in the gap between them for that. "The bank is further down the road," she said. "You can't miss it."

She kept her composure as she turned to face Cade. His expression was entirely devoid of curiosity, though he must have been wondering about the scene playing out in front of him.

"I originally came in here looking for Papa." She forced the change of topic.

"He and Andrew are boxing up some things for Mrs. Carol."

Paisley managed to nod. "Keeping both of them busy is a good idea."

She felt the first tears puddle in her eyes. This was no time for an emotional breakdown. She met Cade's questioning gaze, but no words came. Joshua Delancey stood not ten feet behind her. She made the tiniest gesture of helplessness.

Cade apparently needed no more than that. He looked over her shoulder. "Bank's right at the turn in the road, Delancey," he said. "Lewis is expecting you."

"But, Paisley," Joshua objected. "We need to talk."

She didn't look back at him. "The time for talking passed years ago."

"Paisley."

Cade cut him off with a raised hand. "If Miss Bell wants to talk, she knows where to find you."

Joshua sputtered a moment but eventually accepted the edict. "I hear there's a hotel in town. I'll be staying there. Please come by."

Paisley kept perfectly still as the sound of Joshua's footsteps retreated behind her. As silence descended once more, she allowed herself to finally breathe.

She rubbed at her temples. "Six months I waited for that man to write to me. I actually held out hope for another six months that he'd come back. And now he just casually shows up in my town."

She shook her head. She wrapped her arms about her middle and wandered to the front window. The tranquil scene outside contrasted painfully with the turmoil inside her.

"Why did he have to come here, of all places?" she muttered.

"Feel free to tell me to go hang, if you must," Cade said, "but I'm fair dying of curiosity."

Soon enough the entire town would be. "This is not a story I have shared with anyone. Not in detail, anyway."

"Not even with Gideon?"

She shook her head.

"I'll not insist you tell me—I know enough of your stubbornness to know that wouldn't work anyway." He joined her at the window. "I only thought you might find it helpful talking to someone before you have to talk to *him*."

She ran her fingers along the top of the half-wall as she walked absentmindedly away. The Savage Wells rumor mill turned fast and seldom stuck to the facts. She'd rather Cade have the true story from her.

"Joshua worked as a clerk at my father's bank in Abilene," she said. "That's how I first met him." She dared a glance at Cade, and pressed forward with her tale. "He paid me special attention. That attention grew to courting. After a few months, he asked for my hand, and we were engaged."

"Your father mentioned that," Cade said.

He had probably talked about it while his thoughts were in the past, not realizing he was revealing her secrets.

"Joshua felt that Abilene was not a good place to begin a life together or raise a family."

"I can't argue with that," Cade said. He was still at the window but had turned to watch her.

"He accepted a position in Omaha and left. He meant to find a place for us to live and to make certain the job was secure enough before sending for me." She ran her thumb along the corner of a stack of papers on the desk. "He never came back."

"Did he say why?"

She shrugged a single shoulder. "He never wrote to me. Not even once. So I can't say what it was that kept him in Omaha, but I have a fairly good guess what kept him away from Abilene."

"Cowardice and idiocy?" Cade suggested.

"Me." She let her hands hang limply at her sides. Her energy was quickly disappearing. "I came to the conclusion years ago that he changed his mind about marrying me and chose to end things with silence rather than conversation."

"I'd say that man owes you a conversation, and I think you oughtta make him pay up."

She sighed and looked away from him. "But what if his explanation is he never really loved me, and Omaha was only an excuse to get out of telling me so?"

"Then he's an even bigger lout than I'd suspected."

She could laugh at that.

"Either way, you need to talk to him. You owe yourself an answer."

He was right. She didn't like the prospect of having things out with Joshua, but she needed to do it. She was nervous, uncertain. And she, who had endured the battlefields of Missouri and the death toll in Abilene, was afraid.

Chapter 27

Paisley stood at the hotel desk waiting for Joshua. She'd sent a note up to room five, where Joshua was staying.

Paisley's mind sat heavy and burdened. She'd thought many times what she would do or say if he ever came back. At first she hadn't pictured herself doing anything other than throwing herself into his embrace and never letting go again. But as time had passed, the confusion and pain and the reality of his abandonment had rendered her heart, if not entirely indifferent, certainly no longer attached to him. Now he was in Savage Wells, and she realized the wounds he'd left were still unhealed.

Cade was right; Joshua owed her an explanation. Perhaps knowing why he'd left would help her close that chapter in her life for good.

The sound of footsteps pulled her eyes to the staircase. He'd always been a handsome man, something that had turned her head the first time she'd met him. But he wasn't as polished and refined as Gideon, and he certainly didn't have the authoritative air and confident manner Cade had.

"Paisley, you came. I've been trying to decide all afternoon what to say to you." He reached out as if to embrace her, but she stepped back.

"I'll make it simple for you," she said. "Just tell me the truth."

Dinner was in full swing at the restaurant, which occupied the ground floor of the hotel. A late stage had stopped in town. If Paisley had still been working nights, this would have been a long one.

"Is there somewhere a bit more private?" Joshua echoed her exact thoughts.

"Let's go for a walk." They'd have a bit of privacy without being entirely alone. She preferred it that way.

They stepped out, and Joshua offered his arm. She didn't accept. It was, perhaps, uncivil of her, but she was embarking on a potentially humiliating conversation. Manners could wait.

"Why didn't you ever write to me?" Paisley never bothered beating about the bush.

"I did."

"If you mean to begin with lies, then there's no point—"

"I did write," he insisted. "But you never wrote back. After a while, I assumed you'd changed your mind."

She looked up at him fully. "Assuming any of that is true, why didn't you come back to Abilene when you didn't hear from me?"

He tucked his hands in his coat pockets as they walked. "I wanted to. I wanted to see you again, to finally bring you to Omaha as we'd planned."

"Why didn't you?"

They'd passed the telegraph and stagecoach office, then the barbershop. Paisley only vaguely noted their progress.

"There was no reason to if you weren't writing to me," he said.

He hadn't heard from her, didn't know what had happened, and, yet, couldn't think of a reason to go back home? "You knew more people in Abilene than just me. Did you ever write to any of them to ask after me?" That seemed like a pretty minimal thing a man could do to reconnect with his fiancée.

Joshua began fiddling with his pocket watch, pulling it in and out of his vest pocket but never looking at it, and certainly not looking at *her*. "It was a . . . private problem," he said. "I didn't want to make things awkward for you."

Being abandoned by a man every person of her acquaintance knew she was engaged to had been extremely awkward. It seemed the person he'd meant to spare was himself. What was a little discomfort if he'd really loved her?

They turned back once they'd passed Mrs. Carol's shop, where Main Street gave way to the open expanse beyond the end of town. There were still too many unanswered questions for any sort of easiness between them.

"In hindsight, I can see that I didn't try very hard," he admitted.

"As it turned out," she said, "there wasn't much worth trying hard for."

He stopped on a dime, facing her with a somber expression and pulled brows. "But we're together again. Fate has given us a chance to try again, to make things right."

The thought filled her with something very near dread. No, there would be no trying again. That was her past, and she was a different person now. She would likely always wonder about what went wrong between them, but it wasn't important enough to her to be worth walking that path again.

"I hope, in a very neighborly way, that you are happy in Savage Wells," she said. "But neighborly is all we will ever be, Joshua."

"I'm not giving up so easily this time."

She sighed inwardly. For someone who hadn't wanted to make things "awkward" for her four years earlier, he seemed determined to do just that now.

*   *   *

Cade watched Paisley and Delancey walk down the road. The reunited couple weren't holding hands. They weren't even looking at each other.

"What do you think of Delancey?" Gideon asked, sitting on a chair nearby.

"I ain't sure yet," he answered. "There's something I don't like about him."

"'Something you don't like'? That something wouldn't happen to be their one-time engagement, would it?"

"Does it bother *you*?" After all, Gideon was more justified in disliking Joshua than Cade was.

Gideon shrugged it off, though. "It bothers me that he hurt her and that what he did makes her question everyone's sincerity and trustworthiness. That part bothers me, certainly."

An odd response, that. Cade tried to keep his own answer as casual as he could. "If you need to challenge him to a duel, I'll stand as your second."

"I'm from Washington, not the turn of the century," Gideon said. "Besides, I figure you'll have a shoot-out in the street with the man and take care of it for me."

Cade watched the man sip his glass of water as if the woman he loved wasn't being inconvenienced—or worse—by a lout. "That's a rather yellow-bellied way of defending your woman."

Gideon choked on his mouthful of water. "My woman? Paisley?"

"I know you're not formally courting her," Cade said, "but anyone with eyes can see there's something there. You comfort her, put an arm around her. She talks and laughs with you like no one else. I don't know the whole story, but I ain't blind."

Gideon started to laugh and then couldn't seem to stop. "I've been wondering why you haven't been making up sweet to her," he said between chuckles. "I'm not blind, either, and it has been apparent for a while now that you were pretty far gone on her."

Cade didn't think he'd been that obvious. "I'm not a cad," he said. A decent sort of man simply didn't try to win the affections of a woman who was already being courted, not when the one doing the courting was his good friend.

"Not a cad, perhaps, but not the most discerning fellow, either. I've told you all along that I am very fond of Paisley and I care a great deal for her, but not in a courtship-and-romance kind of way."

That didn't make any sense. "How could you not be? You know her so well; you know how amazing she is."

"I do," Gideon admitted, then took another sip of water. He was clearly fighting a grin. "But I'm rather obligated to think well of her. After all, what would Granny Aisling say if I spoke ill of my cousin?"

"Your—Granny—" Cade's mouth momentarily quit working while his brain attempted to sort out what Gideon had just said.

Gideon laughed, and, just as before, he didn't seem able to stop. "You thought . . . we were . . . courting."

"It was an understandable mistake. You're obviously fond of each other, and very well acquainted."

"We're family." Gideon shuddered even as he continued laughing. "That's . . . disturbing." He shook his head as if trying to clear away the thought.

Cade's mind spun. "She's your cousin?"

"Her late mother was my father's cousin," Gideon said. "So we're second cousins once removed, or first cousins twice removed, I can never keep it straight. But it amounts to the same thing. She's my cousin. A family member. A relative." He shuddered again and made a noise of distaste, but his laughing grin took any insult out of it.

"Why didn't you tell me?"

Gideon shook his head. "Do you usually require a glance at the family Bible when making a new friend?"

Cade gave it a moment's thought. There really hadn't been anything in Paisley and Gideon's interactions that couldn't be explained as the closeness of family members. Cade had assumed a romance existed, but, now that he was looking at it with open eyes, the two never embraced, never gazed into each other's eyes. They laughed and pricked at each other, but never in a flirtatious way.

"She's rather like a sister to you, ain't she?"

Gideon nodded. "Exactly like one, though I only met her in person for the first time when I arrived here. I've known her through family correspondence ever since we were children. Her father had heard through the family that I was a doctor looking for a place to set up a practice, and, since there wasn't a man of medicine within hundreds of miles, he wrote to me asking if I'd consider coming out West. They've only ever been Cousin Barney and Cousin Paisley to me."

Cade's mind was beginning to accept his suddenly very different circumstances. "You truly aren't—"

"If you ask me once more if I am courting my cousin, I will punch you in the face."

Cade laughed out loud; he couldn't help himself. It was such an out-of-character thing for the gentle doctor to say. "Truce," he said. "She's your family. I understand that now."

"Now that we've straightened out that matter, Sheriff O'Brien, here's your next question. Will you be clearing the field of Delancey by fair means or foul?"

"Both?" He could think of a few foul means of taking care of the nuisance.

"Either way, I'm behind you," Gideon said. "Paisley deserves better than a man who ran out on her, and you'd best make certain she knows that."

He planned to make *very* certain of that.

Chapter 28

Cade put on his best shirt and cleanest trousers, took extra care with his razor, and set out for the Bells' home. The whispers about town put Delancey at the Bells' place nearly every night since Mr. Bell had returned home after convalescing at Gideon's. It was a situation that needed looking into.

He didn't think Paisley was foolish enough to allow Delancey back into her life fully. But he wasn't entirely sure *he* had found his way back there yet, and it was time and gone he put his full effort into that.

He knocked at the Bells' door. He hooked his hand near his holster. If Delancey answered the door . . . Well, Cade would prefer things get off on the proper footing. But it was Mr. Bell who opened the door.

"Good evening," Cade greeted. "Is Paisley about?"

Mr. Bell nodded. Cade stepped inside. He set his hat on a hook near the door. Voices sounded from the parlor.

"I appreciate the gesture," Paisley said, "but we don't need you to bring us food."

"The town talks often enough of your straitened circumstances," Delancey replied.

Cade glanced through the threshold into the parlor. Paisley and

Delancey faced each other near the low-burning fire. Delancey watched her with pulled brows. She looked more than a little put out with him.

"You are struggling," Delancey said. "I make a decent wage; I can help you."

That is the wrong way to go about it, Delancey. Prick her pride and she'll fight you ever harder.

"We have not yet sunk to being a charity case," Paisley said.

"But I've seen people in the town give you things. Food, supplies."

Paisley pointed a warning finger at him. "They are our friends. They have that right."

"But I am—"

"—little more than a stranger."

To Mr. Bell, Cade quietly asked, "How long've they been arguing about this?"

Mr. Bell shook his head, vaguely. "I . . ." The words stopped, but his head shaking didn't.

The man needed an escape. "Have you had dinner?"

"No."

"Has Paisley made anything yet?"

"I think so." He didn't look at all certain.

"Go see if there's food waiting in the kitchen," Cade said.

"But, Paisley—"

He clapped a hand on Mr. Bell's shoulder. "I'll send Paisley in. You go eat."

He took the excuse Cade offered. Now to deal with the one causing all the trouble.

Cade stepped into the parlor. Paisley and Delancey eyed one another from a safe distance. They put him firmly in mind of two dogs standing guard, neither willing to turn its back on the other.

"You are being irrational, Paisley," Delancey said.

"Not a wise thing to say to a woman who's armed," Cade warned, casually entering the conversation.

They both startled a little, but quickly recovered.

Delancey eyed Cade's gun belt then glanced back at Paisley's. "Does everyone in Savage Wells walk around armed?"

"The ones that ain't dead."

Delancey wasn't satisfied. "It's not right for a woman to wear a gun."

Cade shifted his gaze to Paisley. "Your pa's wandered into the kitchen looking for some food."

"I hadn't meant to delay his meal. He grows more agitated when he's hungry." She stepped toward the doorway, toward Cade.

Delancey stopped her with a hand on her arm. Cade held his tongue.

"I'm being overbearing, aren't I?" Delancey said.

"Yes, you are." Paisley wasn't one for mincing words.

"I'm sorry. It's only that, seeing you again, after all that happened—" He held his hands up in a show of helplessness. "I'm stumbling about, I know, but—second chances don't happen often. I don't want to waste this one."

"Fate *has* thrown us together again," Paisley said.

Cade's heart dropped to his feet.

"But," she continued, "that doesn't mean this is a second chance."

His heart climbed right back to its proper place.

"I don't give up easily," Delancey insisted.

"You gave up quite easily four years ago."

There was the razor-tongued Paisley he loved.

"I hate to break up a good spat," Cade jumped in, "but Mr. Bell's likely to get antsy and try cooking something on his own."

Paisley turned away from Delancey and crossed toward the door.

Cade stopped her as she reached his side. "I like a woman who wears a gun, no matter what some fellows might have to say about it."

She smiled. Delancey hadn't made her smile once that Cade had seen. She stepped out into the corridor and headed for the kitchen.

Delancey looked directly at Cade. His wasn't so much an angry expression as a jealous one. "You seem to enjoy assuming the role of her champion."

Cade hooked his thumb over his gun belt and slowly sized Delancey up. "She don't need me fighting her battles, but I'll keep an eye on anything—or any*one*—who hurts her."

"She's in no danger from me," Delancey said.

"History says otherwise."

To his credit, Delancey's regret appeared sincere. "I'm not one to repeat my mistakes."

Cade held his gaze. "A great many people in this town care about her. We won't allow you to cause her any pain."

Delancey raised an eyebrow. "I get the impression you're intending to emphasize the 'I' part of 'we.'"

"Indeed." Cade let that hang in the air between them.

Delancey squared his shoulders. "You don't frighten me."

"I should."

Delancey didn't respond, but simply turned toward the front door.

Quitting the field already?

Cade meant to make a slower departure. He'd taken time with his appearance, after all. It would be a shame to waste the effort. He pushed open the kitchen door.

Mr. Bell sat at a worktable, gazing out the small window. Paisley met Cade's eye. "Did Joshua leave?"

He nodded. "There's a bit of tension between the two of you."

She wiped her hands on a dishrag. "He's trying to help. But he's trying to begin right where we ended."

"Is that something you want?"

Paisley set a glass of milk in front of her pa. "I have no desire to waste any more tears on someone I cannot trust."

Tears. Delancey had made her cry. Cade disliked him more all the time.

Paisley watched her pa with worry. "He's having fewer and fewer good days."

Cade took her hand in his. "Anything I can do?"

With her free hand, Paisley pushed a small bit of ham toward him. "Would you slice some meat for the sandwiches?"

"A big task, that. I might have to rest partway through."

She attempted to smile at his humor. "If you manage, I'll let you stay and eat with us."

"I'd like that. Anything else you need for dinner?"

Her eyes dropped away from his. "We don't need another charity basket."

"Paisley—"

She turned away. "Never mind. I'll pull out the bread for the sandwiches."

Cade stepped up beside her again and quickly pressed the briefest of kisses to her cheek. He forced himself to step past her before the temptation to kiss her fully proved too much. They weren't on firm enough footing to tread that path again.

"What brought that on?" She looked surprised but not offended. Her face had colored up nicely, in fact. Cade held out hope that she wasn't as indifferent as he feared.

"You seemed to need it." He returned to the ham. If Paisley wanted it sliced, he'd slice it.

Mr. Bell spoke into the silence of the kitchen. "Your mother isn't ever out this late. Where did you say she'd gone?"

Paisley froze on the spot. For a moment she said nothing. "She is— She's visiting a neighbor."

"At this late hour?" Mr. Bell pressed.

"It's only six o'clock, Papa."

"It is not," he snapped. "It's ten o'clock at least."

Paisley set a plate of sliced bread next to Cade's platter of ham. "Do you mind assembling the sandwiches?"

"Happy to."

"Which neighbor is she visiting?" Mr. Bell demanded. "I'll go fetch her home."

"No, Papa. She's—She's fine where she is." Emotion crept into Paisley's voice.

"I would rather she were home." Mr. Bell paced to the window.

"So would I," Paisley whispered.

Her father looked back at her. "Then I will go get her. We'd both rather have her here."

Pain filled every line of her face. "She can't come home just now. I am certain she wishes she could, just as we wish she was here, but she can't come back."

"If she's just at the neighbors'—"

"They're ill," she said quickly. "Mama is nursing them. It would be a shame to pull her away when they need her so much."

"I suppose," Mr. Bell mumbled and turned back to the window. "How long do you think she'll be gone?"

Her chin quivered. She closed her eyes a moment and pressed her lips together so hard the color disappeared.

Pain ached through Cade at the sight. He set a hand gently on her arm, unsure what else to do.

"She won't be gone long, Papa." Her whisper shook. "We'll hardly notice she's been away."

"And then the two of you can begin working on your quilt again," Mr. Bell said. "You keep putting it off. Your mother isn't at all sure you'll manage to finish it."

"You're right, Papa. It ought to have been finished long ago."

Cade quickly assembled a sandwich and set it on the table near Mr. Bell. Hoping that would keep the man occupied for a while, Cade turned back to Paisley. A tear trickled down her cheek. Cade motioned her out of the kitchen with a jerk of his head.

They stepped into the hallway. Paisley leaned her forehead against the wall. Her shoulders rose and fell with each strangled breath. "I can't keep doing this, Cade. Talking about Mama as though she's still alive, as though she'll walk through the door at any moment . . . I miss her so much it's like a knife in my heart, and Papa just twists it."

"I'm sorry." He truly was. "How often does this happen?"

"More all the time." She turned to lean her shoulder on the wall. She wiped at her cheeks with the heel of her hand. "Gideon says he'll grow worse. Eventually he won't remember anything about Mama. I dread it, but in a small way I'm looking forward to it, which makes me think I must be the most horrible sort of person."

Cade reached out and brushed at a tear slipping down her jaw. "It doesn't mean you're horrible, love. Only worn to a thread."

"I miss him," she said. "He's here every day, and I miss him." She wrapped her arms around herself. "I work around the clock trying to care for him, to keep him calm and comfortable. I'm tired, and I'm frustrated and lonely. And as much as I insisted to Joshua that we don't need the food he brought, I'm failing there as well."

Cade settled an arm around her shoulders and walked with her toward the parlor. He could think of nothing to say, so he kept quiet.

"Papa has no one but me, and I am letting him down." Another tear escaped her eye.

Cade held her hand, gently, wishing he could do more. He brushed his lips along her forehead. Thoughts of kissing her again had kept him up at night. The memory of her in his arms haunted his days. Now she was there, letting him hold her.

A shuddering, half-sigh, half-sob escaped her. Now was not the time to try kissing her again. She was hurt and worried and vulnerable.

"Sit by the fire and warm up, love," he said, putting her a little away from him. "I'll fetch your pa and you a few sandwiches and be back."

She smiled at him. "For someone I didn't like at all at first, you're not entirely terrible."

"Good to hear," he said with a laugh. "My next goal is to be 'mostly fine.'"

She sat in the chair nearest the fireplace. "We can work on that."

We most certainly can.

Chapter 29

Paisley came by the jail the next day, something Cade chose to see as a sign she'd meant what she'd said about working on learning to like him better.

"You're wearing your gun," Cade said, noticing it as he always did.

"Don't you start yelping at me." She was apparently on the warpath. "I'll wear what I choose to wear, whether or not—"

"I wasn't complaining. I was only wondering if something had happened or if you were expecting something to and if that something required a pistol."

Her defenses didn't immediately drop. "I have worn a gun almost daily for years. I do not need a special reason, neither do I need permission from you or Joshua to do so."

"I told you last night that I like your gun." He really did. "You wear it well. You wear it *real* well."

Her mouth tightened, and her nostrils flared a bit. "Do not poke fun at me, Cade."

He sidled up close to her, near enough to enjoy the scent she always wore. "A gun slung low on a woman's hips might not appeal to every man, but it sure turns the head of this one. Has from the very first, love."

"So maybe it's really you and not Joshua who's a bit touched in the head." At least she was smiling, which was more than could be said for him.

He didn't like how easily Delancey pricked at her and made her doubt herself. "Why do you put up with him?" he asked.

"Because he keeps coming around." Her smile only grew. "He's not a bad person, or wasn't when I knew him, at least. He simply didn't love me as much as either of us thought he did. If I shunned every man who didn't fall in love with me, I'd not have a single male acquaintance."

"I'd beg to differ," Cade muttered. Not only had he fallen in love with her, he knew of several others who were more than a little fond of her themselves.

"How did the bank delivery go this morning?" Paisley asked.

He wasn't surprised that she still kept an ear pressed to the ground on matters of law and order in Savage Wells. She hadn't made a go for the job strictly for the salary or prestige, after all.

"Without a hitch," Cade said. "Jones and Tansy were the perfect additions. You've a mind for these things, after all."

"A mind for planning heavily-armed deliveries of money? That is not generally the way a woman wants to be described." But she smiled amusedly.

"Oh, should I have said you were 'prim and proper' instead?"

She winced. "That's almost as bad as 'dainty and demure.'"

Cade chuckled. "Demure? It ain't a bad trait, it just don't suit you."

"You don't seem to think that's a failing in me." The tiniest hint of pleading he caught in her eyes tugged hard at him.

Here was the need for reassurance he had seen in her many times. Maybe if she was constantly demanding compliments and such it would be bothersome. But this was Paisley, who shot like a gunfighter, commanded attention like a general, and didn't back down from the things that mattered, no matter how lopsided the odds. A kind word now and then wasn't much to ask.

"I never cared for prudish women," he said. "But a woman with fire and determination, well, that's another thing entirely."

"Yes, well, not everyone feels that way," she said.

They stood near enough to each other for him to slip an arm around her waist and pull her closer to him. She set her hand on his chest, looking up at him with that same uncertainty.

"A woman doesn't change so someone'll love her. Any man who thinks she should doesn't deserve her affection."

She turned her head, resting it against him. Saints, she felt good in his arms, leaning on him. He could easily grow accustomed to this.

"You are very warm," she said with a sigh. "It is freezing outside today."

"Is that the only reason you're letting me hold you like this?" He asked like it was simply more teasing. It wasn't.

"It's the only reason I'll admit to."

That was good enough for him.

For now.

Chapter 30

Paisley worked an average of a dozen different jobs over the course of a week. They were all tiring, but the two days she spent serving lunch to the stagecoach passengers topped them all. She never sat. She never stopped moving.

Bounty hunting might be more dangerous, but surely it would be less exhausting.

Cade's words of warning filled her mind as they did any time she so much as thought about taking up Marshal Hawking's suggestion of pursuing that risky vocation. *"Putting holes in people strictly for money would turn you into someone cold and sick inside."*

She stepped out of the restaurant after one particularly long day at the restaurant. A cold wind tore at her. Winters were brutal in Wyoming, and they'd not even reached the thick of it yet. Paisley buttoned up her coat all the way to her throat.

Only a moment after she began walking toward Gideon's house to fetch Papa, Mr. Thackery hurried up toward her. He'd walked her home a few times. His attentions were flattering, and he seemed a nice enough fellow, but he didn't make her heart flutter or her cheeks heat. Only one man did that. One she was beginning to hope might feel the same way about her.

"Good day, Miss Bell." Thackery held his sweat-stained hat in his hand, spinning the brim around and shuffling his feet. "Are you headed home?"

"To Dr. MacNamara's, actually."

Papa hadn't been well the past few days, mind or body. Each successive episode struck him harder than the last. He didn't recover as quickly. She worried a great deal about him.

"The weather has been cold these past few days." Thackery cleared his throat, hat still spinning in his hands. "Too much colder and I'll be sent out to break up frozen ponds out on the grazing land."

She couldn't say if he was excited by the prospect or not. He was so fidgety. And he didn't look at her. He hadn't been nervous around her during their sheriff competition. His more personal attentions toward her had turned him into a mess.

"Can we keep walking?" she requested. "I think we'll be warmer that way."

He nodded and kept pace with her, but didn't seem to have anything else to say. Joshua's arrival spared them both any need for conversation.

"Paisley. I came to walk you home." Joshua spared only the slightest glance for Thackery. "And I brought a warm blanket." He held it up. "I know your coat isn't very thick."

"I'm only going as far as Dr. MacNamara's," Paisley said. She could already see his house.

"Well, you can still use the blanket until you get there." Joshua made to put it around her shoulders.

Paisley sidestepped him and kept going.

"You'll freeze," he insisted, double stepping to catch back up with her. "I'll be fine."

"But—"

Thackery jumped in. "If Miss Bell says she doesn't need the blanket, you ought to believe her."

"*I* am concerned for her well-being."

Mrs. Abbott and Mrs. Jones happened past in that moment. Their eyes darted in unison from Thackery to Joshua to Paisley and back again. In an instant, the women's heads were together and whispered words flew between them. They continued down the road, deep in discussion.

More fodder for the Savage Wells gossip mill.

Paisley climbed the steps to Gideon's front porch and knocked at the door. She'd normally just walk in—Gideon had long ago told her she could—but Joshua and Thackery were there, each fighting for the spot beside her. She would have been flattered if she wasn't so annoyed by the entire thing.

Gideon opened the door. He looked at her companions. "Have you been hired as a bodyguard, Pais?"

She gave Gideon a tense-lipped glare as she stepped past him. "They followed me."

"Shall I leave your puppies on the porch?" Gideon asked.

She probably should be nicer to them. They were trying to be kind, after all. She turned and offered them a smile. "Thank you both for walking me over. But my father needs me now."

They were both very understanding and left with solemn promises to see her later. She breathed a sigh of relief when they were gone.

"Two suitors at once," Gideon said. "A fine position to be in."

She shook her head. "Not when neither suitor is the one I want."

"Well, now. This is something." Gideon's tone grew dramatic as they made their way to the staircase. "So who *is* the suitor you want?"

"After so many years on my own, I've simply resigned myself to being a spinster. I'll begin wearing outlandish clothing and will collect large numbers of chickens, all of whom I'll name Annabelle." She hazarded a glance in his direction.

He was grinning, just as she'd assumed he would be. Her brother, Tom, had been the same way: quick with a smile, fond of a joke. "And you don't have any alternatives to the Annabelle farm?"

They'd reached the second-floor landing. It was the perfect moment to switch topics before he tricked her into a confession she was not yet ready to make. "How is Papa doing today?"

Gideon accepted the new direction. "His lungs have cleared significantly. There's still a cough, but it doesn't sound as worrisome."

"That is a relief."

Gideon nodded toward Papa's bedroom door. "His throat doesn't appear as raw, either."

She didn't step inside. "You are sticking very close to the subject of his physical health, which makes me worry that his mind isn't quite so good."

"The last time I checked on him he asked me to ask his mother if it was time for supper."

Papa's mind had returned to his early childhood? He was almost never that far away. Her heart sank clear to her toes. The time had come to ask the question she'd been dreading. "How long before he stops returning to the present?"

"I wish I could tell you," Gideon said. "There is so little we understand about the mind. So very, very little."

"But he *will* eventually stop returning." Paisley had tried again and again to accept that truth. "Someday he won't be my father anymore. He'll be a very confused stranger."

"Doc?"

They both turned at the sound of Andrew's voice. Paisley stole a moment to swipe at the tears in her eyes.

"How's Mr. Bell?" Andrew asked. He stood at the base of the stairs, looking up at them.

"He's still very ill," Gideon said.

Paisley spoke to Andrew. "Would you like to go visit him?"

Andrew shook his head. "If he's ailing, he needs to rest."

"You are so kind to him."

Andrew gave a half shrug. "He doesn't treat me like I'm batty the way most people do."

She blinked back a tear. "Someday, Andrew, he won't know who you are."

He didn't hesitate, not one moment. "He doesn't always know now. But he doesn't need to know my name to play checkers."

"Come by tomorrow," Gideon said. "Maybe he'll be feeling better."

Andrew nodded and slipped away. She'd worried about Andrew for four years. She'd worried about her father for most of the last two. A tiny bit of that worry eased, knowing they were helping each other.

Gideon opened the door. "Let me know if you need anything or if he seems to grow worse."

She stepped into the dim room and was greeted by the sound of Papa's snoring. She didn't want to wake him, but she also didn't want to leave him. "Would you mind if I stayed with him tonight?"

"Of course not. There's a pillow and blanket on the chaise, but if you'd rather sleep on a real bed, the other rooms are empty and, as you know, the linens are freshly laundered."

"Thank you. For everything."

She cherished Gideon's presence in her life. He was the only family she had outside of Papa. Beyond that, the steadiness of his friendship helped her more than she could say.

But the person she longed for most as she sat in Papa's room, so alone, so overwhelmed, was Cade. He was supportive without being pitying. He smiled at her in a way that melted her from the inside, but he could get under her skin like no one else. Hearing him call her "love" the way he did and seeing the twinkle in his eyes did wonders for her every time. Sometimes he would hold her and everything in the world felt right, but then he'd act as though nothing had occurred.

She had been mistaken about a man's affections before. This time, she meant to be far, far more cautious.

Chapter 31

Cade stood in the parlor of Ellis Lewis's house, waiting for the start of a social gathering. Gideon had dragged him there. He'd rather be cleaning the outhouse behind the jail. Still, coming meant he could watch Delancey make a spectacle of himself. That would make for an evening well spent.

"It is pretty," Paisley said to Delancey, once again attempting to return something he'd given her. "But I cannot accept such an expensive gift."

"Don't let the cost bother you," Delancey answered, setting his hand on Paisley's arm. Cade didn't indulge in the urge to snatch Delancey's hand away; he didn't have to. Paisley pulled her arm back. Again. "I am not a pauper. I have all the things I need and money enough. I paid off your debt at the smithy and the mercantile."

"You did *what?*"

It was a good thing Paisley wasn't wearing her gun. Based on the look she gave Delancey, Cade would've been cleaning up a murder scene.

"It was not your place to do that," she whispered urgently.

His brows pulled down in immediate confusion. "But I care for you. We were once engaged."

"I have allowed you to be my friend again," Paisley answered curtly.

"But paying my debts is far too personal and presumptuous a task for a friend to undertake."

His features softened. "Please don't worry that I resent it. I was happy to fix the problem."

Her jaw clenched. "That is not what I said."

Gun or no, Cade could see he needed to step in before Paisley broke Delancey's nose. As much as he'd enjoy that, Miss Dunkle would probably faint and expect him to catch her.

He strode the rest of the way to Paisley and Delancey. "I've not seen you around lately, Paisley."

Delancey eyed him up and down. "We were having a conversation."

"Yes. So everyone heard." He pulled a folded bit of paper from his vest pocket and held it out to Paisley. "Hawk sent this to you inside his last report."

"Did he?" She eagerly unfolded it.

"Who is Hawk?" Delancey asked.

"He's a federal marshal." Paisley didn't look up from her letter.

"Why is a federal marshal writing to Paisley?"

"Believe it or not, there are a great many men who *do* write to women rather than simply saying they will," Cade said.

Delancey didn't try to defend himself but watched Cade with a hard stare. But what could he possibly have said? A man who truly loved a woman would have dug deep into the mystery that Delancey had faced all those years ago. He, however, had simply shrugged it off after a single unanswered letter.

"Oh, heavens." Paisley stared at the paper in her hands. "He's recommended me for a deputy federal marshal."

Cade hadn't heard such unmistakable excitement in her voice in weeks, not since they'd been knee-deep in the sheriffing competition. He knew she'd had her heart set on being sheriff but perhaps hadn't realized just how much it had meant to her.

She faced Cade directly. "Do you think Hawk is serious in his offer?"

"Completely."

Her eyes unfocused a bit as her thoughts wandered. "I've missed wearing a badge."

"You'd have one again with this job." Cade didn't like the idea of her living away from Savage Wells for long stretches of time, but he couldn't deny her the moment of pondering. And deputy marshal was a far sight better than bounty hunter. "You'd be deucedly good at marshaling."

"You are actually considering this?" Delancey reentered the conversation. "It sounds dangerous."

Says the man who abandoned her in Abilene, arguably the most dangerous town in the West.

"I've seen her shoot," Cade said. "*She* ain't the one likely to end up dead."

Delancey pierced him with a glare. "I, for one, am not willing to take that risk."

"You aren't the one who'd be taking the risk," Cade tossed back. "Paisley can make her own decisions."

"I'll need more information to make this one," she said. "And a lot would depend on Papa. I can't leave him here alone while I'm off deputying."

Cade's smile pulled wide. "'Deputying' ain't a word, love."

"I am making it a word." She inched up to him, eyeing him with a laughable bit of false pompousness. "Are you wanting to argue over it?"

"Argue? No. I ain't wanting to *argue*." He laid the flirtatious tone on thick and heavy.

"Good, because as a deputy marshal, I'd have the authority to boss you around."

He leaned in close. "I'd like to see you try."

Delancey cleared his throat loudly. Cade didn't step back. He liked being as near to her as he was, and she wasn't objecting. Delancey's opinion on the matter was of little concern to him.

"Congratulations on the offer," Cade said. "You've been wishing someone would give a woman a chance at proving her worth in this line of work. Whether or not you accept the offer, there's pride in knowing you earned the right to try."

He raised her hand to his lips and pressed a kiss to the backs of her fingers. She didn't snatch it away like she so often did with Delancey.

In the background, Lewis drawled on about the two-thousand-dollar delivery the bank had just received, about the accolades he was receiving from Omaha. Mrs. Endicott was somewhere nearby telling whoever would listen about everything she'd heard that week from the many people she'd visited.

Delancey didn't have anything to say. Cade preferred it that way.

* * *

A loud knock woke Cade from a light sleep. He opened a single eye. Another knock sounded. He slid from his bed, snatching his pistol from the bedside table. He moved quickly to the side of the doorway, having learned long ago that bullets can cut through doors like a hot knife through butter.

"Who's 'at?" he barked out.

"Santa Claus," was the dry answer.

Paisley. He unlocked and opened the door. "Are you plumb out of your skull? Do you know what time it is?"

"You can lecture me later. This is important."

He motioned her inside. "Give me a moment to light the lantern."

She closed the door while he pulled down the box of matches. He lit the wick and set the glass cover back on the lantern. The room went from black to dim.

"You don't have a shirt on." Paisley sounded almost shocked.

"I was asleep, you madwoman." He pulled open a bureau drawer and snatched out a shirt. "I might have shot you, you know."

"Nonsense. You're not reckless."

"Not when I'm awake." He slipped the shirt over his head but didn't bother tucking it in.

"I need you to help me do something." She held his gaze. "Something extremely important."

"What?"

Without the slightest hint of guilt or discomfort, she said, "I'm going to break into the bank."

Chapter 32

Break into the bank? "I may have learned to turn a blind eye to our moonshiner friend, but I've strong objections to bank robbers."

"Hear me out." She set her hand on his arm, her gaze steady. "I have a hunch."

As odd as her notion sounded, he trusted her judgment. "Tell me." He jerked his head in the direction of his table and chairs.

She sat, facing him. "How much money did the bank receive during the last delivery?"

"Twenty-two hundred."

She nodded. "Mr. Lewis must have mentioned the delivery a dozen times tonight, but he said, repeatedly, that the bank received 'two thousand dollars.'"

Cade sat on the trunk at the end of his bed. "The numbers are close."

"Perhaps there's nothing to it," she admitted. "But I doubt a man as proud as he is of the money he's responsible for, would accept two hundred dollars less credit for his achievement."

She was absolutely right. How had he not caught on to that?

He held up his hand. She'd made her point well. "What do we need to do after we break in?"

Her brows lifted in a quick look of surprise. Her lips turned up in a smile. "I need to look at the bank account book and make certain he recorded a delivery of two thousand two hundred dollars."

"You think Lewis is falsifying his records."

"That's one possibility. The other, of course, is that someone stole the money *before* it was recorded, and Mr. Lewis really did receive only two thousand dollars."

"That'd be hard to manage. The box is locked in Omaha, and only Lewis has matching keys."

She thought on that a moment. "Like I said, there may be nothing to this. But we won't know if we don't find out exactly how much he recorded in the bank ledger."

She had a point. If the ledger said two thousand two hundred dollars, then Lewis was little more than an inaccurate braggart. If the account books showed only two thousand, then there was a matter of two hundred missing dollars. Simply asking Lewis would tip their hand. Secrecy was their best option at the moment.

He grabbed a pair of stockings from a drawer and slipped them on, then pulled his boots on as well. "Your father looked worn out by the time you left dinner tonight."

"He was quite tired," she said. "But he fell asleep easily and is resting well."

"Sleeping the sleep of the righteous whose daughter is about to break into a bank." Cade snatched his coat off its hook and buttoned it up all the way.

"What Papa doesn't know . . ." She let the sentence dangle unfinished.

He grabbed the lantern then motioned her through the door. They slipped through the dark behind the jail and mercantile, all the way to the bank. Cade set the lantern on the ground by the back door. It'd be locked. Cade knew the habits of every business in Savage Wells. "If we shoot open the lock, the damage'll be obvious come morning."

"Not necessary," Paisley said. She reached into her pocket and pulled out what looked like a small shaving kit. "Hold the lantern up here so I can see."

She opened her kit and pulled out several long, narrow bits of metal. With an ease that spoke of experience, Paisley slid the implements into the lock.

"I'd forgotten you're a picklock."

"I don't remember telling you that I was." She kept at her efforts.

"You didn't. Gideon spilled your secret."

She closed her eyes as she worked. "My brother and I taught ourselves how when we were children."

He could easily picture her as a troublemaker sort of child. "If you end up becoming a deputy marshal, that'll be a useful skill."

The more he thought about her accepting that job, the more uncertain he was. She'd be good at it, and heaven knew she'd be happier working as a deputy than as a maid or waitress. But the job meant she would be in danger. While she could handle it better than almost anyone he knew, he still worried.

Her mouth twisted in concentration as she worked at the lock with all the elegance of an artist. She turned her pick the tiniest bit.

"There we are." With a satisfied nod, she turned the knob and pushed open the door.

She was a wonder. "Just when I thought I couldn't like you more."

"Oh, yes. Nothing secures a man's good opinion like a woman who can pick a lock."

He heard the dryness in her tone and knew the self-doubt for what it was.

"I don't say things I don't mean, darlin'. I like that you can pick a lock and wear a gun and shoot as well as I do."

"*Better* than you do," she corrected with a laugh.

"And I even like that you've dragged me into bein' a blasted criminal, breaking into a bank in the dead of night."

"I love a good break-in." She wiggled her eyebrows teasingly. At times the temptation to kiss her was almost too much. But he couldn't yet say if she would welcome the attention, so he held off. He ought to win medals for his self-control.

She stepped past him into the dark bank. Cade followed, holding the lantern aloft. Mr. Lewis's office door wasn't locked.

"If he follows the same methods as Papa, the current account book will be in the top drawer of his desk."

Cade set the lantern on the desk and sat in Mr. Lewis's deep-green leather chair. He pulled open the top drawer. Just as Paisley had predicted, a thick, hardbound book sat alone. He took it out and set it on the desktop.

"I've never read one of these." He thumbed the pages.

She sat on the arm of his chair and pulled the book closer to her. "I have. I ran the bank during the last few months my father was still in charge."

She'd taken over for the last sheriff. Ran a bank for a time. Was there anything she couldn't do?

"This is your seat, then," he said.

But she shook her head. "This'll do."

He leaned against the opposite chair arm. Paisley flipped through the account book, her eyes scanning the pages. She grew more beautiful every time he was with her. It didn't seem to matter what she was doing or wearing. He drank in the sight of her.

She paused a moment. Her eyes darted over the page, and she made a "thinking" sound.

"Did you discover something?"

"Mm-hmm. I discovered Lewis shouldn't do mathematics in ink."

He laughed silently. "I'd wager you do all your ciphering in ink."

She met his gaze with an adorable smirk. "Of course."

He added that to his list. He liked that she was smart and wasn't ashamed to be.

"Here's the entry for the delivery." Paisley tapped a page in the account book. She leaned over the book. So did he.

"Two thousand dollars," she read aloud. "So the question remains, did Mr. Lewis keep the missing two hundred dollars and only record two thousand, or did he only receive two thousand?"

"And," Cade jumped in, "if he only received two thousand, where is the rest of it?"

She closed the book. "If the box is locked in Omaha and unlocked here, then the money likely disappeared sometime after arriving at the bank. Unless the deliveryman has had keys made."

"It's possible, but not something we're likely to have a chance to look into." Cade tapped his fingers on the desk as he thought through the situation. "We'd do better to find out if the money's going missing after it gets here. Of course, that'd mean our culprit'd have to be Lewis or Delancey."

He watched for any reaction to the possibility of her former fiancé being a thief. Other than a look of pondering, he saw none.

She carefully slipped the account book back in its drawer. "So, what's our battle plan?"

"First, we cover our tracks here."

Paisley pretended to be surprised by the suggestion.

"Second, we go back to the jailhouse and put a pot of coffee on."

"Step three?" Paisley asked.

Cade shrugged. "We'll sort that out during step two."

They left no trace in the bank. Under a cloud of darkness, they returned to the jailhouse. Paisley offered to start the fire in the corner stove while Cade filled the coffeepot.

"Joshua had a conniption when I built the fire a few days ago," Paisley said when Cade returned. "We had a girl-of-all-work in Abilene. Joshua can't seem to wrap his mind around my new circumstances."

"Have I called him an imbecile often enough since his arrival?" He set the pot on the stovetop.

She laughed. "I do realize what a bad match we were. You don't have to convince me of it."

"Happy to hear it." And he was. "I hope you aren't too disappointed."

"Any hopes I had for Joshua died years ago. Besides, I'm a different person than I was in Abilene." She stood up, having started a fine fire. "Those were hard years. But, then, things aren't exactly easy now."

"Life ain't easy, is it?"

"Things have been over between Joshua and me for years," she said, "but I still hope he isn't our thief."

He could understand that. "We won't know anything until we talk to the two of them. But we'd best not tip our hand."

She nodded slowly. "I'll see if I can glean anything from Joshua."

He slipped his arm around her. She didn't object. So he slid his other one around as well and linked his hands together behind her back. "I'll work on Lewis. I have ways of getting secrets out of people."

"Somehow I don't, though." The mischief in her eyes was more alluring than the most flirtatious look most women could produce. "You told me once your name isn't actually 'Cade.'"

"So I did." He pulled her ever closer. "And it isn't. 'Cade' comes from my middle name, Caden."

"And—?" She very heavily hinted.

"And, I've not told a soul my true given name in fifteen years, so you'll have to bide your time a bit longer, love."

She hooked her finger around one of the buttons of his vest. "I do like when you call me 'love,' though I suspect it's more of a general endearment than one specific to me."

Liked it, did she?

"I heard it a lot in our Irish neighborhood in Boston, so I'd say I picked up the habit there." He saw disappointment enter her expression. "But, then again, I don't use it for anyone but you, so it can't be too general."

The smile that graced her lips was the softest he'd seen from her. "It's a nice change of pace. Thackery started calling me 'Miss Bell' when he switched from competitor to would-be suitor, but being 'Miss' all the time is tiresome. Joshua calls me 'Paisley' but in a tone somewhere between begging and frustrated. And Papa—" Her face fell. "He has started calling me by his sister's name."

Cade pressed a kiss to her forehead, lingering over it. "I'm sorry about your pa. I truly am."

She sighed and stepped away. His arms hovered for the tiniest moment where she'd been. How quickly he'd grown used to her being near him. Every time she pulled away, he felt as though a bit of him had severed itself.

She sat at the desk. "You said it yourself. Life ain't easy."

They drank their coffee in silence. It was a somber way to end their adventure that night. His heart ached for her. She'd lost so much in her life. He knew the weight of loss far too well. He wished he could ease that burden for her.

She stood and stretched. "These late night break-ins are going to catch up with me if we do this too often."

"Don't blame me," Cade said. "You're the one who knocked on m' door at an unearthly hour."

She smiled at him. "Are you complaining?"

"Not in the least." He slipped his fingers around hers. "I'll break into a bank with you any time."

"And then listen to me grumble about my problems?" she added.

He pressed a brief kiss to her cheek, but kept himself to nothing more than that. "Any time, love. Any time."

He meant that promise to include so much more than listening to her worries, but also to hold her when she needed an embrace, to be with her in her loneliest moments, and to someday kiss her again, but truly and deeply. Though it might take time, he fully believed he could eventually earn enough of her regard to make that possibility a welcome one for both of them.

Chapter 33

Cade didn't care a whit for Lewis, but he had to admit the man ran his bank well. He watched every detail, managed every minute and person. It was little wonder people thought him tedious; he *was* tedious. The two of them spent the better part of a half hour discussing the coming delivery.

"Who will you have acting as guards?" Lewis asked.

"Same as last time," Cade said. "Will Delancey be about again?"

Lewis nodded.

"You trust him?" Cade asked, keeping the question almost offhand.

"He has given me no reason not to trust him."

Careful wording. Hesitant tone. "Not a heap of praise, that."

Lewis hemmed a moment. "Mr. Delancey's experience as a clerk and his keen mind for numbers is an asset to any bank. He came highly recommended by the bank officials in Omaha. He is being groomed to become a manager himself someday."

It wasn't evidence one way or the other. "Is there anything you're wanting to see changed in the deliveries? Maybe have the money brought directly to your office rather than the teller's counter?"

"The teller's counter works best." Lewis didn't look at all suspicious at the questioning. Neither did he seem eager to have the money come straight to him behind closed doors. Either he was playing his part well, or he didn't have plans to nip away a few hundred dollars by tucking it away in the comfort of his office. Perhaps his plan was more complicated than that.

"All's been well with the other banks who've sent men to pick up their share of these deliveries?" Those amounts were smaller, so Cade hadn't been asked to oversee them; that'd have to change if the amounts increased.

"Perfectly fine," Lewis said. "Their days are staggered, so it isn't terribly complicated."

And not seen by anyone other than those already in the bank. Now that was a potentially suspicious arrangement. "Who generally hands over the money?"

"Mr. Delancey counts it and has the funds bundled and ready," Lewis said. "When the bank representatives arrive, I am there to see to it they sign for their money so there is a record."

So Delancey did the money counting. It didn't explain how the money disappeared from the original deliveries, but it did put him fully in the thick of dispensing it. And what was to stop Delancey from handing the pilfered money over to someone coming in under the guise of a customer? There were so many different ways the thieving might've been accomplished.

"How much, *exactly*, will be delivered this next time?" Cade asked.

"Three thousand," Lewis read off a paper on his desk. "Of course, they said two thousand two hundred last time and ended up lowering the amount."

Now he was getting somewhere. "They told you they lowered it?"

"Well, no. But that was all we received. I sent a telegram regarding the change but haven't heard back."

That was interesting. "Did you, now?"

"Actually, Mr. Delancey sent it. He runs errands for the bank quite regularly. One of the advantages of having a teller."

That was more incriminating than anything Cade had heard yet. The bank in Omaha would've said something in two weeks' time about two hundred missing dollars. But only if they'd been told. If Omaha hadn't heard and Delancey had been the one charged with sending word . . .

Still, it wasn't anything close to proof. He'd have to very nearly catch Delancey in the act. But how to manage that without tipping his hand and giving Delancey unwanted warning?

"I mean to go forward with the delivery as planned," Cade said. "I've more than enough guards, even with the extra money."

"If you think so." It was somewhere between agreement and skepticism.

Cade had never cared what Lewis thought of him; he still didn't. "Let me know if anything changes," he said.

"I will."

Cade passed through to the bank lobby. The counter was unmanned. A Will Return Soon placard sat on the counter where Delancey would've been. It was about lunchtime.

"Is Delancey at lunch, do you think?" Cade called back toward Lewis's office.

"He asked for the afternoon off. He hasn't asked for time off in two weeks, so I granted it."

Delancey was either very conscientious, or he needed extra time at the bank. Cade thought that over as he strode down the road. They were focusing on securing the deliveries, but he needed to keep the money safe *after* its arrival as well.

He stepped inside the jailhouse to find Hawk sitting at his desk.

"I ain't got any prisoners for you," Cade said. "But if you're handy with a broom, the cells could use a good sweep."

"Not my kind of cleanup job, Cade." Hawk grinned as he leaned back in his chair. "I've come on a matter of a few thousand dollars."

"Has there been a robbery?" Nothing had been mentioned in the recent telegrams.

"I meant the bank deliveries here," Hawk said. "Word's spreading throughout the territory about little Savage Wells being the new gold rush."

"I've been worrying about that." Cade checked the low-burning fire in the potbellied stove. The jail was growing colder as winter drew near. "Our idiot of a banker agreed to the deliveries before giving the town a chance to prepare."

"Then I hope that idiot's kissing the ground you walk on, Cade. I'd wager you're the only reason he isn't already in deep water."

Cade pulled up the stool. "We'll be up to a full three thousand dollars with the next delivery."

Hawk whistled appreciatively. "Even your reputation's not gonna be enough in the long term with that kind of money coming in. How long before the town has enough funds to hire you a deputy?"

Cade had asked that very question every council meeting. "The money only passes through here, very little of it actually stays. Unless the town grows quick and the increase brings the council more money, it's just me standing between Savage Wells and bloody anarchy."

"And *that* is what *I* was afraid of," Hawk said. "For the next few weeks, months maybe, I'm moving my headquarters here to Savage Wells."

Cade folded his arms over his chest. "Are you taking over m' job, Hawk?"

"Not at all. You'll still be sheriff. You'll still run things." He crossed his booted feet on the desktop. "I'll just be another eye on the town, another reason for thieves not to try their luck here. The fate of this town affects the western half of this territory and up into Montana. I'm not risking it."

Cade nodded firmly. "I gave Paisley your letter. Do you really mean to recommend her as a deputy marshal?"

"I have already. From all I could learn of her, she'd do a fine job. Though she'd not have all the opportunities a man would, it'd be something."

It was exactly what she'd been asking for. A chance to prove herself.

"Has she given an answer yet?" Cade asked.

"Not yet. But I'll be here until your council quits dragging their feet. She can give me an answer when she's ready."

If Cade didn't have complete confidence in Hawk, he'd have wondered at the man's motives. But arrows didn't come straighter than John Hawking.

"Speak of the devil," Hawk muttered, getting to his feet and nodding toward the doorway.

Paisley was stepping inside. "Hey, there, Cade. Howdy, Marshal. What brings you around?"

Hawk offered her his seat, but she didn't take it, preferring instead to lean against the cell bars.

"He's come to lend a menacing air to Savage Wells," Cade said.

Paisley nodded her approval. "We need it." She turned to Cade. "Did you tell him about our troubles with the bank?"

Cade caught Hawk up in a few minutes, then shared with them both what he'd learned at the bank, which was, admittedly, nothing rock solid.

"That's not much to go by," Paisley said. "And I haven't seen Joshua yet, so I don't have anything to add."

Cade leaned his shoulder against the wall beside the desk. "Our culprit's keeping things quiet, that's for certain."

"Culprit?" Hawk shook his head. "I'd reckon what you have are culprits."

"I hadn't thought about this being a group undertaking." Paisley paced away absentmindedly. "What if they are both part of this? They'd be able to cover their tracks very well."

"We need to sniff 'em out, but carefully," Cade said. "Are you two up for a bit of strategizing?"

Paisley's eyes danced with mischief. "Always."

Cade couldn't say if Hawk was nodding his approval of Paisley's answer or his agreement to Cade's challenge. Either way, Cade kept himself close to Paisley's side. Delancey hadn't proven much competition, Thackery only slightly more. Hawk very well might.

"Unless our thief is passing his bounty off to someone, he has to be stashing it somewhere. If we could find it, or find evidence it'd been nearby, that'd point us toward the guilty one."

"Search their homes, you mean?" Paisley didn't look entirely supportive. "Asking for permission might warn them off, but sneaking in would likely mean whatever we found wouldn't be accepted by a judge."

She was right, of course. "That's where my friend Hawk comes into the picture."

"You want me to request a warrant from the judge in Laramie?"

Cade gave a quick nod. "But you'd need to send the telegram yourself. I don't want anyone but the three of us to know what we suspect."

"I can send it today and likely have a response no later than tomorrow—perhaps even tonight if we catch Judge Barclay before he leaves the courthouse."

Cade had long ago learned that Hawk knew how to get things done quickly and correctly. "Even with the warrants, we'd do well to time our searches so they aren't noticed by either man—or by *anyone*, if at all possible. Lewis's house'll be more difficult, but Delancey's rooms at the hotel are more accessible." Cade kept to the topic at hand. Letting the two of them see his jealousy would do him no good. "But we can't let Delancey catch us at it. We'd best keep it quiet and small."

"Once we have the warrant, I'll chat with Delancey at the bank as a distraction," Hawk said. "As a marshal new to town, he'll figure I'm just being nosy."

Paisley stopped her pacing right beside Cade's stool. He preferred that to her taking up a position next to Hawk. "Do we intend to ask for keys at the hotel desk or should I keep my lock-picking tools handy?"

Cooper ran the hotel. While Cade didn't peg the man as a scoundrel, he wasn't precisely a saint. "I vote we climb in a window."

"That's what I hoped you'd say." Paisley raised a triumphant fist. "Just give me a shout when all the t's are crossed and i's are dotted. I'd enjoy another breaking and entering."

Hawk laughed. "*Another* breaking and entering?"

"What you don't know can't hurt us," Cade answered. "Hawk, go send that telegram. I want to get on with this as soon as possible."

* * *

Apparently, Hawk's telegram caught Judge Barclay at the perfect time. Not an hour after Hawk sent his request, the judge sent back the word that the warrant had been issued.

Hawk pulled on his heavy overcoat. "When we're done with this bit of detective work, Miss Bell, I'd like to talk to you about that job offer."

She nodded her agreement. Hawk headed toward the bank. Paisley and Cade crossed the road to the side of the restaurant.

"How long do you need?" Cade asked her.

"A minute or two." She slipped in the back door of the restaurant.

Cade took his time walking around to the front. He spotted Hawk through the front windows of the bank. With slow steps, Cade made his way into the restaurant and back to the hotel's check-in counter.

"Sheriff O'Brien," Cooper greeted. That fake English accent of his never failed to fall short of the mark. "What can I do for you?"

"I'm checkin' on things. Any difficulties of late? Troublesome tenants? Customers?"

"None," Mr. Cooper answered. "Not that we have many."

"How many are there?" That'd be a helpful thing to know even without the problems at the bank.

"Mr. Brown was in room one, but he checked out yesterday. There's a Mr. Darrow in room two. He arrived a few days ago, thinking of moving here."

Cade would need to keep an eye out for those two.

"Mr. Thackery moved out when he took the ranch job, and Mr. Rice left after the council didn't pick him for sheriff." Cooper looked over the hotel roster. "Rooms three and four are empty at the moment. Mr. Delancey is in room five, but you know him already."

Cade nodded as if he was only vaguely interested.

"Mr. and Mrs. Jones are in room six. They are in town visiting their son, Mr. Jones, whose wife rather prefers that her in-laws stay here when they visit."

The hotel only had six rooms. That was everyone, then. He wasn't concerned about the Joneses. He'd check into the recently departed Mr. Brown and the newly arrived Mr. Darrow later.

"Do you mind if I take a look around upstairs?" he asked casually. "I haven't checked things here in a while."

"Go right ahead."

That was easier than expected. "I'll show myself out when I'm done."

Cooper nodded his agreement.

Much easier than expected.

The stairwell was empty. The corridors were empty. The doors were closed and locked. All except for room five. Paisley stood in the open doorway.

"Nice work."

She straightened imaginary cuffs. "I *am* good with a lock. Perhaps that's why the US Marshals are so desperate for me to join them."

"Or maybe it's because you've got experience, good aim, and a cool head."

She shrugged. "There is that. I'm also far better looking than any of the other marshals."

"I don't know about *far* better looking."

She threw him a look of shocked amusement. "You're just itchin' to be shot, aren't you?"

Saints, he loved when she bantered with him. "We can settle this with a shoot-out later. At the moment, I have some drawers to dig through."

"Have fun," she said.

He threw caution to the wind. "How 'bout a kiss for good luck?"

Her eyebrows shot up in surprise. She watched him for the length of a breath, not saying a word. "Do you always start investigations this way?"

"I'm starting a new tradition." He leaned in close. "What do you say? Kiss for luck?"

"You're on duty, Cade. You don't need any distractions." She stepped into the doorway. "Now, get to work. I'll keep an eye out."

He looked around the room. If he were a low-life bank robber, where would he hide his ill-gotten goods? Cade checked under the bed, under the clothes in the bureau, the dim corners of the armoire. Nothing.

Delancey might be hiding the money at the bank. They'd have to check there as well. Cade opened the small drawers in the writing desk and carefully flipped through the small stack of papers. Most were scraps with notes jotted on them, nothing of importance, but halfway down the stack he found something intriguing. A bit of arithmetic, splitting two hundred three ways, then adjusting the answer a few times.

Cade returned to the room's door and inched it open. "Paisley," he whispered loudly.

She looked back at him. "Did you find something?"

"Possibly. Come in for a second."

She did, and he closed the door. Cade kept his distance. Every time he got close to her he nearly lost his head. He handed over the note, careful to keep its place in the stack.

"This could be nothing," Paisley warned. "Or it could mean he's working with two other people."

"It ain't proof," Cade acknowledged. "But it's something to go on." He slipped the paper back into the stack and returned it to the desk drawer. "Let's see if Hawk found out anything."

She stepped out with him, locking the door behind them. "It's good having the marshal around while we're sorting this out. He'll be an asset."

They took the back steps down to the street. "You seem fond of Hawk."

"He's a fellow lawman who treats me like an equal," she said.

"So do I," Cade pointed out.

"Which is why I like you."

He followed in her wake. "The only reason?"

"I didn't say that."

He liked that answer. He liked it a lot.

Chapter 34

"Well, Miss Bell, you can out-cook Mr. Cooper, that's for certain." Hawk had accepted an invitation to supper. Paisley had been looking for a chance to ask him about the deputy marshal job.

"Being a better cook than Cooper isn't much of an accomplishment." The restaurant's offerings weren't *bad*, they simply weren't all that good.

"Cooper'll have to do better before someone jumps in and gives him some real competition."

"Do you really mean to operate as marshal out of this tiny backwater?" Their town had always been something of a joke in Wyoming Territory. It was too quiet and small to be anything but quaint.

"Savage Wells is set for a boom. If it'll keep this town peaceful, even with all the money coming in, it'll be worth a bit of inconvenience."

Papa's head drooped drowsily. Paisley tucked a blanket around his legs then stoked the embers in the fireplace. She lowered her voice so as not to disturb him. "It's possible, then, to operate as a marshal, or a deputy marshal, from a town like this?"

"You're considering the job, then?" He sounded hopeful. Outside of Cade and Gideon, no man had seen her interest in sheriffing and law keeping as anything other than entirely odd. Thackery didn't seem to mind, now that she thought on it. Maybe there would be others who accepted her as well.

"What're your arguments against the job?" Hawk asked. "Maybe I can set your mind at ease on a few points."

"For one thing, my father is ill," she said. "I couldn't move him to a big town where he'd be even more lost than he is here. And we've lived in violent towns. I don't want to go back to that."

"Understandably."

Paisley returned to her own chair. "And I'm not entirely convinced your offer is a serious one. Your first job suggestion was a bounty hunter, and that was a joke."

"At first, maybe," he said. "But I looked into it a little more. You have an impressive list of accomplishments."

"How would you know that? Sheriff Garrison never gave me credit for anything."

He smiled at her, something that likely turned quite a few feminine heads and hearts. "Cade and I are smarter than the average, unfocused small-town sheriff. It didn't take much digging to figure out which things Garrison did himself and which were the work of his unofficial deputy."

Cade had been part of the digging? Who'd have guessed the man who'd arrived in Savage Wells as her enemy would have become her advocate?

"I'm convinced a female deputy marshal is an ingenious idea," Hawk said. "Even if it was my own."

"Is my being a woman significant?" She wasn't looking to be a token deputy or a figure of fun.

"The West can be a terrifying place for women and children," he said.

"Believe me, I know."

"Too often the people we're trying to help are afraid of us," he said. "We need someone who can handle the danger of the position but offer a softer touch when it's needed. I'm convinced there'd be a great many times when a woman would warrant greater trust than a man ever could."

"I'm not looking to be a nanny with a badge." If that was the offer he meant to make, he was wasting his breath.

He waved that off. "You'd be a fully-fledged deputy marshal, with all the same rights and same type of duties. But we'd utilize you in those special cases when having a law*woman* instead of a law*man* would set some minds at ease."

She wasn't sure she liked that. "I'd rather be a regular marshal than a special one."

"I think in time you could be," he said. "But people'll need time to get used to the idea of a woman marshal."

She knew that all too well. "My being a woman stopped this town from taking my bid for sheriff seriously. Even if I'd won out, I think a lot of people would never have respected the badge so long as I was wearing it."

"You'll encounter plenty of that if you take this job," he said. "It's one of the reasons I've offered it to you. The doubt and curiosity wouldn't come as a surprise, and I'd wager you'd know how to deal with it."

He made a good point. "Are you trying to talk me into taking this job?"

"I'm doing my all-fire best." He leaned forward with his elbows on his legs. "The folks back in Washington'd likely think I'm cracked, but I know this territory better than they do. Women and children get the short shrift too often. There are too many orphans left alone, too many desperate women with no options other than bawdy houses. I for one am tired of it happening in this territory."

"You make a good argument. But if this town ever gets around to paying for a deputy, that would be a very tempting job too. And I wouldn't have to leave home. I would be here among people I know."

"Which could be a downside, as well," Hawk said. "What's that saying about a prophet in his own country?"

Another good point.

"You could make a bigger difference with the marshals," Hawk said. "And I could pay you more than this town will likely ever agree to pay a deputy. They'd require you to prove yourself worthy of *that* job, just as they did with the job of sheriff. I already know you're more than worthy. And there's no waiting. The job is available now."

He was making deputy marshaling sound more and more appealing. "Keep this up, and I just might say yes." A knock sounded at the door. "Maybe that's Cade come to convince me not to listen to you." She walked toward the front entryway.

From behind her, Hawk said, "You and Cade seem to get along well."

"We do, though we rather hated each other at first." She didn't hate him now. Not at all. She pulled the door open, excited at the thought of seeing Cade again. She'd not seen him all day.

But it wasn't Cade. Joshua stood on the front step.

"What brings you here?" she asked him.

He flashed a smile. "I was passing by and thought I'd say hello."

Passing by? There wasn't much on the south side of town. Almost no one simply passed by.

Hawk came and stood in the entryway.

"Delancey," Hawk greeted curtly. Knowing Joshua was one of their bank thief suspects had soured whatever opinion they originally had of him.

"Have you come to ask Paisley a lot of probing questions about her relationship with the bank?" Joshua was on the defensive. Just what had Hawk said during his visit to the bank?

"He's a federal marshal, Joshua. It's his job to ask a lot of questions."

Joshua's eyes darted from Paisley to Hawk and back again. "Did I interrupt something?"

"Marshal Hawking was attempting to convince me of the merits of the federal marshals."

Joshua's gaze narrowed. "Any federal marshal in particular?"

Hawk laughed. After a moment, Paisley couldn't help laughing herself. Joshua was jealous. He, who hadn't put in the effort to track her down all those years ago when the very bank he was working for knew where she was—when the entire town of Abilene knew—now stood on her porch, jealous. Ridiculous.

"Sheriff O'Brien seems intent on courting you," Joshua said. "Thackery's doing his best. Now the marshal. You and I have found each other again, yet I am the only one making an effort to reconcile."

"Maybe you're the only one who feels like a reconciliation ought to happen." She hated discussing something so personal with Hawk right there, but Joshua was leaving her little choice.

"I'm not ready to give up on us, Paisley."

"I wish you would," she muttered.

Hawk pulled his hat off the peg near the door and popped it on his head. "Give some thought to my offer. You'd make a fine deputy marshal."

"I will," she said. "I need to get Papa to bed so he can sleep. The two of you can head back to town together."

"Of course, Miss Bell." Hawk gave her a respectful bow.

Joshua eyed her more closely still. "But I only just arrived."

"Go back to town, Joshua. There's no reason for you to stay." It was perhaps cruel, but being subtle and gentle hadn't worked at all.

With an air of resignation, he took a step back on the porch. Hawk made his way out as well.

The praise he'd offered stayed with her throughout the night, even keeping her awake long after she'd retired. *"You'd make a fine deputy marshal."* And she realized in those quiet moments, lying in her bed, that Marshal Hawking was right. And if he was right and she was this excited at the idea of the assignment, then maybe she'd finally found what she was meant to be doing all along.

Chapter 35

Paisley soaped the inside of Gideon's parlor windows. If anything was likely to firm up her shaky inclination to accept the job with the marshals, it would be the chance to give up window washing.

They'd hoped to keep their investigation entirely between the three of them, but Gideon was a resource they couldn't overlook. He knew everyone.

"Mr. Darrow is a tailor," Gideon said to her and Hawk. "He's living at the hotel but is actively looking for a place to set up shop. He came with supplies for his business. I don't think he's in on the bank robberies."

They'd been hypothesizing on possible suspects all afternoon.

"I've met Darrow," Hawk said. "I don't think he's part of this."

"There was a Mr. Brown living there until recently," Gideon added. "Maybe he syphoned off the two hundred dollars and fled town."

Paisley dipped her rag in her water bucket. "He couldn't have managed that without having access to the bank books. Someone who works at the bank has to be involved."

"But are we looking at a long-term resident or a newcomer?" Gideon asked.

Paisley wiped down the windows as Hawk questioned Gideon about the various people at the nearby farms and ranches. Savage Wells had gone from a sleepy little town to a place mired in mystery. And Joshua was right in the middle of it.

Was he truly guilty? If he was, had he always been a scoundrel and she'd misjudged him or had the past few years changed him?

Through the now-clean windows she spotted Cade coming up the front steps. She left her bucket and rag behind and slipped out of the parlor to the door. She'd missed him, no matter that only forty-eight hours had passed since she'd last seen him. She was half-gone on the man, though she wasn't entirely certain of his feelings. She suspected he liked her, hoped he *more than* liked her. She pulled the door open just as he reached for the handle.

"Hey, there, stranger." She tossed out the greeting as if she wasn't actually quite happy to see him.

"If you'd come by the jail now and then, you neglectful woman, I'd not be such a stranger." His grumpy style of teasing was welcome.

"You know where I live. You might have visited *me*."

He slipped a finger under her chin and tipped her head up toward his. "You had a gentleman caller over last night, love. I know better than to visit under those circumstances."

"'Gentleman caller?'" She grinned. "Hawk would be as surprised as anyone to hear that description."

"Not as surprised as you might think." Cade's hand dropped away, and his eyes darted toward the voices in the parlor. "He and Gideon in there?"

"They are. Andrew and Papa are playing checkers at the dining table."

Cade nodded and stepped into the parlor. He stopped in the doorway and looked back at her. "You're comin', ain't you? We've a criminal to catch, and I'm not about to attempt it without your help."

Oh, yes. She definitely hoped he *more than* liked her. She wanted his thoughts on the deputy marshal position. She was eager to hear his theories on the bank robberies. More than anything, though, she wanted to spend time with him again.

She walked with him back into the parlor. When she made to return to the windows, he stopped her. "The windows can wait, love." He pulled her by the hand to the desk where Hawk and Gideon sat.

"You look like a man who's made a discovery," Hawk said, eyeing Cade.

"Lewis told me a few days back that when the delivery amount didn't match what he'd been told to expect, that he had Delancey send a telegram to the bank offices in Omaha." Cade eyed them all as he spoke. "So this morning I sent a telegram to the bank offices in Omaha myself, and I just received a reply."

Paisley held her breath. She could sense the importance of what he was about to say.

"No telegram was ever sent."

Hawk nodded slowly. "Sure points a finger, don't it?"

They began debating who the other conspirators might be, whether or not he actually had any, how to catch them. Paisley tried to focus even as the last delusions she'd once harbored about Joshua died. Had her judgment been lacking from the beginning of their relationship? Had all of it been lies?

Maybe he'd been skimming funds from the bank in Abilene and had been using their romance as a distraction. Maybe that was the only reason he'd tried to reconcile with her once he realized she was living in the next town he meant to victimize.

Pull yourself together, Paisley. You have a job to do. What good would she be as a marshal if she let her personal frustrations distract her so easily?

"We know Delancey was south of town last night," Hawk was saying. "Do we know if he's spent much time north?"

"Andrew would know," Paisley jumped in. "He hasn't been up in his tree as consistently since the snow came, but he still keeps a very close eye on things."

Cade turned in his chair in the direction of the entryway that separated the parlor and dining room. "Andrew, we've got a question for you."

"What is it?" Andrew called back.

"Have you seen Joshua Delancey head north of town much since he's been in Savage Wells?"

"Sure. He's out there all the time. At the old Parker place."

Paisley held up her hands in a show of self-assured triumph. "Easy as that, gentlemen. You just have to know who to ask."

"She's brilliant," Hawk said, approval shining in his face. "I'll have you signed on as a marshal, Paisley, if I have to pay you in gold bars."

"Now that *is* tempting." She stood. "I'll leave you men to come up with something equally brilliant to capture the villains while I finish up my work here. Until those gold bars start arriving, I have some windows to wash."

She kept her ears perked, listening to the men. They weren't half bad strategists, though nothing ingenious was suggested. In the end, they decided their best approach was to make the criminals antsy enough to make a mistake. Abbott and Clark lived not far from the old Parker place. The two chicken farmers could be counted on to help. A rumor or two that the sheriff was making extra trips out that direction ought to get the thieves fretting a bit. And rumors were easy to start in Savage Wells.

The conversation wrapped up, and Hawk headed back to the jailhouse.

Cade peeked into the dining room. "We're all done here," he told Andrew and Papa. "Are you two coming or staying?"

Andrew looked up. "We're stayin'. Doc said we could."

"Thank you, Andrew." Paisley hoped he knew that she was grateful for more than just that day's checker games.

"Where're you headed?" Cade asked her as they stepped out onto Gideon's front porch.

"This was my last job today. So I'd say I'm headed to the poorhouse." She looped her scarf more fully around her neck as the bitter winter air crept down her back. The wind bit at her face as they stepped away from the porch. "I hope Hawk kept a fire going in the stove at the jailhouse. I could use a bit of warmth."

"Could you now?" Cade shot her something of a wicked grin.

He teased her often enough, but she never worried about him being anything less than honorable. She liked that about him. She also liked that he wasn't so straightlaced that he was boring.

"Have you made a decision about the deputy marshal job?" he asked.

She started to shake her head but changed it to a nod only to shift that into a shrug. "I don't know. I need the money, and I'd enjoy the work. To know I was helping so many people—I want that. I want that badly. But I can't leave Papa alone for days or weeks at a time. And I know it'll be dangerous, so I need to make certain the risk is one I really want to take."

"All good arguments," he acknowledged. "Having spent a lot of time choosing that risk, I can tell you it ain't something to take lightly."

"But I'd be helping people," she countered. "I keep returning to that. I'd be helping not just the victims of crime in the territory, but also other women who'd like a fair shake at jobs they aren't usually allowed to hold. And, truth be told, I've been dying a little inside having to be a cleaning lady when I know I would have been so blasted good at being a sheriff."

"And, though I hate to admit it, you'd be 'blasted good' at being a deputy marshal."

They stepped up onto the porch of the jailhouse. "Why do you hate admitting it?" He'd never been like so many others who weren't willing to give her credit.

"For all the reasons you listed: the danger, the toll it'd take on you and your pa. And"—his expression turned mulish—"you'd be gone all the time."

She hid her smile. "You'd miss me?"

"Not at all." He let her step inside the jail ahead of him. "It'd be boring being the only sharpshooter in town is all."

"Hawk'll be here." She motioned to the marshal, who was adding coal to the stove in the corner.

Cade slipped an arm around her waist from behind and whispered in her ear. "But Hawk ain't nearly as much fun to kiss, darlin'."

"You said it was my *shooting* you were going to miss," she whispered back.

"That, too." He brushed a kiss to her neck just below her ear before stepping around her and over to the desk.

Paisley was certain she'd stopped breathing entirely. She stood rooted to the spot, her neck tingling, her face turning hot with a blush. Heavens, she hoped he wasn't teasing when he said and did things like that. And she desperately hoped he'd do it again.

Chapter 36

Delancey always had a long lunch on Thursdays, and he spent that time at the mercantile. Cade knew more about the man's schedule than he ever thought he would. The information was critical, however.

Paisley was positioned down at the hotel. Hawk was at the bank. Cade was in the mercantile watching Abbott and Clark set their trap. They had specific instructions and were following them to the letter.

Delancey was filling a small paper sack with penny nails. Why did a man who lived in a hotel need nails?

"It's on account of you snatching up all of Annabelle's best eggs," Abbott told Clark in a voice just loud enough to be overheard by the others. "Sheriff probably thinks our feud is heating up again."

"I haven't been snatching eggs," Clark shot back. "The sheriff's probably sniffing around your place since you're the one who always starts the trouble."

Abbott shook his head firmly. "He rode past my place right up the road toward yours. And the marshal was with him. I'm telling you, Clark, all your underhandedness is catching up with you."

Cade took his cue and sauntered past Abbott and Clark. They stopped him.

"Which of us have you been keeping an eye on?" Clark asked. "It's Abbott, isn't it?"

"Not me," Abbott insisted. "Am I right, Sheriff?"

Cade hooked his thumbs over his gun belt. "Let's just say the marshal and I are keeping an eye on things *generally* up on the north end of town."

Clark's eyes opened wide. The man played his part well. "Is something going on north of town?" he whispered loudly.

"I ain't sayin' a word," Cade answered firmly.

He made his way to the counter. He could feel Delancey's eyes on him. *Perfect.*

"What can I get for you, Sheriff?" Mr. Holmes asked.

Cade slipped his O'Brien six-shooter from his holster and spun it around in his hand. He gave the move all the expert flourish he could. It'd do Delancey good to see how at ease he was with his weapon. He held the pistol up within view.

"I'm needing more cartridges," he said. "Especially seeing as they fit m' rifle as well."

Mr. Holmes wasn't in on the game, but he played right into their hand. "Are you expecting to need them in the near future?"

Cade gave a vague shrug. "Just being prepared."

Mr. Holmes snatched the ammunition from a high shelf and returned to the counter. "Is this on account of the bank deliveries? There's been some concern among the citizens that we'd begin seeing criminals trickle into town."

Well done, Holmes. Abbott and Clark, along with a few others in the mercantile, including Delancey, had stepped closer, waiting for Cade's answer.

"Rest easy, men," he said. "Marshal Hawking has set up headquarters here in Savage Wells, and he and I have our ears to the ground. We're already seeing to the things we're hearing."

"Then there *is* something going on?" Clark asked.

Cade had been very vague about the reason for their playacting. He hadn't meant to cause the man any worry.

He assumed his most confident stance. "I've earned myself a reputation. Criminals don't last long in my town. And the marshal has more notches on his gun belt than the James brothers combined. Anyone trying anything in this town'll be sorry he was ever born."

That seemed a good note to end on. He paid Mr. Holmes for the ammunition and strode from the mercantile, letting the clank of his boot heels emphasize his words. He stepped onto the porch and spotted Paisley up in the first-floor window of the hotel, gazing out onto the street. Their eyes met. He gave her a nod. She returned it.

She set to washing the window, though he knew better. She was acting as lookout.

Cade continued on to the jail, careful not to give away the ruse. He could trust Paisley to do her job. Hawk was tucked away near the bank, hoping to overhear a conversation between Delancey and his accomplices.

There was nothing for it but to wait. He stoked the fire in the stove. Wyoming was proving to be as bone-rattlingly cold as he'd been warned. He slung his long leather coat over the back of the desk chair. Mr. Bell was at the Gilberts' house, enjoying his checkers with Andrew. Mrs. Wilhite wasn't selling her ribbons today. The jail was quiet.

In all his weariness with shooting folks, he'd forgotten the thrill of racing the clock. They were a step ahead of Delancey and his men. If they were smart and careful, they just might trip up the criminals. They were so close.

"That's the grin of a man who's terribly pleased with himself." Paisley stood in the doorway, watching him.

"Where did Delancey go?" He could feel his excitement growing.

She chuckled. "You're enjoying this."

"It's like my birthday's come early." It was all he could do to stop himself from crowing. "There ain't nothing like catching someone at their own nefarious game."

"I know the feeling well." She crossed to the potbellied stove. "Heart pounds. Mind spins. Little bits of the puzzle fall into place, and I swear I can already see the end play out. I don't dare declare victory, but in my mind I'm shouting in triumph because staying a step ahead of the evil-doers will save innocent people a lot of heartache, might even save lives."

She understood. Cade had known that kind of camaraderie in other men, but he had never expected to find it in a woman. She was a treasure.

"Where did he go after leaving the mercantile?" he asked again.

She turned toward him but stayed near the warmth of the stove. "Where did *who* go after leaving *what* mercantile?"

He pointed a finger at her. "Don't push me on this, woman. I'm full dyin' to know."

"Quit being such a grump."

"I'm only being a grump because you're being so difficult."

She set her hands on her hips. "You only think I'm being difficult because you're being so impatient."

He stood nearly nose-to-nose with her. He repeated his original question, slowly. "Where did he go?"

The mischievous twinkle in her eye nearly brought his laughter to the surface. Very nearly. The woman was withholding information, after all. "I figure this ought to be worth something."

"You're as bad as Grace O'Malley."

Her teasing smile disappeared, and her eyes narrowed. "Who is Grace O'Malley?"

"She was a pirate," he muttered back, running a hand down her arm.

To which she grinned. "I like her already."

He wove his fingers through hers. He leaned in and brushed a whisper of a kiss along her hairline. "Well, then?"

"Well, then, *what*?" she answered breathlessly.

"What did Delancey do after leaving the mercantile?"

"Hmm."

Cade inched back. His attentions were distracting them both.

Paisley seemed to recollect herself. "He lugged the nails and the boards he bought down the walk and met someone at a waiting wagon. They talked for a while. The mystery man drove off—I never did see his face—and Joshua returned to the bank."

Building supplies and meetings with strangers. "We may be on to something here. Though I wish I was more certain."

"So do I. But we know more than we did a week ago." The doubts and second-guessing that too often plagued her were nowhere to be seen. "Give us a few more days, and we'll have this sorted out. I know it."

He wrapped his arms around her middle. "I think you enjoy the hunt as much as I do."

"I've never admitted it to anyone, but I do." He didn't know if her blush came from their closeness or from her excitement over tracking down criminals. "The day I brought in the Grantland Gang, it was all I could do not to crow in triumph right in front of them."

"You should've," he said.

She shrugged. "I'd already shot the poor dears. It seemed unsporting to laugh at them too."

"How often've you been told how beautiful you are?" he asked, drinking in the sight of her bright eyes.

She fidgeted, not quite meeting his eyes.

"And smart and witty?" he added.

Her chin dipped down even as her ears turned red. He knew she struggled to see herself clearly, but embarrassing her wouldn't help. She'd pull into herself again, protecting herself from the ridicule she feared so much. A bit of laughter would help set her at ease.

"And stubborn and frustrating?" he added.

She raised a single eyebrow. Yes, this approach was working much better.

"As odd as a five-legged dog?"

"*A five-legged dog?*" she repeated in shocked tones.

Her exasperation made him laugh, and his laughter brought out hers.

"It's a good thing we're on the same team, Cade O'Brien."

"A *very* good thing."

He cupped her face in his hands, running the pad of his thumb along her cheek. A slow breath eased out of her, even as her eyelids fluttered closed. If ever a woman looked ready for a kiss, she did.

He slid his arm down her back to wrap around her waist. The warmth of her stole over him. He'd ached to hold her, to kiss her like she deserved to be kissed. He lowered his head, hovering a breath away from her lips, giving her a chance to let him know if she objected. That hesitation proved a moment too long: Hawk strode inside.

"They didn't say anything too—" Hawk froze on the spot, watching the two of them.

Paisley's eyes flew open, deep red staining her cheeks.

"Didn't realize I'd be interrupting," Hawk said. "Do you two want me to step out again? Give you a moment for some sparkin'?"

Paisley pulled free of Cade's embrace and moved swiftly to the desk.

Cade forced a tense breath. He was too on edge to sit, to even think. He made short circuits back and forth beside the desk.

"All right, then," Hawk said, returning to the topic at hand. "Delancey sent his associate off with the supplies and instructions to 'finish securing things.'"

"That's an odd turn of phrase," Cade said.

"Suspicious, depending on how you look at the thing," Hawk said.

"Securing stacks of money," Paisley said. "That's what you figure he meant?"

Slowly, one breath at a time, Cade forced himself to focus on his job again. Having Paisley in his arms, coming so close to kissing her, hovered in the background, keeping him from remaining entirely calm. She twisted him around in ways no one else did.

"Nothing either of them said was very specific," Hawk said. "And none of it was truly incriminating."

Paisley's brow pulled down in thought. "What if we're following the wrong trail here? What if Joshua isn't part of this?"

She'd maintained that she didn't have feelings for Delancey, but her defense of him made Cade wonder. Was she being blinded by sentiment?

"I haven't entirely convicted him in my mind," Hawk said. "But there's too much pointing in that direction to ignore."

She sighed. "I agree. I just feel like we're missing something." She did have a tendency to question herself.

"We have very little to go on because our criminals are playing it so close to the vest," Cade said. "But we're also keeping our eyes and ears open. Our best bet is to figure out when they mean to skim from the delivery. Short of catching them red-handed, they aren't likely to be convicted."

Cade continued thinking on it as he paced.

Paisley spoke first. "The scam depends on pulling out the money before Lewis counts it. The theft would have to occur straight off. But the thief won't want to be wandering around with hot money burning through his pockets."

She kept saying "the thief" and not "Joshua" when talking about the crime. She clearly wanted to believe the best in her one-time fiancé. Catching him in the act would also help Paisley settle her thoughts on that matter.

"We didn't find any money in his room," Cade said. "The trick'll be figuring out where they mean to hide the money this time around."

"We'll have to make that decision for him." Hawk met Cade's eye. A lot of weight hung in that single look. Cade had seen it before, the time they'd smoked out a band of train robbers in western Wyoming. They were going to catch themselves a thief again.

Cade rubbed his chin as he took another turn beside the desk. "We need to force Delancey to take the money out to the old Parker place, since we know that's where he is when he's north of town."

"But we know Joshua has spent time south of town as well," Paisley said. "The plan will only work if we can make certain he doesn't go south."

"So we block his path southward," Cade said. "If he is carrying pilfered money, he'll want to be rid of it as soon as possible, to reduce the chance of being caught with it."

"That means cutting off his access to the hotel, as well," she added.

"Mark my words," Hawk jumped in, "I'll have the two of you joining the marshals if it's the last thing I do. We could use two people with a head for plotting."

Cade was already shaking his head. He'd been refusing that offer for years. "I picked the quietest corner of Wyoming on purpose, *amigo*. Savage Wells is proving exciting enough for me."

"Which brings me to a question I've been meaning to ask you," Paisley said to Hawk. "How often do you think I'd be called on these 'special assignments' if I joined up?"

"It's hard to predict," Hawk said. "It wouldn't be constant, though. As the territory grows, we'd have more need of a woman deputy marshal. I'm confident you'd be successful enough that we could lobby for more women joining up."

Paisley was intrigued, anyone could see that. Cade vowed he'd find a moment to tell her frankly what law enforcement was like outside the peaceful streets of Savage Wells. If she meant to ply her trade in those waters, she needed to know the true nature of the raging deep.

Chapter 37

Paisley had never seen so many people in the town council chambers. Odder, still, only one member of the town council was even present.

"Quite the party you're hosting here, Gideon."

He held up his hands in a gesture of innocence. "Cade's the host tonight. You'll have to discuss the guest list with him."

"It's an odd assortment, isn't it?"

"Indeed." Gideon motioned toward Mrs. Carol and Mrs. Wilhite gabbing in the corner. "The over sixty-five contingency."

"Be nice, Gid."

He nodded toward Tansy and Dead Ned. "We're also joined by the criminal brigade of Savage Wells."

Paisley spotted Bill Nelson and Andrew standing apart from the others. "And, of course, the usual delivery-day deputies."

"Not to mention the delegation from Canada." Gideon smiled at Mr. Jones and Mr. Oliver, who were deep in a cheery conversation. "And, of course, with you and Hawk both here, we have a pair of marshals as well."

"I haven't firmly decided, you know."

"But you are certainly leaning in that direction." Gideon offered her a chair, but she wasn't in the mood to sit. "The possibility of you joining the marshals is about all Cade talks about anymore, outside of the bank troubles. He's turning into a regular bore, you know."

Paisley didn't know whether to be flattered or nervous. "What does Cade have to say about it? The marshaling, not the robberies."

"Well, there has been a lot of crying." Gideon's very serious expression bordered on the ridiculous. "He said something about how you get all the pretty things."

She shoved his shoulder. "Be nice, or I'll write to my uncle, who will write to your uncle, who will write to your parents. Then you'll get quite a tongue-lashing."

Gideon chuckled.

"What does Cade say?" she repeated.

"He says you'll make a fine deputy marshal," Gideon said, finally in earnest. "Good grief, Pais, he's so proud of you it's nauseating."

"Truly?" She didn't used to blush so much.

"Truly. But I can also see he worries about you being in danger, and he's trying not to admit how much he'll miss you when you're gone. Not very manly to fall to pieces over a woman, you realize."

Even when Joshua had been courting her, he hadn't ever come close to "falling to pieces" over her. He'd liked her well enough, but she'd never seemed *that* crucial to his happiness.

I was so blind. But she wasn't the same naive, weak-willed person she'd been then. She'd grown, and she'd earned the respect of her neighbors. Maybe it was time she started showing herself that same respect.

Cade's voice carried across the room. "I'm obliged to you all for coming on such short notice." When had he stepped inside? "We've a challenge on our hands as a town, and I—"

His eyes searched the crowd, stopping when he found her. He motioned for her to join him. She shook her head. *He* was the sheriff, not her.

"Blast it all, Paisley Bell, I haven't all day to wait for you to give over. We've a crisis to see to."

"There's no 'we' about this crisis, Sheriff O'Brien. I'm an invited guest. You're the host."

His lips pressed hard together. "Saints preserve us all from stubborn women," he muttered.

Not very manly to fall to pieces over a woman. She grinned.

"On behalf of stubborn women everywhere, I'd ask you to leave the Saints alone. They have enough trouble without needing to look after you as well."

Hawk covered what sounded like a laugh with a less-than-believable cough.

Cade spared her a momentary look of amused reprimand before returning his attention to the crowd. "I've brought you all here because I need your help. We've a trio of lawbreakers hidin' out in this town, and we need the cooperation of everyone in this room to catch 'em."

He had their full interest. He had *her* interest piqued as well. Clearly Cade and Hawk had devised some kind of formal plan.

"Now, before you start twistin' your hankies in worry," he continued, "the only ones who'll be in any danger are Hawk, Paisley, and me, along with Tansy and Andrew, who have been temporarily deputized for the bank delivery."

Andrew? Paisley's gaze shot to him, and her jaw nearly hit the floor. There he stood, shoulders squared, chin held high. For the first time since she'd known him, Andrew held himself like an unbroken man, confident and determined.

"What do you need us to do?" Mr. Jones asked Cade.

"All this will be happening tomorrow afternoon, a few moments before five o'clock. You'll each have your role to play. Jones and Oliver are in charge of creatin' a diversion on Main Street. Nothing shady, just a very . . . *Canadian* disagreement. Bring your wagons in, sleighs if there's too much snow, and get into a difference of opinion over who's charged with giving way to whom."

Paisley could easily picture it. "You pull your wagon ahead." "No, I insist. *You* pull ahead." They'd be at it for hours. *Ingenious.*

"We can do that," Mr. Jones said.

"I've no doubt you can." Cade turned to Mrs. Wilhite and Mrs. Carol. "I need the two of you in front of the hotel. Lots of fluttering of hands and—"

"—twisting of hankies?" Paisley tossed out. She knew where this plan was going.

"The hankie twistin' is optional," Cade answered, giving her a wink. "I simply need you to make it inconvenient to get into the hotel."

"We can have the ladies' auxiliary committee meeting at the front doors."

Cade nodded appreciatively. "That sounds very inconvenient."

The look of pride on the older women's faces was priceless. Paisley counted off the objectives in her head. The disturbance in the street would slow Joshua down on his way out with the money. The ladies at the hotel would prevent him from taking his ill-gotten goods up to his room. They need only block off his southward options, and the only ones present whose job hadn't been laid out were Nelson and Dead Ned. What did Cade have planned for them?

Cade answered her unasked question. Dead Ned was charged with playing the role of a troublemaking lawbreaker. Nelson was to make the arrest slowly, awkwardly, and in as drawn out a manner as possible, drawing as many spectators as he could manage. The answer came on the instant: another "inconvenience." Nelson was always deputized on delivery days. Dead Ned was always itching to be arrested.

It was a fine plan. It might even work.

As the others chatted excitedly about their roles in the upcoming ruse, Paisley caught Cade's eye and called him over with a hook of her finger. He obliged, his head tipped and eyes narrowed with curiosity as he approached.

"You've been busy," she said when he reached her. "It's quite a plan you've concocted."

"But is it a good one?" He seemed to genuinely doubt it. "Hawk and I went over and over it, but his knack for strategy, impressive as it is, ain't as keen as yours."

A man who valued her mind. That was a welcome change. "Where will you and Hawk and I be during all of this?"

"I'll be in town, overseeing the money delivery. I always do, so it'd raise suspicions if I wasn't there." He was right on that score. "You and Hawk'll be out near the Parker place watching for Delancey or any of his partners."

That was a good idea, indeed. "My only concern is where you mean to put Tansy and Andrew."

"The rest is sound?" he pressed.

"I believe the word I kept repeating in my head was 'ingenious.'"

Relief flitted over his features. While she appreciated his faith in her, she'd rather see the somewhat pompous expression he usually wore. It would inspire more confidence going into this potentially dangerous undertaking.

He walked with her to the other side of the room. "Tansy will watch the front of the Parker place. Andrew'll watch the back."

She immediately shook her head. "We need Andrew up high. He feels most comfortable there."

His lips pressed together as they did when he was thinking deeply. "Can't say how we'd pull that off." Cade took her hand absentmindedly. "All the trees out that way are bare. He'd be spotted in an instant."

That was something of a pickle. "Tansy's barn is on that side of her property. What if we had Andrew up in the loft? It's near enough to see what's going on, and even get off a rifle shot if need be, but he wouldn't be seen."

Cade gave that a moment's thought. "That'd put Andrew in view of the front of the Parker place."

"So move Tansy to the back. She can tuck herself wherever she can find cover."

"I knew I'd best talk with you before making anything final." He pressed a kiss to her cheek. "I'll go update Tansy and Andrew."

"Come by for dinner after you're done here," Paisley offered. Why did the invitation make her so nervous? He wasn't likely to turn her down.

He brushed his thumb along her lower lip. "I'll see you this evening, love."

Love. What she wouldn't give to hear him call her that always.

Chapter 38

Once upon a time Paisley had been able to serve fine meals to her guests. That night, she had to make do with a watery stew for supper. Cade hadn't complained, and she truly didn't think he'd minded, but she'd flushed with disappointment and embarrassment the whole time they'd sat in the dining room.

She'd wanted to make the night special. Even the after-dinner socializing was proving less than extraordinary. Papa was asleep in his usual chair, his head tipped back, mouth hanging open. Cade sat on the sofa beside Paisley, not saying much of anything. He'd likely either die of boredom or run all the way back to town to escape the monotony.

On top of it all, the house was almost frigid. She had spent what little she'd saved from her jobs to replace Papa's badly worn winter coat. She usually bought firewood from the mercantile, not having a wagon to collect any herself. With her money so short, she was having to scrimp on the wood to heat the house.

"I'm sorry it's so cold." She was too embarrassed to look at him, bundled under a blanket as he was. "I used today's allotment of wood to cook dinner."

"Are you short on firewood?"

Her pride pricked at her on the instant. "I'll buy what I need from

Mr. Holmes when I've saved a bit. Papa and I will simply have to bundle up until then."

"I was only asking because I'm planning to borrow a wagon and go cut some wood myself next week. I'd be happy to throw some in for you as well."

She leaned forward with her elbows on her knees. "I'm doing it again, aren't I? Assuming someone means the worst. I am trying to be better about that."

The blanket she was using for warmth slid off one shoulder. Cade pulled it over her again. She turned her head to thank him and found him watching her intently.

"Is something the matter?"

He let out a puff of air. It actually clouded in front of his face. "Do you really mean to join the marshals?"

"I think I'm equal to the challenge."

"I don't doubt you are," Cade said. "I'm already feeling right sorry for the criminals in this territory, and you haven't even put on that deputy's badge yet."

"Fine praise from someone who figured I wasn't worth my weight in plug nickels when he first arrived in town." She turned fully toward him, grinning at the memory of their early antagonism.

"I never thought that," Cade insisted. "And I gained a quick appreciation for your sheriffing abilities." He moved closer to her. "If I could convince the town council to find the funds for a full-time deputy—a real salary, not a pittance—would you consider staying? A deputy sheriff ain't near as prestigious as a deputy marshal, but you'd be home. More than that, you'd be safer."

"Gideon said you'd been worrying about me." He'd also said Cade was bursting with pride. Paisley liked that particular combination.

Cade's hand slipped out from under his blanket and gently ran the length of her arm up to her shoulder. "Savage Wells is a quiet place. The rest of Wyoming is not. I just want you to go in with your eyes wide open." He brushed his fingers along her jaw.

She leaned her head into his hand, relishing the tenderness of his touch. "That's one benefit of being a special deputy marshal. I'd not be patrolling the streets or chasing down gangs of thieves—like I'll be doing tomorrow afternoon, for example."

He smiled at her in a way that simply melted her inside. "I'll sure miss you. I can't help hoping they'll not have need of you too often."

"Is that your way of saying you like me?" Her heart flipped in anticipation.

"I've been saying that for weeks."

"Have you?" She added a theatrical degree of doubt to her words. "I don't remember hearing you say it."

"Maybe I didn't say it in so many words, but I've been clear as glass."

She leaned back, folding her arms under her blanket. "'Clear as glass'? Though I have my guesses, I can't say I'm *sure* what you think or feel about me. There is nothing about us that is clear as glass, Cade Whatever-your-actual-given-name-is O'Brien."

"I flirt with you like mad," he said. "Heavens, woman, I kiss you every time we're together, or near about anyway."

She wanted to think that meant something, but she didn't dare get her hopes up. "Kisses don't mean much to men, I've learned."

His brows pulled sharply downward. "You think I've been kissing you just for the fun of it?"

"Men do that all the time," she answered.

"Not this man." He jerked his thumb at his own chest. "I ain't a blackguard. I don't kiss a woman unless I mean it."

To her shock, she realized she'd offended him. His gaze slid to Papa before settling on the empty fireplace. Paisley pulled her legs up beside her and leaned her shoulder against the back of the sofa. The silence was anything but comfortable.

She set her hand on his arm, hoping he would hear what she had to say. "The only man, other than you, who has ever been sweet to me is the very man we're setting a trap for tomorrow. And, looking back, I realize he likely courted me only so he could steal from my father's bank without raising suspicion."

She hadn't admitted that out loud to anyone else. Cade didn't look at her.

She pressed on. "When I was at that impressionable age when most young women are first learning what to expect from men, I was living in Abilene. I learned quickly to assume the worst in them."

"And nothin' over the past weeks made you *un*assume the worst in me?" he muttered.

She knew her doubts were unfair. Cade had been her adversary. They'd often been at each other's throats, but he'd never shown himself to be a scoundrel. He'd also never come right out and told her how he felt. Doubts were her particular weakness. He knew that. Surely he could understand why she needed him to simply say, with no hemming or hawing, what his feelings were.

"I suppose you'll start calling me 'Chip' again. And I suppose I'll deserve it. Gideon has told me often enough that my fretting and doubting and worrying was more than any man could be expected to put up with. If he weren't family, I probably wouldn't let him say such things." She swallowed against the lump in her throat. Though she'd done her best to strike a lighter tone, the truth underneath her words stung. "I had hoped I was doing better, or better enough for you to at least not give up on me."

"This ain't me giving up on you, darling. It's just me being human and getting frustrated."

She tried not to get her hopes up. "You're sticking around?"

He gave a quick nod. "Yes'm."

He wasn't giving up on her. She smiled inwardly. "It's a shame you aren't thinking of joining the marshals as well. We could be partners and clean up this whole territory in no time."

"It'd never work, sweetheart."

He'd been talking about taking her on as a deputy only a moment earlier. Had he changed his mind? "Why not? We're a good team."

He tipped her a look. "Because I'm suddenly realizing it'd be inadvisable for us to spend weeks on end exclusively in each other's company. We'd pass all of our time either arguin' or kissin'. The criminals would get away with murder."

"Maybe, but we'd sure enjoy ourselves." She knew her grin was overly broad, but she couldn't help herself. "And after a few months, I'd probably be a lot more sure of your feelings for me," she added.

He actually rolled his eyes. Tough, grumpy Cade O'Brien rolled his eyes. "For such a bright woman you sure can be thick."

She scooted closer to him and stretched upward to press a kiss to his jaw. "I'll miss you while I'm off saving the world."

"I'll be here when you get back."

"Promise?" she pressed.

He kissed the top of her head. "I solemnly vow."

"You really do like me?"

"Saints preserve us," he grumbled. "If I have to tell you one more time—"

"Don't you dare call me stupid again, O'Brien." She pulled back and speared him with a look of reprimand.

"I never said you were stupid, you thickheaded she-cat." He wrapped one blanket-covered arm around her and pulled her up next to him. "Snuggle up close again, will you?"

"You're hoping to do a bit of sparking?"

"Not at all. It's so blasted cold in here I need you for the warmth."

She wrapped her arms around his middle. "You do beat all, you know that?"

He settled his arm around her as well. "Much better, love."

She smiled to herself. Underneath Cade's grumblings was a tender affection she simply adored. "I should warn you, though Papa is dozing and not doing much chaperoning, he's a light sleeper."

"I'll behave myself," he said, adjusting his blanket and settling in as if he didn't mean to go anywhere any time soon.

They'd spent several long, cozy minutes when Cade spoke again quite out of the blue. "Fergus," he said.

"Beg your pardon?"

He gave her a half-smile. "My given name is Fergus."

She tried the name on her tongue and found it wasn't as at home there as "Cade." Still, there was a certain formal ring to it. "I believe I'll call you Fergus when I'm put out with you."

"I didn't know there was a time when you *weren't*."

"It's rare," she said dryly. "Now, let's settle back in like we were. After all, we need to rest up. We have a few scoundrels to catch tomorrow."

"You're the boss, Deputy Bell."

"You just do your utmost to remember that, Fergus."

He pulled her closer and held her as the minutes ticked by. Paisley couldn't remember ever feeling so content in another person's company. He respected her and liked her quirks and oddities. She admired the good man he was and how hard he worked to keep people safe and secure. Though he found her self-doubt frustrating, he hadn't chewed her to bits over it. And he'd promised to be there when she needed him. For a woman who'd been on her own as long as she had, that promise meant more than all the flowery words a man might summon up.

Chapter 39

As soon as the week's delivery money came inside the bank, Cade's recruits took up their positions up and down Main Street. He took a quick peek out the front window of the bank, just to make sure.

"Where do you want to count this?" the deliveryman, Stevenson, asked. The strongbox looked heavy, and he clearly was more than ready to set it down.

Cade usually kept to the front porch during the counting, but knowing this was the most likely moment when the money was disappearing, he stationed himself inside at the front windows instead. He kept his gaze on the street, though he could see the handover out of the corner of his eye.

Lewis directed Stevenson to set the strongbox on the teller counter not far from Delancey. Cade took slow, unconcerned strides to the next window so he could see the exchange better. Lewis sent Delancey for the bank ledger, then flipped through the keys on his key ring, stopping at the ones for the strongbox.

He put the first key in the first lock and turned it. "You're a little early," he said to Stevenson. "You must have had an uneventful journey."

"I suppose," was Stevenson's reply.

Delancey returned, the bank ledger in his hands. "The delivery isn't more than twenty minutes earlier than it has been," he said. "That's not so drastic." He set the ledger on the counter.

Lewis gave him a look of tired patience. "I was making conversation." He turned the second key, then opened the lid. Lewis moved a few things around inside the box. Apparently satisfied, he gave Stevenson a nod of acceptance.

"I just need your signature," Stevenson said, holding out a ledger of his own.

Lewis touched the top of his head and frowned. His other hand fished about in his pocket. "It seems I've left my spectacles in my office. Step in with me; I'll sign the paper in there. Mr. Delancey, will you begin counting and distributing the funds into the boxes for the other branches?"

"Of course." Delancey took up a position directly in front of the strongbox.

Lewis and Stevenson stepped into the back. How often did the scene play out this way, with Delancey given the task of counting without supervision? It was a miracle more money wasn't missing.

Cade continued watching clandestinely, but nothing truly condemning happened. Delancey counted money and moved it into designated boxes. Stevenson left with his signatures and the original strongbox. Lewis marked the amount in his bank books when Delancey said the total was two thousand three hundred dollars. Then, without incident, the boxes for the scattered bank branches were locked up in the bank's safe.

Either Delancey was quite good at sleight of hand or he hadn't taken any money this time. Still, Cade meant to move forward with his plan. Delancey had slipped money from the deliveries before without Lewis noticing. He'd likely manage it again.

Cade moved to the door. "Afternoon, men." He tipped his hat then slipped outside.

The players were all in place. Cade gave them each a nod as he passed, moving toward the jailhouse.

"Sheriff O'Brien!" Lewis called out before Cade had reached the mercantile.

He turned back.

Lewis hurried up beside him. "Could we speak?"

"I'm all ears."

Lewis made a quick check of their surroundings, then, in hushed tones, said, "Two thousand three hundred."

Cade had no patience for puzzles. He simply watched Lewis and waited for him to explain.

"The delivery came to two thousand three hundred dollars, but we were expecting three thousand," Lewis said. "I double-checked with Omaha before this delivery left, and they confirmed the amount: three thousand. We're missing some, just like before."

"Not a good sign, that." So a bit of money *had* been slipped out during the handover.

"It's worse than that," Lewis continued. "The telegram I asked Mr. Delancey to send a few weeks ago about the missing funds wasn't sent. Mayor Brimble and the bank in Omaha both confirmed that."

Cade had learned that himself. But now that Lewis knew, there would be no keeping the situation quiet for long. "Do you have any suspicions about where the money's gone?"

"There's only one reason I can think of for Mr. Delancey not to send the telegram and then lie to me about it."

Cade nodded. Lewis had it sorted through very well. "Give me time to see what I can figure."

Lewis nodded his agreement. "But I have to send a telegram to Omaha. They need to know what's happening."

"Just give me a day or two," Cade repeated. "We have to make certain we have the right man." He didn't need days, really. He simply didn't want Lewis tipping their hand.

"I understand." Lewis returned quickly to the bank.

Cade headed directly to the jailhouse and made his way around back, where Jeb was waiting with Fintan saddled. He mounted swiftly and set Fintan northward. The success of their plan depended on him reaching the Parker place before Delancey did, but he also needed to get there without being spotted by any of Delancey's partners.

He took a roundabout path, his mind reviewing everything he'd seen, everything they knew. Anticipating what came next in a confrontation had kept him alive for ten years as a sheriff. He wasn't about to jump into this situation without some idea of what to expect.

Money was being skimmed off the delivery very quickly. Very deceptively. No doubt Delancey had it in his pocket right now. He was brash, that was for certain, something Cade wouldn't have guessed about the man.

And he was a little sloppy for someone stealing money from the very bank where he worked. Why not send the telegram reporting the missing funds? Not doing so only pointed suspicion directly at him. Unless he meant to skip town once he'd been figured out.

Cade looped off the north road, taking a longer but less conspicuous path. Tansy had agreed to let him stable Fintan in her barn. He'd be there in another minute or so.

What other proof do we have? The note in Delancey's room. Again, he'd been sloppy. Something that incriminating should have been burned.

Who are his partners? That was the impossible question to answer. For all the clues he'd accidentally given that *he* was involved, Delancey had managed to keep the others' identities a secret.

He came up to Tansy's barn. Andrew had been assigned as a lookout in the loft; he had, no doubt, already spotted Cade. A stall was cleaned and ready. Cade tethered Fintan inside. He quickly climbed the ladder to check on Andrew.

"Seen anything?" he asked.

"Two fellas rode up and went inside the Parker place," Andrew said.

That'd likely be Delancey's partners waiting for the stolen money. "Anyone we know?"

"Both of 'em." Andrew never looked away from the house he'd been assigned to watch. "The first was that fellow who was trying for the sheriff job."

Thackery? That didn't seem likely. Rice, maybe. "The one with the blue kerchief?"

Andrew gave a quick nod.

It was Rice. They'd not seen hide nor hair of him since the council's decision. Cade had assumed he was long gone. There'd always been something a little sinister about the man. Cade should have paid more attention, but he'd been distracted by a pair of dancing eyes and a finely-worn gun belt.

"Who else?" he asked. It'd sure be helpful to know who he ought to aim for if bullets started to fly.

"I don't know his name," Andrew said. "But he's the one who carries the money into the bank when it's delivered. He wears a kerchief too."

Stevenson, the deliveryman. He must've come directly from the bank. Which could mean the funds were skimmed before ever reaching Savage Wells. *No, he wouldn't have keys.*

Cade knew Rice was good with his weapon. There was no doubt Stevenson was as well; he'd have to be, working as a guard for such large sums of money traveling across the open West.

"Keep your eyes trained, Andrew. I've a terrible feeling this could get bloody if we aren't on the alert."

Andrew nodded solemnly. "It seems odd, don't it?"

"What's that?"

"The deliveryman's been bringing money here for years; I've seen him from my tree. The same man for years. But Mr. Delancey has only been here a few weeks. It seems odd that they worked out how to steal this money so quick like. And if Mr. Rice is in on it . . . Well, he left town, or we thought he did, before Mr. Delancey ever got here."

That was odd, actually. The money first started disappearing almost the moment Delancey arrived in town. That was hardly time to meet Stevenson and convince him to go in on a scheme. Odd, indeed.

And there was another example of carelessness. Why would he start stealing money straightaway? Why not wait a few weeks to avoid suspicion? It was almost as if he wanted to get caught.

Cade stopped midstride. They had more than enough evidence pointing to Delancey to have put them on his scent almost instantly, so much that Judge Barclay had issued the search warrant without delay. It had been easy. Too easy. Far too easy.

Jumpin' gopher mites. Delancey was being framed. Quick as lightning, Cade was sure of it. They were all being set up. Someone else was stealing the funds, and Delancey was going to take the fall for it.

Him not sending the telegram had seemed condemning. But what if he'd never been asked to send it? What if that had been part of the plot all along?

"Andrew, can you imitate a hoot owl?"

He answered with a well-executed hoot. *Perfect.* He was supposed to whistle like a bird in response to Paisley. Cade didn't want the signals getting confused. "Keep your eyes peeled for Lewis," Cade said. "If he comes anywhere near that house, you hoot. Understand?"

"Sure thing, Sheriff."

Cade didn't waste another minute. None of the others knew they'd been had. They'd be watching for the wrong man and, in their watching, might very well be in great danger.

Chapter 40

Paisley couldn't say if her heart was pounding more from nerves or anticipation. The wait in the cold confines of Tansy's moonshining shack had been a long one. Hawk had told her more about the marshals and what her job there would be like. She'd asked a hundred questions. All the while, neither of them took their eyes off the old Parker place.

They had seen Mr. Rice, one-time candidate for sheriff, arrive with a man Paisley had only vaguely recognized. Hawk had identified him as Stevenson, the bank delivery driver. They knew who the accomplices were; now they just needed to wait for the ringleader.

"Here comes the feather in our cap," Hawk said.

"Joshua?"

He nodded. "Walking up to the door of the house."

"But Cade's not here yet."

"No time to wait," he said. "This is it. Signal to Andrew and Tansy. We'll move in slowly so none of them can leave."

She hopped up and made for the door of their hideout. The air outside was nominally colder than inside the moonshiner's shack. She kept low and out of sight. Andrew was stationed in the loft of the nearby barn with his scoped rifle at the ready. Tansy was tucked behind an outcropping of rocks. Both had insisted they didn't mind the cold.

Paisley slipped two fingers in her mouth and made a bird call. It was a little out of place so late in the season, but not so much so that they were worried about drawing attention. After a moment, an answering whistle sounded. *Tansy.* Paisley waited and listened. Another whistle. *Andrew.*

Paisley tucked her head back inside the hideout. "We're ready. Do you think Cade is on his way?"

"I'm certain of it." He checked his pistol.

Paisley made a quick check of her weapon as well.

"Are you up for this?" His tone was unfailingly somber. "You were engaged to this man after all."

That did weigh on her more than a little. But she knew what needed to be done. "We have a town to protect and people who are counting on us. I'm not afraid to do what needs to be done."

Hawk gave the go-ahead nod. They inched their way forward, keeping a close eye on the place. Hawk and Paisley took up a position in front of the porch, hunched low so they couldn't be seen from inside the house.

She held her pistol at the ready. The plan had initially been for all three of them to go in at once, but they'd talked through how to approach it if Cade didn't make it in time. The goal was to get at least one of the men out of the house so that she and Hawk wouldn't be outnumbered.

Hawk tossed a pebble at the front door, ducking the instant after he threw it. A couple more, slightly bigger rocks, finally brought someone. They heard the door open.

"Who's there? Show yerself."

Paisley didn't recognize the voice, so it wasn't Rice or Joshua. It must have been Stevenson.

Footsteps came to the edge of the porch.

"Who's there?" Stevenson said again.

Cade had said he didn't want anyone dying if it could be avoided. The trick would be luring the driver far enough away from the house to take him down without the others knowing.

He came down the first step.

Paisley met Hawk's eye. He nodded.

Stevenson came down the second, then the final step. His feet were on the ground. That was the key moment. Hawk dove, catching him from behind and slamming him down, hard. He flipped the man onto his back and landed a punch to his jaw. Paisley handed over the gag they'd brought. They couldn't risk him calling out a warning to the others. Together, they pushed him up against the porch stairs and tied him to the newel post.

One down. Two to go.

They slipped up the steps. Stevenson had left the door open. They'd need to be extra careful not to be spotted. The front steps had recently been repaired, so at least they didn't squeak. Hawk stepped onto the porch. Paisley moved up right behind him.

No voices came from inside. A shutter, hanging by a single, bent hinge, blew against the house. Somewhere in the distance an owl hooted. Hawk nodded toward the door, then, pointing to himself, mouthed, *Me first.*

She nodded. Both armed and alert, they entered.

Joshua laid on the ground not far from them, facedown and unmoving. A door leading outside to the back end of the house stood wide open. Rice had made a break for it.

"I'll head after the runaway," Hawk said, already heading for the back door. "See if Delancey's still alive."

Still alive. Even knowing he was a criminal, the thought of Joshua dead hit her like a rush of cold water. But she had a job to do.

"Joshua?" She crossed to him. "Answer if you can hear me. Answer in whatever way you can."

A shot rang out from somewhere behind the house. Then another from further away. She hoped Hawk had found Rice and not the other way around.

"Joshua?"

Still no answer.

In the back of her thoughts, she swore she could hear Cade's voice. *Be cautious. Assume anything could be a trap.*

Joshua might very well be feigning whatever injury had laid him out. She nudged him with her foot. He didn't move. Paisley carefully crouched beside him. Gideon had taught her how to find a pulse in the wrist. She checked Joshua's. It was there but very faint. That likely meant he really was injured.

She holstered her pistol long enough to turn him over, but pulled it back out immediately thereafter. She wasn't taking unnecessary chances. An enormous bump jutted out from Joshua's forehead, a trickle of blood running down his face. He'd been hit.

Had there been a mutiny among the thieves? Maybe he'd returned empty-handed. Or maybe they'd intended to take all the money for themselves. Either way, she needed to find Hawk, see if Rice had escaped, and then get Joshua to town and over to Gideon's house.

Joshua's eyes fluttered open. He looked at her, though there was undeniable vagueness in his eyes. "Waiting." He took a pained breath. "They were waiting. For me."

What did he mean?

"Knew I was coming. Planned it all."

Planned it all. Did he mean Rice and Stevenson? Of course they'd planned it. *Joshua* had planned it.

His eyelids were nearly closed again. "Go. Danger."

He was warning her? That was hardly the behavior of a hardened criminal.

A gunshot rang out, rattling the windows. Pain seared through her back and shoulder, burning, tearing, ripping at her. Her arm dropped limp at her side, her pistol slipping from her dead grasp. She stumbled forward, trying to catch herself using the only arm that would move.

Someone grabbed her from behind before she hit the ground. The grip was rough and jerked her backward from the house.

Chapter 41

Andrew had given his owl hoot. Hawk and Paisley didn't know where the real danger was coming from, and there'd already been three gunshots. Cade ran at full speed toward the Parker place, all the while studying every inch of his surroundings. He would be coming up from the side of the house, but he had no idea where anyone else was.

He'd reached the barren side garden and very nearly to the house when he caught out of the corner of his eyes a glint of afternoon sunlight flashing off metal.

"I'd advise you to toss down your weapon, Sheriff." Lewis.

Cade spotted him, not thirty feet away, holding a gun to Paisley's head. He met her eyes. There was worry there, but not panic. Her holster was empty. Lewis had disarmed her somehow.

"I'm not bluffing," Lewis shouted, slipping more fully behind Paisley. "Both of you."

Hawk was only a few feet away from Cade, but his arm was bleeding badly. They had Lewis outgunned, but he had a human shield.

"Toss your gun," Cade told Hawk. He'd not get Paisley killed if he could help it.

"Quit being so yellow-bellied and shoot the man, Cade," Paisley called back.

Was the woman daft? Lewis might panic and actually pull the trigger.

Lewis dragged her backward, putting more distance between them all. If only Andrew or Tansy were closer.

Paisley captured Cade's gaze. She mouthed, quite clearly, the words, *Shoot him. Now.*

He did still have one gun tucked out of sight under his coat. But shooting Lewis without hitting Paisley would take every bit of skill he had.

"Take the shot," Hawk muttered under his breath. "You're the only one who can."

"I might hit her," he answered back, careful not to move his mouth too much. He didn't want to tip off Lewis.

"Do you really think he'll let her live? At least this way she has a chance."

Blasted blazes. Hawk is right. Lewis had taken a single step backward, pulling Paisley with him. He kept his gun to her head. Everyone held their breath, no one daring to so much as flinch.

"One chance," Hawk warned. "Make it count."

One chance, and a powerful big chance it is. "I need a diversion," Cade said. "Gun's at my back."

"Got it," Hawk said.

Cade tensed. A lifetime of shooting people, of honing that deadly skill, came down to this one moment. If he could pull it off, it'd be worth every sleepless night, every regret, every moment that haunted him.

Hawk stumbled to the side, crying out loudly as he clutched his bloody arm.

Cade worked off pure instinct. Flip coat out of the way. Draw pistol. Raise. Aim. Fire.

Lewis fell backward.

Paisley reached across herself and pulled Lewis's second pistol from its holster as he fell. In one fluid movement, she spun and shot at something just beyond Cade. The telltale thump of someone dropping to the ground followed.

He spared enough of a glance to identify him—Stevenson. Paisley was the only one who'd seen him sneaking up from behind with a gun in hand. Cade needed no more details than that.

He made straight for Paisley. She'd dropped to her knees. Cade matched her posture, grasping her arms. She moaned and pulled away from his grasp.

"Are you hurt?" He held tight to her shoulders, searching for signs of injury.

"Quit squeezing my arm, Fergus, or I'll shoot you too."

He opened his hands, only then noticing the blood seeping between his fingers. "Did I—?" he asked, eyeing the red stain spreading over her sleeve.

"Lewis shot me from behind." She looked down at her wound a moment, before pushing out an exhausted breath. "That's how he got my weapon away from me."

She was hurt, but not badly. "Tansy took down Rice, but only after he'd shot Hawk. I think Rice is probably dead."

"What about Lewis?" She ducked her head to where the banker lay prone on the snow-crusted mud.

Andrew was standing guard over Lewis. He must have run the whole way from the barn; he was still out of breath. The tiniest rise and fall of the banker's chest told its own story.

"Still alive," Cade said. "Gideon'll sew him up enough for a trial." He looked back to Hawk, standing over Stevenson. "Dead?" he called out.

"No," Hawk called back. "But it's bad."

"He was tied up," Paisley said. "I don't know how he got loose."

Dusk was coming quickly, and the temperature was dropping.

"Hawk." Cade motioned the marshal over. "You and Paisley get to town. Give Doc a chance to look at you both. Tansy and Andrew and I'll meet you there with these three."

"First you shoot at me, and then you get rid of me?" Paisley objected weakly. "I'd hate to see your approach with women you *don't* like."

"I ain't ready to joke about this yet, Paisley." He didn't know if he'd ever be. He fought the urge to pull her into his arms and simply hold her. But they had a mess to clean up first. "Tell Gideon to take good care of you," he said.

"He wouldn't dare do anything less," she answered with a smile.

Cade turned to Hawk. "If you let anything happen to her—"

"I know, you'll shoot me. Get in line."

Cade allowed himself one drawn out moment to reassure himself she was whole and well and that they'd both survived the shoot-out. "I love you, Paisley Bell," he said.

"You'd better," she answered.

Chapter 42

"I don't need a sling," Paisley declared firmly. Again.

Gideon was unimpressed. "You're a doctor now, are you?"

"You have given me a little medical training."

"Telling you where I keep the camphorated oil does not constitute medical training."

There was no arguing with the man when he was on his medical high horse. "I feel stupid, is all. It's just a bullet hole, and you got the slug out. This"—she motioned to the sling supporting her left arm—"seems pretty unnecessary."

"It's a good thing Cade likes stubborn women," Gideon muttered. He scrubbed at his surgical implements with a particularly pungent liquid. His usually cheerful expression was replaced with tightly drawn lips and deeply furrowed brow.

"Is something the matter?"

He kept at his work. "It's never easy losing a patient. Even if that patient was bound for prison anyway."

Stevenson hadn't survived, though Gideon had worked hard to save him. "He was going to shoot Cade," she reminded him quietly. "It wasn't enough just to slow him down. I aimed to stop him." She'd shot him in the chest. "I have a feeling there was nothing you could have done to keep him alive after that."

He shook his head. "There wasn't. But it's still a difficult thing."

"Is this the first time you've had a patient die?"

"No," he said curtly.

She sat at his desk. "Well, it's the first time I've killed someone. So if you have any tips on coming to terms with that, I'd appreciate hearing them."

He closed up his medical case. "If you decide to become a deputy marshal, you'll have to learn to deal with it. Have you changed your mind?"

"If anything, today has solidified my determination." It was an odd realization, but she couldn't deny it was true. "There are bad men all over this territory hurting people, killing them. I worked for Sheriff Garrison without credit, without pay, because I wanted to help, I wanted to improve people's lives. I'd be doing that every day as a deputy marshal. Taking a life isn't an easy thing. But saving a life—that's something worth taking a risk for."

"Does Cade know?" Gideon asked.

She nodded. "He muttered something about missing me when I'm gone." She smiled at the memory of his grumpy confession in her freezing cold house. "But he seems to think I'll do a fine job and says if it's something I want to do, I ought to do it."

Gideon sat in an armchair near the crackling fire. "I'm going to get sentimental for about thirty seconds, mostly because Cade's my best friend and you are—and I mean this with complete sincerity—by far my favorite cousin. I don't think I've met two people better suited for each other than you and Cade. That's a rare enough find in a big city where a person has plenty of people to choose from. Out here in the middle of nowhere, that's downright miraculous." Underneath his praise of her and Cade's connection, Paisley heard a note of loneliness.

"Maybe some unmarried woman who loves noxious medicines and

blood and gore will move to Savage Wells, and you'll find *your* perfect fit," she said.

His doubtful smile was more than a bit self-deprecating. "I, for one, am not holding my breath."

"I would be willing to scout out any eligible women in the territory while I'm out deputy marshaling. It likely is part of my job."

It was good to hear Gideon's laugh. "That's just what we need, a federal marshal in charge of matchmaking."

"Is that what your assignment's going to be?" Cade asked as he sauntered into the room. He looked as tired as Paisley felt. He eyed her sling, and concern filled his expression. "Is your arm bad as all that?"

"Gideon's just being an ol' fuss. He didn't make Hawk use a sling."

Gideon pointed an accusing finger in her direction. "Hawk didn't need to have a bullet dug out of his arm, missy. You had a lot more damaged tissue than he did."

"Is she well enough to go to the jailhouse?" Cade asked. "Mr. Larsen needs to get her statement."

Gideon indicated she was free to go.

Paisley paused as she passed his chair. She set a hand on his shoulder. "You're a fine doctor, Gideon, and a good man. Try to remember that when you're feeling discouraged."

He patted her hand. "Thanks, Pais."

She followed Cade to the front door. He helped her with her coat, she having only one free arm. "What was all that with Gideon?"

"He's kicking himself for Stevenson dying during the operation."

Cade watched her closely. "You shot the blackguard in the chest. A man doesn't usually recover from that."

The gravity of her actions was settling with greater weight on her heart. "I had to," she insisted. "He would have killed you. There was no time for a less messy approach."

He slipped his arm about her waist and pulled her up next to him. He didn't speak; he didn't have to. She knew he understood the struggle she was having inside and that it was one she had to pass through on her own. Paisley held tighter to Cade. How she loved this man, so strong when he needed to be, but so gentle as well.

"Gideon said Joshua will be fine enough to testify against Lewis," she said. "He was being framed the whole time. We had it all wrong, Cade. We took the bait and ran with it."

"I seem to remember you kept telling us you weren't sure about it, that something didn't seem right." His hand rubbed her back in long, lazy circles. "I thought it was sentimentality."

"Because of my history with Joshua?"

He didn't answer out loud, but she felt him nod.

"I'll not doubt your instincts again, love. Not ever."

*　　*　　*

The bright ribbons hanging from every bar and filling the shelves in every corner stood in stark contrast to the day that had just passed. The cells were empty. Lewis was recovering at Gideon's from the bullet that had shattered his shoulder. Tansy was standing guard in front of his room. Mr. Jones would be relieving her overnight. Nelson had volunteered the morning shift. Savage Wells was taking the future of their town very seriously.

Over the next fifteen minutes, Mr. Larsen peppered her with questions, taking a thorough accounting of her answers. Hawk wanted to make certain Lewis, the sole survivor from the group of thieves, didn't get away with his crimes for want of thoroughness on their part.

Joshua had already given his statement. He explained how Lewis had never instructed him to send any telegrams, that the note found in his hotel room was not in his handwriting. That Lewis knew he had bought the old Parker place by virtue of having written up the note he'd purchased it with, and how he had used that information to point suspicion back at Joshua. The idea of framing the new bank teller had likely been formed even before Joshua's arrival. It had also likely been the reason Rice had tried for the sheriff's job. Stealing the funds would have been even easier if the local law turned a blind eye.

Cade held her hand while she gave her accounting. She held fast to him as well. He'd sworn he didn't kiss a woman if he didn't mean it; she figured he wouldn't hold her hand if he didn't mean that as well.

"I feel, in the spirit of full honesty, I need to tell you, Mr. Larsen, that, unlike Cade and Hawk, I'm not an official lawman of any kind, and unlike Tansy and Andrew, I was never temporarily deputized for this undertaking. I know that means I have less leeway when it comes to gunning people down."

Mr. Larsen nodded solemnly. Cade's expression grew suddenly quite serious. Apparently the possible ramifications of Paisley's actions hadn't truly settled on his mind until that moment.

"I have her papers granting her the title of United States Deputy Marshal," Hawk jumped in. "They're signed by the necessary people in Washington and by me. While we're still missing her signature, I think it at least implies that, in the eyes of the United States government, Miss Bell has quite a bit of leeway when it comes to enforcing the law and keeping the peace." Hawk met her eyes. "Not that I'm trying to force you into accepting the position. I just don't want to see you in trouble for today's work."

"She won't have any trouble," Mr. Larsen insisted. "There is enough evidence that she was acting to save a life when she shot Mr. Stevenson. I doubt any judge would rule her actions as anything other than completely justified. But the deputy marshal appointment, whether or not she accepts it, will help guard against any arguments of impropriety of her presence during the raid. And Mr. Lewis holding her hostage takes on an added degree of severity when her role as an agent of the federal government is understood."

"I should have deputized you," Cade whispered, clearly angry with himself. "I didn't even think of it."

Mr. Larsen gathered up his papers. "I'll go over these and get everything organized so Marshal Hawking can take them to Laramie tomorrow when he's ready. I think you have more than enough here to see to it that Mr. Lewis isn't free to rob more banks any time soon."

Hawk walked Mr. Larsen out, discussing the situation in low whispers. Cade remained behind with Paisley.

"How are you holding up?" he asked. "Shooting a man dead ain't an easy thing to come to terms with."

"I haven't let myself think about it much yet." She stood and paced away. "At some point I'll have to, but at the moment, all I can think about is how obvious it was that Stevenson was going to kill you, shoot you from behind. I knew it the instant I saw him sneaking up. I knew it as surely as I knew Lewis meant to kill me in the end."

"Oh, Saints above, Paisley."

She turned at the sound of his moaned words. He sat at the desk, hunched over with his head in his hands. He didn't look up, didn't move. She brushed her fingers through his hair and then slipped her hand around his.

"What if I'd missed?" he muttered. "He was standing so close to you. What if I'd missed?"

"You are the only person in the world I would trust to make that shot, Cade O'Brien. And you made it."

His troubled gaze turned upward at last. "I've a feeling I'll be reliving that moment in my nightmares for a long time. If I'd been off even the smallest bit—"

Paisley set her hand on the side of his face. She meant to say something reassuring but found her mind empty of words. This man who had made a career out of split-second decisions and understanding the necessity of occasional bloodshed sat there haunted by the possibility that she might have been hurt. She was touched, deeply. And yet she couldn't let him fret over this. He had enough regrets weighing on his soul as it was.

"Time to put on your big-boy britches, Fergus," she said sternly.

That golden eyebrow of his arched right on cue. "I'm in trouble, am I?"

"I've had a horrible day. I was shot, then endured having a bullet dug out of me. I need you to quit your wailing and hold me."

He obliged without hesitation. His embrace was warm and reassuring. "I don't ever want to pass another day like we've just had, darling."

She held more tightly to him with her good arm. "Neither do I. Seeing Stevenson poised to kill you, knowing I couldn't do anything because I'd stupidly allowed myself to be surprised and disarmed—" She leaned against his chest.

His next breath trembled as it escaped. "I've never been shaken that much while doing my job before."

"That is a firm argument against me working as sheriff's deputy here," she said. "Even if the town council ever agreed to pay for one."

"You've the right of it, I'm afraid. It's a shame, though. We make a good team, you and I."

She smiled up at him. "I suppose we'll have to find a different way of combining forces."

His smile was a touch crooked. "I can think of a few ideas." He held her gaze as he leaned ever closer.

His kiss was tender in an almost inexplicable way. There was a gentleness to it that spoke volumes of how fragile she apparently seemed to him in that moment, as if he sensed that she'd nearly been snatched away. Her heart melted at the painstakingly slow kiss. He, who never seemed scared of anything, had truly been afraid for her.

He broke the kiss and pressed his forehead to hers. "If you get yourself shot while deputy marshaling, I'll kill you," he whispered.

"Understood."

Worried as he was, he wasn't going to argue against her taking the job. She'd never imagined there could be a man who understood her as completely as he did, let alone one who truly valued and respected the person she was.

"I love you, Cade," she whispered.

"You'd better."

Chapter 43

Paisley stood a few steps away from the only occupied cell in the jail-house. She'd grown more quiet during the past five days. Cade couldn't decide if she was stewing over her decision about marshaling or regretting her role in the roundup.

Cade set an arm around her and stood at her side as Hawk and his newly arrived deputies pulled Lewis from his cell and out the front door. Delancey stood on the porch, his forehead still bandaged, a look of anger on his face that would have left even a hardened criminal quaking.

"You'll be held in the territorial prison in Laramie," Hawk said. "And your trial will be held there. Are you clear on that?"

Lewis didn't answer.

"We'll be on our way, then," Hawk said. "Unless Sheriff O'Brien or Deputy Marshal Bell has something to say."

Lewis's expression turned mocking. "*Deputy?* She'll never be anything but a joke."

Paisley didn't flinch, didn't respond at all. She simply watched him with an obvious dose of bored patience.

"She'll be a fine deputy marshal." Delancey of all people made the declaration. "She caught *you*, didn't she?"

Cade blinked in shock at hearing Delancey support Paisley's decision to join the marshals. He had been quite vocal in his objections before.

"The prisoner has a long journey ahead of him," she said to Hawk. "Best not delay."

Lewis was dragged into the sleigh. The largest of the deputies tied him in, then sat beside him, arms folded, mouth tight. Lewis was in for a rough trip to his final destination.

"I suspect we'll discover he did even more than we realize," Cade said.

"That is why I don't care how much the territory laughs at the idea of a female deputy marshal." She sat at the desk with her elbows propped up, her hands clasped in front of her. "The West is full of scoundrels like Ellis Lewis who are hurting innocent people. I mean to help put a stop to that."

"I hope you noticed, love, no one was laughing just now. You've more than proved yourself."

"I would have rather made that point in a less violent way." She rubbed her eyes with the palms of her hands.

"Has Stevenson's death sunk in yet?" Cade knew of no kinder way to ask the question.

"With a vengeance," she answered on a sigh. "I'll likely always wonder if I might have managed the thing without killing him. And even though the answer always comes up 'no,' it doesn't stop the wondering."

"It never does."

A sadness hung over her that tore at him. "I'm going forward with the hope that I'll not have to shoot too many more," she said.

"And if you do?"

She gave him a half-smile. "Then I'll likely come running back here, begging you to tell me I'm not a terrible person."

"I'd prefer you come running back here for happier reasons."

She rose and crossed to him. "Cade?"

"Yes, love?"

She took a shaky breath. "I think I need you to hold me again."

He happily complied. "As often and for as long as you'd like."

There was a need in her that echoed a need in him. Life had treated them both badly. But they were stronger together. He knew she felt that, too. It was the reason they so easily turned to each other in difficult times, the reason they found such ready comfort in each other.

"Are you takin' me up on my offer?" he asked.

"What offer is that?"

He pressed his cheek to hers. "To hold you any time, any place, forever and always."

"I come with a great many troubles. I think ill of myself too often and far too often doubt others. I've a father who'll only grow more ill and broken." Hesitation sat heavy on her brow. "And I don't take big steps quickly. Too many of those steps have tripped me up."

He understood entirely. Life's disappointments had taught her to proceed with caution. "I think you'll find, darlin', that I can be real patient when needed."

She set her hand on his cheek. "Then you'll understand when I ask you to make your offer again in a few weeks' time."

"And in a few weeks' time, you'll . . ." he prompted.

"Probably insist you ask again a few weeks after that. And then again a few weeks after that."

"You mean to keep me waiting?"

Her eyes grew heavy. "Are you willing to wait?"

"Forever if need be, love. Forever."

Chapter 44

Snow blanketed the buildings on Main Street. Families walked about, bundled against the cold. Wheeled wagons had been replaced by sleighs. The shoot-out was still spoken of, but otherwise the town was peaceful again.

"My game!" Mr. Bell clapped his hands gleefully.

Andrew laughed and reset the board. A shaft of sunlight from the window glinted off his deputy sheriff's badge. Tired of waiting on the council, and having seen what the chance to work and help out had done for Andrew, Cade hired him on himself and paid him out of his own salary. It wasn't much, but Andrew seemed more than happy with the arrangement.

Mrs. Wilhite smiled at them fondly as she packed up more of her ribbons. She was moving her Ribbon Emporium to the millinery. She and Mrs. Carol were excited about the change. Cade was relieved. The women would look after each other.

Cade had only just returned from running a few boxes of ribbons across the street. He would miss having Mrs. Wilhite around, but Mr. Bell and Andrew would be at the jailhouse every day. Gideon came by regularly. He'd have company enough.

"Only a few more boxes," Mrs. Wilhite promised him. "We'll be all moved and out of your hair by the time your lady love returns."

"Am I that obvious?" He glanced out the window like he'd been doing all day.

Mrs. Wilhite gave him a maternal hug. "You've missed her while she's been gone. There's nothing wrong with that. In fact, I'd say there's everything right with it."

"Hawk said she'd be back in a fortnight, which was extended to seventeen days. But her last telegram said she'd be home today." He didn't see any sign of her coming down the street. She'd promised to stop at the jail the moment she arrived from Laramie.

"Do you plan to marry her?" Mrs. Wilhite never had been one for beating around the bush.

"Paisley ain't one to be convinced of anything quickly. But, yes, I mean to marry her once she's ready. The instant she's ready, in fact."

Mr. Bell joined them at the window. "I've been asking my Mary-Catherine for months to marry me," he said. "I think she might say yes the next time I ask."

Like mother, like daughter. "It's fortunate you aren't one to give up easily," Cade said to Mr. Bell. They'd agreed that going along with his mental wanderings was easiest on him.

Mr. Bell nodded. "She's the kind of woman who's worth waiting for."

Cade couldn't think of a more perfect description for Paisley. He ought to know. He'd been waiting for the woman these past seventeen days. *The kind of woman who's worth waiting for.* "I know just what you mean."

"You found one of those yourself?" Mr. Bell asked, his understated smile indicating he already knew the answer.

"I have, indeed."

Mr. Bell nodded his approval, then wandered back to the checkerboard.

Cade caught Andrew's eye. "All's well?"

"Everything's just fine," he answered with confidence. He was a different man from the one Cade had met a short few months earlier. A smile tugged at Andrew's lips. "And everything's looking up for you as well."

An odd thing for him to say, to be sure.

"This is a fine 'welcome back.' Nothing to greet me except the back of your head."

Paisley. Cade spun around. There she was, framed by the doorway, her gun belt slung low on her hips as always, and a look of amused challenge on her face. Seeing her never ceased to bring him a feeling of having come home.

She set her hands on her hips and arched an eyebrow. "Do you mean to offer me a howdy at least?"

He'd fully expected to greet her with enthusiasm. He'd meant to throw his arms about her and pour every lonely moment he'd spent without her into a deep and heartfelt kiss. But having her back, hearing her voice again, froze him to the spot.

He all but sighed her name.

Her expression softened. "I'd say you missed me, you hardheaded man."

"That I have."

She closed the distance between them. She wrapped her arms around his neck, laying her head against his shoulder. His arms were around her in an instant. For the first time in more than two weeks, Cade felt complete again.

"You were late, darlin'," he whispered. "Fourteen days is hard enough. Seventeen is downright cruel."

She pressed a kiss to his jaw. "But you're still here, just as you promised you'd be."

"Just as I promised, love."

He moved his head in order to kiss her properly. His fingers threaded through her hair. Each touch of their lips he filled with every moment of missing her. He pressed her tightly to him, trying to convince himself that she really was there with him and doing his utmost to forget that she would, eventually, have to leave again.

"How long are you home for?" he asked before lightly kissing her forehead.

"I don't have another assignment yet. You might be stuck with me for months."

"Perfect," he whispered.

Cade was lost once more. Kissing her was the only logical course of action. The past two weeks had been torturous. If not for her obvious love of her work and how proud he truly was of the good she was doing, he'd likely have begged her to never leave again. As it was, he was already learning to live for the days when they were reunited.

His efforts at welcoming her home stopped short at the sound of a clearing throat. He felt Paisley's laugh even before he heard it.

"Next time," she said, "let's undertake our 'welcome home' with fewer onlookers, shall we?"

She pulled back a bit, then settled quite comfortably into the crook of his arm. She kept her own arm around his waist.

"Is this the woman you were waiting for?" Mr. Bell asked. He nodded in approval. "She seems lovely."

Paisley closed her eyes and took a slow, deep breath. "He doesn't recognize me."

Cade pressed a kiss to her temple, pulling her ever closer. He could only imagine how terrible her father's illness was for her.

"He has been quite vague on a great many things these past days," Cade said.

Paisley leaned more heavily against him. "Being around Papa can be painful, but he has seemed less afraid now that he doesn't realize how lost he is. I'm grateful for that."

Cade could do nothing but hold her close and hope he offered some comfort.

"Thank you for looking after Papa while I was away. I didn't worry knowing you were here."

"And I will worry less now that you're home again." He walked with her toward the far corner of the room. "I have a welcome home gift for you."

"Do you?"

He brushed his hand along her hair, then slipped his hands down to her shoulders. "I'll fix you dinner tonight, as well, so you can get settled back in."

"Is that a threat?"

Saints, he loved her. "I *can* cook, you troublesome woman." He reached into his vest pocket and pulled out a long, gold chain.

"A necklace?"

"Not just a necklace, sweetheart." He stepped behind her and fastened the clasp. "It's meant as a reminder each time you're away deputy marshaling that you've a gun-toting sheriff waiting for you back in Savage Wells."

She looked down at the necklace. "There's a ring on the chain."

"It's a Claddagh ring, an old Irish tradition." Not one to let an opportunity pass, he pressed a kiss to the back of her neck. "The heart is for love. The hands holding it mean friendship. The crown over the heart is for loyalty. Giving someone a Claddagh is a promise, one that's not made lightly."

She turned to face him, clutching the ring and chain. "Thank you. I'll treasure it."

"I'm glad to hear it. The ring was my ma's."

Her eyes opened wide. "You'd give me something that important to you?"

"Eventually you'll realize that *you* are that important to me." He kept her close, pressing his cheek to hers. "It's a grander thing than I've words to explain, love, having you home again, well and whole. Life's empty when you're gone."

"I missed you so much," she said. "But I never once wondered if you would be here when I came back. I never worried that you would change your mind." Her arms wrapped around him again. "That is a very new experience for me."

He could have shouted with triumph. His Paisley, who doubted and struggled to trust, had faith in his promises. She believed in him.

"I will be here every time," he vowed.

"For the rest of forever?" she asked with a smile.

"For the rest of forever."

He kissed her. Then he kissed her again. And once more for good measure. She settled into his embrace. He had waited his entire life for a woman like Paisley.

He'd found home, and he'd found *her*, and he didn't mean to ever let either one go.

Acknowledgments

With gratitude to the following:

The Wyoming State Historical Society, the Lane Medical Library at Stanford University School of Medicine, and The Farmers' Museum in Cooperstown, New York, for invaluable information and insights.

Jewel Busch, who read innumerable versions of this book and helped me sift through the bad ones to where the best was waiting. I could not possibly have done this without you.

My critique group—Annette Lyon, Heather B. Moore, J. Scott Savage, Michele Paige Holmes, and Robison Wells—who continue to be a desperately needed source of support and encouragement. And LuAnn Staheli, who is so very missed. This book was the last one she gave me her exceptional feedback on, yet I know the things I learned from her will continue to influence everything I write.

My agent, Pam Howell, who has on more than one occasion been the only thing standing between me and giving up on this entire crazy business. Your calming and reassuring influence keeps me moving forward, and your hard work and knowledgeable insights give me the confidence I need to keep dreaming big.

My editor, Lisa Mangum, for making this story so much better than

ACKNOWLEDGMENTS

I could have on my own, for your kindness and generosity, and for your dedication to creating amazing books.

To all the readers who have waited so patiently for another book. The drought is finally over!

And to my wonderful family. Your unwavering support and love means the world to me.

Discussion Questions

1. How does Paisley's history—being forced out of her home by warfare, losing her mother and brother, coming of age in a violent frontier town, plus a broken engagement—impact her ability to trust people? Do you think that will always be a struggle for her?

2. Cade comes to Savage Wells looking for a job in a peaceful town. With the expansion of the bank and the inevitable growth of the town, do you think Savage Wells will remain peaceful? What would it take to keep the peace in a boomtown? How would that affect Cade?

3. In nineteenth-century America, women were barred from many professions. Women weren't granted the right to vote until two decades into the twentieth century. What reasons might nineteenth-century Americans have had to justify these restrictions? What practices do we embrace today that might be considered outdated by people one hundred years from now?

4. In the 1870s, America was still recovering from the effects of the Civil War. In what ways does that conflict impact the residents of Savage Wells?

5. Do you think Andrew will ever fully recover from the impact of war? What could the townspeople do to help him?

6. Gideon tells Paisley that he's given up on the prospect of finding love. Do you think he has lost hope because he knows single women are scarce in the West? Or do you think there is more to his discouragement than that?

7. Hawk holds a position of authority and is well respected by his fellow lawmen. How might his selection of Paisley as a deputy marshal influence the opinions of others in his profession?

8. Tansy takes up her own version of "moonshining" after being abandoned by her family. Why do you think she tries so hard to emulate them even after they were unkind and unloving toward her? Why do we sometimes seek the approval of people whose opinions shouldn't matter to us?

9. Why do you think the attorney, Mr. Larsen, avoids coming to town? Is he hiding something? Shy? Avoiding someone?

10. What future do you imagine for the various characters in *The Sheriffs of Savage Wells*? What triumphs, hardships, or challenges do you see them facing down the road?

About the Author

Sarah M. Eden is the author of several well-received historical romances, and her previous Proper Romance novels, *Longing for Home,* won the Forward Reviews 2013 IndieFab "Book of the Year" award for Romance, and *Hope Springs* won the 2014 Whitney Award for "Best Novel of the Year."

Combining her obsession with history and an affinity for tender love stories, Sarah loves crafting witty characters and heartfelt romances. She happily spends hours perusing the reference shelves of her local library and dreams of one day traveling to all the places she reads about. Sarah is represented by Pam Howell at D4EO Literary Agency.

Visit Sarah at www.sarahmeden.com

FALL IN LOVE WITH A
PROPER ROMANCE

JULIANNE DONALDSON

JOSI S. KILPACK

SARAH M. EDEN

  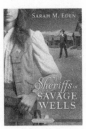

NANCY CAMPBELL ALLEN

Available wherever books are sold

SHADOW
MOUNTAIN